THE OTHER ANNIE

BRIAN O'SULLIVAN

This is a work of fiction. Names, characters, places, and incidents either are the product of the author's imagination or are used in a fictitious manner. Any resemblance to actual persons, living or dead, events, or locales is merely coincidental.

THE OTHER ANNIE

Copyright @20224 **Brian O'Sullivan**

All rights reserved.

ISBN: 979-8-9853830-5-8

Published by **Big B Publishing**

San Francisco, CA

No parts of this publication may be reproduced, stored in a retrieval system, or transmitted in any form or by any means, electronic, mechanical, photocopying, recording, or otherwise, without the prior written permission to the copyright owner.

This book is sold subject to the condition that it shall not, by way of trade or otherwise, be lent, resold, hired out, or otherwise circulated without the publisher's prior consent in any form of binding or cover other than that in which it is published and without a similar condition including this condition being imposed on the subsequent purchaser. Under no circumstances may any part of the book be photocopied for resale.

❀ Created with Vellum

This book is dedicated to the "Psychological Thriller Readers" Facebook group. My book sales have jumped 25% since I joined it, and the members have been a pleasure to interact with!

CHAPTER 1

BOBBY MCGOWAN

"Her name was Annie Ryan. She was born on December 11th, 1983. And she went missing on December 24th, 1998. She hasn't been seen since."

I was talking to William Ryan, Annie's uncle, at his palatial estate in the Hollywood Hills—the same house Annie had gone missing in all those years ago.

The room we were in, which William identified as his study, was the size of a small house and had views of the Pacific Ocean.

William had heard about my investigation into my mother's murder and the eventual death of the man responsible for it, Conrad Drury.

Apparently, he was impressed because he had invited me to Los Angeles to pitch me on the idea of taking on another seemingly unsolvable case: the disappearance of his niece.

"So, how do you want to do this, Bobby?" William asked.

Bobby McGowan, that's me.

"Why don't you just tell me everything you know," I said.

I pressed record on my phone and let William Ryan talk.

ANNIE RYAN WAS BORN in Los Angeles, the first child of Connor and Emily Ryan.

She had a younger brother born three years after her, but he died of SIDS at fourteen months.

Annie had already been the apple of her parents' eyes, but she became everything to them after her brother's death. She was raised in Chatsworth in the San Fernando Valley, and her parents doted on her, sometimes to the chagrin of others in the extended Ryan family.

Connor and Emily often repeated Annie's accomplishments in school.

If Annie memorized her multiplication tables quicker than her older cousins, her parents would let it be known. Once Annie could identify all fifty state capitals, they'd find a way to forge it into a conversation. This rubbed some relatives the wrong way, but because they'd endured the tragedy of losing their son, they let it pass.

For the most part, Annie lived up to the expectations she was burdened with. Being an only child, and a brilliant one at that, placed added pressure on her.

She excelled in school, achieving straight A's during her freshman year of high school. To boot, she was a very pretty young lady, and everyone knew she would become a beautiful woman.

Annie wasn't perfect, however.

She was a bit rebellious, and it sometimes gave her parents grief. Annie would ditch school once or twice a month and always used the same refrain when her father confronted her: "Maybe if I'd gone to school today, I'd have improved on my straight A's. Oh wait, that's not possible."

Connor would tell Annie there would come a time when taking shortcuts would come back and haunt her.

"I'll let you know when I hit that point," she'd say.

Annie could be quite sardonic, but her parents chalked it up to being a teenage girl.

So, while Annie continued to be the light of Connor and Emily Ryan's eyes, she wasn't without a few flaws.

Then again, Connor hadn't exactly been the perfect child himself. He was in and out of juvenile hall as a teenager, ranging from petty crimes like stealing beer to more serious things like spray-painting his neighbor's home while they slept.

Connor would tell himself that maybe this was all karma and he deserved some of the grief he was getting with Annie.

But he certainly didn't deserve what happened on December 24th, 1998.

No parent deserved that.

∼

ON THE NIGHT IN QUESTION, Annie attended a lavish Christmas Eve party at her uncle William's monstrous house.

Over fifty people were there, the majority of whom were family. The rest were family friends, a few valet drivers, and two women who catered the party.

The party started at 4:30, and Connor and Emily arrived with their daughter a little before 5:00.

Annie was seen many times over the next hour, and several people saw her sit down for dinner at 6:00. At some point, she left the dinner table and was never seen again.

After dinner, the Ryans held their yearly tradition of Secret Santa, in which each family member was randomly chosen to buy a present for another family member.

Annie had bought a poster of The Backstreet Boys for Ginny Ryan, her sixteen-year-old cousin and the self-professed "Biggest Backstreet Boy Fan in the World."

When only a few presents were left to exchange, Emily Ryan went looking for her daughter. Annie had been so excited about the present she'd bought that she knew Ginny would love it, so Emily was surprised that she wasn't there to give her gift away.

After looking for ten minutes without luck, she returned and asked her husband to help her find their daughter. They weren't alarmed yet. William Ryan's house was huge, and it wasn't uncommon for the kids to play in one of the many rooms or the expansive backyard. Annie was a good swimmer, so the pool and hot tub weren't the immediate worries they would have been with young kids.

When they still couldn't find her, Connor and Emily returned to the living room and asked some other family members when they'd last seen Annie. Three different kids told them they'd seen Annie when they first sat down for dinner but that she'd gotten up from the table about ten to fifteen minutes after dinner started. None of them had seen her since.

At this point, Connor and Emily started to grow concerned. They checked the pool and the hot tub to be safe, but Annie wasn't in either. They checked each of the eight bedrooms, but still, nothing. They walked outside and yelled Annie's name to no avail.

They talked to the valet drivers William Ryan had hired and asked if they had seen a young girl run off. None had.

They talked to the two women in charge of catering the event, but they hadn't seen anything either.

Connor went to William and his wife, Penny, and asked if they could think of any place that hadn't been checked. They couldn't.

People were starting to get frantic.

What had started as a Christmas party had turned into a search party - the worst kind of party.

Another half-hour went by without a trace of Annie.

Finally, with no other options, William Ryan, at the behest of his brother Connor, called 9-1-1 at 8:36 p.m.

ALTHOUGH NOT THE oldest member of the extended family, William Ryan had become the most recognized face and, for all intents and purposes, its de facto leader.

There were a few reasons for this.

One, William was the most charismatic member of the Ryan clan. If you walked into a room and all eyes were on one man, it was almost inevitably William Ryan speaking. He was handsome—which didn't hurt—but it was more the easy confidence in which he spoke that made him so charismatic.

The second—and more important—reason was that William Ryan was the most successful member of the Ryan family. He'd started a production company in Hollywood in his early thirties, which grew in stature during the 1980s and 90s, eventually putting out blockbuster movies starring Brad Pitt, Julia Roberts, and Denzel Washington, among others.

William was raised in a small, three-bedroom house, where he and Connor shared a bunk bed until William was thirteen and Connor was eleven. His lone sister, Sophie, was blessed with her own room, and the sometimes feuding brothers were jealous. William's father worked in construction, and his mother was a stay-at-home mother. Money was tight for the family of five.

William excelled in school and attended USC on an academic scholarship, graduating Magna Cum Laude at the ripe old age of twenty-one. He had majored in marketing, but instead of joining a marketing firm, he was hired by the William Morris Agency, one of the biggest talent agencies in the world.

He quickly advanced in the company, and by his late twenties, some people thought he was the one truly running the place. At thirty-one, he'd built up quite the client base within William Morris but abruptly decided to leave and start his own agency.

A few of his clients left William Morris and joined him, and several of those who didn't initially join did in the years that followed.

By thirty-five, William Ryan was worth ten million dollars. By forty, he was worth over twenty million. And by the time his niece Annie went missing on Christmas Eve of 1998, he was forty-eight years old and worth close to forty million.

∼

"And why does all this matter?" I asked William Ryan.

He'd been incredibly forthright about himself. Some might say too much so. Calling himself charismatic, handsome, and even extolling his virtues over the rest of his family. It was alarming.

"Because I've always worried that Annie was abducted because of my success. No one else in the family had any money worth speaking of."

"But you never got a ransom note or anything signifying that her disappearance was about money?"

"No, but I thought maybe that had been the intended plan. And then things went awry."

By using the word 'awry,' I knew he meant that Annie had been killed before they could follow through with a ransom request.

"Who would have wanted your money?" I asked.

"Who didn't want it?"

"Are you referring to family?"

"God, I hope not. The only thing that could make this worse than it already is would be if a family member were involved."

"Well, wasn't the party almost exclusively family?"

"There were friends of the family, the valet drivers, and the women who catered the event. The rest were family."

He grabbed a piece of paper and slid it across the table to me.

"This is a list of everyone who was at the party."

I looked down at the sheet of paper. It was intimidating.

He'd separated it into four categories.

Family, of which thirty-nine people were listed. Friends, of which there were seven. Valet, which had three people. And caterers, of which there were two.

Fifty-one people to look into. Fifty-one alibis to confirm. Fifty-one motives to check out.

Making things even more challenging, Annie had gone missing over twenty-five years ago.

"So, do you want to take the case?" William Ryan asked.

"Am I investigating this as a missing person's case or as a murder?"

"Wherever it leads you, Bobby. But I imagine it's, sadly, the latter."

I didn't respond for quite some time.

"Well?" he prodded.

As daunting as it sounded, I was also fascinated. It was like solving a massive jigsaw puzzle.

I probably should have taken my time; maybe thought about it for a few days.

Instead, just like when I reached for my family's photo album, I made an impulsive move.

"I'll take the case," I said.

CHAPTER 2

When I finished my meeting with William, he suggested I meet with a man named Earl Razzle.

I'd heard of him. Everybody had.

Earl Razzle was a private investigator to the stars and a famous one at that. And really, he was more than just a PI. He was like a confidant, PI, and best friend all rolled into one.

He had been on the news many times over the years, usually with a famous star sitting next to him. And Razzle would inevitably steal the show.

He was loud, entertaining, and fearless. His dark, spiky hair went in all different directions.

Razzle had to be in his mid-fifties by now, but there wasn't a gray hair to be seen. I'm sure some dye was involved.

His tan was always on point. His clothes, always impeccable.

With Earl Razzle, the look was half the thing.

He looked like a rockstar and acted like one as well. For all intents and purposes, Earl Razzle was the rockstar. He was certainly more interesting than most of the famous people he represented.

Earl would smile at the camera with his big pearly whites and explain why the tabloids had it all wrong. His client was a golden god who could do no wrong. His client - who had been caught with a prostitute - was just doing research for his upcoming movie where he played a pimp. You get the idea.

The unintentional comedy at his press conferences was off the charts.

The public loved Earl. This well-tanned handsome man with the whitest of teeth, explaining why his likely nefarious client was a pillar of the community.

And while William Ryan was more of a behind-the-scenes guy and not exactly famous, his money was as green as theirs.

∼

I HEADED down to Razzle's office in Beverly Hills.

The same Beverly Hills where I'd be living for the next month.

After I agreed to take the case, William booked me into a room at the Beverly Hilton Hotel. It was June 1st, and he reserved it until the same date in July.

When that time came to a close, William and I would jointly decide if it was worth continuing my investigation. He would inevitably make the final decision—he was the one with the checkbook, after all.

William stated that a week or two wouldn't be long enough to investigate this complicated case, and I tended to agree with him.

He asked if I could start right away, and I told him I didn't see why not. I told him I could drive back to Santa Barbara later that night and return with clothes, toiletries, etc.

He was ecstatic that I both took the case and agreed to start immediately.

I couldn't check into the Beverly Hilton until two p.m., so, with an hour to kill, I parked my 2015 Honda Civic - boy, did it stand out in Beverly Hills - and walked to Earl Razzle's office.

To my surprise, once I told his secretary my name, she immediately escorted me to his office. William must have called ahead.

The man I'd seen on T.V. numerous times extended his hand.

"Earl Razzle," he said.

His tan was on point. Razzle was the George Hamilton of Celebrity PI's. I reminded myself that I was only thirty-two and too young to make George Hamilton references.

"Bobby McGowan. It's nice to meet you," I said.

Besides Razzle himself, my view was of Rodeo Drive, a street full of Tiffany's, Saks Fifth Avenue, and other places I'd never shopped at. Amongst all these high-end stores was Earl Razzle's office.

He noticed my eyes wandering.

"Not a bad location, right?"

"Not too shabby," I said.

"Here, take a seat."

During my previous investigation, I was used to sitting in uncomfortable chairs across from police officers who were equally uncomfortable.

Not here. Not now.

Razzle - that couldn't be his real last name - led me to a huge, three-piece black leather couch. It was comfortable as hell. He pulled up a portable black loveseat and sat next to me. This had to be the most informal meeting I'd ever had.

"I've been told you're here about the Annie Ryan case?"

"I am."

"William Ryan called me and said you might be coming."

I nodded.

Razzle immediately started talking again. I imagine Razzle could filibuster for hours if you didn't get a word in.

"Annie Ryan is one of the cases that has always irked me," he said. "I can't believe I never discovered what happened to that young girl."

I was getting a case of deja vu. I remember Mark Patchett, the detective assigned to my mother's murder, also telling me that my mother's case was the one he could never get out of his mind. The one that got away.

"Why did this particular case stick with you?" I asked.

"Because of the family. Connor and Emily lost their only daughter. Their only remaining child. And the extended family was never the same. As I'm sure you noticed, William Ryan is still consumed by it to this day. The guy is now in his early seventies, and it's still all he thinks about. He used to host raucous family functions, which have basically become non-existent. I guess you can't blame him. Everyone would be throwing a suspicious glance at other members of their family. No one knows who killed or abducted Annie on the night in question, so everybody has their own opinion on who did it. I feel like everyone is a suspect in one way or another."

"Did you ever land on one specific suspect?"

"I landed on twenty. That's the problem. No one really had an alibi. If you were there, you were a suspect. People claimed they never left the dinner table, but then someone else would say they saw them use the bathroom. This case is like watching fifty people play telephone, where everything changes the more you talk to them, and nothing is as it seems."

"There must have been someone you suspected more than others."

"A lot of people were suspicious of Rex Zell."

"William didn't mention him."

"He's not a family member. He was the twenty-five-year-old boyfriend of Vanessa Ryan, one of Annie's many cousins. Rex's family had their Christmas Eve party earlier that day, so Vanessa invited him to William's, who was fine with it. The more, the merrier had always been William's motif. As you can probably guess, the guy loves a big show, being a Hollywood guy and all."

"I got that impression," I said.

"Quite the house, isn't it?"

I guess William had told him I'd been there.

"One hell of a place," I said, but I wanted to get back to discussing the case. "Did Rex have an alibi?"

"Yes and no, just like everyone else. He says he was at dinner the whole time, but most of the party thinks he left for at least five or ten minutes. Alibis are relative when it comes to this case. I mean, everyone was there. It's like a game of Clue."

His reference took me to the game.

'It was Rex. In the living room. With a paperweight.'

"So you were suspicious of Rex?" I asked.

"No, I said the family was."

"Did they have a motive for why he might have done it?"

"Not really. He was just the one person that most people agreed had left the dinner for a considerable amount of time."

"Doesn't sound like much."

"Agreed. I think the family kind of wanted to blame it on Rex."

"Because he was an outsider, and they wouldn't have to look inward?"

"That's very good, Mr. McGowan."

"Thank you, Mr. Razzle," I said, responding in kind with his last name.

He shot a glance in my direction. He'd noticed. I shouldn't have been surprised. He was a famous PI, after all.

"A Mr. McGowan should fit in just fine with a bunch of Ryans," he said.

I almost asked what kind of last name Razzle was, but I resisted.

"We'll all sit around and eat corned beef and cabbage," I said.

Razzle laughed.

"So it doesn't sound like you think it was Rex?" I asked.

"Anything is possible, but I never found any more on him than others. Rex was a pothead who liked listening to the Grateful Dead. He never struck me as the violent type."

"What was the killer supposed to have done to Annie?"

"There's another twenty opinions on that as well."

"Give me a few," I said.

"Some people thought the killer strangled her in a fit of rage and then somehow got her body to their awaiting car."

"But weren't all the cars valeted?"

"Bingo, Bobby."

He'd obviously used my first name because it went well with *'Bingo.'*

"Did anyone not valet their car?" I asked.

"William and his wife. Everyone else had to. You saw that steep hill. It would be hell if twenty or so cars had to navigate that themselves, parking at bad angles and blocking people in. It was better to have the valets make some sort of order out of it."

"So what do you mean when you say 'get her body to their awaiting car?'"

"After the fact. You saw the massive amount of trees down past the backyard. Potentially, the killer could have done away with Annie, hid her body in the woods, and then come back with their car later and picked up the body."

"Sordid stuff," I said.

"Indeed."

The number of cars got me thinking.

"Do you have the rundown of how many people drove their own cars and how many people were driven there?"

"I sure do."

"Can I get that?"

"Of course."

"Thanks."

"I also have the rundown on how many people were either too young or too old to have killed or abducted Annie. She was a pretty strong fifteen-year-old, so I eliminated any girls twelve and younger and any ten and younger boys. Annie could have overpowered them if needed. I also eliminated any of the relatives over eighty. Could an eighty-year-old man have killed Annie? Maybe. But I had fifty-one people at this party, including the valet guys and the caterers, so I had to eliminate some of them. Now, if they told me that Grandpa Gary had it in for Annie, I obviously looked at Grandpa Gary, but none of the octogenarians seemed to fit the bill."

I wondered if Grandpa Gary was a real person. I'd find out soon enough.

"You've spent a lot of time on this case," I said, stating the obvious.

"You have no idea. So I was surprised when I heard William brought in a guy with basically no experience."

"I caught my mother's killer when the police hadn't accomplished jack shit in twenty years."

I sounded defensive, as if I needed to prove myself. It wouldn't be the last time.

"I know, and that was quite impressive. If you solve this, I'll be even more impressed," Razzle said.

"Do you have a spreadsheet with the breakdown you're talking about?"

"Oh, I have a lot more than that."

Razzle rose from his loveseat and went to the desk on the other side of the office—the one that looked directly out on Rodeo Drive.

He waved at a strikingly beautiful woman who walked by.

"That's one of Kim Kardashian's best friends," he said.

I couldn't give two shits.

I'd found Razzle quite likable, but if he name-dropped another celebrity, I might change my mind.

He turned around and handed me more than just a printed-out spreadsheet. It was a binder six inches thick. There wasn't a loose paper in the mix. Everything was in order.

"Jeez," I said.

"Yeah, jeez."

"How much is here?"

"Approximately a hundred and seventy pages."

"I've never heard of a police report that comprehensive," I said.

"This is more than just a police report, but that's in there, too."

Mr. Razzle had certainly done his homework. And yet, he'd never caught the man or the woman responsible for Annie Ryan's disappearance.

What chance did I have?

"You can reach out again if needed," Razzle said. "But this will tell you everything I've learned over the years."

"I appreciate this, Mr. Razzle," I said.

"You're welcome. With that, I have to bid you farewell. The Governor of California is waiting outside."

I wouldn't have believed it myself, but sure enough, as I walked out of the office, the Governor was patiently waiting for Earl Razzle.

CHAPTER 3

Connor Ryan agreed to meet with me.
After some cajoling from his brother William.

As Annie's father, you'd think he would have been eager to talk to me, but as I learned over the course of our conversation, he didn't think any good would come of my investigation.

I met him at his house in Chatsworth, a nondescript city in the San Fernando Valley. The differences between his home and his brother William's didn't have to be stated. They were obvious.

I wondered if there was any family jealousy over William's success. There had to have been some. None of his siblings or extended family had achieved the wealth and status that he had—not even close.

"Come on in," Connor said.

In his rundown, Earl Razzle dedicated five of the first thirty pages to Connor, the most of any individual related to the case, with the exception of Annie herself. I planned on finishing Razzle's binder later that night.

Did that mean Earl Razzle considered Connor Ryan a suspect? Not necessarily. He was the girl's father, after all.

Connor was sixty-nine years old, and had been widowed for some time.

Twenty-five years had passed since Annie's death. A lot of the parents at the time were now approaching seventy. William had already passed it. It was odd, looking at people older than my father and wondering if they might have committed murder. Was this all going to end with a frail, oldish man being taken off to jail?

It was possible I'd never catch the killer.

But if I did find the person responsible for killing Annie Ryan, they were going down for it. I don't care if he was led away on a walker.

∼

"So, how's the investigation going?" Connor Ryan asked.

We were sitting on a ratty old gray couch. This was neither William's study nor Earl Razzle's office.

"This is only day three, but I'm trying to learn more each day."

I'd spent the previous day driving to Santa Barbara and packing my car with a month's worth of clothes.

"At that rate, you'll catch Annie's killer in 2083."

He managed a slight smile, but there wasn't much effort behind it. From our brief phone call and the short time I'd spent before him, I began to think Connor Ryan was a broken man. It would be hard to blame him.

He'd had two children. One died as an infant, and the other one was likely killed as a fifteen-year-old at a family Christmas event, which only made things worse.

"Are you all but certain she was murdered?" I asked.

"Yes. The alternative is worse."

I was pretty sure what he was alluding to, but I still had to ask.

"Which alternative?"

"That she was taken by some prostitution ring or something like that. Or, some crazy sex fiend somehow kidnapped her and has had her in a dungeon for the last twenty-plus years. It's easier just to assume she's dead."

I couldn't disagree with him.

"It doesn't seem likely a prostitution ring or a sex-crazed monster would be at William Ryan's house on Christmas Eve," I said.

"Maybe you're right. The other alternative isn't much better. That one of my relatives killed Annie."

He bowed his head.

"I know this is tough, Mr. Ryan. I'm sorry."

"There are too many Ryan's to keep track of. Call me Connor."

He'd said verbatim what William Ryan had said. I wonder if it was oft-repeated in their family. It made sense. The fact that Ryan was also a common first name only added to the confusion.

"Connor, it is. I hate to ask this, but I wouldn't be doing my job if I didn't. Did you ever suspect any family member of the crime?"

He raised his eyes to meet mine.

"What exactly is your job?"

"William hired me to look into your daughter's disappearance."

"People have been looking into her disappearance for twenty-five years. What makes you think you can do better than the cops?"

I hated to toot my own horn, but if there was ever a time, this was it.

"My mother was killed a few years after Annie went missing. The cops looked into her murder for almost two decades as well, without any luck. I was able to catch her killer, though. By myself."

He looked me over.

"Oh, shit, I know who you are now. William told me he had hired someone. He didn't tell me it was you. That's some pretty amazing shit you accomplished."

It was my fault since I'd brought it up, but now I didn't want the attention.

"I just went where the evidence led me."

I sounded like a generic cop show.

"Well, maybe lightning will strike twice. But even then, what does that get me? She's going to be dead regardless."

"Wouldn't you like to get closure?"

"I guess, but at what expense? Let's assume it's someone from the family. Do you think we could ever have a family event again?"

"From what I've been told, you don't have many these days, anyway," I said.

"That's true. I guess I'm saying that I don't know if I want to find out who killed Annie. Say hypothetically, it was one of William's kids. It's not; I'm just using them as an example. Would I ever talk to my brother again? Maybe not. It seems like more bad than good would come from knowing who killed Annie."

"I'd want to know," I said.

"If you knew a family member had killed your mother, you wouldn't have felt that way."

"Maybe not," I conceded. "You never thought it might be one of the valet guys? Or one of the caterers?"

"You can rule out the caterers. They were two women in their late fifties who'd probably never met Annie. As for the valets, there were only three of them. The other two would have known if the third was gone for a while."

"What about a family friend?"

"It's possible, but that opens its own can of worms. Whichever family member brought or invited them will be vilified for the rest of their life—rightfully so, I might add."

"Did you ever suspect Rex Zell?"

"No, he got a raw deal. People were looking for someone to blame in the first few months, and two or three people said they thought he might have left the dinner. Well, twenty people left that dinner to go to the bathroom at some point. I talked to many people in the younger generation, and none of them thought Zell was involved. Every single one said he was a good kid. But still, the rumors continued. I just felt bad for him."

Neither Razzle nor Connor Ryan thought Zell was involved, so I decided to move on to a different line of questioning.

"If Annie was killed in or around the house, what do you think they would have done with the body?"

He didn't answer for a few seconds, and I realized my question was too much.

"I'm sorry for my straightforwardness," I said. "I know these questions are tough for you."

"You're just doing your job, right?"

He didn't seem convinced that was enough.

"Yes."

"The cops always assumed the body was left by the trees to be transferred later."

"That seems to be the popular opinion," I said. "But the police report says they searched around those trees."

"At what, ten at night? The cops came for a missing person. It's not like they came with dogs to comb the area. At least not that night. They did the next day, but by then, the body was probably gone."

I noted that I wanted to go back to the house for a more extensive search of the circumference, especially where the trees were. Was it possible for the police to miss a body that was lying there? Late at night, the answer was probably yes.

"Were all the cars parked by the valet drivers except William and Penny's cars?"

I knew the answer was yes, but I pushed the conversation along, hoping he might say something worthwhile.

"That's right. Their cars were already in the garage."

"Could their children have had access to their parents' cars?"

Connor shook his head.

"I'm sure William would appreciate you insinuating his kids might have had something to do with it."

I found that ironic coming from the guy who'd just used the example of William's son having killed Annie, but I didn't mention it.

"I'm just asking questions," I said. "I'm not accusing them of anything. And I told William I would go in whatever direction this case led me. He was fine with that. And let's be honest, Connor. My investigation was always going to involve his extended family."

"Your immediate family is different."

"That's true," I said. "But he never said they were off-limits, and if he had, I never would have taken the case. Plus, like I said, I'm not accusing them of anything. I'm just trying to figure out places where Annie could have been hidden. Maybe a friend of their kids knew the cars were there."

"And then what? Said something like, 'Oh, before I go, I need to go back in your garage and grab a dead body?' No, William and Penny's cars have nothing to do with this."

He made a good point. Maybe I'd asked a dumb question, but it helped eliminate a line of thinking, so it wasn't a total loss.

"That sounded rude," Connor said. "I'm sorry."

"Don't be," I said. "If I were in your situation, I'd probably hate having someone dig up all this old shit that you'd rather remain buried."

I regretted using the phrase, fearing the word 'buried' had its own connotations with his daughter.

"I don't want it buried. I'm just not sure what good can come from this."

"Is there anything peculiar about the case? Something you don't think has been examined enough?"

"I mean, there's one thing that stands out like a sore thumb."

I had no idea what he was talking about.

"What is it?"

"Did William mention the name Kai Butler?"

"No, not that I remember."

I'd only read the first thirty pages of Razzle's summary but was pretty sure I hadn't seen his name.

"He's Annie's first cousin. He was my sister, Sophie's son."

"And what, you suspect him?"

"Well, I can promise you if he did this, he'll never be prosecuted."

I knew where this was likely headed, but I played along.

"And why is that?" I asked.

"Because he's dead. Kai killed himself about three months after Annie went missing. He was only seventeen years old."

"Jeez."

"Yeah. They never had any evidence against Kai, and he didn't leave a suicide note incriminating himself. Still, you have to admit it's a pretty big coincidence that a family member kills themselves so soon after her death."

"Were Kai and Annie close?"

"They were thick as thieves."

Why hadn't William or Razzle mentioned this?

"You're the first person to have mentioned Kai."

"It's not exactly everyone's favorite subject to talk about. You can understand why."

"I can, but it shouldn't be ignored, either."

"Just to be clear, I don't think Kai did it, but I always feared maybe he knew something, and that's what led him to take his life."

"Do many people share your opinion?"

"The police looked into Kai after his suicide, but they never found anything connecting him to Annie's disappearance."

"Do you know if Earl Razzle ever looked into his death?"

I reminded myself to read the entire binder—soon. I felt like someone who had come to a job interview unprepared. If Razzle had written about Kai, I should have known about it before talking to Annie's father.

"Yes, I'm positive Razzle looked into him. The guy is kind of a jerk, trying to get on the news any way he can. But I'll give him one thing: he was thorough. I'm sure he looked into Kai."

"So you think Razzle is a good investigator?"

"Damn, I hate to admit this, but yes, I do."

Connor Ryan was shuffling around in his seat. I wasn't sure if he was nervous or maybe just old and getting a little tired of sitting down. We had been talking for quite a while.

"I'll get out of here after a few more questions, Connor. Can I contact you again after I've done some more investigating?"

"Sure, why not? You seem like a nice young man. Taking this job was probably a fool's errand, but I'll help you if possible."

"Thanks."

"What's your next question?"

"If you had to guess, do you think Annie's disappearance was perpetrated by one of the younger generation or one of the older generation?"

Connor Ryan took several seconds to mull it over.

"That's an excellent question, but I'm unsure I have an answer."

He thought for a while longer.

"I guess, if I had to choose one, I'd say it was someone from the younger generation."

"And why do you say that?"

"The kids could roam free at any family function, especially at William's huge house. They were in and out of rooms, making messes, causing disturbances, etc. If one of the adults followed her around or, God forbid, went into a room with her, that would have stood out."

"What do you mean by going into a room together?"

"I'm not saying anything was going on sexually. I have zero evidence of that. But Annie was fifteen years old and physically mature. It's not impossible."

He bowed his head again.

I couldn't end the interview with this being the last thing we discussed.

"Tell me about one of your favorite memories with Annie, and then I'll get out of your hair."

Connor smiled for one of the few times.

"This one is easy. Annie loved the boy bands of the 90s. I was no big shot, but I knew my brother was, so I asked William for a favor. Justin Timberlake was the lead singer of a group called NSYNC and, by far, their biggest star. It was Annie's 15th birthday, and we were having a family dinner in Hollywood. We were from Chatsworth, so going to Hollywood was a big deal for Annie. She could get pretty starstruck, as most teenage girls could. William had called in a few favors, and after dinner, just as we started singing Happy Birthday to Annie, who walked up to the table and started singing along? That's right, Justin Timberlake. Annie let out the happiest scream you've ever heard. I can still hear it to this day. She leaped from the table and gave him a hug, before we had even finished singing. Her smile at the moment made it all worthwhile. It's the lasting image I have of her."

Connor Ryan started wiping away a tear.

"God, she was so happy that night," he said.

CHAPTER 4

I spent the next two days submerged in Earl Razzle's case summary.

It was titled "The Disappearance of Annie Ryan."

On the bottom, it read, "Researched by Earl Razzle."

The line mentioning his name was in bigger font than the top line mentioning Annie.

I'd thought Razzle was pretty down to earth for a celebrity, but it was apparent he also had a massive ego.

He could write, though. I'll give him that. The file was immaculate and exhaustive. He had done a lot of work.

There were a few things that stood out.

HE WAS unconvinced that Kai Butler had killed or abducted Annie.

Razzle said that Kai and Annie spent a lot of time together and got along famously, but he'd found no evidence that they were at odds. No reports of them ever fighting or even getting into a minor argument.

Kai had killed himself by jumping off a bridge. He didn't leave a suicide note. No foul play was suspected, and the cause of death was ruled a suicide.

Kai's father was Doug Butler, who married Sophie, William, and Connor's sister.

THE OTHER ANNIE

Although the Ryan clan was a big Irish family, they started marrying people with different heritages.

Connor's wife, Emily, was of French descent.

William's wife Penny's family had come from Holland.

And Sophie's husband, Doug Butler, had come from England.

Yes, the extended family was predominantly Irish, but they were becoming a blend of cultures, as all families eventually become.

Doug Butler seemed like a standup guy and was beloved by the family. Unlike Connor, he had managed to move on from his son's death (as much as a parent could) and was an excellent father to their other two children. At least, that's how Razzle's summary portrayed him.

The fact that Annie was Connor's last surviving child had a lot to do with his inability to rebound from it. He had no children to fall back on.

Doug Butler had to persevere for the sake of the rest of his family.

I'd get in touch with him at some point.

∽

EARL RAZZLE only spent a paragraph on each of the two caterers. No one seemed to believe they were suspects, and I tended to agree. They were in their fifties, and this was their first time meeting the Ryan family. They had zero motive and were busy throughout the entire dinner.

He didn't spend much more on the valet guys.

The head valet was Ramon Estrada, who owned and operated Victory Valet, the company William had hired for the night.

On that day, he had two young men working with him: Luis Ignacio, who was twenty-four, and Victor Fuller, who was twenty-two. None of the three had any connection to the Ryan family, and like the caterers, this was their first time at the Ryan house. The three were together the whole time except for a few quick bathroom breaks.

Razzle was dismissive of them as suspects. Once again, I tended to agree.

∽

THE NIGHT in question sounded like a festive occasion.

There was prepared eggnog, a punch bowl that included rum, many cases of wine, and a full bar. The caterers even made some Irish coffees that some of the guests had after finishing dinner.

Jameson, Bushmills, and West Cork were your whiskey choices. The

Ryan family had emigrated from West Cork in Ireland, so William Ryan included that whiskey with the heavyweights of Jameson and Bushmills.

So, there was plenty of booze at the party.

It likely had nothing to do with Annie's murder, but if someone got drunk and, for some reason, had it in for Annie, it could have been a starting point. We all know how alcohol can exacerbate the worst in some people.

∼

AFTER READING Razzle's findings a second time, I made an executive decision. I would focus on one or two individuals at a time. The sheer amount of names was overwhelming.

First, Kai Butler. His suicide was an obvious place to start. Even if he had nothing to do with Annie's death, maybe he had discovered something which caused him to take his own life.

Second, I was going to do a deep dive into William Ryan. No, I didn't think he had killed his niece. He'd hired me, after all. No, that didn't eliminate him as a suspect, but he just didn't strike me as a killer.

Then why look into him?

Because he was the money bags of the family, and if his fear was correct, and this might all have been a ransom gone wrong, I'd need to look into William's connections, which were probably endless.

So, for the time being, I'd be looking into a young man who took his own life and an older man who'd accomplished a lot in his.

All the other family members could wait.

CHAPTER 5

Gina Galasso had a hard name to forget.

And it turned out Gina was hard to forget as well, but not in a good way.

She was forty-two going on seventeen, which was ironic because I wanted to talk about her teenage years.

Gina had been dating Kai Butler when Annie went missing, and in fact, Gina had been at the Christmas Eve party on the night in question. She was one of the seven family friends who had been there.

And she was still dating Kai when he committed suicide a few months later.

We met at her tiny, run-down apartment in Santa Monica. She sounded odd on the phone and initially didn't want to meet with me, but I eventually wore her down. I can have that effect on people.

"Thanks for meeting with me," I said.

We were sitting across from each other at the lone table in her apartment. Clothes were spread all over the ground, some used ashtrays were scattered around the room, and the air smelled stale. Those last two were undoubtedly related.

"Sure. Don't know what you'll find twenty-five years later, though."

I was tired of mentioning having solved my mother's twenty-year-old case and decided not to mention it unless asked.

"I come at it with fresh eyes," I said, using my new go-to line.

"I'll tell you what ain't fresh? Annie's body. She's been dead a long time, and ain't nothing going to bring her back."

"How are you so sure she's dead?"

"She's been gone twenty-five years. The only way she's alive is if she's underneath some pervert's house in some dungeon. So, if you look at it that way, maybe it's a blessing she's gone."

It was a view shared by Connor Ryan.

"Have you always thought she was dead?"

I found it helpful to try to get people's points of view both now and when Annie originally went missing. The differences can tell you a lot.

"Since about two weeks after she disappeared. I guess I held out hope for that long. After that, I knew it was 'Sayonara, Annie.'"

If you were feeling generous, you could say Gina Galasso spoke her mind. I just found her to be crass.

"Did you know her well?" I asked.

"Probably better than some in her own family."

"Why do you say that?"

"Kai and I would hang out with her a lot back then, and everyone knows that teenage girls don't like to tell their parents anything."

"What type of things did she keep from her parents?"

"Pretty much everything. Guys she liked. Pot she smoked."

"Was she dating a guy when she went missing?"

There had been no mention of a boyfriend by William, Connor, or in Razzle's binder.

"Certainly not someone she'd introduce as her boyfriend."

"But she was seeing a guy?"

Gina Galasso laughed.

"More like guys."

"She was seeing more than one guy?"

"Annie was a pretty girl. She could have a lot of guys if she wanted."

"How many was she hanging out with?"

I tried not to sound judgmental.

"It's hard to remember. I know she was talking to a few guys, but I don't know how many of them she was balling."

Gina took out a cigarette and lit it. I couldn't remember the last time I'd seen someone smoking in their own house—or, in this case, an apartment.

"I'd ask your permission, but this is my place, and I'll do what I want," she said, seemingly reading my mind.

"It is your place," I said, not exactly condoning her actions.

"Where did we leave off?" she asked.

"You said you didn't know how many people Annie was sleeping with."

"That's right. I didn't know. Could have been two or three, I guess."

"Could it have been zero?" I asked.

Gina took a drag of her cigarette and pondered the question.

"I guess it's possible. Annie was such a flirt, though; I just assumed she was balling at least a few of them."

"Would Kai have known?"

"Annie wouldn't have told him if that's what you mean. They were close cousins, but a girl doesn't go and tell her male cousin who she's sleeping with."

"Fair enough," I said. "Were you and Kai friends with the guys she hung out with?"

She inhaled another drag of her cigarette.

"We met them a few times but didn't know them well since Kai and I went to a different high school. When Kai and I would hang out with Annie, it was often just the three of us. It would give Annie a break from her people, which everyone needs occasionally, especially in high school."

"So you didn't suspect any of the guys you saw her out with?"

"None of them was at the Christmas party, so no."

I decided to move on.

"What do you remember from that night?"

"I remember having a great time right up until she went missing. A few of us teenagers stole a handle of vodka, and we hid it in one of the rooms."

"Was Annie ever in that room?"

"Yeah, but early on. It was within ten minutes of her getting there. Word must have traveled fast amongst the under twenty-one crew."

Gina then laughed, coughed, and took a drag of her cigarette, all in one fell swoop.

Her eyes were glazed over, and it looked like she was high on something. And I don't mean nicotine.

"Did she stay in the room long?"

"No, she was in and out in a few minutes."

"Did she have a drink when she was there?"

Razzle had mentioned that Annie had been in a room with the other teenagers, but he hadn't mentioned that they were drinking. Either Razzle thought it didn't matter, or none of the teenagers had ever mentioned it. That seemed unlikely, with a police investigation and all.

"No, she didn't have a drink."

"Do you guys remember if you mentioned the alcohol to the cops?"

"I don't remember, but I'm sure we admitted to it. The cops didn't care about underage drinking. Not when a girl was missing."

She had confirmed my suspicions.

It was weird to look at the forty-something across from me. The way she talked and dressed reminded me of a high schooler. This seemed to be a case of arrested development. Gina Galasso had never grown up.

She had the cigarette stains on the carpet to prove it.

"Who did you think might have killed Annie?"

"I can tell you one person it wasn't."

"Who's that?"

"Kai. I know people suspected him, especially after he offed himself, but trust me, he had a good heart. He wouldn't never do nothing like that."

Gina's grammar had never made it past high school, either.

"They were close, though, right?"

"Sure they were. I think they were the closest in age of any of the cousins, so that helped. No, maybe that Ginny girl was closer. Well, whatever. They were close in age."

"And you said they'd hang out socially sometimes?"

I tried circling back to the time she and Kai spent with Annie.

"Yeah, we all would. As friends. What are you trying to say?"

"No, that's not what I meant at all," I said, finding myself on the defensive. "You said you and Kai would see Annie out socially?"

"Oh yeah, you mean we would see her out together."

"Yes," I said.

"I already told you we did. And sometimes, they'd use each other as excuses."

"How do you mean?"

"Like Kai would tell his parents that he was hanging out with Annie, and because they were cousins, they were cool with that. And then Kai would come to see me, or we'd go and do things we shouldn't be doing. But Kai's parents didn't worry because they thought he was chilling with his cousin."

I had so many questions.

"What type of things shouldn't you be doing?"

"Drinking. Smoking weed. You know, the basics."

"And neither set of parents would call the other parents and get suspicious?"

"No, because they'd say they were hanging with each other. And we didn't have cell phones back then, so they just let us do our thing."

It made sense, but it still seemed odd that you'd use your cousin for something like this. Isn't that what friends were for?

"I'm sorry to do this, but can I bring up Kai's death?"

"You can say suicide, you know? Ain't no reason to sugarcoat it now. He's long gone, just like Annie."

"Did you have any inkling that he was depressed?"

"Inkling? That's an odd word to use."

She was right. I should have chosen something different.

"I'm sorry," I said. "Did you have any idea?"

"Yeah, I had an inkling," she said, laughed, and then ashed her cigarette, only getting half in the ashtray.

"We had lots of inklings," she said and laughed again. "Lots and lots of inklings."

"I get the point," I said.

Razzle's summary said that Kai was depressed but didn't go into too much detail.

Gina put on a straight face.

"We all knew he was depressed. It wasn't like he was shy with that information."

"What type of things would he do?"

"It's less about that and more about what he would say."

"What would he say?"

"I'm going to commit suicide."

Gina laughed again.

This woman who was ten years older than me - but acted fifteen years younger - was getting on my last nerves.

"Was he ever committed?"

"No, not officially. But he met with some psychologists or psychiatrists or one of those doctors."

"Had he always been this way?"

Gina turned serious for a moment.

"Maybe a little bit, but it got worse a few months before Annie got killed."

This was interesting.

"Did he ever tell you why?"

"No. He said it was nothing."

"And you're sure it started getting worse in the months right before Annie was killed?"

"Yeah, I think so."

"On a scale of 1-10, how positive are you?"

"I don't know. How about a 7.6352," Gina said. "Is that close enough for you, Mr. Interview Man?"

Safe to say, I didn't like this woman very much. She was being obnoxious for no reason.

"Did anyone else notice that he was acting weird?"

"No. Just me."

"How can you be so sure?"

"Because it wasn't something he liked to share with his parents, and it's not like he had that many friends."

"Could he have told Annie?"

"Maybe, I guess."

Gina lit up another cigarette, which I took as my cue. I'd likely see Gina again, but for now, I was ready to be done with her.

"I have one last question."

"Shoot."

"Did you ever think that Kai's death was anything other than a suicide?"

She pondered the question.

"He walked by that bridge every day, and he'd talked about suicide before. I think he just snapped and impulsively jumped one day."

"Did many people know he walked by there every day?"

"Yeah, I guess," she said.

"Thanks," I said. "I'll be in touch."

"Can't wait," she said sarcastically.

I showed myself out as Gina Galasso remained seated while attempting a smoke ring.

CHAPTER 6

Kai Butler's parents, Doug and Sophie, had moved out of Los Angeles less than a year after Kai committed suicide.

I couldn't blame them, but for the purposes of my investigation, it made things more difficult. Kai seemed an important part of this massive puzzle, but I wouldn't be able to meet with his parents in person unless I traveled to Des Moines, Iowa.

I called them the morning after I'd met with Gina Galasso.

As you may have guessed, they weren't delighted that I was reopening old wounds.

"What did you say your name was?" Doug Butler asked.

"Bobby McGowan."

"And William hired you to look into Annie's death?"

"Yes."

"Why would he do a thing like that?"

"I guess you'd have to ask him."

"Unlikely. We're not exactly pen pals since we moved all those years ago."

"Does your wife still talk to her brother?"

"You're getting a little personal here, guy."

"I'm sorry. I'm just trying to look at every possibility regarding Annie's death, and since your son died less than a few months later, it seems important."

I heard him let out a sigh on the other end.

"I can respect that you're just trying to do your job, but you must understand this is incredibly tough for me and my wife. Even all these years later."

This was becoming a recurring theme.

"I understand. I'll try to keep this as painless as possible."

"Okay, what do you want to know?"

"When did you notice that Kai was first getting a little depressed?"

"He'd been that way his whole life if we're being honest."

"Gina Galasso told me that she thought it started getting a lot worse a few months before Annie died."

"She told you that? I liked her when she was dating Kai, but from what I've heard, she's fallen off a cliff in recent years. We had Kai seeing a psychologist by the time he was ten years old. His depression never really went away. So Gina's wrong to suggest it got worse leading up to Annie's death. And I don't like the suggestion behind that."

I tended to believe Doug Butler. Gina hadn't left a positive impression, which made me wonder if maybe she was wrong about Annie being promiscuous as well.

"She wasn't insinuating that," I said. "She defended your son."

"Okay," Doug Butler said, calming down a bit.

"Did you keep in touch with Gina over the years?" I asked.

"I saw her a few times after our son's funeral, but not much. My wife kept in touch with her for a year or two, only to hear stories about Kai. If memory serves, I think she moved to Colorado after high school. At some point, my wife started to think she might be using drugs, and she realized there were better ways to remember Kai."

"But you've heard she's not doing that great?"

"Just from people who still live in LA. Rumors are that she has a drug habit. But I'm telling you, that wasn't the girl my son was dating. That girl was sweet."

"That's too bad about Gina."

"Sure is."

"Is your wife home right now? I just wanted to ask her a few quick questions."

"No, she's at the store. I could have her call you, but please promise to keep it brief. She gets depressed just talking about Kai."

"I promise it will just be a couple of questions."

"Okay, then. And are we almost done?"

"Just one more question."

"What is it?"

"Did you ever suspect anyone in Annie's death?"

"Nice to hear someone finally calling it what it is. People would talk about Annie's disappearance for years as if she would walk through the door someday—false hopes if you ask me. And no, I never suspected anyone. It was a day for the family. How could anyone kill our sweet little Annie?"

It was becoming evident that Annie was viewed differently depending on who you talked to.

"I'll let you go for now, Mr. Butler. Can I call again if something comes up?"

I'd continue asking this politely, even though I knew that if I needed a question answered, I'd call back, regardless of what they said.

"Yeah, I guess," he said.

∼

THIRTY MINUTES LATER, his wife Sophie called back, and I talked to her for about five minutes. I mentioned that I had spoken to William and Connor, and she lamented that she hadn't seen her brothers in years.

Doug had made it sound like he and his wife weren't close to William, but I could still feel the pain in Sophie's voice.

We moved on to Kai, and she talked about how he was such a smart kid and that maybe his mind was too busy for this world.

"He couldn't get out of his own way," she said. "He was a classic over-thinker and never achieved peace of mind."

"He seemed like a great young kid," I said.

"Thanks," Sophie said.

She had little more to add, and it was apparent that it was very tough for her to talk about Kai.

I got off the phone as quickly as I could.

∼

I STILL THOUGHT the Kai Butler angle was intriguing, but since he and Annie were dead, his ex-girlfriend was a crackpot, and his parents were far away in Iowa, I decided to put him on the back burner for the time being.

I'd double back if and when necessary.

I called William Ryan.

"Hello, Bobby. Are you making any progress?"

"I'm learning more every day, but nothing groundbreaking yet."
"That's good. I'm sure you'll come up with something."
I found that an odd thing to say.
"Listen, I'd like to come back to your house."
"No problem. For what reason exactly?"
"I want to get a better read of the house's layout. And when I'm done doing that, I'd like to ask you a few more questions."
"Okay. How does tomorrow at nine a.m. sound?"
"I'll be there."

CHAPTER 7

The Beverly Hilton was a plush hotel, and part of me just wanted to sit by the pool and conduct my interviews over the phone. It was June, after all.

But no, I had a job to do.

Telling William that I wanted to get a better feel for the house wasn't just lip service. I didn't feel I got a good enough look that first time. I'd met him and decided to take the case, but I hadn't walked around the house and got the lay of the land.

That had only been four days ago. It felt much longer.

When you're dealing with the murder of a young woman - and the suicide of a young man - days can feel like weeks.

I ARRIVED at William's house a few minutes before nine. I parked on top, where all the cars would have been valeted all those years ago.

In his case summary, Earl Razzle included a section dedicated to all the cars at the party and the people in each vehicle. That may become important as my investigation progresses, but there wasn't much I could do with it for now.

William Ryan met me up top.

"How are you, Bobby?"

"Okay, I guess. Not that I have to tell you, but this is a pretty heavy case."

"I'm sure this can't be easy. That's why I'm paying you the big bucks," he said and smiled.

"It's nice to see you again in person," he added. "Sounds like you've been talking to a lot of people."

"I talked to your sister yesterday."

"I know. She called me. It had been several months since we'd talked, so I guess I owe you a thanks."

"I don't deserve credit for that."

"Well, even if you never catch Annie's killer, maybe you'll get more people talking in this family again. I'd consider that a win."

I didn't know how to react, so I just nodded.

"Did you want me to walk you around the grounds?" William asked.

"I thought I'd do it myself. After all, I'm the new eyes on the case, and I'd like to look at the house without any built-in biases."

"What do you mean exactly?"

"Well, you might say something like, 'It never could have happened in this room because dot dot dot.' And you may well be right, but I'd like to come to that conclusion myself."

"Okay. I get where you're coming from."

"Are all the doors to the house and the rooms open right now?"

"The rooms should all be open. I'll unlock a few of the house doors that may be locked. Will that work?"

"Yes."

"Give me five minutes, and then you can enter the house. I'll be in the study where we met last time. Come find me there when you are done."

"I will. Thanks, William."

"Is there anything else?"

William's wife Penny hadn't come up once, and now, she hadn't been at the house on either occasion I'd visited.

"Does your wife still live here?" I asked.

I saw a rare show of emotion from William. He'd remained unflappable when discussing Annie. But by bringing up his wife, I'd caused a reaction.

"She's currently in the Swiss Alps, and I think she goes to Morocco after that. Martha's Vineyard is sometime later this summer. You see, Penny and I have basically been separated for the last ten years. We won't get divorced because there are so many tax implications, so instead, she just travels around the world on my dime, which I'm okay with. She bore me two beautiful children."

Come to think of it, his children hadn't come up much either.

"Where are they right now?"

"I think my son is in the Swiss Alps with my wife. And I'm not sure exactly where my daughter is at the moment. Probably with that deadbeat husband of hers. So, why don't you come see me in the study when you're done?"

That was William's way of saying that this part of the conversation was over. The multi-millionaire's family life was a disaster; that much was obvious. I wasn't sure if he talked to any of the three.

It appeared he lived in this massive house all by himself.

I don't know many people who would enjoy that.

FOR THE NEXT SEVENTY-FIVE MINUTES, I walked around almost every step of the property.

That may seem like a long time, but for a house with eight bedrooms, I needed every minute of it.

The house itself was long but not very wide. The upper parking area was a vast blacktop that probably could have accommodated twenty cars. There were sixteen cars up there on the night in question, and I'm assuming it could have fit a few more.

From there, you take a small set of stairs down to the house's front door, where you are greeted by a giant dining room - where the dinner was held - and an open-air kitchen beside it. Past the kitchen, there is an extremely long hallway where seven of the eight bedrooms are located. The master bedroom was in its own area, nestled about fifty feet behind the dining room.

I was most interested in the seven bedrooms along the hallway. I walked into them all and spent at least a few minutes looking around each.

The rooms that didn't have a door to the backyard didn't interest me as much. If the room only opened into the long hallway, I considered them an improbable place to kill Annie. It would be exceedingly risky to bring a body out of one of those rooms. With fifty people at the party, it's almost inevitable one of them would be walking down the hallway at any given time. The exception would have been dinner, but even then, hauling the body of a fifteen-year-old would take time, and someone would likely see you.

You wouldn't have that problem with the rooms that had a door opening to the backyard.

In that case, you could have dragged Annie's body out and possibly placed it in the woods nearby.

I spent most of my time in those three bedrooms but tried not to hover too long.

It had been twenty-five years; it was not like I was going to find a blood stain.

∽

AFTER FINISHING THE LONG HALLWAY, I went outside. At the far end of the house—on the opposite side of where everyone's car was parked—was a hot tub and a black-bottom pool.

A massive lawn ran parallel to the house, and then there were the woods.

This was the Hollywood Hills, and you probably wouldn't imagine it as some sort of forest, but almost every house was surrounded by large trees, which helped to give each home some privacy —something that millionaires desired more than most.

The trees at the end of the lawn were large, probably sixty feet high, and they went on for a good fifty yards until you reached the closest neighbor's home.

Could the killer have taken Annie's body into the mass of trees? It was possible, maybe even probable.

The only problem with this theory was that the police had searched the woods that night and found nothing. It would have been dark, however, and the police reports suggest they only took a cursory look at the area, so I think it's very possible they could have missed her body.

The assumption was that the killer returned later that night or early the next morning to transfer the body. The LAPD returned at eight a.m., and they thoroughly checked the woods that morning and found no trace of Annie. So, if the popular theory was correct, someone came back and removed her body before the police returned.

Leaving her body in one of the rooms wouldn't have been possible because the LAPD searched every room on the night in question.

Could the killer have hidden Annie's body in the back of a closet and covered it with clothes, and the police - and the guests - just missed it?

Highly unlikely.

~

I FOUND William after I'd finished my walkthrough.

"So, what do you think?" he asked.

I didn't want to tell him every theory I came up with. I had no idea who did this or knew who William might mention this to. The more tight-lipped I was, the better.

That said, I didn't see the harm in telling him my working theory, and it's not like I was breaking new ground.

He heard me out and nodded.

"It makes the most sense. It always has."

"How many of your rooms were being used on the night in question?"

"Well, our kids each had their rooms. And we had two of the oldest people in the family staying the night, so they'd each had a room as well."

"I'm most curious about the three rooms with doors into the backyard."

"Ah, yes. My son, Henry, had one of the rooms with a backdoor, but my daughter Amy's room did not. And I think one of the elderly people might have been using one of the rooms with a backdoor. About details like that, I'm not positive. And I don't think it matters who was staying in them."

"Why is that?"

"Annie went missing during dinner when no one was in their rooms, anyway. It doesn't seem important whose room it was."

I disagreed. I found it unlikely that Annie would enter one of the older people's rooms. But I didn't say that to William because then it might sound like I was suspicious of his son or, at least, his son's room.

I wanted to ask Gina Galasso if she could remember whose room had the booze. Since it had been full of the younger generation, it seemed possible that Annie could have been tempted—or lured—back to that room.

"You're probably right," I said to William, not wanting to delve deeper into the subject. At least, not yet.

"Is there anything else you'd like to know?" he asked.

"Do you have any connections with the LAPD? I'd like to meet with a few detectives who worked the case."

"The first homicide detective who worked the case is gone. His name was Phillip Chide. He died about six months after he took the case."

"How did he die?"

This case had me on edge, and hearing about the detective's death, I immediately became suspicious. You never knew if they could be related.

"He had a heart attack. It was devastating to me. I thought he was a bulldog of a detective, and he'd eventually get his man. Or woman."

I hadn't given much thought to Annie's killer being a woman, but there was always that possibility. It was hard to imagine a woman carrying her dead body into the woods, but you never know. I reminded myself not to rule anyone out.

"The police report most often mentioned a guy named Mike Minter," I said.

"Yeah, he took over for Chide. I immediately didn't like Minter, and that continues to this day. He has not been nearly as helpful as I would have wished."

"Does Mr. Minter still work for the LAPD?"

"Yes."

"You have his number?"

"I do," he said. "Hold on, I have to scroll through my phone."

He started doing just that.

"And I had another question," I said.

"Shoot."

"Why didn't you mention the name Rex Zell? Or Kai Butler?"

"I've already told you why."

"Remind me," I said.

"Because I didn't want you to have any built-in suspicions before you started investigating. Fresh eyes, didn't you say that? Or was it me?"

I smiled.

"I can't remember at this point, either."

"Me neither," William said. "I just shared Minter's number with you."

I looked down at my phone.

"Got it."

"His precinct isn't far from here, so if he's in, you could see him now."

"I will."

"But be on guard. He's not the friendliest of cops."

∼

I COULDN'T DECIDE if Mike Minter should have played in the NFL or the NBA. On one hand, he was probably 250 pounds and built like a linebacker. On the other hand, he was around 6'5", and I could have seen him as a great small forward. Charles Barkley came to mind.

The only difference was that Mike Minter was white. He did have the same bald head as Sir Charles, however.

We met at the LAPD precinct on North Wilcox Avenue, which served the Hollywood Hills.

Someone at the front desk greeted me, and when I mentioned my name, Mike Minter walked over.

I imagine the fact that Annie Ryan's killer had never been found was a stain on the Los Angeles Police Department, specifically the Hollywood division. The fact that they never found her body made it even worse.

"Detective Minter," he said and extended his hand.

What followed was an aggressive handshake from a guy with an aggressive aura. I could tell that in the few seconds I'd been in his presence. I doubted very many people fucked with Mike Minter.

"Bobby McGowan," I said.

"Follow me."

As Minter walked toward his office, a detective in his early forties approached him.

"Hey, Reggie," Minter said.

"Hey, Mike."

After he passed, Minter looked at me and said, "He can call me Mike. You can't."

I could tell this was going to go well.

We entered his office, where three coffee cups and two huge files were splayed across his desk.

"Excuse the mess," he said.

He wasn't the first police officer who'd had a messy desk. It seemed to run in the "family."

We both sat down.

"Your reputation precedes you, Mr. McGowan."

"Oh yeah?"

"Sure. I heard about your mother's case and all you did to catch the guy. What an unbelievable accomplishment. You should be very proud of yourself."

He was laying it on pretty thick, and a sneer came with it. I got the impression he was mocking me. This guy was a real piece of work.

"Thank you," I said, deciding not to rock the boat just yet.

"You're welcome, Mr. McGowan."

I was only thirty-two years old and didn't like being called Mister.

"Mr. McGowan is my father. Call me Bobby," I said.

It reminded me that I hadn't talked to my Dad since the day after I took the case. It was time to call him.

Detective Minter nodded at me, and his face turned serious.

"How can I help you, Bobby?"

He'd been polite, but it was perfunctory. Mike Minter didn't like me.

"I've got a good overall grasp of the night Annie Ryan went missing, but I wanted to hear from someone working this case since the beginning."

"It sounds like you got yourself some faulty information there, Bobby. I didn't start the case until six months after the murder. Phillip Chide was the lead before then."

I swore at myself under my breath. What an amateur mistake on my part.

"I knew that. I'm sorry."

"That's okay," he said, but there was a slight smirk as if he was happy to see me fuck up.

"What did Chide think of the case? And what were your initial impressions after taking over from him?"

"Let me just say one thing first," Minter said, leaning toward me. "I'm only giving you this time as a favor to William Ryan. You're not a detective. You're not even a P.I."

He wasn't wrong.

"Well, I just appreciate the time. Very generous of you." I said.

He stared at me, trying to get a read. Was I now the one being sarcastic? He was attempting to figure that out. I was, but I'd never admit it.

Instead, I just got another sneer from him. One thing was certain: Mike Minter would not be starting a Bobby McGowan Fan Club.

"I agreed with Phillip Chide for the most part. At least to start. We both believed something tragic happened, and someone tried to cover it up."

"Do you care to elaborate on that?" I asked.

"We tended to think the death was accidental."

"Why?"

"Because who plans on murdering someone when fifty other people are in the same house as you?"

"Makes sense. But it could have been an unplanned murder. Like someone goes crazy and strangles Annie."

"That's possible, but our investigation never led us in that direction. No one had a motive."

"To me, and I understand I just started on this case, it seems unlikely someone would cover up an accident. If one of Annie's cousins and she were playing around on a bed and Annie fell and broke her neck, why not just come clean and say it was a horrible accident? Why go and hide or get rid of her body?"

"I've seen that exact scenario dozens of times. People accidentally kill someone and then panic and try to cover it up, making matters worse."

While what Detective Minter said was possible, it still didn't ring true.

"Let's stick with my cousin scenario," I said. "You think a teen or early twenty-something would have the wherewithal to go hide her body and come back and pick it up later? And I didn't even mention that Annie weighed a hundred and twenty pounds. That's a lot of weight for someone to carry around."

"Once again, I've seen it before. People can be crazy strong when they need to be."

He glared at me as if to say that line of questioning was over.

"Where do you think Annie was killed?" I asked.

"Maybe one of the rooms. Maybe outside. We just don't know."

"Hadn't Annie been at the dinner table when they started serving?"

"Yes. What's your point?" Minter asked, but not in a pleasant, question-asking type of way.

"Doesn't it seem more likely that she'd stay in the house? I mean, who leaves a huge family dinner to go outside?"

"Teenagers."

I nodded.

"That's fair."

I hated to agree with Detective Minter, but his point was valid. I knew many teenagers who would love to leave a family dinner whenever possible. Shit, I had been one of those kids.

Neither one of us said anything. Minter continued to be pretty tight-lipped, surely on purpose. I hadn't got much out of him, and the whole "it was an accident" thing didn't satisfy me. It seemed disingenuous. I knew he wouldn't like it, but I doubled-back to it.

"If you really thought this was an accident, you probably wouldn't want to commit many man-hours to it, especially now that twenty-five years have passed."

He stared at me for a few seconds.

"Are you saying we didn't give the investigation its proper due?"

"I'm not saying anything. I'm asking a question."

He leaned in closer.

"Ask it again."

"If you thought this was all some random accident, would you spend as many man hours as you would on a suspected murder?"

"Your question sounds the same the second time."

"You still haven't answered it."

"We would still spend the same amount of time on it," he said.

I probably shouldn't have said what I said next, but I was fired up. Mike Minter was a jerk.

"So, you would spend as much time investigating a kid dying from a trampoline fall as you would if that kid was murdered?"

He hopped up from his desk, obviously pissed.

"You're a sarcastic asshole, aren't you?"

"I hadn't planned on being one," I said. "I just don't believe you think this was an accident. I feel like I'm being stonewalled."

"Well, like I said, you're not a cop, nor a P.I. Here, let me check my rule book and see what it says about stonewalling private citizens."

He made a fake production like he was thumbing through the pages of his non-existent book. He then sat back down.

"Oh, looky here. It says there's no law against it," he said, and he fake-shut the book that wasn't there.

I wasn't going to get anything more out of him—that much was obvious—but I couldn't let him bully me, so I decided to press his buttons.

"It's too bad for the Ryan family that Philip Chide passed away."

"Are you suggesting he would have solved what I haven't?" he asked.

"No, I would never suggest that. I'm sure this is your year," I said.

Minter rose from his chair a second time, shoved it back, and leaned toward me. He looked like he wanted to take a swing at me.

"This meeting is over. Good luck with your investigation, Mr. McGowan."

I couldn't resist one last snide response.

"Don't you remember? It's Bobby."

"Get the fuck out of here," he said.

So I did.

I'd pissed off the lead detective and knew he wouldn't be helpful from here on in.

Good job, Bobby.

CHAPTER 8

THE KILLER

When I first heard the name Bobby McGowan, it meant nothing to me.

He was just another in a long line of private investigators hired by William Ryan in hopes of catching Annie's killer.

Who just happened to be me.

But as I did with the rest of the overmatched PIs, I decided to read up on Bobby. Be prepared, as they say.

I'll give it to Bobby. He was more interesting than the rest, with the possible exception of Earl Razzle, who was quite the character. Not that it had helped him. He'd been looking into the case for twenty years and never came to suspect me. Sorry there, Earl. At least you look sharp on TV.

Most of the PI's bios were pretty much the same. They caught this guy. They caught that gal. They worked with this lawyer. They worked with that police department.

Blah Blah Blah.

Bobby McGowan was different. He wasn't a PI at all. More than anything, he was a son who was pissed off that his mother's killer was never caught and took things into his own hands, accomplishing the impossible.

McGowan had done this on his own, and the killer, Conrad Drury, didn't sound like a dumb criminal—the opposite, in fact. He'd had an escape plan that was second to none.

And yet, McGowan had somehow still found Conrad - and then killed him. I hated to admit it, but I was impressed. Maybe I was selling Bobby McGowan short.

Conrad Drury also intrigued me. I started reading about the murders he had committed. We shared a lot in common. He might have even been crazier than I; I mean, this fucking guy framed innocent people for the murders he committed. Who does that?

You have my respect, Conrad Drury, but you still lost your life at the hands of Bobby McGowan. That will never, ever happen to me. I'm too intelligent.

I liked that Conrad conversed with McGowan. I appreciated the flair.

He wasn't just some no-name, easily forgotten killer. He was among the greats, just as I was. The noticeable difference was that he was no longer with us while I was still wreaking havoc.

After debating with my inner demon - yes, mine is a singular beast - I began considering reaching out to Bobby McGowan. No, I wouldn't be a schmuck like Conrad Drury and do it via some random website. I was going to give this some thought. Make sure I was hidden behind approximately twenty firewalls. Ensure that there was no risk on my end.

I hated to admit it, but life had become a little boring. It was time to spice things up.

One gem I discovered about Bobby - in some random article I found online - was that his given name was Robert, but in his own words, he 'hated being called it.'

Well, guess what? That's your name from here on in.

Robert. Robert. Robert. Robert.

This is going to be a lot of fun.

Be talking to you soon, Robert.

CHAPTER 9

BOBBY

After my antagonistic meeting with Mike Minter, I returned to the Beverly Hilton and called my father. A few days later than I should have.

I told him about the case's progress and how it was slow-moving in the same way that my mother's had been. There were a lot of similarities. Both crimes took place a long time ago; there was no DNA to speak of, and obviously, the police had never found their man.

All I could do was meet and interview people, hoping that would lead somewhere. I viewed each interview as a jigsaw puzzle piece. I wasn't going to solve the case with just a couple of pieces, but as I got more and more under my belt, the giant puzzle might start to slowly come into view.

My analogy wasn't perfect, and my father told me so.

"You need every single puzzle piece to finish a puzzle," he said.

"It's a work in progress."

I heard my father laugh. That was happening a lot more often since I'd put an end to Conrad Drury. If catching my mother's killer was the most important thing I'd accomplished, having my father return to being a happy man was a close second.

"When are you coming back up here?" he asked.

"I'll find my way to Santa Barbara in the next few weeks. I promise."

"Okay, great. Be good to see you. Now get back to working on those puzzle pieces."

∼

UNFORTUNATELY, despite my father's encouragement, the puzzle pieces were coming in slower than I'd expected.

I knew the reason why. I was going about this like a TV police procedural does. Step A to Step B to Step C. Slow, gradual, linear progression.

Annie's murder investigation had likely been done this exact way from the beginning. I certainly wasn't going to catch the killer in a month by doing the same as everybody else.

I needed to throw a monkey wrench in my way of thinking.

I needed to think outside of the box.

A crazy theory. An off-the-wall suggestion. Anything to break the monotony.

I wanted to hear Cousin A say why he thought Uncle B did it. Or grandson C say why Grandpa D had been Annie's killer.

Even if I had to listen to some off-the-wall theories, those might lead me to indirectly learn something important. And hopefully, a few more puzzle pieces might start fitting into place.

∼

I CALLED WILLIAM RYAN.

It had only been two days since I'd spent over an hour looking around his house.

"How's the investigation going, Bobby?"

"I feel like I'm covering ground that's been covered by plenty of people already."

"Well, that's only natural. You're learning about all this stuff for the first time."

"I understand that, but I'd like to look in a new direction for a few days."

"What do you have in mind?"

"Actually, I was hoping you could help."

"Sure. How?"

"This will sound like an odd request, but does someone in your family have some wild theories about what might have happened to Annie? Maybe someone who is kind of the crackpot of the family."

"We've got a few of those, but one stands above everyone else."

"Who is that?"

"Annie's second cousin. His name is Adam Toon. He's a bit whacky."

"And he's got some theories on Annie?"

"Oh, I'm sure he does. He's got theories on everything."

"Perfect. How do I get ahold of him?"

"He still lives in LA. I'll give you his number. But first, you have to guess his nickname. Remember, his name is Adam Toon."

CHAPTER 10

"Toon the Loon. That's me."

"You sure you don't want me to call you Adam?" I asked.

"Whatever you want. I don't mind being called Toon the Loon. That's what everyone has been calling me since I was like twelve. I take it as a badge of honor."

"If you don't mind, I will go with Adam."

"Whatever floats your boat."

I was sitting across from Adam Toon, a.k.a. Toon the Loon, at his apartment in Santa Monica. And yes, I had guessed his nickname immediately.

Adam lived three blocks from Gina Galasso's apartment but felt worlds apart. His complex was much more modern, and his apartment was clean. There were no lit cigarettes or dirty ashtrays to be seen.

However, he did have some interesting artwork, including a whale/shark/dolphin/human all morphed into one. Was it trying to say that we humans came from the sea? I had no idea. I'm sure his nickname hadn't come out of left field.

"Thanks for meeting with me," I said.

"You're welcome. It's not every day some guy says he wants to hear some of your crazy theories. Usually, it's the exact opposite, and they tell me to shut up."

"I was tired of doing and hearing the same old thing every day."

"Join the club. That's like my motto in life."

Adam had seemed pretty normal to this point, but while I sat in the love seat he'd pointed me to, he sat Indian-style on the floor. That was a bit odd, I had to admit.

"So, William told me you are Annie's second cousin?"

"See, you're already agreeing with my line of thinking."

"I don't follow," I said.

"You said 'are' not 'were' regarding Annie as if she's still alive. One of my crazy theories is that Annie wasn't killed on that Christmas Eve so many years ago."

I'd asked for this.

"Alright, let's hear that theory."

"You know how they say all the best lies have an element of truth?"

"Yes."

"Well, my theory is based on truth. Even if my conclusion turns out to be false."

"Okay, I think I'm following."

I had a feeling shit was about to get weird.

"To get to my point, I'm going to ask you some rapid-fire questions," Adam said.

"Okay, sure."

"Do most people think Annie was killed on the night in question?"

"Yes."

"On the premises, correct?"

"Yes."

"And yet, her body was never found there, right?"

We both knew the answer, but I decided to play along.

"That's correct."

"And they had cops at the house that night, right?"

"Yes."

"And they checked the woods behind William's house, right?"

"Yes."

"And the next day, they came back again?"

"Yes."

"With dogs this time, right?"

"Yes."

"And they searched the woods again?"

"Yes."

"But the dogs never picked up any scent of Annie, right?"

I had to think back to the police report that Earl Razzle had given me.

"Correct. The dogs didn't pick up on any scent."

"And they never found anything signifying that Annie had died in the house or that her dead body was left in the woods for any amount of time?"

Adam had switched up how he asked the question, and it would be my first no.

"No, they didn't."

"And yet, they all still think she died that night, right?"

He switched back.

"Yes," I said.

"Which brings me to my point. There is no evidence Annie was killed in the house. Not one drop of blood. Nothing. The same goes for the house's outside and the surrounding woods. The dogs picked up no scent. And she was not carried dead to one of the waiting cars since there were valet guys there. So, where did the body go? Could it have gone unseen by the cops on the night of, and then someone comes back and gets her body the next morning? Maybe, but I'm not convinced of it like everyone else."

Toon the Loon paused momentarily and took a breath. I had been starting to doubt whether the guy needed to breathe like the rest of us.

"So, Bobby, ask me what I think happened?"

"What do you think happened?"

"I think Annie left dinner and then ducked out of one of the rooms and walked through the backyard to the bottom part of the house where the lawn and the valets couldn't see her. Then she had someone pick her up and drive away."

He paused, signifying he was done.

"So you think she's still alive?" I asked.

"I'm not sure if she's still alive, but my main thesis is that she didn't die that night."

"You came up with this elaborate theory. What are your other thoughts? See it to the end," I said.

Adam smiled. He was happy that I wanted to hear more.

"So, he was an older man because otherwise, her parents or friends would have known about the guy. Let's say he was in his early twenties. He couldn't tell his parents, obviously. He was twenty-one, and she was fifteen. This isn't rural West Virginia. So, he had to be subtle. He and Annie were starting to fall in love, and he told Annie they could fake her disappearance and travel the country together, unencumbered by her parents. Or his. And what better day to get this all started than Christmas Eve? None."

He took a deep breath, but I didn't dare interrupt. He was on a roll.

"They traveled together for a few months. They got out of California, where the cops were looking for her. Their first stop was probably to dye her hair or do something to make her look older. I don't know. Maybe matching tattoos would make people believe they were a couple. And maybe they did this for a while. It's unlikely they went to Europe. I don't know if Annie even had a passport, and the older guy must have known that the cops would be alerted if Annie's passport was used. So, instead, they just drove around the U.S., staying at divey motels on his credit card. She'd never use her ID or do anything to bring attention to herself. Now, here's the problem."

He took a quick breath and continued a second later.

"After about three months - maybe less - Annie starts getting homesick. This older guy was fun and exciting and showed her things she'd never seen, but now she was starting to miss her family. And she realized that what they'd done was pretty darn horrible. Her parents would be worried sick. While initially enjoying being on the run, Annie started feeling bad for what she was putting her parents through. She chastised herself for being so selfish. So, Annie made the colossal mistake of asking the guy if they could go home. He knew this was an impossibility. He'd be charged with kidnapping, statutory rape, and probably ten other things. No, thank you. Returning her or turning themselves in were both out of the question. He tried to sell Annie on the idea that this was a massive crime and she'd be charged as an adult. She might spend twenty years in jail. Annie wasn't buying his pitch. She said she didn't care. She wanted to go home, and if she had to spend some time in jail, that's a chance she was willing to take. And that's when Mr. Twenty-one-year-old decided that he had to kill her. Which he did."

"Where?" I said, continuing this thought exercise.

"At some cornfield in Nebraska. Or Iowa. He took her to the middle of the cornfield late one night, killed her, then dug a huge hole and buried her in it. Never to be seen again."

This time, I was the one taking a deep breath.

"Now I know how you got your nickname," I said.

He laughed pretty loudly.

"So, what do you think?"

"The overall thesis is not entirely impossible," I said.

"See, I knew you'd believe it."

"'Not entirely impossible' is hardly the same as believing it."

"Okay. You didn't not believe it. Is that better?"

I smiled and shrugged.

"I guess."

"Why did William hire you?"

"To find out what happened to your cousin. I told you that."

"I know, but why you? A million PIs are out there, and you're not even one of them."

We'd reached the point that every conversation seemed to reach these days: *Why was I qualified to investigate Annie's disappearance?*

"I solved a decades-old murder. Do you know what I'm referring to?"

"Yes. I Googled you before you came over today, and what you accomplished is amazing. I'm just trying to make sure William didn't hire you for ulterior motives."

"Like what?"

"I don't know, so that he could keep you under his finger? A licensed PI has connections and can go in his own direction. Do their own thing. They are harder to keep on a leash."

"Why would William want to keep me on a leash? Are you saying he was somehow involved?"

"I doubt he had anything directly to do with Annie's death."

"Directly?"

"You know what he does, right?"

"Yes."

"You know how much he's worth, right?"

"Yes."

Adam was definitely taught the Socratic method at some point in his life. The questions never stopped with this guy.

"And you do know that money makes the world go round?"

"I've heard the expression."

"Well, maybe somebody took Annie to ask for a ransom from our family's only wealthy member. Maybe William didn't go to the cops and tried to pay the ransom himself, but something went terribly wrong. And maybe he'd rather have someone like you to monitor more than a real PI."

It was time to switch this game around.

"I've got a couple of questions for you," I said.

"Let's hear it."

"Is Earl Razzle a PI?"

"Yes."

"Did William hire him?"

"Yes."

"Is he an attention-seeking PI?"

"Yes."

"Does Razzle seem like a guy you can keep on a leash?"

"No."

"Have there been other PIs besides Razzle?"

"Yes."

"So your point about William not hiring PIs doesn't hold water?"

"All fair points. You're pretty good at this," Adam said, and we shared a laugh.

"Maybe he just thought I really would bring a new set of eyes to this," I said.

"Maybe you're right."

In one quick, impressive move, Adam went from sitting Indian style to rising off the ground without ever putting his arms down to touch the ground. I'd never seen anything like it and knew I'd have no chance of accomplishing the feat.

"I'm grabbing some tea. Would you like some?" he asked.

"I'll take a water if you have one."

"Coming up."

He set off to the kitchen. I could have excused myself at that point, but there were a few other questions I wanted to ask him first. He had no filter, and his openness was invaluable in a family that seemed so guarded about this tragedy.

He returned a minute later, handing me my water, then slinking back to the ground without using his hands. Impressive stuff.

"How well did you know Annie?" I asked.

"If we were doing a pie chart about how well all the cousins knew Annie, I would fall somewhere in the middle. My little orange triangle would take up like 8% of the whole chart."

Toon the Loon continued to live up to his name. It was becoming harder to imagine him as an Adam.

"I've heard that Kai Butler was close to her," I said.

"He was. It's such a shame about Kai. I liked him a lot."

"Did you always think it was a suicide?"

He looked me over.

"I wish I could give you some great conspiratorial story like I did with Annie. The truth is, I'm not sure about Kai. He had been treated for depression over the years. Everyone in the family knew it. Plus, he'd lost his best friend in the family. So, of course, it's possible. But he never seemed like the type who would go through with it. I don't know what to think about his death. I never have."

He covered his face in his hands.

"I'm sorry, Adam."

"Thanks. It was such a shitty time for our family."

I decided to change the subject.

"How exactly are you related to Annie?"

"My father was one of William's many cousins."

"I can't keep track of all of you guys."

"Don't feel bad. Neither can I."

We laughed.

"On the night in question, did you see Annie much?"

"I saw her when she walked in. I was hanging out with a few other cousins by the front door when Annie, Connor, and Emily walked in. She gave us all a big hug, but then her Dad called her over and said she should go thank William for throwing the party."

"Was that odd?"

"Kind of. Do you have to thank the host in the first minute of getting there?"

"It sounds like you're not the biggest fan of William Ryan."

He smiled, but it was an odd, indifferent smile.

"How can I not love the guy who gave me my nickname?"

"He gave it to you?"

"Yup."

"Not exactly the nicest name to burden a young kid with. What did you say? You've had it since you were twelve?"

"Yeah, right around then. And yes, it's not the greatest nickname to bequeath a young kid. But it stands out in this buttoned-down family, so it can't be all bad."

He took a sip of his tea. He looked suddenly vulnerable, like maybe the nickname had caused him grief over the years, and he just didn't want to admit it.

I felt bad.

"Hey Adam, I think I'm going to get on the road in a minute," I said, intentionally referring to him by his given name. "It was nice meeting you. If I have some more questions, can I contact you?"

It's how I was closing every interview.

"Of course. You want some more crazy theories?"

"Next time."

"How about one more quick one?"

"Let's hear it."

"I'll make this one extra quick."

"Okay."

"Like one sentence quick."

I didn't respond so he'd get to the point, which he finally did.

"What if the hierarchy of the Ryan family already knows Annie's fate, and you're just a patsy?"

"A patsy for what?"

"I don't know, but I'd look both ways before I crossed the road."

"What are you saying, Adam?"

"Oh, I'm just being Toon the Loon, the craziest member of the Ryan tribe."

Now, he was officially starting to get odd.

I stood up.

"I hope to see you again, Mr. Patsy man," he said.

"It's been twenty-something years. What would be the point in hiring a patsy? And to what end? If I find nothing, what does hiring me accomplish?"

"I don't know, but time will tell."

If Adam Toon were a movie, he would have been great for the first ninety minutes but fell apart for the last fifteen. Had he put something in his tea?

I took a few steps toward the door.

"Hey, one more thing before you go," he said. "I've got someone you should see. She's the smartest Ryan I know. And that includes Mr. Rich Guy, William."

"Sure. Who is it?"

"Her name is Amber Ryan. She is a recently divorced mother of three and has a lot on her plate, but I bet she'd be willing to meet with you."

"How's she related to Annie?"

"She's a second cousin like I am. Her father is William's first cousin, too. Our fathers are brothers."

"Didn't I just tell you that your family tree is going to be the death of me," I said.

Adam Toon laughed.

"Ain't that the truth."

I had made my way to the door.

"Hold up, one second," he said. "I'm going to call Amber right now. She lives in LA. Would you be willing to meet with her today?"

"Of course."

He made the call, and I had another interview lined up a few minutes later.

"Thanks," I said.

"You're welcome."
"I'll be in touch. You take care, Adam."
"Look both ways," he said.
I walked out of his apartment and made my way to my car.
Was everyone in this family half crazy?

CHAPTER 11

Amber Ryan lived in Pasadena and was the mother of three.
Immediately upon answering the door, one of Amber's children ran by her and me and headed toward the street.

"Get back here, Bonnie," she said.

Amber had strawberry blond hair that represented her Irish roots well. She wore it quite long, something you didn't see as often anymore. She was pretty.

Her daughter returned, and as we walked into the house, I was greeted by two more children, another girl, and one son.

"Can you all say hi to Bobby?" she said.

She treated me like an old friend despite having just learned my name on the phone an hour before.

Or had she learned my name from another family member before Adam Toon contacted her? This got me thinking about whether my name —and what I was doing—had spread through the Ryan family over the last week.

"Thanks for meeting with me," I said. "Cute kids. How old are they?"

"Ten, nine, and seven."

I quickly glanced at Razzle's file when I returned to my hotel before this meeting. Amber Ryan—she had been Amber Ryan Beauford, but she was recently divorced—was older than Annie by two months and was also fifteen on the day Annie went missing.

If my math was correct, she was now forty-two years old.

"Must be tough having three so close in age," I said.

"It can be a pain in the ass," she said, smiling. "Luckily, my oldest, Jesi, is pretty good at helping me. Good thing because the other two are rowdy as hell."

Before I could answer, she called Jesi over.

"Jesi, can you look after your brother and sister for a bit? I'm going to have a quick talk with our new friend here."

I assumed Jesi was short for Jesibel or Jezebel.

"Okay, Mom," she said. "I'll make sure they stay inside."

"Thanks."

"Adorable," I said.

"Life would be easy if they could all be like Jesi."

I smiled.

"Would you like a coffee? I just made some."

It was after noon at this point, and probably not the ideal time for coffee, but maybe when you have three kids running around, you need to stay caffeinated at all times.

"Sure, I'll take some. Thanks."

She poured us a coffee and led us outside to a little table.

It was a hot day for early June, but there was a nice breeze, and it felt nice to sit outside. My investigation always occurred in offices, houses, or apartments. I was in Los Angeles, and the weather was beautiful. I wanted to be outside whenever possible. I told myself that the next interview I conducted would be at an outdoor coffee shop or eatery.

"So, what did you think of my cousin, Adam?"

"I liked him, but I also understand how he earned his nickname."

Amber laughed.

"You can say that again. He's got a good soul, though. And he's odd in a benevolent way, not a scary one."

"That was the impression that I got," I said.

"So, I heard you're investigating Annie's death."

I could now get an answer to the question I'd pondered earlier.

"Did you find that out from Adam or already know?"

"I already knew. I got a call from another cousin about four or five days ago saying that William had hired someone new to look into the case."

"So the word is out," I said.

"It is. You're so busted."

I laughed. It was safe to say that I liked Amber Ryan right away.

"So, what's the feeling in the family about William hiring me?"

"My guess is you won't be that popular. No offense."

"None taken."

"Some people are just tired of it. I mean, it has been twenty-five years; I guess I can't blame people in that camp."

"But you're not in that camp?"

"No, I want to find out what happened. It still eats at me often, and I'd love to get a resolution."

I thought back to what Connor Ryan said about there being no good end result.

"Even if it's a fellow family member?" I asked.

"Yes. At least then, you know who it is. Otherwise, you just suspect everybody at least a tiny bit, and that's far worse."

It made perfect sense.

"Who do you suspect a little more than a tiny bit?"

"Ah, you want to get right down to it?"

"I met the kids. We've had some coffee. Why wait?"

Amber laughed. I had a feeling she laughed often.

"You're right. We're like old friends. Okay, on to more serious topics. I'm not sure I ever suspected only one person, but I did suspect a demographic."

"Which demographic would that be?"

"My age group."

"You thought one of the teenagers was involved?"

"Well, I should clarify a bit, I guess. I'm talking up to about twenty-five. I think that was the age of our oldest cousin at the time."

Connor Ryan had thought the same. That one of the "kids" was most likely to be involved.

"Why do you think that?" I asked.

"There are a few reasons. One, there's just more drama between people your own age. Now, drama doesn't usually lead to murder, but there could at least have been some jealousy or anger or something else between Annie and someone around her age. What would a forty-five-year-old parent have against Annie?"

"I'll buy that. What's another reason?"

"So, once we all would sit down for a family dinner - and we used to have two to three of these a year - the adults usually stayed seated. They were adults for a reason. Kids were different. They'd sometimes get bored while waiting for food and maybe get up and run around the house for a while longer."

"I'm with you so far."

"My point is that if one of the adults had gotten up and left the dinner table for a protracted period, people would have remembered. Also, an adult walking around the house while dinner was served would have stood out. That would have registered with the kids running around. But from what I remember, there was no mention of any adults having left the dinner table or being seen walking around the halls."

Adam Toon was right. Amber was an intelligent woman. She'd thought a lot about what happened to Annie.

"I like the logic, but adults must also use the bathroom."

"Using the bathroom is different than leaving the table and being gone long enough to commit a crime."

"Point taken," I said.

We both sipped our coffees when something random came to mind.

"I just realized I've talked to an Adam and an Amber about an Annie."

"Indeed. And we're not the only three. There's a cousin named Able and another one named Ashley. Shit, I might even be forgetting one or two off the top of my head."

"How many of your cousins still live in LA? Approximately. It seems like a lot of the family has stayed here."

"It would be a total guess, but I'd say two-thirds have remained in LA. Better for your investigation, right?"

"I certainly prefer interviewing people face to face."

"Probably able to better gauge whether someone is lying to you."

"I'd like to think so."

"Well, then you are properly screwed if the killer is off in Bumfuck, Idaho, and you'll never meet them in person."

She'd managed to squeeze in a 'screw' and a 'Bumfuck' in the same sentence. Impressive stuff.

"Did anyone suspiciously move out of Los Angeles after Annie went missing?"

"I know it's not exactly what you mean, but does Kai Butler count?"

"Yeah, I guess he does. We'll get back to him, but did anyone else either move or seem like they got more distant?"

"Not that I remember, but remember that I was only fifteen."

"Of course."

"Sorry, but nothing stood out."

"No problem. Okay, on to Kai, who I feel I've talked about more than any other family member besides Annie. Were you and Kai close?"

"Not particularly. I was kind of on the dorky side. I went to school, went to band practice, and then came home and did my homework.

Rinse. Repeat. Kai had more of a social life than me. He wasn't Mr. Popular, but at least he had a girlfriend. He was also two years older, which was a big gap back then."

"Annie was your age and still hung out with Kai."

"That's true, but Annie was also very mature by fifteen. Hanging out with some seventeen-year-olds wouldn't be out of the ordinary for her. She was on her way to being a knockout, and I'm sure the teenage boys loved her. I was the ugly duckling."

"I doubt that," I said.

"It's true," Amber said. "But thanks."

"Do you think Kai and Annie drank together or did anything more substantial?"

"There was definitely drinking. I have no doubt about that. And I'm sure Annie partook in that. Then again, a lot of fucking teenagers drank back then. As far as drugs, weed might have been smoked, but that's it. Annie was a good kid. I feel like I'm putting her down a bit. And Kai was a good kid, too. I guess I didn't just fit into their crowd. Like I said, I was about the most fucking boring buttoned-up teenager in the family."

"And now you cuss like a sailor," I said.

When Gina Galasso swore, it was egregious and unnecessary. Amber's seemed well-timed. Or maybe I only thought that because I liked Amber and couldn't say the same about Gina.

"Having three kids will do that to you," she said.

We both laughed.

She then blushed.

"The swearing isn't that bad, is it?"

"No, you're fine."

I was not looking to hit it off with a recently divorced woman with three kids who also happened to be ten years older than me, but we were having a moment.

I decided to get back to the issue at hand: Annie Ryan.

"Gina Galasso and Adam have said there was another Annie different from the one she presented at family functions. Do you think that's true?"

"I mean, don't we all have another person behind our public persona?"

"Some are more pronounced than others."

"I'm not ready to paint Annie with that broad a brush. She was fifteen years old. Name another teenager who doesn't act differently between family and friends."

"You," I said.

Amber Ryan laughed.

"That's not a bad call. I was a goody two shoes. I was probably just as big a dork in front of family as I was to my friends."

"What was Adam Toon like back then?"

"Oh, Toony."

"Toony?"

"Well, once Toon the Loon caught on, it kind of morphed to Toony the Loony, at least amongst us kids."

"I found him quite interesting, and maybe not as out there as his name suggests—at least for most of our conversation."

"Sometimes, he's perfectly normal. Other times, like if you ask him about extraterrestrials, you'd think he's the one from a different planet."

Amber paused and then continued.

"But like I said earlier, he's as harmless as a fly. I can guarantee he had nothing to do with Annie going missing."

"That never even crossed my mind," I said. And he thinks Annie got out of that house alive—or, at least, has a theory that says so."

"It's possible, I guess. I mean, if Annie really did have this other persona, who's to say she didn't escape the party to go somewhere else."

"Do you think that?"

"If I'm being honest, no, I don't. Annie might have been a little wilder than me, but she was still a nice young woman. Her parents and all of her relatives were there. If she just left mid-party, she had to have known people would get worried. And if memory serves, she'd bought a gift for our cousin Ginny for Secret Santa. She looked up to Ginny, and I'm sure she'd want to give her that present and see her reaction."

"She'd bought her a Backstreet Boys poster," I said.

Amber blushed.

"Oh, the things we teenage girls liked in the late 90s."

"If it makes you feel any better, I thought I was going to marry Britney Spears when I was like ten."

"Shit, I feel like I'm the same age as Britney. How young are you?"

"I'm thirty-two."

"You're just a kid. I've got a decade on you come September."

"You look young," I said.

"I don't feel it with the three kids, but thank you. And you realize you'll always be interviewing people older than you? Annie went missing twenty-five years ago, and I doubt you'll be interviewing the seven-year-olds who were at the party."

"I don't know, I've started to suspect this one five-year-old."

I quickly realized my joke was in poor taste. I was talking about a murdered teenage girl, after all.

"That's a bit morbid," Amber said. "But it's also pretty funny."

I sighed with a sense of relief.

"Phew. Thought I'd gone too far with that one."

Just then, her lone son approached.

"Mom, the girls are fighting over the remote and pulling each other's hair."

"Oh, shit. I've got to take care of this, Bobby. Do you want to reconvene this in ten minutes?"

I'd learned enough from Amber for the time being.

"No, I'll get out of your hair. Let's talk again soon, though."

"Get out of my hair? Was that a joke at my daughters' expense?"

I laughed.

"No, I'm not that quick."

"Well, you have my number. Call me if you have any more questions," Amber said.

"I will."

We stood up and walked back into the house. Amber pointed me toward the front door, and as I approached the door, I looked into the adjoining family room and saw her two young daughters yelling and grabbing at each other's hair. Amber yelled at them to stop and stepped between them.

I couldn't imagine the stress of being a single parent to three kids.

I'd probably resort to swearing all the time, too.

∽

I RETURNED to the Beverly Hilton after stopping at Taco Bell on the way. No, it wasn't the healthiest lunch, but I hadn't eaten since nine a.m. and was starving.

Overall, I thought I'd had a productive morning, conducting two interviews and learning more about Annie. No, there wasn't a smoking gun yet, but that wouldn't be this type of case.

It was just as I'd imagined it: a giant jigsaw puzzle. And maybe I'd found a few more pieces today, even if I didn't know exactly where they fit just yet.

Amassing more information was my goal for the time being.

Now, if a relative came to me and said, *I've been holding back something important all these years,'* then I'd be pleasantly surprised. I just wasn't expecting anything like that.

I parked my car in the self-parking garage—it didn't deserve to be valeted—and entered the hotel.

I took the elevator up to the 6th floor and headed to Room 614.

As I began unwrapping my first taco, I saw the light beeping on the hotel phone.

I was starving, but hated eating when something was hanging over my head. I'd be thinking about the message, not the food, so I called the front desk.

"Hello, Mr. McGowan. You have some mail down here for you."

"Like actual mail? Snail mail?"

"Yes."

Who the hell would be sending me mail? What was this, the 1980s?

"I'll come right down," I said.

As I walked out the door, I glared at my Taco Bell; as if it was to blame. I took the elevator down and was greeted by a polite middle-aged woman running the front desk.

"Hi, I'm here to pick up..."

"Yes, Mr. McGowan, I have that mail for you right here."

Did she know my face, or had she assumed it was me since we just got off the phone? I didn't feel like asking.

I saw her grab a small postcard and hand it over to me.

"Thanks," I said.

I took it from her and decided I'd wait until I got back upstairs to look at it. A minute later, I was there. A postcard in one hand and my Taco Bell mere feet from me. Damn, I was hungry.

The postcard, addressed to me, featured a great picture of the St. Louis Arch and the surrounding skyline.

I turned it over, and five words were written in big, bold lettering.

"HOW'S THE INVESTIGATION GOING, ROBERT?"

That was it—five little words. Most people would have thought the words sounded good-natured as if they were rooting for my investigation to succeed.

I knew better. They had used my given name to mock me. I had no evidence of this - how could I? - but I was sure of it.

I suddenly didn't feel so hot, and the tacos I'd been craving would go uneaten.

HOW'S THE INVESTIGATION GOING, ROBERT?

What the hell had I got myself into?

CHAPTER 12

THE KILLER

I'd decided to keep the first letter short and sweet.

I didn't gloat and say I was the one who killed Annie. I preferred keeping it vague.

HOW'S THE INVESTIGATION GOING, ROBERT?

Shit, I could have just been a concerned citizen asking how his case was doing.

But I knew Bobby McGowan was no dummy. When he saw the name 'ROBERT' in big block letters, he'd know this wasn't some Helpful Harry here to provide his support.

At least part of Bobby would think he was hearing from the person responsible.

I'd have paid anything to have been a fly on the wall at the Beverly Hilton when he received the postcard. I'd have loved to see his face drop when he realized this wasn't just some benign, decades-old case in which he had nothing to fear.

No, this case was ongoing, and if Bobby/Robert didn't watch himself, he might be joining Annie in the afterlife.

CHAPTER 13

BOBBY

Of all the things I hated about the letter, the fact that he'd addressed me as Robert pissed me off the most.

Whoever this jerk was, he'd done his research and knew that I'd always gone by Bobby, despite my birth name. Robert was my father, not me.

And I knew from the second I'd read the letter that this wasn't some well-meaning "fan" of mine encouraging me to catch Annie's killer.

Did that mean it was definitely the killer reaching out? No, I wasn't ready to go that far. I'd already amassed a few enemies, and it wouldn't shock me if someone like Mike Minter did this just to get a rise out of me. Gina Galasso came to mind as well.

Well, whoever had sent it had accomplished their mission. I was on edge, more so than at any time since taking the case.

I DECIDED to reach out to Amber.

The layman would probably assume I was calling her because we'd gotten along so well, but that wasn't the case. Since Adam had raised a warning flag about William Ryan, I would try to avoid going through him whenever possible. It was unavoidable with questions about his house and things of that nature, but I thought Amber could give me the current information I needed without involving William.

To be clear, I still had zero reason to think William was involved. But he had hired me—someone with only one case under his belt—to look into a highly complex case. Just in case he thought I'd be his lap dog, I was going to be careful.

A crazy idea popped into my head.

Could William have been the one who sent the letter?

I wasn't ruling anything out.

∽

"Hello?"

"Hey, Amber, this is Bobby McGowan."

"Wow, back-to-back days."

I hoped I wouldn't regret calling Amber first. The last thing I wanted was for her to think I was calling for personal reasons.

"I'm sorry. It's just that you seem to have a good grasp of the family, and I had a few follow-ups for you."

My question wasn't a follow-up from yesterday's meeting, but it sounded like a convincing reason to call her.

"I was just busting your balls. What do you want to know?"

"If I ask you a question, can you promise to keep it between us?"

"Sure."

"Have any of the extended Ryan family moved to St. Louis?"

She took a few seconds to reply.

"Yes. The Yardleys did, probably about ten years after Annie died. Sue Ryan was William's cousin, and she married Gus Yardley. They have one child named Nathan."

"Do you happen to have their number?"

"I'm sure I do. Can I call you right back? I'm shitty at looking at my contacts while talking on the phone. I'm sure you don't have a problem with that as a young buck of thirty-two."

I laughed.

"Talk to you in a bit."

She called back a minute later.

"I have Sue's and Nathan's number. He is just a few years younger than me."

"I'll take both."

"Sue's is 314-582-9555 and Nathan is 314-222-2998."

"Thanks, Amber."

"You don't want to tell me why you're suddenly interested in a family in St. Louis and arguably the nicest family of all the extended Ryan families?"

"Next time we talk, I'll let you know. I'd like to keep it to myself for now, but they are not suspects, so don't think that."

"Okay, I understand. I mean, you are the pseudo-private investigator, after all."

"Ouch. That hurts."

She laughed.

"Goodbye, Bobby."

"Bye, Amber."

~

Before I called Sue Yardley, formerly Sue Ryan, I had to remind myself not to be too accusatory.

Amber had said they were arguably the nicest family of all the Ryans. Not that I necessarily put a lot of stock in that. You never knew what happened behind closed doors of any family. Sometimes, the seemingly most well-meaning ones had the biggest skeletons in their closets.

But the main reason not to be accusatory was a pretty obvious one. Why would the person who sent me the postcard be so obvious as to have it addressed from the city they live in? They'd rightfully assume that's where my investigation would lead. Unless that's exactly what they wanted: me to get closer to them.

I did a little reading from Razzle's file before I called Sue Yardley.

The family was small—just Sue, her husband, Gus, and their son, Nathan.

Nathan was thirteen years old on the day Annie went missing.

He was old enough that I couldn't rule him out entirely.

Sue and Gus were in their early forties on Christmas Eve, 1998. There wasn't much more information about them in the file. Everyone seemed to think the three remained at the dinner table when Annie was likely abducted.

This was probably a useless excursion, but I had to give them a call. Any private investigator would—even a pseudo one.

THE OTHER ANNIE

~

"Hello?"

Sue Yardley answered a phone call from a random number. Maybe they'd adopted some of the friendliness synonymous with the Midwest.

"Hi, Sue. My name is Bobby McGowan and William Ryan has hired me to investigate Annie Ryan's disappearance."

I'd managed to lump three names into one sentence. And her name in the sentence preceding it.

"It's nice to meet you, Bobby. I had no idea William still had people looking into that tragic event."

Her voice was hushed, and I struggled to hear her.

"Maybe it's grasping at straws at this point, but they decided to give me a chance."

"Well, good luck. You'll probably need it after all this time."

I was going to ask her about Annie quickly. I could close the call by asking about the postcard.

"What do you remember about that night?"

"I remember all of it. The initial fun of seeing everyone for the cocktail hour, and then all of us sitting down and enjoying a nice dinner. Then, going to William's massive family room for the Secret Santa game. And then it all turned into a tragedy when they couldn't find Annie."

"That must have been very tough."

"Maybe this just shows I've been lucky with my own family, but that is still the worst day of my life. At least when my parents passed on a few years back, they were approaching ninety years old. Annie was a teenager in the prime of her life."

"Was your son Nathan close to her?"

"Not really. They knew each other, obviously, but we lived about an hour south of Los Angeles, and they lived in the Valley. So it was mostly family functions."

"Did you and your husband know Annie well?"

"Not great, no. Connor was my first cousin, so we knew each other pretty well, but once I got married, as I said, we moved pretty far south compared to the rest of the Ryans, and I didn't get to see him as much once our kids started growing up. So I never felt like I got to know Annie that well."

"It seems like the vast majority of the Ryans stayed in and around Los Angeles—at least before Annie went missing. Do you know why that was?"

I noticed that I had used 'disappearance' and 'went missing' when describing Annie. Was I trying to will her back alive? Like everyone else, I knew there was a 99.9% chance she was deceased.

"I think we all had a great sense of family and enjoyed those huge family functions that William hosted. That's probably not reason enough to stay in Los Angeles, but it was certainly a big selling point."

"That seemed to change after Annie," I said.

"It sure did. For one, the Christmas parties ceased altogether for several years. Annie's going missing was just too fresh in our hearts and minds. And when they did return about five years later, they were much more sparsely attended. As you said, some people moved out of Los Angeles after that. It's like the innocence of the Ryan family ended that day, and there was no more reason to stay in Los Angeles. It was almost like the city had jinxed us. And I know many people stayed and still live in LA to this day, but moving was the right decision for us."

"Annie's disappearance had a longer-lasting impact than I first realized."

"You can say death. She's not coming back twenty-five years later."

"Do you think she was killed on the night in question?"

"Yeah, probably."

"Any guess as to who?"

"Don't think I haven't wracked my brain hundreds of times over the years about that, but I have no idea. I had secretly hoped it was a family friend or a valet, so it wasn't one of our immediate family, but that's just for selfish reasons."

"Do you think it could have been an accident, and then someone panicked?"

Mike Minter's hypothesis still seemed like a long shot, but I threw it out there.

"That's possible, I guess. But why not just say it was an accident? That's much better than disposing of a body after the fact. That should go without saying."

Sue agreed with my way of thinking.

"So you think it was planned?" I asked.

"Maybe. Or maybe it was in the heat of the moment. Either way, I think it was murder."

"A lot of people seem to think the likely killer would have been from the younger generation. Do you agree with that?"

"Yeah, I'd probably say so. Why would an adult want to hurt Annie?" Sue asked.

"Why would a kid want to hurt Annie?" I countered.

My question went unanswered for several seconds.

"You're right. They wouldn't. But having had a young son myself, you just don't always know what's going on with your kids. Maybe there was something there that we just all missed with Annie. Some connection that was bubbling under the surface but never came to light."

"Maybe," I conceded.

"Have your interviews led to any discoveries?"

"Not exactly. I'm still very early on in my investigation. Just over a week."

"Well, I wish I could help, but I can't add much."

It was time to ask her about the postcard, but I already knew nothing would come of it.

"I received a postcard with the St. Louis Arch on it. It came from someone who pretended to be interested in my investigation. Is there any chance you, your husband, or your son sent it?"

"A postcard?"

"Yeah."

"Why would we send you a postcard? Ten minutes ago, I didn't even know who you were."

It was the first time her voice had raised even a little bit.

"Any chance your son or husband knew about me?"

"Doubtful. We don't talk to our relatives much anymore. I'm pretty sure neither my husband nor my son knew anything about your investigation. We kind of do our own thing these days. My son is married with a couple of kids and lives in the suburbs of St. Louis, and my husband and I are just a couple of retired sixty-somethings."

"Is your husband with you right now?"

"No, he's fishing today. He can't get enough of it since he retired."

This was a dead end; I'd known it would be from the beginning. Still, I had to make the initial call and ask. I didn't even bother asking for her husband to call me.

"Thanks for your time, Sue. If you think of anything about Annie, please don't hesitate to contact me."

"Okay, will do."

She hung up, and I knew I'd never hear from her again.

AFTER I HUNG UP, I looked at the postcard again.

"Who sent you?" I said aloud.

The postcard contained some minuscule stamped letters and numbers. Was there a way of finding out where the envelope was mailed from? Ten to one, it wasn't St. Louis.

I knew nothing about how that worked.

But I imagine an old cop friend might.

And I didn't mean Mike Minter.

CHAPTER 14

"Patchett speaking."

"Hi, I think some cupcakes might have been poisoned," I said.

It had become a running joke between me and Detective Mark Patchett of the Santa Barbara Police Department. He'd been the lead detective on my mother's case for twenty years, and we were sometimes at odds but had become friendly since the death of Conrad Drury, my mother's killer.

"How the hell are you, Bobby? You're lucky it all ended well for you. If not, you would have been known as that weird cupcake guy for the rest of your life."

"Glad I wasn't burdened with that."

"So, is this a friendly call?" Patchett asked.

"Not exactly. I called to ask for a favor, and it's a big one."

"I'm listening."

"Did you hear that I took a case in Los Angeles?"

"I did. You're climbing up the ladder quite quickly."

"I think this might be a one-time thing. This work is monotonous."

"Now you know what it's like to be a detective. It's the same things over and over: reading police reports, interviewing people, and then re-interviewing the same people."

"You just described my last week plus."

"Get out while you can—not from this case necessarily, but from the whole private investigator/vigilante thing you're currently undertaking."

"First time I've been called a vigilante."

"You could have called the cops on Conrad Drury but went after him yourself."

I had no good response to that.

"Cat got your tongue?" he asked.

"So, on to my favor…"

Patchett laughed.

"Let's hear it."

"What can you tell from a postcard?"

"I'm not sure what you mean."

"I got a postcard in the mail. Can I tell from the postcard itself what post office it was sent from? What day? What time?"

"If you go into the post office, they will mark it, but not if you just drop it into a standing mailbox. That will get marked at their closest processing center, and there would be no way to pinpoint where it came from. At least, that's how I understand it."

"This doesn't sound like your specialty."

"No, it's not. That is something that the feds are better at than your local police departments. Do you want the number to the FBI?"

Patchett was joking.

"In the future, I just might."

I wasn't joking.

"Anything else, Bobby?"

"What about fingerprints?"

"You said it's a postcard?"

"Yeah."

"And it's just the postcard?"

"What do you mean?"

"It didn't come in an envelope?"

I realized where Patchett was going with this.

"No."

"Do you know how many people have probably touched that postcard along the way? The person who sent it, assuming they weren't wearing gloves. The clerk at the post office. A few people who work the conveyor belts and sort out the mail. Two or three people at the post offices the postcard got transferred between. A few more when it ended up in its destination city. The mailman himself. And then whoever handed it to you."

I hated to admit it, but Detective Patchett was likely correct.

"Damn," I said.

And then I thought of something.

"If he sends me another one, then we could do a little process of elimination based on fingerprints, couldn't we?"

"Yeah, if the guy who sent it wasn't wearing gloves. But if it was a bad guy sending it, he likely had them on. That's pretty much criminology 101 these days."

"Yeah, you're probably right."

"And what makes you think he will send another letter?"

"Call it a gut feeling," I said.

"Keep in touch."

WITH THE POSTCARD seemingly a dead end for the moment, I came up with a new idea.

And I didn't think Connor Ryan would enjoy it.

CHAPTER 15

My latest phone call began with that familiar refrain.
"Hello?"
"Connor, this is Bobby McGowan again."
"Oh, hey."
He sounded even more down than when I'd initially met him, and he wasn't exactly a bed of roses then.
"I wanted to know if you have an old box of Annie's things. I know she had some sort of diary, but I'd also like to see her old toys. Stuffed animals. Board games. Whatever you may have kept. I will return them in a day or two."
It may have sounded odd to ask to look at stuffed animals and board games, but I wanted anything that might give me a sense of Annie's personality.
"We've got several boxes of her stuff. Emily and I never could bring ourselves to part with them."
I knew that Emily Ryan had died from cancer several years back. I wondered if the stress from losing both her son and daughter had made her more prone to catching cancer. I wonder if there had ever been a study to see if there was a cause and effect? I know stress was a substantial mitigating factor regarding your overall health. Could the ultimate stress of losing kids contribute to getting cancer or expedite your demise once you contract cancer?
I often pondered random subjects like this.

"Are the boxes at your house?" I asked.

"Yes."

"Could I swing by and pick them up?"

"Sure. You remember where I live, right?"

"Yes. Is later today alright?"

"Fine," he said and hung up.

I'm not a doctor, but Connor Ryan sounded clinically depressed.

Two hours later, I'd picked up five boxes of Annie's stuff and set them in the backseat of my car.

I told Connor I was making progress in hopes of perking him up, but he only gave me a few perfunctory smiles. I feared that he might be a lost cause.

"Do you know if her diary or journal is in there?" I asked.

Earl Razzle had alternately referred to it as both a diary and a journal. I'm not even sure if I knew what the difference was. I assumed that a diary would be considered more personal.

"Yeah, it's in there."

"Great. Thanks. I'll have this back to you in a few days."

"Keep it for as long as you want," Connor said.

I'd worried that Connor wouldn't like me asking for Annie's personal stuff. It was worse; he was indifferent.

An hour later, I was back at the Beverly Hilton going through Annie's old things.

I'd felt a connection with Annie early on, but this ratcheted it up a level. I was now going through things that meant a lot to her. An old easy-bake oven. Some stuffed animals. A Barbie doll.

Connor had kept many things, even things from Annie's childhood, that she surely would have been embarrassed by at fifteen.

I would eventually look through it all, but for now, the diary interested me most. I found it in the third box I searched.

It was a pink book, probably about half the size of a textbook. It had some ruffled feathers of some kind on the spine of the journal. And on the cover, ANNIE'S DIARY: DON'T TOUCH.

I smiled at those last two words. It's almost like I could hear Annie saying, *'DON'T TOUCH,'* even though I'd never met her.

It was odd to think that Annie would be eight years older than me if she were still alive. Her pink diary and easy bake oven ensured she would be fifteen forever.

Annie was dead. I knew it. Everyone else knew it. Whether they'd admit it or not.

As I'd told myself more than a few times, there would not be a happy ending in this case.

I opened the diary, feeling a tinge of guilt for looking at her personal thoughts. That guilt was quickly overridden by my desire to catch her killer.

The first page was titled *"Classes I love, Classes I hate."*

The fifth page was *"TV shows I can't get enough of."*

On the twelfth page, I found something worth looking into. The title was *"Boys that I might like in the future."*

The entry was written on August 11th, 1998.

There were six names on there, and only one of them, Colton Weatherly, rang a bell. I was fairly certain he'd been at the party, but I'd have to check Razzle's summary. With fifty-one names at the party, I couldn't always remember every name.

I took a screenshot on my phone and told myself I'd ask Adam Toon or Amber about them later. William Ryan could be accommodating, but not when it came to knowing Annie's high school crushes.

Maybe Gina Galasso would recognize a few of the names—great, another meeting with the chain-smoking one.

Annie spent five pages on how she butts heads with her parents - especially her father. That must have been extremely difficult for Connor to read. In the end, Annie concedes that her parents are good people, but that's after a few pages of bashing them.

She does talk about good times.

How she loves two of her teachers - in history and math. How she has three or four great friends. How she loves ice cream, especially Salted Caramel Chip by McConnell's. How she can't wait to go to college somewhere on the East Coast, so she can see that side of the country.

She dedicated a few pages to her 15th birthday and how she met Justin Timberlake. She is ecstatic, and the happiness emanates from her diary. She goes out of her way to thank her parents and Uncle William.

A few passages had been blocked out by Annie scribbling over them.

As much as I tried to decipher what was below them, it was useless. They were lost to time.

Overall, Annie came off as both a happy and a semi-troubled teenager. Yes, it's possible to be both. In fact, I'd say that characterizes a great deal of teenagers.

To close out her journal, Annie had about ten loose pages of drawings.

They were mostly portraits and a few drawings of birds and butterflies, one of which was a beautiful drawing of a Monarch. She wrote her initials, AR, in small letters on each one, signifying she was the artist.

The Monarch was truly a phenomenal drawing. She had some genuine talent, which made me all the more sad she was gone.

∼

I TRIED Amber and Adam Toon, but neither could be much help with the names of the boys that Annie listed. They remembered the name Colton Weatherly but didn't know much about him. Amber thought Ginny might have known him, but wasn't sure.

I hated having to do what I did next, but it was my best option.

∼

"WHO'S THIS?"

Even a nice hello was too much for Gina Galasso.

"Hi, Gina, this is Bobby McGowan."

"Who?"

"Bobby McGowan. We talked about a week ago. I'm investigating the disappearance of Annie Ryan."

"Oh, yeah. You."

Gina had lost none of her charm.

"Could we meet up again?"

"No, I'm good. I'm swamped the next couple of weeks."

I highly doubted that.

"You couldn't sneak in like fifteen minutes?"

"We'll see. Hit me up in a week."

I didn't want to wait a week.

"Well, since I have you on the line right now, can you give me two minutes?"

"Fine. Go."

I rattled off the six names that Annie had listed.

"Were any of these guys at the Christmas Party?"
"Only one."
"Which one was that?"
"Colton Weatherly."

She'd answered that question correctly. I'd read Earl Razzle's summary after I found the boys Annie had mentioned. Only Weatherly had been at the party, and the write-up on him was less than a page. Reports were that he never left the dinner table. From what I could tell, he was never considered a suspect.

"What was Colton like?" I asked.

"He was a jock. I think he played basketball and football. Tall guy. Handsome."

"How about his personality?"

"Like I said, he was a jock."

That got me to laugh. It was funny that Gina thought that all jock's behaved the same. In her defense, when you're in high school, it might seem like they all do. They certainly have a similar vibe.

"Was he a nice jock or an asshole jock?"

"For jocks, he was pretty nice."

"Do you know if Annie ever went out with him?"

"I don't think so, but who knows? Kai and I didn't know everything about her dating life."

"Last time we talked, you suggested that Annie might have flirted with a few guys."

I decided to go with flirting as opposed to screwing or hooking up, which is what Gina had initially insinuated.

"Yeah, I might have exaggerated that part of our conversation. My bad."

Gina was a piece of work.

"So you don't think she had a few guys vying for her?"

"I don't remember. It was so long ago."

I'd circle back to that some other time.

"Why was Colton at the Christmas party?"

"I'm not sure. Two of Annie's cousins went to the same high school. Maybe they invited him."

Had Earl Razzle mentioned that two of Annie's cousins went to high school with her? I don't remember reading that.

It seemed like something worth checking into.

It made me realize that I was almost solely focused on the younger generation and that I shouldn't rule out someone older having killed

Annie. After all, they would be more likely to have the strength to drag her body to the woods. And while the idea of a forty-plus-year-old man wanting to kill a fifteen-year-old girl brought about some sick scenarios, it wasn't impossible.

"Who were the two cousins?" I asked.

"Ginny Ryan, for sure. And I think Carrie Thompson was the name of the other one."

I remembered seeing the name Carrie Thompson. She was Annie's second cousin and the only child of her parents, the mother of whom was a cousin of Connor and William Ryan.

Ginny Ryan had been Annie's Secret Santa. Annie not coming to the family room to give Ginny her gift had been the impetus to start searching for her.

"Do you know if either Ginny or Carri still live in LA?"

I realized I was asking a Gina about a Ginny.

As if all the names weren't complicated enough already.

"This is a lot more freaking time than you requested," Gina said. "And no, I have no idea if they live around here. Remember, since Kai's death, I've been ex-communicated from the Ryan clan."

Calling them the Ryan clan was a not-so-subtle jab at them.

"And you don't know anyone else's name on the list?"

"No. I didn't go to high school with Annie. I just remember Colton because he was at that party and was kind of famous in our area since he was such a good athlete."

"Anything else you can think of, Gina?"

"I can think this has been going on for about five minutes now, and you asked me to give you two. You're not a very good judge of time," she said.

"Always a pleasure," I said, and she quickly hung up.

CHAPTER 16

I found out through Adam Toon - he and Amber had become my liaisons as much as William - that neither Ginny nor Carrie still lived in Los Angeles.

He said that Carrie had never been an integral member of the extended family, and he didn't have her phone number. He thought she had moved to Michigan but wasn't positive.

Ginny lived in New York and worked on Broadway.

"Usually in really small plays," Adam said.

"They call that off-Broadway," I responded.

"Look at the big brain on Bobby," he said, giving me the number.

∼

MAYBE THAT BIG brain was just working overtime, but before I called Ginny, I wondered why she'd gone to act in New York when she was related to a famous producer right here in Los Angeles.

Was I reading too much into it? Probably.

And although I still didn't think William Ryan had anything to do with Annie's disappearance, he didn't seem to be all that popular amongst his family. None of the ten or so people I'd interviewed had said, "Oh, you got hired by William? He's such a stand-up guy."

Now, maybe this family wasn't the lovey-dovey type, but I still found it odd that I had yet to hear one compliment about the most well-known member of their family.

～

I DIDN'T GET AROUND to calling Ginny until five p.m. my time. I hoped it wasn't too late in New York.

She answered on the third ring.

I bet that actors and actresses were more likely to answer random phone numbers in hopes it was someone calling to say they'd booked a job. The rest of the public - myself included - looked at stray phone numbers as the plague.

Well, that was me as recently as a year ago. Not anymore. I usually felt obliged to answer random numbers when working my mother's case then and Annie Ryan's case now.

"Hello. This is Ginny."

She had a distinctive voice; I imagined it would stand out on stage.

"Hi, Ginny. My name is Bobby McGowan, and I'm investigating the disappearance of your cousin, Annie."

"I figured you'd be calling at some point. I heard William had hired a new guy."

"That would be me."

"So, what do you want to know? I'm not sure I have any information that you wouldn't have already heard from somebody else."

She was probably right, so I jumped into Annie's list of boys she might like.

"What can you tell me about Colton Weatherly?"

"Colton? Jeez, I haven't heard that name in a long time. I went to high school with him, and we dated briefly. Or hooked up. Isn't that what the kids say these days?"

"It's more than just kids who say that," I said.

"Oh yeah, you've got the pulse on America?"

She said it in a comical way, not mean-spirited.

"I'm a pop culture wonder kid," I said, unsure exactly what I was trying to say.

"What are you, a teenager?"

"Nope. Thirty-two."

"Shit, that feels like a teenager to me these days."

I'd had a very similar talk with Amber Ryan.

"What are you, like forty? That's the new thirty, they say."

I knew better than to mention a woman's age, but I was trying to shine it in a positive light.

"Nice ass-kissing, Bobby. And I'm forty-one."

I passed the test.

"Safe to say, I didn't expect our conversation to start like this," I said.

She laughed on the other end.

"Me neither."

"Alright, you ready to start with the more serious questions?"

"Let's do it," she said enthusiastically.

Ginny had a great personality. You could tell that from a mere phone call.

"So, you and Colton were dating. Were you guys together at the time of the Christmas Party, and were you the one who invited him?"

"Yes, and yes. Everyone thought Colton had a perfect life because he played all the big sports, but he had a shitty home life. His Dad was in the army and deployed overseas for most of the year, and his mother was an alcoholic. She hadn't planned anything for Christmas Eve, so I asked my mother if we could invite Colton to the party. She asked William if that was okay, and he said it was fine. So that's how he ended up there."

I decided not to tell Ginny that Annie had listed Colton as a guy she might be interested in. I didn't see the point. If I ever started focusing on Colton as a suspect, that could change, but there was no need for it now.

"Did Colton sit down for the dinner itself?"

This was another question I knew the answer to, but it helped push the conversation along. I often found myself in this situation since Razzle's summary had been so comprehensive. I knew a lot of the answers to the questions I was asking.

"Yeah. He sat next to me, and we didn't leave the table once. You might wonder how I'm so sure, but when the cops ask everyone that question ten times in the days that followed, it kind of gets imprinted in your mind."

"I get it. It seems like that would be a tough night to forget."

"Exactly. Which sucks because it's one of the few nights in my life I'd actually like to forget."

"Did you ever suspect anyone?"

"Not really."

"What does that mean?"

"No, I never suspected anyone specifically. Obviously, our family had a couple of screw-ups, but what family doesn't have them? And it's not like every screw-up murders their cousin or niece."

"Who were the screw-ups?"

"There was an older couple named Quincy and Chandra. I know they had been in trouble with selling drugs at one point."

Razzle mentioned them in his report, but they were in their sixties when Annie went missing. They were not considered suspects.

"Anyone else?" I asked.

"I mean, I hate to say this, and it's probably not fair, but people talked about Kai and his mental health issues. Does that count as a screw-up?"

"No," I said adamantly. "Any person can be burdened with that."

"You're right. What a dumb thing for me to say. I'm sorry."

"You're fine. What did you think of Kai?"

"I liked him. He seemed to always put on a good face when I saw him. I'd heard the stories that he'd been seeing psychiatrists from a young age. Shit like that gets around in a family. But we always got along."

"Did you know his girlfriend, Gina?"

"I know who she was, and I knew they hung out with Annie sometimes, but I never hung out with them socially."

"Any reason why?"

"No. I just never totally hit it off with Kai. I don't know why, and like I said, I had nothing against him. He was always friendly to me."

I was getting tired of talking about Kai all the time. He was dead, and I felt that, in some small way, I was trampling on his good name.

"Any of the other adults considered screw-ups?"

"From the viewpoint of William Ryan, they probably all were. No one achieved what he did."

It would have been perfect timing to ask Ginny why she didn't use William's connections in L.A., but I decided it could wait.

"You're not a screw-up just because you don't make a million dollars," I said. "I'm asking if anyone in the family might have - and excuse me for saying this - had eyes for Annie. Do you see what I'm getting at?"

"It's not overly subtle, so yes, I get what you're saying. And no, I didn't see anything like that. I was a teenager like Annie, and none of the uncles ever touched or tried to hug me too long or anything creepy. In fact, the only family member who hugged us for too long was Grandma Esther. It was like a bear hug. Everyone tried to get away from those."

"Maybe I should check up on her," I joked.

Ginny started laughing on the other end.

"Thanks. I needed that. This is not exactly the most upbeat conversation I've ever had."

"I'll grant you that. I had a personal question if you don't mind."

"Okay," she said, but her voice sounded suspicious.

"If you have an uncle who's a well-known producer in Hollywood, why come all the way to New York to act in off-Broadway plays?"

"That's not too personal. I thought you were going to ask why my husband doesn't buy me flowers more often."

"That was my next question."

Ginny laughed again.

There was a lot of divorce and separation in the Ryan family, so it was nice to hear that Ginny was still married. For all intents and purposes, William was divorced. Before Emily Ryan died, she and Connor had been divorced. Amber had recently divorced.

I realized those were all people who had stayed in L.A. Ginny, the Butlers, and the Yardleys were all still married and had moved out of L.A.

Maybe the secret was getting out of Los Angeles and the city's curse over the Ryans.

"Actually, Uncle William helped out early in my career," Ginny said. "He got me on a few commercials and a guest spot on a famous sitcom. But that didn't feel like real acting to me. Movies, TV shows, and commercials are great and all, but I wanted to perform live. There's so much more pressure being a theater actor. If you screw up a take in a movie, oh well, you just film it again. Not on stage. If you screw up, there's no rewind button. There's just hundreds of faces staring at you, letting you know that you screwed up."

"And you like that?"

"Yeah. I like the added pressure."

"Very admirable," I said.

"Thank you. And I know you said off-Broadway, but I've been in a few major Broadway productions."

"Oh, I'm sorry. I didn't know."

"Don't worry about it. I have as much respect for the actors who do off-Broadway as any actors in the world. And I'm including Leo DiCaprio, Margot Robbie, or any famous Hollywood actor."

"I think I get why."

"If you're ever in New York, let me know, and I'll get you some tickets to one of my shows. Better yet, tell William that some clues have led you to New York, and you need to be flown out here for a few nights."

"I might just take you up on that," I said. "Although I'm not sure William is going to buy the reasoning. Or the plane tickets, for that matter."

"He can afford it."

"What do you think of him?"

"He's a good guy at heart, but I do think he looks down on a lot of the family. Maybe it's only natural. He worked his ass off and accomplished a hell of a lot. He probably looks at some of his contemporaries and wonders why they couldn't have done the same. Or, at least, approached it."

"He doesn't seem to be the most popular, but just speaking from my interactions with him, he's been very fair and supportive of my investigation."

"I believe that. I know this case has haunted him greatly. If I were Annie's killer, I wouldn't want to be stuck in a dark alley with William. I don't care how old he is. That guy has some serious bottled-up anger. This has affected William more than anyone other than Annie's parents. Being that it happened at his house only adds to it."

"Connor seems like a broken man," I said.

"That's nothing new. He's been like that since the moment Annie died. Truth be told, Emily was the same way before she passed. Since they'd lost their other child so young, Annie meant everything to them. People thought Annie was going places, which made the tragedy even sadder. Maybe that's why William took to Annie. He saw greatness in her."

"Some people would say being a Broadway actress is quite an achievement."

"I'm not exactly Meryl Streep, but thanks. And I was alluding to William's generation. In my generation, quite a few of us have had successful careers."

"During my investigation, a lot has been made of the generations, and most people seem to think the likelihood is that someone from the younger generation was involved in Annie's murder. Do you agree with that?"

"Well, like I said earlier, no creepy uncles stood out. So there's that. But it's not like I can see someone from my age group wanting to harm Annie, either. That's why this is such a great mystery, even twenty-five years later."

I was enjoying my conversation with Ginny. I'd place her in the same category as Adam and Amber. On the other side of the ledger was Gina Galasso and Mike Minter.

Ginny, good. Gina, bad.

Earl Razzle was his own entity. I told myself I should visit him soon.

"I've been working on it for two weeks now, and I'm not sure I'm any closer than the day I took the case."

"I don't believe that," Ginny Ryan said. "Because of your legwork, you're now prepared."

"Prepared for what?"

"In case someone lies to you, you'll catch it. Or maybe a seemingly meaningless fact comes to light, but now you'll know its importance."

"Thanks. That's a good way to look at it."

I heard some bustling around on her end.

"Hey, I hate to end this, but I'm meeting with a casting director in about thirty minutes."

"This late?"

"Haven't you heard New York is the city that never sleeps?"

I laughed.

"Touché."

"If you need any more questions answered, just let me know. Good luck with your investigation, Bobby."

"Thanks for the time, Ginny."

CHAPTER 17

"Bobby McGowan. You're a man about town. Sounds like you've talked to half of the Ryan family already."

"I've been putting in my due diligence," I said.

I was back at Earl Razzle's office in Beverly Hills, mere blocks from my hotel.

The only difference is that my stay in Beverly Hills was temporary; Razzle's office was here for the long haul.

And I was okay with that. I was enjoying my time in Beverly Hills, but it's not a place where I'd like to live permanently. And it wasn't just that I couldn't afford it. It was a little too ritzy for me. But for a month, I could slum it.

"So what have you found out?" Razzle said.

He wore black leather pants, a black shirt with the top three buttons unbuttoned, and a white cowboy hat.

"The more I learn about this case, the more I realize I don't know anything."

"Ain't that the truth?"

"I often feel like I'm wasting my time."

And then I remembered what Ginny Ryan had said to me: that this was all just preparing me for what was to come.

"Well, if you think you're wasting your time after two weeks, how does that make me feel? That means I've wasted twenty-plus years of my life."

I intentionally moved my eyes around the office, settling them on Rodeo Drive.

"If William Ryan's money helped in a small way to build this office, it wasn't a waste," I said.

"Good point. You're alright, McGowan. I wasn't sure I was going to like you."

Depending on the circumstances, Razzle continued to switch from my first name to my last name. Maybe it was to keep me off guard. Razzle seemed to enjoy a lively back-and-forth.

"Can I give you a brief rundown on everyone I've talked to, and you can tell me if I've overlooked anything."

"Sure. Give it to me."

I spent the next ten minutes reviewing everything I'd learned, including the postcard I'd received. Razzle rarely interrupted but gave me some valuable added information when he could. With his persona, you wouldn't think he'd be able to play second fiddle, but he proved to be a good listener. Earl Razzle continued to grow on me.

He was adamant that I shouldn't believe a word Gina Galasso said. She'd lied to Razzle several times over the years.

"And that's basically it," I said once I finished.

Razzle smiled.

"You've been even busier than I thought. You've met most of the main characters. And you've met some of the loons - and I don't just mean Adam. I'm impressed. If I were you, I'd sit at the Beverly Hilton pool and talk to the girls that walked by, not getting any work done."

"Trust me, it's crossed my mind," I said. "Not sure that's what William is paying me for, though."

Razzle smiled.

"No, I guess not."

"I'm just not sure all these interviews have got me anywhere," I said.

As Razzle looked up at me, his face turned serious.

"Stop feeling sorry for yourself. You've done some great work, and it's not like you were going to solve this in two weeks, anyway. You now understand the case enough that the puzzle pieces might start making sense."

He'd also used a puzzle analogy.

"This is one complicated puzzle," I said.

"Well, no one said it would be easy, Bobby."

I nodded, getting his point.

"What do you think of the postcard?" I asked.

"Honestly?"

"Yes."

"90% chance it's someone screwing with you."

"And the other 10%?"

"If you were somehow certain it was legit - and you can't be - I'd spend every waking moment trying to find out who sent it. That should become the sole focus of your investigation. But again, I doubt it's actually the killer. I investigated this case for a long time and never got a letter. Why would he choose you?"

"Maybe it's so far removed, he thinks he'll never be caught now."

"Possibly. I mean, the guy or gal committed one of the most brazen crimes I've ever come across - killing someone at a Christmas Eve party with fifty family members present. You'd think he'd want people to know about his accomplishment."

Razzle shook his head.

"Sorry, accomplishment was the wrong word to use," he added.

"Don't worry about it," I said. "I knew what you were getting at. You're surprised he hasn't gloated once or twice over the years."

"Exactly. Nothing from him at all."

"Well, maybe he's finally come out to play."

This time, Razzle nodded.

"Maybe…"

CHAPTER 18

The day after I met with Earl Razzle, William Ryan called and gave me some devastating news.

Connor Ryan had taken his own life. I was crushed.

He had killed himself via carbon monoxide poisoning while sitting in his car in the garage. William said he'd left a note and that Connor blamed this on Annie's death and how he never fully recovered from it. He'd long considered taking this final step and hoped he'd now find some peace.

"I'm so sorry, William. Connor was your brother. You must feel terrible."

"I feel terrible that he had to resort to this. But, and don't take this the wrong way, I think he'll be happier in death than he was ever going to be in life."

I was tired of all the misery associated with the Ryan family. I longed to be back in Santa Barbara.

"Will there be a funeral?" I asked.

"Yes. It will be next Friday—a week from today. We're working on the logistics," William said.

"Will I be invited?"

"Of course, Bobby. There will be a lot of the family there, so I expect you to be as well."

William didn't say it was part of my investigation, but he sure insinuated it.

"I'll let you know when we get the specific details," he said and hung up the phone.

I sat back on the couch in my hotel room and put my head in my hands.

No, I couldn't exactly call Connor a friend, but I'd met and talked with him a few times, and it was readily apparent how much his daughter's death had affected him. Both back when it happened and for the twenty-five years since.

I felt a deep compassion for him.

I'd thought he was a broken man more than once, and I'd been proven correct. I wish I'd been wrong.

The funeral was scheduled for next Friday, and I would be there.

Would the killer be there, too?

THE NEXT SEVERAL days were more of the same.

Interviews and research. Research and interviews.

I reached out to people I'd yet to contact. That included several more of the extended Ryan family, a few family friends at the party, and even the lone surviving caterer.

I learned a few small things that weren't touched on in Earl Razzle's summary, but nothing that turned the case on its head.

If something didn't change soon, the month would have passed, and William Ryan would have a decision to make: keep me on retainer or cut his losses. While I hated dealing with Annie's death and the grief that the family still endured, I equally despised the idea of leaving the case having accomplished nothing.

But I knew it wasn't up to me whether I stayed on. The ball was in William Ryan's court.

THE DAY BEFORE THE FUNERAL, I returned to the Hollywood Hills and interviewed William Ryan's closest neighbor. It's probably something I should have done earlier.

The man, Myles, was now eighty-six years old and the only neighbor still living in the same house as he did in 1998.

Myles said he had walked over to William's the following day when the police started canvassing the neighborhood, but as for the night in question, he had neither seen nor heard anything. Myles wasn't sure if he'd ever met Annie, and even though he was neighbors with William, he didn't know him very well.

It didn't surprise me. Being a neighbor in the Hollywood Hills wasn't the same as being a neighbor on a typical suburban street where houses were contiguous.

William's house was on several acres of property and was surrounded by trees on all sides. Just because you were theoretically a neighbor doesn't mean you'd see him very often. It was just a different style of living from how I grew up in Santa Barbara, where we'd have block parties, and I'd know every family that showed up.

I thanked Myles for his time and headed back to the Beverly Hilton. The funeral was scheduled for eleven a.m. the following morning.

As usual, I parked my car in the garage.

As I walked by the front desk toward the elevator, I saw one of the staff stare at me.

"Mr. McGowan," he said.

The staff had begun to know my name. That happens when you stay at the same hotel for weeks on end.

"Yes."

"We have a letter for you," he said.

My eyes quickly met his. Since starting my stay here, I've only received one letter—the postcard!

I walked the ten feet to the front desk.

"Well, really, it's more of a postcard," he said.

Bingo!

He started to hand it over to me. I watched as he grabbed the top right of the postcard, using his thumb and forefinger.

"Here you go, Mr. McGowan."

I was taking this to Patchett. I didn't care if he said that fifty postal employees handled the damn thing. If that were the case, then I'd knock on fifty doors. I wasn't exactly swimming in new theories, and these were undoubtedly the best things I had to go on.

Not that I needed Earl Razzle's confirmation, but he'd said as much.

I grabbed the postcard in the lower right-hand corner, trying to touch as little surface space as possible. I could see the front, and it said, "Come Visit Los Angeles."

That piqued my interest.

Have you come back to the scene of the crime?

"Thanks," I said.

THE OTHER ANNIE

Once again, I decided to wait until I got upstairs to read the postcard. I got off the elevator, walked to my room, and locked the door behind me as if Annie's killer was somehow following me down the hall.

The front of the postcard was replete with Southern California destinations: Disneyland (located in Anaheim), Universal Studios, the Santa Monica Pier, and the Hollywood Sign. I turned the postcard over. It had the same block lettering as the first one I'd received, and my suspicions were confirmed. This was from the same guy.

This time, there were two sentences, thirteen words in total, and once again, a shiver went down my spine.

'*See you at the funeral. I'll be the one in the dark suit.*'

I CALLED Detective Patchett the next morning at 9:30 a.m., ninety minutes before the funeral was to start, and ten minutes before I would start driving to the valley.

He wasn't in the office yet.

The dispatcher asked if I wanted to leave a message, but I declined.

Before I hung up, I quickly thought of something. If I were to have Patchett run a fingerprint check, I'd have to deliver the two postcards in person.

"Will the detective be in on Monday morning?" I asked.

"Yes. Probably between eight and nine."

"Can you tell him that Bobby McGowan will be stopping in?"

"I'll let him know," she said.

I could meet Detective Patchett and then grab lunch with my father, whom I hadn't seen since starting the case almost three weeks ago.

CHAPTER 19

St. John Eudes Parish was a beautiful Catholic Church in Chatsworth with a huge steeple rising toward the sky. The fact that it rose toward the heavens wasn't subtle, but it was dramatic.

I intentionally arrived early, getting there at 10:15 for an 11:00 a.m. funeral. I didn't want to risk missing a thing.

Was Annie Ryan's killer going to jump out of his car at 10:35 and declare that he was the man I was looking for? No, but maybe I'd overhear something that stood out. Something that didn't ring quite right.

I exited my car and hung out in the parking lot, hoping to exchange pleasantries with people I'd interviewed over the last few weeks. I'd received a text from Ginny Ryan that she wouldn't be making the trip from New York, but I knew that Adam Toon and Amber Ryan would be there.

Amber arrived first, and she beelined directly toward me. Her kids hung back, deciding to hang with themselves.

I couldn't imagine how tough this must be for all the Ryans. In the back of their minds - and the front of mine - they had to be wondering if Annie's killer was still amongst them. Making it worse, Connor Ryan had committed suicide. Those funerals were always tougher.

Kai Butler's funeral must have been brutal. A suicide directly on the heels of Annie's death. Making it even worse - if that's possible - is that some people in the family feared that Kai may have had a part in Annie's death.

The tension at that funeral must have been palpable.

Whenever someone new arrived, I'd look in their direction and wonder if the man sending me postcards had just arrived. And was he the killer or just some lunatic trying to screw with me?

Amber and I created some small talk for a few minutes. We certainly didn't want to talk about Connor's death. The thought of him intentionally breathing in carbon dioxide to end his time here on earth wasn't exactly feel-good stuff.

Adam Toon arrived soon after that. He and Amber exchanged a long hug, and then we shook hands. It was evident that Adam and Amber got along very well. After all, it was Adam who had encouraged me to meet Amber.

We talked about how hot it was getting in LA—it was already eighty-four degrees at 10:45—and might approach 100 in Chatsworth. We did anything to avoid the issue at hand.

"Can you guys point out any relatives I might not have met yet?" I asked.

"Jeez, Bobby, this is a funeral—not a meet-and-greet," Amber said, but she smiled when she said it.

"Bobby thinks this is a social hour," Adam chimed in.

"I got it. You guys are laying it on a little thick," I said.

They both smiled. Once again, anything to avoid talking about Connor.

At 10:45, William Ryan arrived, looking resplendent in a dark suit and a dark blue tie. I'm sure looking good at the funeral was important to him. This was his brother's funeral, and a great many family members would be here.

He came over and exchanged pleasantries with the three of us. I felt some eyes moving in my direction. I assumed they wondered who this non-Ryan was hanging out with William, Adam, and Amber.

If they didn't know who I was already.

I'm sure the bulk of them wish William had never hired me.

Adam tapped me on the shoulder.

"That's Phyllis Ryan. She married William's father's brother and is the oldest living Ryan. Is that convoluted enough?"

"You could have said she was the wife of William's uncle."

Adam smiled.

"Yeah, I guess that would have been easier."

He then tapped William, who hadn't been listening to us.

"What is it, Too…What is it, Adam?"

It was apparent William was about to say Toon, and probably Toon the Loon, but then thought better of it. Was it because of my presence or because we were at a funeral? I couldn't be sure.

"How old is Phyllis?"

"Ninety-five," William said. "And seems to be in pretty good health. She'll outlive the whole damn family."

I couldn't decide if it was an inappropriate joke to make at a funeral or the perfect time to say it.

Amber pointed out another family member I'd yet to meet. She looked to be in her late sixties.

Before I knew it, the doors to the church opened, and we all started walking inside. At that point, I parted ways with the other three. I would be sitting in the back of the church. I didn't deserve to sit near the front and wouldn't try to pretend I was more important than I was.

As a McGowan, I had been to a few Irish Catholic funerals over the years, and I always left them feeling exhausted. I wanted to hear why that person was beloved; I didn't need to sing along to four songs I couldn't remember the words to.

The toughest of all had been my mother's funeral. I was a twelve-year-old kid who'd just lost his mother, and now hundreds of people wanted to approach me, hug me, and tell me how much my mother meant to them. Maybe if I had been a little older, I would have taken it better, but at that moment, I just wanted to get out of that church. It was brutal.

As a good Catholic boy—even one who had lapsed long ago—I took Holy Communion and made the sign of the cross.

I passed by Connor's casket, which was closed. I'm not sure what happens to a body after carbon monoxide poisoning, but I guessed that your body probably looks as close to a living human as almost any death besides dying in your sleep.

And yet, they'd opted for a closed casket.

Open caskets seemed much more popular twenty years ago; at least, that was my impression.

About fifteen minutes after Communion, the service mercifully came to an end.

We reconvened outside, and I talked to some assembled guests. I introduced myself as Bobby McGowan, but I didn't know how I knew Connor.

I was rescued by Amber and her three kids, who looked like they'd rather be anywhere else but here.

"Can we go home now?" One of them asked.

"No, we have to see him get buried, and then we have the reception."

All three faces seemed to deflate at once.

"But at the reception, they'll have some good food," Amber said. "Probably some cookies and cake too."

Their faces perked up a little bit.

∼

THE BURIAL OCCURRED at the San Fernando Mission Catholic Cemetery and lasted about forty minutes. Only about half of the people from the funeral made it there. They'd either headed to the reception early or called it a day after the funeral.

I couldn't exactly blame them. Three stops in one day was a lot.

My eyes darted like they were watching a tennis match, but nobody stood out at the burial. Not that I should have been surprised. The killer wasn't going to wear a sign around his neck.

∼

THE DAY'S last stop was the reception. A local restaurant hosted it.

They'd cordoned off the back section, and the food was served buffet-style.

They had lasagna, chicken Alfredo, garlic bread, and a large salad. It was Italian food being served at an Irish funeral.

But hey, the Irish aren't exactly known for their food.

They were known for their love of life, and many Irish funerals were overshadowed by the wakes, which usually took place the night before. The guests would regale each other with what were often drunken stories about the deceased.

Yes, there have been millions of tee-totaling Irish, but their wakes were probably a little less exciting.

I'd always liked the idea of a wake over a funeral. I wanted to be remembered in life more so than in death.

∼

CONNOR RYAN WAS A DIFFERENT STORY. He'd lost both of his kids very early in their lives and had been a shell of himself ever since. It's not like there were a bunch of great stories about Connor having had a few too many and making an ass of himself.

Too bad. It would have made him seem more human. More alive.

Between servings of lasagna, which was quite delicious, I managed to talk to almost everyone who had made it to part three of the day.

Earlier, I'd been reticent to mention why I was there, but I grabbed a glass of red wine and decided to mingle. I decided that if the killer were there - in the dark suit! - I'd want him to look into my eyes. Maybe I'd see a flicker of recognition.

Midway through the reception, I feared that I was starting to look like a political candidate, going table to table.

This was a funeral, after all, and not the time to discuss my investigation. I sat down my glass of unfinished wine and spent the rest of the time watching the conversations without involving myself.

When we were down to about fifteen people, I decided that was my cue to leave. I hadn't accomplished much but I reminded myself that this day wasn't about me.

It was about Connor Ryan and the tremendous hole in his heart, even all these years later.

As I left the restaurant above the exit, I saw a large, blown-up picture of Connor Ryan with his daughter.

Connor had a huge smile on his face. I'd never seen his face come close to lighting up like that. Annie also had a big smile, seemingly happy to hug her father - something rarely seen in teenage girls. My heart ached for both of them.

"I'm going to catch this guy," I said underneath my breath.

I walked out of the restaurant and into the warm Los Angeles air.

CHAPTER 20

I drove up to Santa Barbara early on Monday morning.
I called William to tell him I'd be out of Los Angeles for the day, but it still pertained to the case. That was true, as my first stop was with Detective Patchett of the SBPD. My second stop was a lunch with my father, and while that was personal and not business, William didn't need to know about that. I didn't think he would have cared.

I arrived at the Santa Barbara Police Department's main office minutes after nine and went to the front desk. I knew the place like the back of my hand, having been there many times over the years, always wanting updates on my mother's case.

The front desk clerk told me that Patchett was running a few minutes late. A few seconds later, she tapped me on the shoulder, signifying I should turn around.

"Hey, Bobby."

Detective Patchett was walking toward me.

"Late again?"

He laughed. We had a much better friendship now that I'd caught - and killed - the guy responsible for my mother's death. There had been tension for two decades, but we'd let bygones be bygones.

"Yeah, I had a good reason for being late," he said.

"What's that?"

"I knew I had to meet with you."

I smiled.

"I walked right into that one."

"Speaking of walking, let's head down to my office."

We arrived at his office, which hadn't changed over the years. It was still too small, with one desk and a few uncomfortable chairs. I knew that police officers often got a gold watch when they retired. I bet 99% of them would have traded that in for a bigger office when they worked.

"So, what brought you from LA to Santa Barbara?" he asked.

"It's about that postcard I told you about."

"Okay. What about it?"

I'd been holding a manilla envelope that contained both postcards. I took it out and set it between us.

"I received a second one," I said.

"I told you these things likely have several fingerprints all over them."

"I don't care."

I told Patchett about how I'd knock on fifty doors if I had to.

"This isn't even my case, Bobby. Shit, this didn't even happen in my city."

"I know," I said and stared at him.

I could have said something, but it wasn't necessary. I could have told Patchett that it was me who had caught my mother's killer. That it was me - not the SBPD - who had solved their most high-profile crime in decades. That it was me who had saved his ass from lamenting my mother's case for the rest of his life.

And he knew I could say all that, which made my stare enough.

"I'll see what I can do," he said.

"Thanks. How long does that usually take?"

"The standard is seventy-two hours, but I usually get them back within two days."

"You won't get in trouble, will you?"

"Let's hope not. I'll say there's been a string of car break-ins."

"And they are sending postcards?" I asked.

Patchett started laughing.

"Good point. I'll figure something out."

"Thanks for doing this. It's important, or I wouldn't ask."

"You don't have another Conrad Drury on your hands, do you?"

"Let's hope not," I said, and he knew that's all he was getting.

"How's your father, by the way?" he asked.

"I'll tell you in a few hours."

"Excuse me?"

"I'm having lunch with him."

"Ah, gotcha. Tell him I said hello."
"I will."
"And your sister. How's she?"
"Still being a Mom back east."
"Give her my best too."
"Consider it done."
"I'll be in touch, Bobby. Likely Wednesday. If not, Thursday."
"Thanks again," I said and turned to go.

I'd been in and out of the police department within ten minutes.

THE PALACE GRILL—WHICH Santa Barbara residents simply referred to as The Palace—had always been my father's and my favorite restaurant, but it only served dinner, so we had to pick a different place.

I let my father choose, and he'd settled on Ca'Dario, a great Italian restaurant tucked just behind State Street on Victoria Street. My father had long enjoyed the ravioli there, and I had no doubt that would be his order on this day.

I met him outside Ca'Dario at noon sharp, and like Detective Patchett, my father was walking up soon after I'd arrived.

I gave him a big hug. I hadn't seen him in three weeks, which was a long time for us. We both lived in Santa Barbara, so I usually saw him quite often.

He was excited about me taking the Annie Ryan case, but I knew he also missed me, so I was happy we could have this lunch.

We were seated and given two menus.

"I already know what I'm getting," he said.

"Ravioli?"

"Am I that predictable?"

"At this restaurant, yes."

Ca'Dario was a small restaurant with probably about fifteen tables. We were given one in the corner of a half-filled restaurant.

I scanned the menu and decided on the PANINO CON BISTECCHINA (yes, it was all in caps on the menu), a panini with thinly sliced steak, caramelized onions, and fontina cheese.

The waiter came by and took our orders, leaving some bread behind.

"So, how are you liking Beverly Hills? Got a bunch of celebrity friends now?"

"Oh, yeah. Tom Cruise and I are like this," I said, locking my middle finger over my index one. "And I've started dating Emma Stone. You're going to love her."

"Isn't Emma Stone married?"

"This is Hollywood, Dad. That shit doesn't matter."

He laughed.

"Well, you haven't lost your sense of humor."

"That's true, but this case is tough. I told you I was at a funeral on Friday."

"Yeah, that sounds terrible. I guess the guy never recovered from losing his daughter."

There was a time when I wasn't sure my father would ever recover from losing his wife.

"It was tough," I said, not needing to draw the parallels. I also wasn't going to tell my father about the second postcard I'd received.

"Do you like the Beverly Hilton?" my father asked, leaving the funeral talk behind.

"It's a great hotel. You'd love it. Want to visit? It's been boiling down there. You could just sit by the pool and soak in the rays."

"Tempting, although I'm sure my doctor wouldn't want me laying out in the sun all day."

"Skin cancer takes years to develop, and you're already an old man," I said and laughed.

At only sixty, my father was quite a bit younger than most of the older generation of Ryans. William Ryan had more than a decade on him.

"I'm young at heart, Bobby. Did I tell you I've started biking again?"

"No, tell me more."

"There's this little group of us who ride around every Sunday. We're all at least fifty-five years old, and there are about ten of us in total. It's a lot of fun."

This made me happy. My father had become a homebody ever since my mother's murder. It was great to see him as a man about town.

Sadly, my mind went to Connor Ryan. He'd never have the third act that my father was now having.

"So, where'd you bike yesterday?" I asked.

"Went around Goleta Beach and then through the UCSB campus."

"I'm sure that's just what all those college kids want: a bunch of geriatrics biking through campus."

My father laughed.

"You like busting my chops."

"I've been gone. I've missed it."

"Well, I'm happy to have you back, even if it's only for lunch."

"Glad to be here, Dad."

"You'll be back soon, right? Wasn't this just a one-month job?"

"William Ryan, the guy who hired me, said we should reassess after a month. I imagine he'll want to keep me on."

"That's good news, I guess. But for how long? Another twenty-five years? Shit, you'll be geriatric at that point."

I laughed.

"Maybe he'll give me another month."

"Do you feel like you're making progress?"

I reminded myself not to mention the postcards.

"Yes and no. I understand the case well, but no suspects are leaping off the police report."

"Just because you solved your mother's doesn't mean you're going to be able to solve every other cold case."

"I understand that."

"I don't want you to be disappointed if you don't crack this case. Didn't you tell me that Earl Razzle was on this case? He's got tons more experience and connections than you, and he didn't solve it."

"Well, anybody with one connection has more than me."

"Did you try to meet with any Los Angeles detectives?"

"Yeah, one."

"And?"

"And he won't be inviting me over for a 4th of July barbecue. Let's just say that."

My father nodded, knowing not to push it.

The waiter brought us our entrees soon after. We spent the next few minutes in silence, eating our respective lunches.

"How's the sandwich?" my father asked.

"Excellent. The ravioli as good as always?"

"You know it."

We ate for a few more minutes without saying anything. My father broke the silence.

"How did the Ryan extended family take Annie's loss? As a whole, I mean."

"They did not take it well. As you know, her father just took his own life. And it's affected the whole family down the line. There are rarely any big gatherings anymore. Every member seems to still have some residual suspicions. There's a sadness that kind of permeates the whole family."

"Sounds like a fun case you've got here, Bobby."

I smiled.

"It hasn't exactly been a barrel of laughs."

"I wouldn't think so."

"But then again, it just makes me want to solve her murder even more. Can you imagine if I solved it? Just what a relief that would be for the family."

"I'm tempted to say the generic *'that will never bring Annie back,'* but I know better. What you accomplished didn't bring your mother back, but it was still monumental to our family. And I imagine it would be the same for the Ryans."

"I've dreamt of a huge party to celebrate Annie's life once the murderer is finally behind bars. And after that, all the Ryans could go about living the rest of their lives."

"Is that realistic?"

"I'm not sure. The family may be so far gone there's no saving them."

"I meant, is it realistic that you're going to catch this guy and put him in jail?"

The waiter came over and took our empty plates. He asked us if we wanted dessert, and we declined, just ordering coffee.

"Realistic? Yes. Probable? No."

"I miss you up here," my father said.

"I've missed you too, Dad. I promise it won't be this long before I visit you next time. You sure you don't want to come down to LA?"

"And lay out at that hotel pool of yours?"

"Yup."

"Maybe. We could find a nice Beverly Hills restaurant to have dinner at."

"There's several within walking distance."

"Alright, I'm sold. I'll come down for a day. Next week good?"

"Perfect."

The waiter returned with the bill, and we headed outside a few minutes later. We hugged, and I told my father I'd contact him next week to solidify his trip to Los Angeles.

CHAPTER 21

I felt a bit homesick over the next few days.

The reason was obvious. I'd gone from spending time with my father in my hometown to coming down to LA, where every time I talked to a Ryan family member, it was about the death of a fifteen-year-old girl. It was my job, and I understood that, but it was still getting tedious.

I was even growing tired of living at the Beverly Hilton. It wasn't the hotel's fault; it was still beautiful. It was just getting a little cramped. If William Ryan extended me another month, maybe I could negotiate for an Airbnb.

And that was fast approaching. It had now been three weeks. William hadn't mentioned that he would end my employment, but it's still a conversation we had to have.

I COULD HAVE CALLED my ex-girlfriend, Ivy Harrington, who now lives in LA, to cure my loneliness.

Unfortunately, when I had finished with my mother's killer, Ivy had made it clear (probably at her mother's behest) that we were no longer to see each other.

I had decided to respect those wishes.

∼

I got the call I'd been waiting for on Thursday at 11:56 a.m.

"I've got your results," Detective Patchett said before I'd even had the chance to say hello.

"Great. Anything interesting?"

"Yes."

He didn't say anything.

"You're killing me," I said. "What is it?"

"There were three sets of fingerprints that appeared on both postcards."

I tried to temper my expectations.

"Okay," I said.

"One set was yours. And I got the other two people's names, numbers, and addresses."

"Wow, Patchett. This is great. Only two doors to knock on. Not fifty."

"Actually, you'll only have to knock on one door. After I found out their names, I did a quick search of both. One of the two people is named Mary Jo Haggarty, and she works at a Post Office in Pleasant Hill, California. It's a city up in the Bay Area. So, it's obvious she just handled both postcards in the office. It's the second person whose door you'll be knocking on."

"And what's his name?"

"Vance Hayes. And he lives less than a mile from the Pleasant Hill Post Office."

"You've gone above the call. Thanks so much, detective. Does it show his profession?"

"No, I couldn't find that. He is only twenty-one years old, however. I'm texting you a printout of his driver's license."

The wind quickly went out of my sails. This guy wasn't the killer. I don't know if he was somehow involved decades after the fact, but I was pretty confident he wasn't committing murders at negative four years old.

The text went through, and I clicked on his driver's license photo. In the picture, Vance Hayes looked like a shy teenager. How could a guy like this be involved?

"Did you get any more information on him?" I asked.

"No, just his address, DOB, and this picture. You sound let down."

I was, but I didn't need to let him know. The truth was, I was fearful that my big break wouldn't amount to jack squat.

"I'm not let down," I lied.

"I want you to listen to me for a second, Bobby."

"Sure. What is it?"

"Be careful. I don't need - or want - to know the ins and outs of your case, but I do know it's a missing person's case. If you think the guy sending postcards is involved, he won't take too kindly to some random guy knocking on his door. Use your brain. I don't care if he's only twenty-one years old. Like I said, be careful. I don't want to hear about some asshole firing a shotgun through his front door and killing a friend of mine."

I didn't like Patchett leaving me with that visual, but maybe a warning wasn't the worst idea. I was already discounting Vance Hayes because of his age. Perhaps I was wrong to do so. Maybe he was the son of the killer. Maybe a tenant in the killer's house. I didn't know what he was, but he'd likely sent me two postcards, which made him part and parcel to my case.

"I'll be careful. I promise," I said.

"Then I don't have much more to say. Talk to you soon."

And with that, he hung up.

~

I FLEW UP to the Bay Area early the next afternoon.

I didn't know anything about Vance Hayes, but if he worked a 9-5, I figured I'd be there waiting when he returned home. I preferred that to flying up at seven a.m. and trying to catch him before he left his place.

And who knows if he even had a job? He was only twenty-one and could have been a student. Maybe he was a bartender and worked nights.

I had no idea what to expect.

I'd booked a rental car and a return flight for later that night. This would be the second time I'd ever flown into and out of the same city on the same day.

A few years back, my buddy had a bachelor party in Las Vegas, and the following day was Ivy's birthday. She was hosting a well-attended brunch at nine a.m., and I didn't trust myself enough to fly back from Vegas at seven and make it to the brunch on time. So I'd booked the latest flight back from Vegas, a 10:00 p.m. flight that night.

Having flown in at eight that morning and started drinking by noon, you can guess the shape I was in when I finally arrived at the airport. Maybe TSA felt generous because they let me on the flight despite a stagger to my walk.

As for my current flight, I landed at Oakland Airport at 3:00 p.m., picked up my rental car, and headed east toward the address on his driver's license: 194 Golf Club Road in Pleasant Hill.

I drove by a sign for a private detective named Quint. Was that going to be me someday? I guess time would tell.

~

He lived in a pleasant - hey, it was Pleasant Hill! - suburban neighborhood with two and three-bedroom houses up and down the street. There were no luxurious homes, but no duds either.

I'd tried to find out a few other things about Vance before I went to his house, but there wasn't much online. There were only a few Vance Hayes's on Facebook or Instagram, and they were all set to private. And considering he was only twenty-one, maybe he only had Snapchat or some other social media I was too old for.

I still couldn't get over how young he was. How the hell had he got himself involved in a murder that took place before he was born? Hopefully, I was about to find out.

I sat in my rental car and debated whether to go right up to the house or wait until someone left to confront them.

"Screw it," I said.

I got out of my car and approached the house.

My eyes were on a swivel, Patchett's warning of a shotgun never far from my mind.

I knocked on the door. No response.

I knocked again—still nothing.

I knocked a third time and pressed the doorbell as well.

Thirty seconds later, the door was finally answered.

"Can I help you?"

The man who answered looked to also be in his early twenties, but it wasn't Vance Hayes.

"I'm here to see Vance," I said.

"He's playing a game right now."

"How long until he's done."

"Who knows with him? Could be five minutes or five hours," the guy said and laughed.

The presence of another person had helped set my mind at ease.

"Can I come in?" I asked.

"Woah, guy," he said. "I don't even know who you are."

"It's very important. I can assure you of that, but I can only talk to Vance about it."

"Wait, did he win the contest? Are you with corporate Dungeons and Dragons?"

I resisted the urge to laugh. He thought I was with corporate Dungeon and Dragons. This was my chance.

"Wow, you're good," I said.

I hadn't exactly confirmed his suspicion, but I certainly hadn't denied it.

"Vance, come here quick!" the man yelled. He was way too excited.

When no one appeared, he left the front door to go and try to find him.

A minute later, Vance Hayes appeared at the door. He was older than the teenager in his driver's license picture but was still easily recognizable.

He had a big smile on his face.

"I thought this day would never happen," he said. "Andy said you're from D and D?"

"Do you have a place we could talk? Preferably away from your friends."

His face lit up.

"Sure, we can go to my room."

He let me inside the house and guided me down a hallway. We passed a room where four or five people were playing some sort of video game.

They gave Vance some words of encouragement.

"Congrats!"

"You deserve it."

"You're a D and D Wizard!"

We approached his room, and as I looked in, I realized I'd never seen a bigger mess in my life. Several blankets covered the floor, a box spring was up against a wall, blocking 75% of the walking space, toilet paper rolls were spread, and at least four unfinished Doritos bags were on the floor.

It made Gina Galasso's apartment look pristine.

He looked at me, slightly embarrassed.

"Why don't we talk outside?" I said. Technically, it was a question, but I'd said it more as a statement.

We walked back through the house, and I heard a few more words of encouragement yelled in Vance's direction.

I'd expected us to go out front, but he opened a sliding glass door to a backyard. There were a bunch of white plastic chairs, and we both sat in one.

"So I won the contest?" he asked excitedly. "I figured that's the only reason you'd show up at my house."

"I'm not from corporate D and D, Vance."

"Andy said you were."

"Andy was mistaken."

Suddenly, his facial expression changed. I couldn't tell if he was just disappointed or if there was some fear, too.

"Well, what are you here for?" he asked.

There was no way to sugarcoat it.

"I'm here about some mail you've sent."

He didn't say anything, but something registered.

"What?"

"Don't play dumb with me, Vance, or I'll have to call the cops."

"For what? I haven't done anything illegal."

"That's yet to be determined."

"Are you a cop?"

"No."

"If you're not a cop, what are you?"

I decided a white lie couldn't hurt.

"I'm a private investigator."

"Investigating what?"

It was time to put Vance on his back heel.

"Did you have anything to do with the murder of Annie Ryan?"

It had worked. He was instantly defensive.

"What? Who?"

"You heard me. Annie Ryan. Did you have anything to do with her murder?"

"I've never heard that name in my life. I swear to you."

"Then why are you sending me postcards?"

"What the fuck? That's what this is about?"

I had him right where I wanted him. His expression told me he was ready to come clean.

"You better tell me now. Before I call the cops."

He shifted around in his chair.

"I was just trying to make a little extra money. The guy offered me $200 to buy a postcard, write on it, and mail it. Who wouldn't do that? And then he had me do it again."

"What guy? Who paid you to do this?"

"Some guy online. I don't know his real name."

"How did he find you?"

"On this website."

"What's the name of the website?"

"52solutions.com"

"Is this like 4chan?" I asked, knowing 4chan was a shady internet website, but not much more about it.

"It's not nearly as seedy, but it does allow you to be anonymous."

"And you can reach out to someone on there to do your dirty work for you?"

"If you're talking about mailing a postcard, then yes. This isn't a website where people go to talk about school shootings and shit like that."

"Can you show me the site?"

"Yeah. I have to go grab my laptop."

Vance walked back inside. His friends and roommates were about to get some bad news.

He opened up the sliding glass door a minute later.

I moved my seat so I could see the screen.

He logged into 52solutions with a password that looked to be over twenty characters long. I was pretty darn tech savvy - I'd formerly worked as a social media manager, but these off-the-grid websites were entirely out of my realm.

He was on the site and leaned his laptop closer to me. 52solutions looked like Amazon on steroids, with fifty different places to go on the home page itself.

"How did he contact you?" I asked.

"He started a thread, asking if anyone in the United States wanted to make $200 bucks by sending an envelope. I responded first."

"Do you have access to his initial post?"

"No. All posts get erased after it's completed."

"You sure this isn't 4chan-ish?"

"It's not that scary, believe me. I've been on 4chan, and 52solutions ain't even close."

"Can you find out the location of the other users?"

"No. That's part of the charm of these websites," Vance said.

"I think charm is going a bit far."

"Fine. Part of the allure is being able to stay anonymous. Both with your name and your location."

"Everyone has to have a screen name, right?"

"Yes."

"And what was the screen name of the person who had you send the postcards?"

"Now, that is something they do save. They have a section of people you've conversed with lately."

He took a few seconds to navigate the website, pressing the laptop keys at an obscenely fast rate.

"Okay, here you go. This is his homepage."

The homepage had his screen name (itstartedwithanAR) and a very disturbing photo.

An animated man stood over several dead animated women; his arms raised high in the air as if he'd accomplished some heroic feat.

"This is the guy you're doing business with?"

"If you didn't talk to anyone with a weird profile picture, you'd be a lonely person on these sites."

I looked at the screen name again. ItstartedwithanAR.

"And the screen name?" I asked.

"I figured he was just a gun nut. You know, an assault rifle. AR."

"AR actually stands for an ArmaLite Rifle," I said.

"Most people think of it as an assault rifle."

He was probably right.

I focused on the screen name. I don't know if it was because the letters were the lone capitalized letters or because Hayes had just mentioned them, but I stared at the letters AR for several seconds.

A sickening thought came to mind.

AR were Annie Ryan's initials.

Could it possibly be that itallstartedwithanAR was referencing Annie Ryan?

No fucking way.

There had to be a different explanation. Hayes was probably right. The guy was a gun nut.

But what if my hunch was correct? What if itstartedwithanAR was talking about Annie Ryan? As if that wasn't scary enough, the person had used the phrase 'started with.' Were there other dead girls besides Annie Ryan? It was just animation, but his profile picture had several dead women.

My head was throbbing.

I saw a small orange light flashing on the corner of his homepage.

"Does that mean he's online right now?" I asked.

"Yes."

My body tensed up. I couldn't believe this was happening.

"I need to talk to this person," I said. "How do I send a message?"

He looked at me and was considering protesting but thought better of it.

He clicked a small icon just above the flashing orange light.

"All you," he said.

"It would be better if you don't watch this exchange," I said.

"Hey, you do what you have to do," Vance said. He didn't like this one bit. "In fact, I'm going inside. I'll come back out here in five or ten minutes."

I nodded at him, and he approached the sliding glass door and walked inside.

Was I about to message Annie's killer? At the very least, it was a distinct possibility.

I started typing.

"Hey, AR. Got any more jobs for me?"

Nothing happened for about forty-five seconds, but then I saw some dots going in and out, which I assumed meant he was typing.

"Hey, SirVanceALot. Nothing for now. This is the first time you've reached out to me. I'm a little suspicious."

"Sorry. I'm just poor right now. I could use another $200."

"Stop begging."

I hoped he'd give away something about himself, but I couldn't be too obvious.

"I apologize. Listen, forget I asked. I'm here if you need me, though."

"Is everything okay, SirVanceALot? You sound different, Chief."

Maybe I should have kept Vance out here and let him type in his own diction. ItstartedwithanAR seemed to sense something was up.

"It's still me," I typed.

"I don't think it is. Who is this?"

Holy shit.

"It's Vance," I typed, instantly realizing my mistake.

"So, now it's Vance. You have never given me your real name."

I had to come up with something.

"I figured you knew it from my screen name."

"Who is this? Really, Chief, your secret is safe with me."

He'd said Chief twice. That registered with me.

Vance had told me there was no way to track people from this site. This might be the one and only time I had to confront this guy. I had to go for it.

"It's Vance. Since I told you my name, why don't you give me yours?"

"I'll pass."

"Then I have a question for you."

There was no response, so I kept typing.

"What does AR stand for?"

Another ten seconds with no response. It felt interminable. Finally, the dots started moving.

"For assault rifle, you silly goose."

Silly goose had never sounded more threatening.

I didn't know what to do, but I had to decide quickly. I couldn't risk him logging out. I'd never have this chance again.

I decided to go for it.

"Are you sure it doesn't stand for Annie Ryan?"

This time, twenty seconds passed before I saw the dots.

His response came through. I don't know what I was expecting, but I was disturbed by what he'd written. Deeply, deeply disturbed.

"I'll be seeing you around, Robert."

Holy. Fucking. Shit.

As soon as I read it, the flashing orange button turned off. He had logged off.

I ran to the screen door and yelled for Vance.

He quickly came to the door.

"I'm afraid this guy is going to close his account," I said. Can I download or save anything that will help me identify the guy?"

"There's not. Like I said, this site allows you to be anonymous."

"Shit."

We approached his laptop.

"Jesus," Vance said.

"What is it?"

"You were right. He just deleted his account."

He grabbed the laptop, lifting it up to show me.

"Fuck," I yelled.

I was not a big obscenity guy, but the last several moments seemed to warrant it.

"What did you say to him?" he asked.

"Better you don't know."

Vance seemed to understand. He'd realized that whatever I was here for was quite serious.

"You're right," he said. "I don't need to know anything."

I thought of one more thing.

"How did he pay you?"

"Through a special payment option on the webpage. Like everything else, it's anonymous. You don't have to give an email, Venmo, or anything like that. That's a dead end. I'm sorry."

There were almost certainly other questions I should have asked in the moment, but my mind was racing, and I couldn't think of any.

"Is there anything else you can tell me?" I asked.

"No, there's really not."

"Have you ever seen that screen name on other sites like this?"

"No, I'd have remembered it."

"And he told you what to write on the postcard?"

"Yes. And he'd had me order postcards from Amazon. The first was St. Louis, and the second was Los Angeles. And he had me write in big, block letters."

"And none of this struck you as weird?"

"Sure, it was weird. But I made $400 for sending two postcards. I go to Diablo Valley City College and have four roommates. $400 is a lot of money."

I believed he was telling the truth.

"I'm going to leave you my phone number," I said. "If he reconnects his account and reaches out to you, I want you to call me immediately."

"Okay, I will."

Vance's expression told me he couldn't wait until I got out of there.

A few minutes later, I obliged.

I walked to my rental car and looked at myself in the rearview mirror.

'I'll be seeing you around, Robert.'

CHAPTER 22

THE KILLER

I never planned on attending Connor Ryan's funeral.
I just told Bobby McGowan, "I'd be the guy in the dark suit," to get under his skin and put him more on edge than I'm sure he already was.

In fact, I had no intention of meeting Bobby McGowan.

So, you can imagine my surprise when SirVanceALot contacted me on 52solutions.com. I knew something was up immediately. This wasn't the type of website where you reach out to see how someone is doing.

I didn't initially assume it was Bobby McGowan, but I thought it was possible once the person on the other end asked what the AR stood for. And when they mentioned Annie Ryan, I knew for sure. I was talking to Bobby McGowan.

In a stroke of genius, I decided to use the word *'Chief'* a few times, knowing I wasn't talking to SirVanceALot. I'm honestly not sure if I've ever used that phrase, but Bobby certainly would have noticed it after I used it a second time.

Let him spend the next two weeks asking people about a mysterious guy who says Chief a lot. Hahaha.

I ended our chat by telling "Robert" I'd be seeing him around and quickly deleted my account. I knew 52solutions was more secure than Fort Knox, and Bobby could never find my location, but I deleted it just to be sure.

∼

I SPENT the next few hours trying to figure out how Bobby had located SirVanceALot, who I now knew was a Vance. Bobby had made a rookie mistake by using his first name.

I'd narrowed it down to two likely options. One, Bobby was able to locate which post office Vance had sent the postcard from, possibly via a timestamp or something like that. And from there, maybe the post office knew who he was or had a video of him. I wasn't quite sure. The second - and more likely - option was that Vance had left fingerprints on the postcard and was found because of them.

I couldn't think of any other possibilities.

I guess, in the end, it didn't matter. The fact that Bobby had found me mattered, but not the manner in which he did.

I knew I should stop contacting Bobby and playing this ridiculous game. I should go back to living my life, which is a pretty great life. I should put this all in my rearview mirror.

Should. Should. Should.

But should is no fun.

I had no doubt Bobby would be hearing from me again.

Maybe in person this time.

CHAPTER 23

BOBBY

The days that followed my meeting with Vance Hayes went nothing like I'd expected.

I'd assumed the case would take off now that I'd caught my first big break. It didn't quite work out that way.

I reached out to William, Adam, and Amber but didn't mention that I'd talked to Annie's prospective killer online. From the start of this case, I'd decided that the fewer people who knew things, the better, and I still believed that.

I did say the word "Chief" during our conversations and then mentioned how nobody uses that word anymore.

"I mean, honestly, when was the last time you heard someone use the word, Chief?" I asked.

It was subtler than asking if any relative used that word regularly.

None took the bait.

I was hoping I'd get lucky, and they'd say that 'Uncle Tyler uses the phrase a lot' or something to that end—no such luck.

I called Mike Minter, who was in a rush when he took my call. I was doing a brief rundown of what I'd found when he had the nerve to laugh at me.

"You think the murderer paid off some random guy from the internet to send you a postcard or two? I'll have to tell my future grandchildren about that one."

I decided there was no point in telling him about my conversation with itallstartedwithanAR. Minter wouldn't listen to me, regardless, so I just hung up on him.

I was incensed.

I considered calling and asking for another detective, but Minter was still the lead on the Annie Ryan case, and I'd be told to contact him.

No, screw the LAPD.

I was done with them.

I was going to do this on my own.

ON THURSDAY, my father called and said he was driving to Los Angeles in the morning. It wasn't the most opportune time to have him visit, but he'd worry too much if I objected to the trip, so I played nice.

It was only twenty-four hours, after all. What could go wrong?

HE ARRIVED at eleven on Tuesday morning, and I met him in front of the Beverly Hilton valet parking lot.

"You must be big time. I still self-park my car," I said.

My father laughed.

"Well, that's probably because your car is a piece of you know what," he said.

I smiled and led him into the hotel. I showed him around the main lobby and the lower level and got him a key for the day.

"Where's the pool?" he asked.

"We'll get there soon enough."

WE ARRIVED AT MY ROOM, and he was genuinely impressed by the view of Beverly Hills.

"Are you sure you want to solve this case?" he joked.

"I'm not sure William Ryan will put me on a permanent retainer. Plus, as great as this place is, I wouldn't want to live here year-round."

"I think I could. Maid service every day. Awesome weather. Beverly Hills right next to you."

"I'm so sorry you have to slum it in Santa Barbara," I said.

"Point taken. I love our town, too."

He set his bag down on the cot I'd delivered for the night. I told my father that the rooms were expensive and that he could stay with me for one night.

Only he'd gotten the arrangements wrong.

"I'm not letting my father sleep on the cot," I said, grabbed his bag, and threw it on the bed.

"You got the bed. I got the cot," I said.

"Thanks, Bobby. You didn't have to do that."

"You're an old man with back issues. It's the least a son could do."

He laughed.

"In that case, I gladly accept."

"Okay, what now?" I asked.

"Do you have work to do?"

"I always have somebody to call or something to read," I said.

"Then why don't you show me that pool you keep talking about. I'll relax for an hour, and then we can go to lunch. I'd rather lay out and then eat as opposed to the other way around."

"Sounds like a plan," I said.

∽

Twenty minutes later, my father was lying by the pool, and I was back upstairs, reviewing more evidence.

For what must have been the sixth time, I was reading over Annie's journal, hoping something would jump out. And for the sixth consecutive time, I was disappointed. There was just nothing that made me think this young lady was in any imminent danger.

∽

An hour later, my father returned to the room. He got changed in the bathroom and was ready for lunch. I realized that this arrangement wouldn't have worked if he had been staying for longer than one day. It was too much to share a room with your father, but for one day, I could manage.

"Have you eaten at The Grill on the Alley?" he asked.

"I've walked by it ten times but haven't stopped in yet."

"It just came highly recommended by the front desk."

"You are making yourself at home here, aren't you?"

"Hey, I've only got twenty-four hours. Might as well make the most of it."

"The Grill on the Alley, it is. You ready?"

"Ready as I'll ever be."

It was a phrase I'd heard hundreds of times in my youth.

"You seem chipper," I said.

There had been enough days over the years where he hadn't been, so I never took for granted how much he'd changed since I'd solved my mother's murder.

"Let's FaceTime your sister at lunch," he said.

"FaceTime? When did you find the fountain of youth?"

"I'm a young sixty, Bobby."

"You keep telling yourself that."

My father laughed, and we headed out the door a minute later.

∼

THE GRILL on the Alley was a Beverly Hills stalwart, and you could feel it as you entered. It had that old-school charm that no new restaurant could match.

We had a fantastic lunch, and my father threw back two martinis. I hadn't seen that in a long time.

"The lady at the front told me that Jackie Gleason and Frank Sinatra both used to eat here," he said. "So I thought I'd go for a popular drink back then. No one drinks martinis anymore."

"You'd be surprised," I said. "They are making a comeback. Everything retro is now becoming cool again."

"Even my clothes?" he asked.

"Okay, almost everything," I said, and he laughed.

My father paid the bill despite my attempt to pay it. It would be the same when he was ninety and I was sixty-two. It's just how he was built. He paid for all lunches and dinners.

∼

WE TOOK a walk around Beverly Hills after lunch.

"Where is Earl Razzle's office?" he asked.

"I've never seen you like this. Drinking martinis because Jackie Gleason did and now wanting to see some celebrity PI's office."

"When in Rome…or, in this case, Hollywood."

"Here, follow me."

I led him down to Razzle's office and walked in. I didn't know what to expect.

"Is Mr. Razzle in?" I asked the secretary I'd dealt with a few times before.

"Let me check, Mr. McGowan."

I felt my father's eyes look in my direction. I knew it was because she'd known my name.

She came back less than a minute later.

"He said to come on in."

"Thanks," I said.

We walked into Earl Razzle's office, where his megawatt smile greeted us. Earl was always dressed to the tee, but he'd outdone himself today. He wore red leather pants, a black leather shirt, and a red and black cowboy hat. And that was all overshadowed by a gold belt buckle the size of a small country.

"Bobby, how are you?"

"Mr. Razzle, this is my father, Robert."

They exchanged handshakes.

"Your son is being modest. He can call me Earl any time he wants."

"You're not tired of this kid yet?" my father joked.

"I can deal with him for a few more months. And then, he'll realize this case is unsolvable and be on his merry way."

"Don't count him out," my father said, coming to my defense.

"Let's just say I'll be pleasantly surprised," Earl said.

He motioned to the massive leather couch where I usually sat.

"Would you like a drink, Robert?"

"I just had two at The Grill on the Alley."

"Then I guess it can't hurt to have a third."

My father laughed. He was like a kid in a candy store. I'm not sure I'd ever seen him like this. It must have been the martinis.

"You want anything, Bobby?"

"I'm alright, thanks. I'll be the designated walker today."

"That's a good son."

"Vodka or gin martini, Robert?"

"Gin."

"Ah, a renaissance man. All the kids have theirs with vodka these days."

Earl Razzle, a private investigator to the stars, spent three minutes making my father an authentic martini. It was surreal.

He topped it off with two green olives and came and sat it on the small table in front of the couch.

"Thank you very much," my father said.

"Don't worry about it. I enjoy it. I recently made a Jack and Coke for a famous Los Angeles Dodger. And he had a game a few hours later."

"You ever going to spill all the beans and write an autobiography?" I asked.

"No. Those secrets will die with me. I might tell them amongst friends like I just did, but I won't publish them for public consumption."

"It would be quite the book, I'm sure."

Earl Razzle let out a smirk.

"You have no idea."

I believed him.

"So, Robert, how long are you in town for?"

"One day. Then I'll let my son get back to his case."

"I already told him he might as well enjoy the amenities. Sit by the Beverly Hilton pool and conduct his meetings there."

"Amen," my father said. "Then run to The Grill every hour and pick up a martini."

My father and Earl Razzle shared a laugh. Was this real life?

"I can leave if you guys want to work on your comedy routine together," I said.

They laughed again, and my father took a sip of his martini.

"Restaurant quality, Mr. Razzle."

"You're not the first guy to have a drink at The Grill and then follow it up with one here."

"I could get used to that."

"Maybe you should stay a week, Robert."

"Don't give him any ideas," I said.

"I'll put you on a job. I've got a very famous Hollywood director who is positive his wife is cheating on him."

"Are you sure you don't want to write that autobiography?" my father asked. "It sounds like you enjoy dishing the dirt."

It could have been construed as mocking him, but Earl smiled.

"Behind closed doors, I'm good with it," he said. "I'd never say anything to a newspaper or, God forbid, a tabloid."

My father took a big sip of his martini and was two-thirds finished. He was going to nap this afternoon; I had no doubt about that.

"Another drink, Robert?"

"No, I think I'll pass on another one. Three is already about two too many for me."

I laughed and made the 'Cut him off' sign to Razzle.

"Well, if you come down and visit again, be sure to drop in."

"Are you kicking us out?"

"Unless you want to sit in on my meeting with a very young supermodel."

"Can I?" my father asked, his booze intake becoming obvious.

"Let's go back to the hotel, Dad."

"No supermodels this trip, I guess," he said.

Earl Razzle was enjoying every minute of this.

We stood up to go.

"Anything new on the case?" Razzle asked me.

I hadn't divulged much information to him, but maybe I should have. He knew the case better than anyone.

"There are a few new wrinkles. I'll drop in soon."

"Looking forward to it."

My father and Earl shook hands.

"Great meeting you, Robert."

"You too, Earl. You're a lot more classy in person than on the TV."

It was meant as a compliment, and luckily, Razzle took it that way. I'm not sure I would have.

My father took the last swig of his martini.

"And you make a good drink."

"Drop by anytime."

We said our goodbyes, and my father and I left his office. Sure enough, just as when the governor had been sitting there, a long-legged supermodel was waiting to see Earl Razzle.

Talk about living the life.

WE HEADED BACK toward the Beverly Hilton, my father's nap fast approaching.

"Thanks, Bobby," he said as we crossed the street to the hotel. "That was an enjoyable two hours."

"I concur."

"That Earl is alright."

"I concur again."

"And that supermodel had long legs."

"Let's make it a trifecta. I concur again."

We entered the hotel and took the elevator up to my room. My father instantly jumped on the bed. The three drinks had taken their toll.

"I'll be fine after a quick nap," he said.

As he said it, I saw the flashing light from the phone. My heart skipped a beat.

Could it be another postcard?

"I'll come back up in an hour, Dad. Have a nice rest."

I looked over and saw that he was already fast asleep.

CHAPTER 24

I took the elevator downstairs.

The amusement at my father's tipsiness had been replaced by nervousness over the flashing light on my hotel phone.

I approached the front desk.

"Hello, Mr. McGowan. I suggested The Grill on the Alley to your father. Did you guys go there?"

"Yes. He loved it. Thank you."

"Of course."

"Listen, my phone was flashing again. Do I have something waiting for me?"

"Hmm, let me check. I'll be right back."

She walked back to talk to another employee, which was surprising. They had the postcard right in front of them the other two times.

She slowly made her way back over. Something was up.

"What is it?" I asked.

"Well, it's kind of odd, but someone called and left a message, and all they said was when you came down here to tell you to answer your phone."

"That's it?"

"That's it."

"Okay, thanks," I said and started to walk away.

I only got five feet until I felt my phone vibrating in my pocket. I took it out and saw it coming from an unrecognized number. There was no way I wasn't picking up.

"Hello?"

"How many Roberts does it take to have lunch together?"

The person on the other end was using some sort of voice changer. It reminded me of *Scream*, where the killers disguise their voices.

A second later, it hit me. He was referring to me and my father.

I walked toward a corner of the lobby where no one was standing. I didn't want anyone to hear what I had to say.

"Who is this?" I asked.

"I believe you know me as itstartedwithanAR."

"What the hell do you want?"

"To meet your father."

It didn't happen often, but I had no idea what to say. I wanted to go on an expletive-filled rampage, but that wouldn't accomplish anything.

"No more postcards?" I finally asked, trying to change the subject from my father.

"I wanted to talk to the real you."

"52solutions doesn't count?"

"I was hiding behind a firewall then."

"You're hiding behind a voice changer now."

I heard a garbled laugh.

"Good point, Robert. Good point."

"We didn't meet at the funeral?" I asked.

"I'm not going to give you the answer to that question. Have you seen the movie *In the Line of Fire* with Clint Eastwood and John Malkovich?"

I had no idea why he was asking me about a decades-old movie.

"Years ago. Why?"

"Malkovich's character says to Eastwood: *'I'll keep you in the game, but I'm not going to throw it for you.'*"

I understood what he was saying despite not knowing the ins and outs of the movie. He thought this was some one-on-one battle of wits. My mind immediately went to Conrad Drury. He had treated it the same.

"I can live with a one-on-one battle," I said. "Just don't bring my family into it."

"Touchy, touchy. I won't harm your old man unless it becomes necessary."

"What do you want?"

"I just wanted to talk to the guy trying to identify me."

"So, Annie is dead?"

The voice continued to be scrambled. And it's not like I could call 9-1-1 and ask this phone call to be traced. I just had to stand here and hope he somehow slipped up.

"Yes, she is. I'm sorry. Were you expecting to find her alive after all these years?"

"No. I knew she was dead, and I was looking for a deadbeat killer."

"Oooh, I'm shaking in my boots."

"Now what?" I asked.

"Now, you continue on your little escapade, and I continue doing what I like."

"Killing young girls?"

"Do you think I'm going to answer that?"

"I do."

"Well, you're wrong."

"Did you kill Kai Butler?"

"Who?"

"Don't play dumb."

"Oh, I remember that name. No, I'm sorry, he jumped off a bridge. You can't just blame every random suicide on me."

"Are you telling the truth?"

"We're old friends now. Why would I lie to you?"

"Why engage with me? Why not Earl Razzle or any of the other PI's?"

"Because of Conrad Drury. I studied up on him."

My Conrad vibes had been spot on.

"Then you know what happened to him."

"But see, you were playing offense versus him. And now you're playing defense versus me."

"Is that the case?"

"It sure is, Robert. How else do you think I know you and your father went to lunch? Or how I knew to call you the very moment you went to the front desk."

Holy shit. He's been watching me this whole time. My eyes started darting around the mostly empty lobby.

"Are you still here?" I asked.

"No, that wouldn't be very smart. I'm long gone. Plus, I was in disguise, and you have no idea what I look like. So it doesn't matter."

The more he talked, the more I got the impression he had been part of the younger generation in 1998. He didn't give off the vibes of being in his sixties or seventies. This guy was young. I was sure of it.

"How many people have you killed?"

"More than one. Less than Conrad Drury."

"You seem very confident for a guy disguising his voice."

I looked around and made sure no one was heading toward me.

"It's because I'm disguising my voice that I feel so confident. I won't make the same mistakes that your friend Conrad made."

"He wasn't my fucking friend. That animal killed my mother."

"If you're so protective of your parents, why are you downstairs in the lobby and not looking after your father?"

Rage built up inside of me. Then fear.

My mind immediately thought of two things. One, the guy was still here somewhere, looking at me. Two, and much more importantly, my father was alone in my hotel room.

I set off for the elevators. I almost ran into a couple as they exited the first elevator that opened. It arrived on my floor, and I sprinted the remaining twenty yards to my hotel room.

I took out my key, and right before I opened it, I told myself to calm down a little bit. I didn't need my father to see me this frantic.

I slowly opened the door and, to my instant relief, saw that my father was asleep in bed. I heard him breathing in and out, so I shut the door and walked back into the hallway.

I was in such a fervor, worried about my father, that it took me a second to realize I'd kept my phone on. I put it up to my ear.

"Are you still there?" I asked.

I slowly walked down the hall, away from my room.

"Yes. Glad to hear your father is okay."

Once again, I wanted to erupt in a flurry of curse words, but it was more important to keep my cool.

"What do you want?" I asked.

"You're giving it to me."

"Giving you what?"

"This. This give and take. I can't believe I hadn't thought of it earlier. It makes you feel alive, you know."

"You have a sick sense of humor."

"I have a sick sense of everything."

I could tell he wouldn't give me anything useful, so I figured, why not swing for the fences?

"Where is Annie's body? You could at least give it back to her family."

"Nice try. Like I said, I'll keep you in the game, but I won't throw it for you."

I needed to get a rise out of him. Maybe then he'd make a mistake. The problem was figuring out how to get that rise.

"Annie must have spurned your advances at the party. And that must have gotten you seriously upset."

A man started walking down our hallway, and just in case, I inched closer to my room, but the man entered an earlier room and shut the door behind him.

"I'd heard such good things about your investigative skills, but when you throw out stupid theories like that, it makes me wonder."

"So she went willingly?"

There was a laugh on the other end. Even the laugh remained muffled.

"It's about time I let you go, Robert. It's been fun."

What to do? He was about to hang up.

"Give me one tiny clue. It can be something you think will never lead me back to you. Just give me something. You said you'd keep me in the game. Be a man of your word."

There was a few-second break.

"Maybe when I get to know you better."

And then the line went dead.

~

I HEADED BACK DOWN to the lobby, deciding to let my father continue his nap and hoping I might see someone draw attention to themselves downstairs.

When I arrived at the lobby, I noticed nothing out of the blue. The only people milling around were a couple in their early thirties.

With one eye still on the elevators, I approached the front desk. I had to be gentle in my handling of this.

"Hello, Mr. McGowan."

It was the same woman as before. She eyed me a bit suspiciously, and I had a feeling what she was thinking: Why does this guy receive postcards and messages to answer his phone?

"Hey, so I took that call," I said. "And it was an old friend."

"Oh, that's nice. Old friends are important."

If I had to guess, I'd say she was being sarcastic.

"But he's playing a trick on me, and it's driving me nuts. He said he's lost eighty pounds and is unrecognizable."

"I'm not sure I follow."

I shot a quick glance toward the elevators. An elderly couple headed toward them.

"He told me I was in his line of sight when I was at the front desk."

"I'm still not sure I follow."

"I was wondering if I could look at your videotapes to see if I recognize him. He had to have been somewhere within eyesight of the front desk."

"Is this a joke?" she asked.

"No."

"I'm sorry, Mr. McGowan. The only people allowed to look at our tapes are upper management or the police. Of which, you are neither."

That last line was a stinger.

"Okay," I said sheepishly.

"And what kind of friend just calls and doesn't show his face if he's nearby?"

"I've got weird friends, I guess."

She gave me a courtesy smile.

"Well, thanks for your time," I said.

If I had been checking out and didn't have to see her again, my tongue might have gotten the best of me, but I still had to deal with her after today.

I didn't say a thing and just walked away.

∼

I HEADED up towards my floor.

I paced back and forth for another fifteen minutes or so. It had probably only been forty minutes since my father first went to bed, but I couldn't take it anymore.

I walked in, and he rustled out of bed.

"How long have I been down?"

"Close to an hour."

"Sure doesn't seem like it."

I felt shitty about lying to him, but it was better than the truth.

"Are you alright, Bobby? You look a little haggard."

"I'm fine," I said, although I was far from that.

"So, what's next on the docket?" he asked.

∼

WE WENT OUT to dinner that night, and I'm sure I was a lousy dinner guest.

The next morning, we had some breakfast by the pool.

I was just waiting for my father to leave Los Angeles the whole time.

I couldn't tell him that, though, so I had to put on a happy face.

FINALLY, at about eleven a.m., he packed up his stuff, and I walked him down to the valet.

When we arrived downstairs, he turned to me.

"Alright, what's really going on, Bobby?"

"What do you mean?"

"You haven't been yourself since after our lunch yesterday."

"Just busy is all."

"Just busy? You were at dinner and breakfast with me. Pick a different excuse."

"I have a lot on my mind. That kind of busy."

"Fine, don't tell me."

I hated to continue lying to him, but the fact was that the truth was worse.

"Did you have a good time?" I asked, changing the subject.

"Yes. Up until I took that nap."

I saw the valet pull up with his car. Mercifully, I didn't have to answer his nap comment.

My father hugged me and started walking toward his car before quickly turning around.

"Oh, I forgot one thing," he said.

"What is it?"

"I hope you don't mind, but I started thumbing through that journal this morning when you were gone."

"No, that's fine. Did you find something?"

"Not exactly."

"What is it then?"

My father was leading up to something, but I had no idea what.

"I was watching an episode of *Dateline* recently. It took place in Los Angeles. The crux of the case was whether a husband killed his wife or not."

I couldn't help myself.

"Aren't they all?" I asked.

My father laughed.

"Yeah, pretty much. Anyway, the husband had written a note that basically admitted guilt. The problem was that some water had spilled on the letter, and some words had smeared. So the LAPD brought in this expert who, I don't know, recreated the old letter or something like that."

My father took a deep breath, building up to his big moment.

"I saw a few examples where words were scribbled over in the journal. I was thinking that maybe you could take that journal to this expert and see if she could make something of it. She had a Russian-sounding name if I remember correctly."

"That's an excellent idea, Dad."

"You think so?"

My guess was that Annie had scribbled over the words hard enough to make them forever unintelligible, but it was still an excellent idea by my father. For the first time that morning, I wasn't lying to him.

"I do. I'll reach out to her later today."

"Okay, great. I can't remember her name precisely, but the guy who killed his wife lived in Los Angeles somewhere, and he was a plastic surgeon. I'm sure you can find the episode online and find out who the expert was."

"I'll find it. Thanks so much, Dad."

With that, we hugged a final time, and he got in his car and drove off.

CHAPTER 25

Within twenty minutes of my father leaving, I was sitting at a Hollywood Starbucks in a corner booth, thumbing through Annie's diary/journal.

I had to get the hell out of my hotel. It was starting to drive me bonkers.

As I scanned the journal, I started leaving Post-it notes on each page where words were scratched out or scribbled over.

I could only find four examples. One was from May 1998, one from August, and the other two from December.

I was most interested in the two from December: the 16th and the 22nd.

I looked at them several times, and it was still impossible to see what had been written below the chicken scratch. You could make out parts of letters, and if I strained my eyes enough, I thought I could see the letter T at one point, but I certainly couldn't decipher a whole word, much less a whole sentence.

Maybe this expert could accomplish the impossible.

I was about to try to find her number when I felt I was missing something.

I looked them over one last time, and that's when it hit me.

Annie's entire diary was written in purple, and the May and August entries were scribbled over in the same purple. But the two entries from December had been scribbled out in blue ink.

Was this a holy shit moment?

I wasn't sure, but it felt like it could be something big.

Why would Annie cross something out in a blue pen when she'd used a purple one for the entirety of her journal?

I didn't have a good explanation, but I was even more excited to learn more about this handwriting expert.

∼

WITHIN A MINUTE OF BEING ONLINE, I found the episode of *Dateline* my father had been referring to.

And once I found that, I quickly found the expert's name: Kira Palova.

I called her office, and she agreed to meet up with me that afternoon.

∼

I WANTED to learn more about Ms. Palova before meeting with her.

Her bio listed her as a handwriting expert, but the *Dateline* case showed that she was more than that.

I found the episode online, read the description, and fast-forwarded until I first saw her onscreen.

It was a murder trial, and Ms. Palova had been hired by the prosecution attorney. The defendant had signed a letter that the prosecution alleges was an admission of guilt. The problem for the prosecution was that the paper had been exposed to some liquid while in the evidence room, and most of the words had become smudged.

The episode didn't mention how the police made such a colossal mistake.

Ms. Palova was hired to reconstruct the letter. The episode didn't go into her methods or how exactly she recreated the original letter, but they showed her on the witness stand, and the defendant was convicted, so I'm assuming she'd done her job well.

∼

AN HOUR LATER, I was sitting outside Kira C. Palova's office, knocking on her door. She was located in North Hollywood, about a twenty-minute drive from the Starbucks I'd found myself at.

"Are you Mr. McGerrity?"

"Mr. McGowan," I said.

"Please, come in. Call me Kira."

Kira Palova was wearing a long, lightweight, free-flowing yellow dress. She had a thick - and I mean thick! - Russian accent that threw me for a loop. Hearing it on the *Dateline* episode hadn't prepared me for deciphering it in person.

Her "office" was just an open studio with a desk in one corner, a couch in the other, and yellow walls filled with writing, mostly of languages I didn't recognize.

"You found me online?" she asked.

"Sort of," I said. "My father had seen the *Dateline* episode you were featured in, and from there, I found you online."

"I see."

"I'm fascinated by your work."

"Well, thank you. Why don't we sit down?"

We sat on the yellow couch - I was sensing a trend - and she noticed the diary I held under my arm.

"What is that?"

"It's what brought me here," I said.

"What is it?"

Her "what" sounded like "Vut."

Her accent sounded like a *Saturday Night Live* cast member exaggerating a Russian character.

I opened Annie's diary and leafed through it until I found the four passages I sought. Kira crept closer to me.

"Do you see where she has scratched out some of her writing?"

"Yes, I do."

I flipped a few pages later and showed her the second one.

"And here."

"Yes."

And finally, the third and fourth ones from December of 1998.

"So, you probably already know my question, but I'm wondering if you can work your magic and find out what was originally written below the scribble?"

Kira smiled slightly.

"If only it were magic," she said. "This is tough, almost impossible work. Not many people can do what I do."

"So, you think you can do it?'

"I can try. No guarantee. May I see the diary?"

I handed it over.

I was surprised, but she didn't initially look at any of the scribbles. Instead, she flipped the page over and started looking at the back of that page. I had an idea of what she was doing.

"You see, Mr. McGavin," she said, butchering my name again. "The page you showed me was last touched by the pen that scratched out the writing. When I flip it over, I can see where the initial writing touched the bottom of the page."

She may not have been good with last names, but she was darn good at her job. I was starting to get my hopes up.

"The problem is, this journal is old, and the initial words and the scribbling have molded together over the years."

Damn.

"So, is it possible or not?" I asked.

"I don't know yet. This is not an easy project. I will have to use telescopes, magnifying glasses, and some of my special ink dyes to try and separate the writing from the scratching. I will use the tiniest scalpel to try and scrape off the newer ink that scratched out the old words."

I had to admit I was fascinated by Kira's process. And to be honest, a bit intrigued by her. She was quite the character.

"I'll pay you whatever your rate is," I said, assuming William would foot the bill.

"This is a two or three-day job," she said. "I'd probably charge about $1,500, and there are no guarantees I'll get what you want. I may find nothing. I may find a few letters. If we are fortunate, maybe I'll make out a few words. And if God himself touches us, maybe I'll come back with a full sentence. But I am your best option. No one does the work that I do."

"$1,500 is not a problem," I said, continuing to be enthralled by the woman in front of me.

"There is one problem, however. I have a few projects in front of yours."

I didn't want to wait any longer than necessary. I needed Kira to start immediately.

"How much would it cost to start on this right away?"

She pondered the question.

"Are you a cop?" she asked.

It was time for one of my famous little white lies.

"No, but I'm a private investigator working on a big case."

"Would I maybe end up in court?"

You could tell this excited her a great deal.

"Yes, I think that's possible," I said, lying again, hoping this would put her over the edge.

Between my father and Kira Palova, I'd lied too many times for my liking.

"Well, since this sounds like a huge case, I might be able to bump you up and start tomorrow morning. Would that work?"

"That would be great. And how much more would that cost?"

"Let's say an extra $500 to start tomorrow, so $2,000 total. That may seem like a lot, Mr. McGilly, but I promise you this is not easy work, and very few people can do what I can."

"If you accomplish what I hope, you'll be worth every penny," I said.

Kira Palova smiled at me.

"How do you take payment?" I asked.

"Credit Card or check. Sometimes cash, but I don't want to walk around Los Angeles with two thousand in cash."

I debated whether to return the next day with a check from William Ryan or just throw it on my credit card now. Anything to expedite this project, I thought to myself, so I handed her my credit card. I was confident that William would reimburse me.

Ms. Palova had one of those small credit card machines and ran my card through.

"It went through," she said.

"Phew," I said, running the back of my hand over my forehead.

Kira Palova thought it was hilarious.

"You Americans are always so funny."

"Thanks," I said, likely blushing.

"So, what is your number? I will call you when I finish."

I gave it to her.

I thought about asking her to call me after her first discovery but realized how silly that conversation might be.

"*Mr. McGoo, this is Kira. We have found a letter R!*"

No, I could wait until she was finished.

"Thank you so much for this, Kira."

"You're welcome," she said, although it came out as *Yor Velcome*.

That's when I remembered something.

"One more thing," I said.

"Yes."

"Please start on the two entries from December and get back to me when those two are finished. I'm less interested in the other two."

"Okay. If it's just those two, I think I may finish this in a day or two."

"Excellent. Looking forward to hearing back from you."

I showed myself out, and as I walked to my car, I called William with the good news: he owed me $2,000.

CHAPTER 26

Kira Palova called me back at 3:00 p.m. the following afternoon. She asked me to swing by.

I sped down to her office like a child coming out of his room on Christmas morning.

She was waiting outside as I approached and led me into her studio, and we both sat on the couch.

"You didn't say much on the phone," I said. "Were you able to accomplish a lot?"

"I will let you decide."

She stood up from the couch and walked over to her desk, returning with Annie's diary and a single piece of paper.

"First, the bad news," Kira said.

Damn.

"I couldn't do anything from the first journal entry—the one from December 16th. Whoever scratched over it did it with great aggression and didn't leave any possibility of me finding what had been written below it. I made out what I thought was the letter N and, later, a W, but I can't even be sure of that. And judging by how big the scratching area was, this was likely two to three sentences, so two letters aren't going to help you."

"I'm ready for the good news," I said.

"I was a little more successful with the second journal entry. The one made on December 22nd."

My heart started racing.

"How successful?" I asked.

She grabbed the piece of paper that she'd set on the couch. It had been sitting there, taunting me. I wanted to know what it had to say.

"So, the scratched-out part on this section is smaller. I think it might only be one or two short sentences. And I was able to pick up several letters."

Kira set the paper in between us.

"Here's what I was able to decipher."

I glanced at it but wasn't sure what I was looking at. There were a few upper-case letters and then several lower-case Xs. It almost looked like hieroglyphics.

"You're going to have to explain this to me," I said.

"So, I believe this second entry has around twelve or thirteen words. One or two sentences, most likely."

I looked down again.

Thx Othxr Anxxie has a xrazx Chrxxtmxx Evx idex. Shoxxd I xx scaxxx?

"The x's are letters that I couldn't make out. And trust me, I used everything in my, what do you Americans call it, my bag of tricks?"

"That's right."

"I did everything I could, including using my microscope that sees everything."

"So, we're going to assume the first word is The?" I asked.

"Yes. And Other is likely the second word. I realize this journal is from a woman named Annie, and I think that's probably the third word. "Has a" are the fourth and fifth words. I'm guessing the next two words are crazy and Christmas, followed by Eve and idea. There are then four words left. Should is first, I think. I is the second. As you can see below, the last two words were hard to distinguish. It could be something like "go scalp," "be scared," or "do scans." There is a big enough break that I think these are two separate words, but there is the possibility that this is one seven-letter word."

Kira paused, giving me time to take it all in.

I looked once again at what she'd deciphered:

Thx Othxr Anxxie has a xrazx Chrxxtmxx Evx idex. Shoxxd I xx scaxxx?

Of her three possibilities for the last two words, "be scared" made the most sense. If I substituted that and took Kira's word for the rest, it read: The Other Annie has a crazy Christmas Eve Idea. Should I be scared?

That was assuming xrazx was crazy, Evx was Eve, and idex was idea. They all seemed like safe bets.

The Other Annie has a crazy Christmas Eve idea. Should I be scared?

The total weight of this hit me at once.

"Yes, Annie, you should be scared," I said.

I thought it was to myself, but when Kira raised her eyes to mine, I realized I'd said it aloud.

"It's nothing," I said to her.

"So, you are happy with my work?" she asked.

"You earned every dollar."

"Hopefully, you will come back with more business."

"I will," I said.

I was still intrigued by Kira and might return down the line to say hello, but Annie Ryan's case now had my full attention.

I thanked Kira and said goodbye.

MY FIRST TWO calls were to Amber and Adam Toon.

I still preferred to use William Ryan only if it directly involved him.

Neither Amber nor Adam knew what it meant.

"Sure, Annie might have acted differently in front of her parents than with our generation, but every teenager did that. She certainly didn't have two personalities if that's what you're suggesting," Amber said.

Before I got off the phone, I told Amber I didn't think Annie was referring to herself.

I looked down at Kira's sheet of paper.

The Other Annie has a crazy Christmas Eve idea. Should I be scared?

I hated to admit it, but if you read it with that assumption in mind, it did sound like someone talking to their alter ego.

Could Annie have had some crazy idea and left the party alone? Is it possible this was all just a runaway? And then something tragic happened after the fact. Or, against all odds, she fled the family and is alive somewhere in this world.

None of those made sense. The killer had been in contact with me, or at least, I thought he was the killer.

Could he just be some crackpot who was trying to rile me up? There were numerous examples of people interjecting themselves into high-profile murder cases.

Was it possible Annie had gone missing on her own, and I was talking to some attention-seeking jerk? I guess it couldn't be ruled out.

∾

My call with Adam went in a different direction.

"See, this goes well with my theory."

"Remind me of that theory again."

"Annie decided to run away with an older guy, and they traveled the country."

"Oh yeah, that one."

"Don't be dismissive, Bobby."

"I'm not."

"Okay, you didn't sound that enthusiastic about it."

"Give me a break, Adam. This case is exhausting."

"Just think about it. Annie says the other Annie has a crazy idea. Maybe that's her saying she'd devised this plan to leave the party and flee the area."

Was Adam living up to his nickname, or was he slightly more insightful than everyone else? It was always hard to tell with him.

"It's not impossible, and the note could be interpreted as her talking about herself," I admitted. "I came at it with the viewpoint that she was talking about another Annie. Not herself."

"There's no other Ryan named Annie, and I never heard her or her friends talk about another girl named Annie."

"Amber said the same thing."

"Wow, you called her first?"

I laughed.

"You should take it as a compliment. You're the one who had us meet."

"Call me first next time," he joked.

"You got it," I said.

I swore Adam to secrecy, just as I had with Amber. I told them that what she'd written in her diary could be a monstrous clue, and I didn't want it to get out to everyone.

They both promised not to tell a soul.

∾

I knew who my next call had to be.

"Who is this?"

The now familiar voice scowled.

Gina Galasso couldn't be bothered to sound cordial.

"It's Bobby McGowan again, Gina."

"Jesus. Am I ever going to be done with you?"

"Only if I solve this case."

"Well, you're not doing a great job so far."

"You're always the charmer."

"That's what my PO always used to tell me."

"You never told me you had a parole officer."

"It's not something I share with everyone, genius. I went on a bit of a stealing spree about a decade ago. Don't worry; no one got hurt. I wasn't that type of criminal. They let me out of jail early, but I still had to see a PO for like six months after being released."

"I thought parole officers were for serious offenders, usually released early from prison."

"Technically, you're right. He wasn't exactly a parole officer; he was more like a liaison to the county jail, making sure I was doing alright. But saying PO just sounds so much cooler."

"I can't figure you out, Gina."

"Good, let's keep it that way."

I was reminded of how Kai Butler's father, Doug, had said that Gina had drastically changed over the years. What had happened to the sweet young Gina? And had her personality change had anything to do with what happened to Annie? With what happened to Kai? Was she harboring some dark secret?

I decided to press the issue, and then I'd return to the main reason for my call.

"Doug Butler said you were a very kind and happy teenager. I get a sense that you've changed."

"Hell yeah, I've changed. Wouldn't every person change after a tragedy like that? Didn't you change when your mother died?"

"Yes, I certainly did. All of my teenage years were filled with angst and regret. But I feel like I've slowly drifted back toward the man I was meant to be."

"That's the first human-sounding thing you've said since you met me."

"Thank you," I said, despite it being a backhanded compliment.

"So you understand how a person can change after a dramatic event?"

This was as open as Gina had been with me. By a country mile. Was she ready to let me in on that big, dark secret?

"Is there something you'd like to tell me, Gina?"

There was a pause, which I took as a good sign.

"No."

"Are you sure?"

"Yeah, but if I ever decide to confess all my sins, I'll be sure to contact you and not a priest."

"Coming clean can be good for the soul," I said, realizing how cheesy it sounded as it came out of my mouth.

"What soul?" she said quietly, and I suddenly felt for Gina.

"Would you like to talk? I could come over to your place."

"No, I don't want to talk, Mr. PI. I just want you to end this damn investigation already."

"That's not going to happen," I said.

"Yeah, I figured."

"When you mentioned the tragedy you went through, were you talking about both Kai's suicide and Annie's murder?"

"Oh shit, Sherlock Holmes is in the building. Did you figure that all out by yourself?"

I decided not to call her out on her sarcasm.

"Which affected you more?" I asked.

"Kai's. I was dating him, after all. Annie was just a sometimes friend. But Annie's death certainly didn't help. Like I said, it only made Kai's depression worse. And they were no longer some lovable family. I'd always liked to come over to Kai's parents or the extended Ryan family's get-togethers, but not after Annie went missing. So yes, Annie's death was also a big part of it."

This was a good time to get to the point of my call.

"I've been reading over Annie's diary."

"Wait, she had a diary?"

She sounded nervous.

"You didn't know?"

"I guess I'd just forgotten. What's in it?"

"Nothing incriminating per se, but I found something interesting."

"What is it?"

"Do you remember the first time I came and saw you?"

"How could I forget the best day of my life?"

Sarcasm was a defense mechanism for Gina.

"When I asked you about Annie, you said she acted differently with you guys than she did with her parents. I think you alluded to her being two different people or something to that effect."

"Maybe I did. Is there a question there?"

"There will be. So, in Annie's journal, she referred to someone named, *'The Other Annie.'* She wrote that the other Annie had some crazy Christmas Eve idea and asked if she should be scared. Do you think Annie was referring to an alternate personality of hers?"

There wasn't a response for several seconds.

"Gina?"

"Why do you have to keep bothering me about this case?"

She sounded like she was near tears. I'd touched a nerve, but I had no idea why.

"What does she mean by the other Annie?" I asked.

"You're probably right. They were talking about Annie acting differently."

She was wholly unconvincing.

"Who's they? This was Annie's personal diary. Why don't you tell me what you know?"

I could hear her crying on her end.

"I'm really busy, Bobby. Can we talk later?"

She was barely able to get that out. Something changed when I mentioned the other Annie. Something important. I was convinced of it.

Most people would have pressed Gina at this point, but I had a better idea. I knew it was easier for her—or anybody else—to lie on the phone than in person. So, I would surprise her at her apartment, look into her eyes, and see if she could lie when put on the spot.

"Sure, Gina. We can talk later."

More muffling cries on her end.

"Thank you. I'm just a little bewildered today."

I was tempted to say, *'You sounded okay until I mentioned the other Annie,'* but I feared losing her for good. I was going to do this in person.

"No problem. I'll call you later," I said.

"Goodbye," Gina said and hastily hung up.

CHAPTER 27

I drove to Gina's apartment within minutes of getting off the phone with her.

My adrenaline was pumping. I'd talked to dozens of people, but this was the first time someone sounded truly nervous, like they were hiding something. My gut told me this was my investigation's most crucial moment yet.

Gina's apartment complex was open-air, so I'd be able to get into the building. The question was whether she'd answer the door when she knew it was me.

I decided to pretend to be an Amazon driver.

As I approached her door, I tried to shield my face as much as possible in case she looked out the peephole.

I knocked loudly on the door and tried to disguise my voice as well as I could.

"Amazon here. I have a package for you to sign."

Did Amazon ever actually have you sign for packages? I didn't think so, but I hoped the loud knock and hearing the name Amazon would inspire Gina to open the door.

Which she did.

"Oh, fuck," she said. "I knew it wasn't fucking Amazon."

She wasn't happy to see me. The double f-bomb proved that.

"What the hell do you want?" she asked.

"To talk to you in person. Can I come in? And don't say you're busy."

Gina shook her head.

"What does it matter anyway? Fine, come in."

Gina escorted me in, took a quick seat on the couch, and lit a cigarette within seconds. She was wearing an old-school Lynyrd Skynyrd shirt and some jean shorts and was sporting a haircut that wouldn't be catching on anytime soon. She was a disheveled mess.

"How are you?" I asked.

"Fine and dandy, can't you tell?"

"If you need help with anything, let me know."

"You're just trying to solve your damn case."

"I'm trying to do that also. Which is what brought me here."

"No shit. Go ahead and ask your freaking questions."

I took a breath and silently hoped that the journal entry hadn't just been another red herring. I got straight to the point.

"What did Annie mean when she wrote, *'The Other Annie'*?"

Gina took a more extended breath than me. She looked directly into my eyes.

"What did she say about him?"

"Him?" I asked, stunned.

"The Other Annie isn't some variation of the real Annie. She doesn't have multiple personalities or anything like that."

There went that theory.

"What did you mean when you said him? Is the other Annie a guy? How can it be? Help me understand."

"I probably should have told you about him earlier, but he wasn't at the Christmas Eve party. How could I ever have suspected him? The police never did, but we know why that was the case. That's a whole other thing, I guess."

Gina was rambling, and I had to get her back.

"Who wasn't at the party? Who is the other Annie?"

A tear started to make its way down Gina's cheek.

"I just lied to you," she said.

"About what?"

"I always kind of suspected him. Even though he wasn't at the Christmas party, part of me knew, or at least thought, he was responsible for Annie's death."

She had dodged the question several times.

"Gina, look at me," I said. "Who is the other Annie?"

A second tear started making its way down her other cheek.

"His name is Wade Bannie."

The name sounded familiar, but I wasn't sure why.

"Who is he?"

"He went to high school with me and Kai."

"And he knew Annie Ryan?"

"Yeah, he met her a few months before Annie went missing."

"How did they meet?"

"Kai introduced them. He didn't want to. Kai and I were seeing a movie with Annie, and Wade happened to be at the theater, also. He came over and asked Kai to introduce him to Annie. Wade was a bully, and people usually did what he said. I'm sure Kai didn't want to do it, but he didn't have much choice."

"So he introduced the two?"

"Yes. Right before we were about to walk into the theater. We were seeing *A Night at the Roxbury*, that silly Will Ferrell movie. I remember it like it was yesterday. Look it up on Google. That movie came out sometime around October of 1998. Check Google right now."

Gina was starting to get a little panic-stricken. I had to steer her back.

"I believe you, Gina. What happened after the movie?"

"Wade ditched his friends and hung out with us. Again, Kai didn't like Wade but was too scared to tell him he couldn't join us."

"What happened next?"

"We decided to head to an In n Out and eat. The four of us sat outside and ate our burgers. Annie and Wade were blatantly flirting with each other. And as we sat at that In n Out, Annie came up with her nickname for Wade."

"The other Annie," I said, but more as a leading question so Gina would continue.

"So, we're sitting there, and Annie asks Wade his last name. He says Bannie. Annie says something like, 'That rhymes with my name. How do you spell it?' So Wade says B-A-N-N-I-E, and Annie gets all fired up because there is an Annie in his last name. I remember Wade joking that if they ever got married, Annie would be known as Annie Bannie, and we all got a laugh out of that. Wade was a bully, but he could also be charming, and he was being charming at that In n Out. I could tell that Annie was infatuated. Wade got a lot of girls in high school. He was handsome and cocky and charismatic, so I'm not blaming Annie for falling for his charms. Anyway, for the next half hour, we talked about Annie and Bannie, and somehow, we thought it was the funniest thing ever. Remember, we were teenagers. We found a lot of stupid shit funny. At some point, Kai asked a question to Annie and she said something like, 'Are you talking to me or the other Annie?' And from then on in, we just referred to Wade Bannie as the other Annie for the rest of the night."

You could have given me a million guesses at what the other Annie meant, and I still wouldn't have come up with anything as crazy as this.

Gina wiped a few of her tears away.

"How did the night end?" I asked.

"Kai dropped Wade off first and then Annie after that."

"Did Wade get Annie's phone number?"

"Yes. Her home number. Remember, this was before we had cell phones."

"Do you know if they kept in touch?"

"Yeah, they did. At school the next week, Wade went back to being an asshole and told Kai that he would soon be banging his cousin. Kai felt terrible and tried to warn Annie, but at this point, she was already smitten. Try stopping a teenage girl."

Gina looked up and tried to force a smile, but with the tears and her now-smeared makeup, she looked like the female version of the Joker. I felt terrible for her.

"And you said this was in October of 1998?"

"September or October. I'm almost positive. Check when *A Night at the Roxbury* came out. We saw it opening weekend."

Now that I had the backstory, I wanted to ensure Gina's memory of the event was correct. I Googled it, and sure enough, *A Night at the Roxbury* premiered on October 1st, 1998. I believed every word that Gina had told me. I never would have expected that after my first few impressions of her. That got me thinking.

"When we first met, you said that Annie might have been sleeping with several guys. Was that true?"

"No, that was a lie."

"Why did you lie about that? Did it have something to do with Wade Bannie?"

"Yes. Kai thought that Annie might be a virgin. So I made it sound like Annie had a bunch of boyfriends in case Wade Bannie came up. Then I could say he was just another in a long line of them."

"I'm trying to give you the benefit of the doubt here, Gina. Why would you want to defend Wade Bannie?"

She tried to wipe away a few more tears.

"It's so complicated," she said.

"Try me."

"Wade kept mocking Kai at school. 'I'm going to bang your cousin' became 'I'm fucking your cousin' to 'Thanks for introducing us, Kai.' This went on for the last few months of 1998. Now, Wade was not a dummy. He didn't say this to anybody but Kai. I'm sure he was sleeping with other girls and wouldn't want this to come out. But he liked pressing Kai's buttons. So, this goes on till about mid-December, and then, out of the blue, Wade stops taunting Kai. He doesn't know why. He tried to bring up Wade to Annie, but she didn't want to discuss it. Talking about romantic partners with your cousin of the opposite sex isn't something a teenager wants to do."

She finished the cigarette she was smoking and quickly lit up another one. I didn't say a word.

"Then Annie goes missing at the Christmas party," Gina says. "Kai hates Wade at this point, but the guy wasn't at the party, so how could it be him? It couldn't be, right? About a week after the party, I got the courage to bring it up to Kai. He went ballistic on me. It was by far the maddest I've ever seen him. 'Wade didn't do this!' he yelled. And 'Don't ever bring this up again!' So I didn't. I was of two minds at that point. One, maybe Kai really didn't think Wade had done it. That would make sense. The guy wasn't fucking there, you know? But the other part of me thought that maybe Kai didn't want to deal with the repercussions if it had somehow been Wade. He had introduced the two, after all. I'm sure he thought about how the Ryan family would look at him if they knew Annie's killer had been introduced to Annie by Kai. Kai never admitted that, but I know it crossed his mind. And then, two months later, Kai kills himself. I didn't know what to think. Was he depressed? Yes. Had he contemplated suicide? Yes. But I never thought he'd do it. And then my mind went to the weirdest place. Anybody who knew Kai knew that he walked by that bridge every morning to go to school and every afternoon to walk home. He had a car, but his parents' house was half a mile from our high school, so he always just walked."

Gina had to stop talking. The tears were now flowing incessantly. I walked the few feet between us and put my arms on her shoulders.

"I'm so sorry, Gina. This must have been weighing on you heavily for all these years."

She leaned out and hugged me, then muffled the tears after a minute.

"I still don't know to this day if Wade killed Annie. And I still don't know if Kai killed himself or not."

"Don't take this the wrong way, Gina, but why didn't you go to the police with your suspicions about Annie or Kai's death?"

"Well, I told you why with Annie. We didn't think Wade had anything to do with it, and Kai was afraid of what would happen if we were wrong and Wade had done it. There was no way Kai would let me go to the police. When he died, I considered it, but I didn't because of who Wade's father is."

"Who is Wade's father?"

"You don't know anything, do you?" she said rhetorically.

And when I didn't say anything, she dropped another bomb.

"Wade Bannie's father was like the most famous cop in the area."

And that's when it hit me. Why the name Bannie had rung a bell. I had seen an E. Bannie on a few of the police reports. He wasn't the first or second lead detective, but he was mentioned once or twice. I was certain of it.

"What is his first name?"

"Ed, I think. Or Edward."

"And you were afraid if you went to the police, they wouldn't listen to you?"

"Yeah, or worse. If Kai's death wasn't a suicide, then why wouldn't they come and get me too?"

"So what did you do?"

"I became a hermit. I went to school and went home immediately after. I tried to stay home from school often, but my mother started to get suspicious, so I had to go. I avoided Wade Bannie in the halls. If I saw him coming, I'd turn and walk the other way. When I graduated in June, I moved away. I told my mother I wanted to attend a Junior College near my father in Colorado. That's the last thing I wanted to do. My father was a creep. But I knew I had to get out of Los Angeles."

"When did you move back?"

"Five years ago. My mother got sick, so I came back and looked after her. She died a few years back, and I think I'm just too lazy to move now. If Wade Bannie ever wanted to get me, it's not like it would be any great loss to the world. I mean, look at this apartment."

And that's when Gina Galasso truly lost it. I'm not sure I'd ever heard or seen crying at this level. Her whole body shook up and down. I now understood that Annie's death had affected Gina more than anyone. Her boyfriend dies two months after Annie, she moves six months later, and she's probably never been the same person since.

I now had great empathy for a woman I had previously disliked immensely.

I walked back over and gave her another hug. She was trying to control her tears but to no avail.

Finally, a good three minutes later, she was ready to talk again.

"I think that's pretty much it," she said. "Any questions?"

"In your heart of hearts, do you think Wade Bannie killed Annie?"

"If you'd asked me a week ago, I would have said 50/50."

"But now that you know he's mentioned in Annie's diary in connection with Christmas Eve?"

"Yes, I think he probably did kill Annie."

"And do you think he killed Kai?"

"That I'm not sure of. It's possible Kai's grief was enough to push him over the edge."

It was a terrible analogy, considering Kai died by going over a bridge, but it's not like I was going to say anything.

"And Wade never threatened you or tried to contact you?"

"No."

"Where is Wade now?"

"I don't know. I've heard he's kind of famous on social media. Instagram, I think. I don't do all that stuff."

I could search for him later.

"Do you know where Wade went after you graduated high school?"

"He moved to the Caribbean, I think."

"Convenient," I said.

"Exactly. He's a very smart guy. I'm sure he could have gotten into plenty of colleges. I'd already decided to move to Colorado but I was glad to hear he was no longer in the country. At that point, I just tried to wash my hands of Annie and Kai's deaths. I tried not to be consumed by them. I eventually stopped talking to Kai's parents. His mother called me for a while and wanted some old stories, but that ended after a few years. It was probably my fault. I was turning into a conceited bitch, which I kind of still am. And from there, I just went on living life. I talked to a few PIs that William Ryan hired over the years, including Earl Razzle. I always felt - maybe mistakenly - that it would be more suspicious if I said I didn't want to talk. But it's probably been five years since I'd talked to anyone about the case before you called me out of the blue."

I needed to lighten the mood. For myself, but more importantly, for Gina.

"Are you okay, Gina? You haven't dropped an f-bomb in like ten minutes?"

She smiled at me.

"I'm sorry for having been such a bitch."

"You're not one, and there's no need to apologize. You've been carrying an incredible burden."

She nodded.

"Thanks. But yes, I have been a bitch. For twenty-five fucking years."

She erupted in laughter. She was so happy to sneak an f-bomb in for me. And then, the laughter turned to tears.

Twenty-five years of guilt were coming out during this one conversation.

"Does anyone else know the nickname that Annie gave Wade?"

"I don't think so. I think it was just me, Kai, Annie, and Wade. Like I said, Wade had a few girlfriends already. I'm sure he didn't want them to know about Annie Ryan."

"Thank you for everything, Gina."

She nodded at me.

I stayed and comforted her for several more minutes before I decided it was time to go.

"One last thing, Gina."

"What?"

"Let's not mention our conversation to anyone."

"Who do I have to tell?" she asked.

It was a sad, fitting last line for our conversation to end on.

CHAPTER 28

I woke up the next morning and asked myself, now what?

It's not like I could go to Mike Minter. Could I call an anonymous tip or contact Internal Affairs?

Not yet.

I didn't have enough.

I knew that Wade Bannie was likely sleeping with Annie Ryan before she went missing. That's all I had. He wasn't at William's Christmas Eve party - at least, no one saw him there - and that trumped everything. I had no case if I couldn't find a way to place him there.

How could I go about placing him there twenty-five years after the fact?

I could go back and talk to his high school friends and ask if he slipped up and mentioned going to the party.

I wasn't even ready to do that.

That would inevitably bring my attention to Wade and his father. I had to be a lot more subtle. If Gina was right, the Bannies were not a family to be taken lightly.

That also meant not mentioning Wade Bannie's name to Amber, Adam, William, or anyone else from the Ryan family—at least, not until I knew more.

I had to be smart going forward.

My first order of business was to learn everything I could about Wade Bannie.

All of my investigations would be conducted online—for the time being—because I was putting a lot of importance into keeping a low profile.

I found Wade Bannie's Instagram page within seconds. Gina Galasso said he was kind of famous on there. He had 9,000 followers, which certainly didn't make you an influencer by today's standards, but it was a healthy following.

His profile picture was him posing with a marlin he'd caught. Bannie had the surfer dude look, and his dirty blonde hair had streaks of bleach running through it. He was handsome and very tan, and even from the profile picture, you could tell he was confident in his skin. He just had that air about him.

Bannie was seventeen when Annie went missing, which would make him forty-two or forty-three now. If the marlin picture had been taken any time in the last few years, Bannie had aged well.

It's impossible to pigeonhole all killers, but Conrad Drury was the more likely killer than Wade Bannie. Drury was short, unattractive, and had a permanent scowl. Women didn't like him, and he didn't have many friends.

Wade Bannie appeared to be the opposite. He had beautiful women in his arms in many of his photos. He also had several photos of him out on the town with his guy friends. They were generally good-looking white guys wearing Vineyard Vines or Tommy Bahama-type shirts. They likely had been in the best fraternity on campus. You know the type.

Which got me even more fired up.

While I hated Conrad Drury with every fiber of my being, at least his existence was lonely: working for Amtrak, getting rejected by women, and living alone.

Wade Bannie was the opposite. This guy was living every man's dream. Out on boats. Fishing for Marlin. Being a ski bum during winter. Surrounded by beautiful girls. Friends with successful men. Traveling the world.

If he'd killed Annie Ryan, he hadn't suffered any repercussions in this life.

I noticed that none of his pictures mentioned a wife or a family.

Considering every other picture was of him with a pretty girl, I doubted he was married or had a long-term girlfriend. He'd have had a lot of explaining to do.

I tried to find out what he did for work, but to no avail. Wade Bannie was not on LinkedIn. I Googled his name along with the following keywords: job, profession, vice president, and owner.

I found nothing.

What did he do? Where did he live? Did he have a home base or just travel the world?

Despite showing his life in pictures on Instagram, he did seem mysterious. There was never a picture of his newly bought house, his local coffee shop, or him rooting on his favorite team.

He was either taking a helicopter ride, on a boat, hitting the slopes, river-rafting down a river, or something similar.

I hated myself for thinking it, but *The Most Interesting Man In The World* from the Dos Equis commercials came to mind.

∼

MAYBE I COULD USE his distinctive look to my advantage.

I could print a few pictures of him and go around the Beverly Hilton to see if anyone saw him.

No, Bobby!

You have to lay low. The one significant advantage you have right now is that Wade Bannie has no idea you know who he is. You may have talked to him, but knowing his identity is entirely different.

I'd resorted to talking to myself.

∼

I SCANNED THE PICTURES AGAIN, hoping something would stand out.

He had a video captioned, "If you know, you know."

It was a famous scene from the movie *Stripes* where the guy says, *"The name's Francis Soyer, but everybody calls me Psycho. Any of you guys call me Francis, and I'll kill you."*

I looked through some of the comments.

'I know better than to call you that.'

'You're secret is safe with me...Francis.'

Was Wade's real first name Francis?

I Googled Francis Bannie, and sure enough, I found a match.

It was a lone match, but it was enough. It was for the website ancestry.com, and there was a Francis Wade Bannie, born in Los Angeles on February 23rd, 1981.

The middle name was Wade, and the birth year was correct; it had to be him.

The proverbial lightbulb lit up above my head.

He liked to call me Robert. Well, two can play at that game.

Be seeing you around, Francis.

CHAPTER 29

Next on my to-do list was looking into Wade's father, Ed Bannie.

Using the internet to investigate people continued to be monotonous work; I Googled multiple different permutations of his name: *'Ed Bannie police officer,' 'Ed Bannie police corrupt,' 'Ed Bannie Mike Minter,' 'Ed Bannie dirty cop,'* and *'Ed Bannie cover-up.'*

I tried those and twenty others.

There was a surprising amount of information on Ed Bannie. Some viewed him as a celebrity cop. In fact, any major drug bust or murder that occurred in the Hollywood Hills between about 1988 and 2015 seemed to have Bannie as the lead detective, with the lone exception being the Annie Ryan disappearance. I hoped to find out why.

An article on his retirement helped me understand the basics about the man.

Ed Bannie was now sixty-five years old, which would have made him forty when Annie was killed. He retired in 2019 at the age of sixty, after having served thirty-five years for the LAPD. He retired older than most cops, and the article insinuated that he had been a desk jockey for the last decade or so of his career. The retirement article was a puff piece, building up Ed Bannie as LA's most decorated police officer.

Other articles weren't as generous.

Several referred to him as *'rough and tumble,' 'combative,'* or *'A man's man.'* I took them to mean he was challenging to work with.

One particular article grabbed my attention.

There was a drug bust that happened back in 1991. A very famous Hollywood actor's house had been raided, and over 100k of cocaine had been found. Now, I don't know much about cocaine consumption, but I can tell you that 100k is way too much for personal consumption. This guy was dealing.

Near the end of the article, in a short paragraph that I easily could have overlooked, I found a passage that caught my eye.

'Bannie, often considered a hothead, was seen in a shoving match with his fellow officer, Greg Quinones, right as the paparazzi arrived at the celebrity's mansion.'

From there, I went on another deep dive, trying to discover who Greg Quinones was. A few crime articles mentioned him over the years, but nothing like Ed Bannie. Quinones certainly wasn't a celebrity cop.

I tried looking for Greg Quinones's address on the internet. There were nine people with that name in the Los Angeles area, and honestly, the last LA Times article I'd seen mentioning Quinones was from 2002. That was over twenty years ago, and he easily could have moved from Los Angeles. There had to be a better way.

What to do?

I looked back at the article. The proverbial lightbulb went off in my head.

The article was written by a *Los Angeles Times* reporter named Cassius Fields. I clicked on his name, which sent me to the *Los Angeles Times'* homepage.

Cassius Fields was a black guy with a steely look in his eyes. He didn't look like a reporter who would easily give you a break. *Dogged* was the word that sprang to mind.

"Cassius Fields was a respected member of the Los Angeles Times from 1985 until his retirement in 2020. He wrote about many subjects but specialized in the crime beat, which he loved more than anyone."

I Googled Cassius Fields and found a Twitter account. I looked at the photos from his time with the Los Angeles Times, and it was him. He'd made a few more years around the sun and had more gray hairs, but he was the same guy.

I typed a message.

"Hello, Mr. Fields. My name is Bobby McGowan, and I have a few questions about some of your old Los Angeles Times articles. I'd greatly appreciate it if you could message me here or call me at 805-555-9527."

And then I pressed send.

I sat there, staring at the screen, hoping to get an immediate response. I was dying to see those three little dots moving back and forth, signifying he was typing; just as I'd been excited seeing itstartedwithanAR type on the 52solutions website.

I glanced back at my message to Cassius Fields, but there was no response.

~

I DECIDED I needed to grab a bite to eat.

I could have ordered room service, but I wanted to get out of the room for a few minutes. I walked downstairs to the general store to pick up a banana, power bar, or something to keep my glucose levels up.

I passed the front desk, and the woman I'd asked to see the tapes was there. She smiled at me if you could call it that. I would be on her radar for the remainder of my stay, that's for sure.

I ended up grabbing a banana and a granola bar that I knew I'd hate.

I quickly walked outside and got some fresh air before returning to my room. I only used Twitter occasionally, and it wasn't even downloaded on my phone, so if Cassius Fields messaged me, I'd only see it from my laptop.

When I returned to the room, I looked at my laptop, and sure enough, he'd sent me a message.

'Hello, Mr. McGowan. Thanks for reaching out. I'll give you a call around 2:30.'

I looked down at my phone. It was 2:16. I'd been investigating Wade and Ed Bannie on the internet for nearly five hours.

~

MY PHONE RANG PROMPTLY at 2:30.

"Hello."

"Is this Bobby McGowan?"

"Yes."

"This is Cassius Fields."

"Thanks for calling back."

"You got it. How can I help you, Bobby?"

Right to the first name. I liked it. It furthered my opinion that he was a straight shooter.

I had to be delicate with how I approached the subject of Ed Bannie. I obviously couldn't come out and say I suspected his son of murder and potentially of him helping cover it up.

"I was curious about some of your old articles for the *LA Times*."

"Which ones exactly?"

"You wrote about crime, and I've been reading about some of the crimes in the Hollywood Hills. I'm especially interested in the police force back then, even as far back as the 90s."

"I'd be remiss if I didn't ask you why you are so interested in crimes from decades ago."

I couldn't just bullshit Cassius Fields. He was too bright for that. So, while I couldn't give too much away, I couldn't give him nothing.

"I'm looking into an old case."

"That's pretty vague, Bobby. If you want to get any information from me, you'll have to do much better than that."

I implicitly trusted this man I'd never met before. I couldn't explain it; I just did.

"Can I trust that this conversation stays between us?" I asked.

"Of course."

Before I could continue, he interrupted.

"And do you know why I'm willing to talk to you?"

"No," I answered.

"Because I followed your mother's case. This is the same Bobby McGowan, isn't it?"

"Yes."

"I'd seen you on a few interviews after the case reached its conclusion, and I thought I recognized your voice."

He was being diplomatic by saying the case had reached its conclusion. In reality, it was Conrad Drury who had reached his conclusion.

"Well, thank you for talking to me."

"You're welcome. Now, what do you want to talk about? Don't sugarcoat it."

"I'm looking into some of Ed Bannie's old cases."

"Ah, Ed Bannie."

"You don't seem all that surprised," I said.

"Nothing about Belligerent Ed Bannie surprises me."

"Was that his nickname?"

"Yes, but it was only mentioned behind his back. You'd get your ass kicked if you said it to his face."

"He was referred to as a man's man in a few of your articles."

"That's a way of saying he was an asshole, but you couldn't just come out and say that in an article."

I laughed.

"So you guys didn't exactly see eye to eye?"

"He hated me, but Ed hated anyone involved with the media. His view was that he'd caught the bad guy and done all the legwork, etc., and here comes the *Los Angeles Times* to report on it and try to sell a few papers. Sure, he hated me, but I was no different than a myriad of other people he also despised. He especially had it in for the paparazzi."

"Well, I can't really blame him for that."

"Indeed. But Belligerent Ed would be a bully. Smash their video cameras. Literally, kick them out of crime scenes. Often by using his boot."

"I'm surprised they let him get away with that."

"I'm talking in the early 90s to the early 2000s. Once the internet hit, Bannie started to mellow out a little bit. By then, he was in his mid-forties anyway, and in cop years, that's like sixty."

"So he did chill out later in his career?"

"A little, I guess. You still wouldn't want to cross him."

I decided there was no better time than now.

"Did you work the Annie Ryan case?" I asked.

"Ah, the Annie Ryan case. That was a tough one for all of us. Yes, I covered it."

"What do you remember most about it?"

"How confusing it was, I guess. How could a teenage girl go missing from a family Christmas event? And I mean to go missing without a trace. No one saw her leave. No one saw her get abducted. No one saw any suspicious family member talking to her. I'm not sure if the LAPD ever had a serious suspect."

Because they were protecting the son of one of their own!

"Do you remember if Ed Bannie had a big part in that investigation?" I asked.

"I'll keep answering your questions, Bobby, but I will have a few for you at the end. Understood?"

"That's only fair," I said.

"Okay. It's a deal. If I remember correctly, Ed Bannie was out of town on the day Annie disappeared."

Hmmm. I knew a lot about Annie's case but missed this fact. Then again, Bannie was barely mentioned in the police reports. How would I have known?

"Do you know where he was?" I asked.

"I think he and his wife were on vacation. And I only remember this because Phillip Chide was appointed lead detective. This must have pissed off Bannie because those two were the head honchos, and Bannie hated to surrender an inch to Phillip. Bannie was almost always the lead on any big case, but he was out of town when Annie Ryan disappeared, so Phillip took over. And once you are appointed lead detective, you don't lose it just because someone returns from vacation."

I noticed he referred to Phillip Chide by his first name and Ed Bannie by his last name. That spoke volumes.

"Thank you. I know Chide died of a heart attack six months later. Why did Mike Minter continue as lead instead of Bannie?"

"Because of the politics I already explained. Minter came on as the second lead because Bannie was out of town. And once you're on the case, either as lead or second in charge, you remain there."

"Gotcha. Do you remember how soon Ed Bannie returned to LA after Annie's disappearance?"

"I have no idea about that. Probably within a day or two because I remember seeing him around William Ryan's house, despite the fact he wasn't the lead detective."

"You sure remember a lot about this case," I said.

"It's not one you easily forget," Cassius Fields said.

"No, I guess not."

"Any more questions before I get to ask a few of my own?"

"Do you remember Greg Quinones? He's a former LAPD detective who got into it with Ed Bannie."

"Jeez, you really have it in for Bannie."

"Just trying to get more information."

"That sounds like a generic answer I would have given," Cassius said.

I laughed.

"Maybe I'm a reporter at heart."

"Good luck with that. And yeah, I know Quinones. Last I heard, he was in Los Angeles. That was ten years ago, though."

"Do you have an old phone number for him?"

"Okay, Bobby, you seem like a nice kid, but you're going to have to give me a lot more than you've given me if you want people's phone numbers. No, I'm not a reporter anymore, but I still abide by a code, and you're not getting Quinones's number unless you give me a damn good reason."

How do I do that without mentioning Wade Bannie and my investigation?

"William Ryan has hired me to look into the disappearance of Annie Ryan," I said.

"Okay, that's a start. How long have you been on the case?"

"A month."

"And this has led you to ask me several questions about Ed Bannie. He wasn't one of the lead detectives. He wasn't even in LA on the day Annie went missing. What's with all the interest in him?"

I had no idea how to get out of this. What could I say?

"A couple of people have mentioned that he was acting suspicious."

"Do better. That's weak," Cassius said. He wasn't wrong. "Listen, Bobby, you obviously have something more than just *'Oh, I heard someone say something.'* I'm hanging up this phone if you don't give me more right now. I said this conversation is between us and will stay that way, but you won't be getting anything more out of me."

I didn't know what to do. Could I trust Cassius to keep quiet? I thought so. Was it worth dropping Wade Bannie's name? Getting Greg Quinones's number, a cop who worked with Bannie, would be huge. I decided it was worth it.

"I heard a rumor that Bannie's son hung out with Annie occasionally."

There was silence on the other end.

Finally, he answered.

"Holy cow. I don't know what I expected, but it certainly wasn't that."

"Remember, this stays between us."

"I remember, Bobby. You don't have to remind me. So, you're considering whether Bannie's son could be involved?"

"I'm just asking questions."

"Stop. We both know it's further along than that."

"I have nothing even approaching evidence. Just some conjecture."

"Then you should be careful who you talk to."

"Exactly."

"I didn't mean me. I meant Ed Bannie. He knows a lot of important people in this town, and I don't just mean cops. So watch yourself. Don't ask the right question to the wrong person."

"Can I trust Greg Quinones?"

"For the most part, yes. He hated Ed Bannie as much as anyone. He told me privately that Bannie was the reason he was given an early retirement."

"Then why did you say, *For the most part?*"

"I haven't seen him in years, but he had an alcohol problem. And when he got drunk, he got combative. I'd tread lightly talking about Bannie's son. If Quinones got information like that, who knows what he'd do with it."

"Point taken. Thank you."

"You're welcome."

"Why didn't you ever write an expose on Bannie?"

"Because I wanted to reach the age that I've reached."

"I can't tell if you're joking or not."

"I'm about 85% serious."

I didn't say anything, letting his words linger. I had to be careful with Ed Bannie; that much was certain.

I told myself not to lose sight of the fact that I was looking into his son. After all, Ed Bannie wasn't even in town when Annie Ryan disappeared.

Could Ed Bannie have been part of the cover-up? Maybe he found out that his son had committed an egregious crime. I was starting to think that was a distinct possibility. Maybe this apple didn't fall too far from the tree.

"Did I tell you enough to get Quinones's number?"

"It's an old one. No guarantees."

"That's fine. Thank you."

He gave me the number.

"Will you keep me posted?" Cassius asked. "I don't expect a phone call every few hours, but I'd love to be kept abreast of anything substantial."

"Keep an eye on your phone in the coming days. I'll be in touch."

"Great."

"And thank you for all of this, Cassius. You've been invaluable," I said.

"Good luck. And be careful."

∽

I CALLED Greg Quinones within seconds of hanging up the phone with Cassius Fields. It was the correct number.

"Who did you say you are?" he asked after my introduction, which didn't go as planned.

"I'm looking into Annie Ryan's disappearance. I just talked to Cassius Fields; he gave me your number."

"Cassius is a good man."

"Yes, he is," I said like I'd known the guy for ten years.

"And what are you, exactly? A private investigator?"

I couldn't help but lie.

"Yes, I am. Cassius said you might be willing to talk to me."

"I've never had a problem talking. My ex-wives can tell you that."

I laughed.

"And you remember the Annie Ryan case?"

"Who doesn't? That's probably one of the most famous unsolved cases in Los Angeles history."

His phone was breaking up, and it was hard to hear him.

"Listen, Mr. Quinones, could I buy you a coffee or lunch to discuss the case? I'm having a hard time hearing you."

"Sure, I'm always up for a free lunch."

I realized I wasn't even sure he was still in LA despite having a 310 phone number. It was time to find out.

"Are you in LA?" I asked.

"Sure am."

"How far are you from Beverly Hills?"

"Twenty minutes."

"Do you want to meet here for lunch? In, say, an hour?"

"And you're buying?"

"Yes," I said.

"In that case, I'm in, but I get to pick the restaurant."

"Wherever you want."

"Have you heard of The Grill on the Alley?"

CHAPTER 30

I was back at The Grill for the second time in three days—or was it four days? I wasn't sure. It had been such a whirlwind since I received the call from the disguised voice, and my father mentioned Kira Palova.

Since then, everything has been done at breakneck speed.

I'd beat Greg Quinones there and requested a table for two. Considering what we would be talking about, I'd have preferred a more secluded coffee shop. The Grill was a hustle-and-bustle restaurant, and you couldn't find a secluded table there. Someone was always within earshot.

I told myself to try and keep it down. You never knew when Big Brother was listening.

A man walked in a few minutes later and looked around as if waiting for someone else. He had a perfectly manicured mustache, and I'm guessing was somewhere in his early to mid-sixties. I don't know how to describe it, but he had the vibe of an ex-cop.

"Are you Greg Quinones?" I asked.

"Yes. You're McGowan?"

"I am."

"You look like a boy scout."

"I'm older than I look," I said.

He looked unconvinced.

I told the hostess we were ready to be seated.

She led us back to a table in the far corner of the restaurant. There were still two other tables within several feet of us, but it was the best I could have hoped for.

Before the hostess left the table, Quinones asked for a drink. She informed him the waiter would be right over to take drink orders.

I had mixed feelings. Cassius had said he had a bit of a temper when he drank, but I also knew that a few drinks tended to produce loose lips.

However, Quinones was a former cop, and they tended to be tight-lipped. Then again, he hated Ed Bannie, which could push him toward talking. Basically, I had no freaking idea what to expect.

The waiter returned, and Quinones ordered a double scotch—Dewar's.

"What are you having?"

Quinones asked me, not the waiter. This was a chance to regain a little trust after he called me a Boy Scout. I was not a double scotch guy, but the circumstances called for it.

"I'll have what he's having," I said.

Greg Quinones smiled.

"That's a good boy scout."

"Where were you coming from?" I asked.

"Santa Monica," he said.

I thought of Gina and Adam's apartments.

"Nice city," I said.

"No complaints here."

Our small talk had been limited to at most five words. It was forced and probably came off as fake.

"Thanks for meeting with me, Officer Quinones. Is it okay to refer to you as that?"

"Well, if you're referencing me being a cop, you might as well go with Detective Quinones."

"You're right. My apologies."

"What do you want to know about the Annie Ryan case?"

I saw the waiter returning, so I held my tongue. He set the drinks down. We both took a sip of our Dewar's, and I tried to prevent making a face. I'd had plenty of drunken days in my life, but I'd never been a scotch guy.

"Let's hear it. This is why you dragged me out here," Quinones said.

We spent the next ten minutes discussing the case and ordering food. I already knew 90% of the information he relayed to me, and the other 10% wasn't anything important.

It was time to get down to brass tacks.

Once again, the waiter beat me to it, arriving with our lunches.

He set them down. I'd gone with a crab cake, and Quinones had ordered a filet mignon with a side order of creamed spinach. And a second double Dewar's as well. This wasn't going to be a cheap lunch.

After we took a few bites, it was time to get down to it.

"What, if anything, did Ed Bannie contribute to the Annie Ryan case?" I asked.

"Oh, that asshole."

He said it loud, and I saw two glances from the closest table.

"Yes, that asshole," I said, hoping to sound like I was in solidarity with him.

"It's funny because he was far and away the most well-known cop in Hollywood back then, but he didn't have that much impact on the Annie Ryan case. He had been on vacation, so Phillip Chide got the case."

This was more information I already knew. I had to probe deeper.

I had a wild theory that once Ed Bannie got back from his vacation, his son told him he'd murdered Annie Ryan. When he found out the LAPD had Annie Ryan's diary in their possession, Ed Bannie went to the evidence room, looked over it, and scribbled over any mentions of 'The Other Annie.'

I couldn't get past the fact that two entries had been scribbled in a completely different color than Annie had used for the rest of the diary.

I was certainly taking a leap, and people might call this theory crazy, but it didn't seem all that far-fetched to me.

There were other questions I couldn't answer. Why wouldn't Ed Bannie just take the diary at that point? Why leave it there at all? Did he think scribbling over it was enough? Would it be too obvious that it went missing when he checked it out? Would he risk a fellow cop seeing him walk out of the evidence room with it?

"This conversation stays between us, right?" I asked.

"If you think I would ever mention this to Ed Bannie, think again. I've hated the guy for as long as you've been alive."

"I'll take that as a yes."

I smiled, but Quinones just took a sip of his scotch. Was he a functioning alcoholic or just taking advantage of a free lunch? After what Cassius Fields had said, I leaned toward the former.

"It's a yes," he said.

"Do you know if Ed Bannie was doing anything behind the scenes on the case?"

"What do you mean exactly?"

"Do you think he ever looked at evidence in the evidence room?"

"It's possible, but he wasn't the lead or even the second lead, so it's unlikely."

"Is there any way, twenty-five years later, to see who checked into the evidence room?"

"I've been gone from the LAPD for a long time, so I'm not sure. But for a high-profile case like that, I imagine all that information has been maintained."

Quinones was about to take another sip of his drink when he set it back down and stared at me.

"What the hell is going on here?" Greg Quinones said rather loudly.

I reminded myself that Big Brother could always be listening.

Ed Bannie knows a lot of important people in this town.

Instead of getting specific, I decided to give a broad statement.

"I think Ed Bannie might have been up to no good," I said.

Quinones leaned back in his chair.

"Well, there's no freaking doubt about that."

"He was corrupt?"

"You're freaking goddamn right, he was."

The drinks were starting to affect Quinones, and it sounded like he wanted to drop an f-bomb during every sentence.

"What type of things?"

"E, all of the above."

"Excuse me?"

"If this were a multiple choice question, the answer would be (e) all of the above. He intimidated. He planted evidence. He stole evidence. He did it all."

"And how do you know this?"

He laughed.

"Everyone who worked with him knew it. They were just afraid of Ed, so they didn't report shit. Or, they were in on it."

"What do you mean exactly?"

Quinones took another sip and looked around for our waiter. His steak remained half-eaten, but his drink would not remain half-drank.

"I mean, he gave some of our colleagues a taste."

"A taste of what?"

"Of drugs. Well, of drug money, I mean. Everyone knew Ed Bannie was pocketing some of it when they did a huge bust. Whether it be drugs or money."

"Were there that many drug busts in the Hollywood Hills?"

"Well, our jurisdiction extended beyond just the Hollywood Hills, but the Hills had plenty of action. And they were the best type of criminals to steal from."

"Why?"

"Because they were rich. They lived in the Hollywood Hills, for Christ's sake. If fifty grand in either drugs or money went missing, they weren't going to raise a fuss with the LAPD. That would have kept their case in the public eye for longer. That's the last thing they wanted. They just wanted their time in the spotlight to end."

Quinones was giving me a gold mine, but it still didn't incriminate Ed Bannie in the Annie Ryan case. The waiter appeared, and Quinones ordered his third double Dewar's. I told the waiter he could take my now-finished crab cakes. Half of my first drink was still sitting in front of me.

"Not to look a gift horse in the mouth, but why are you telling me all this?" I asked.

"You think you're the first? I've told twenty people about this over the years. Nothing ever happens to Ed Bannie. He's bulletproof."

It made me think of something.

"How close were Bannie and Mike Minter?"

"Two peas in a pod. Mike was younger and looked up to Ed. He admired those old-school cops who stepped over the line from time to time."

"And Mike took over the Annie Ryan case from Phillip Chide, correct?"

Another in the long line of leading questions I already knew the answer to.

"He did."

"And did Ed Bannie take over a bigger role after that?"

"It's been a while, but like I said, I don't remember Ed having a big impact on the Annie Ryan case. Listen, I hate Ed more than just about anyone alive, but I don't think the Annie Ryan case is the way to get him."

I'd gone the whole lunch without mentioning Wade Bannie and planned on keeping it that way. Quinones had a big mouth, and I didn't want people to know I was going around asking about Wade.

"How would I get my hands on the old evidence room information?" I asked.

"You wouldn't. You're not a cop. You're just a PI."

"I can't file something to see it?"

"What kind of PI are you? Shouldn't you know this shit?"

THE OTHER ANNIE

He looked at me, and I felt the tenor of our conversation was about to change.

"Why did you drag me here?" Quinones asked, suddenly suspicious.

He took a sip of his drink. I took one of mine, but now he looked at me as an outsider who hadn't even finished his first double Dewar's.

Once again, I felt some eyes on us from neighboring tables.

"I've been upfront with you," I said. "I'm looking into Ed Bannie."

I said his name quietly.

"But why? You're working on the Annie Ryan case, and Ed had nothing to do with that case."

I started to think it would be better to cut my losses and end this lunch soon. It was going sideways fast, in more ways than one.

"I asked you a question," he said, his eyes not leaving mine.

I had to give him something, or there would be a scene at The Grill on the Alley.

"Because I suspect that Ed Bannie took something from that evidence room."

"But why? It wasn't even his case. Why would he take anything?"

I reminded myself that no matter where our conversation went, not to mention Wade Bannie, Greg Quinones was a wild card; that much was obvious.

"That's what I'm trying to figure out," I said, raising my voice slightly for the first time.

It was a tremendous no-response response. I was proud of myself.

The waiter walked back over after having been there a minute before. I had a feeling he was trying to get us out of there.

"Can I take your steak, sir?"

"I'll take a to-go box," Quinones said.

"And can I bring you guys the check?"

He was hoping I'd say yes, which I did.

"Great. I'll be back in a few seconds."

I'd never seen a waiter so excited to clear a table before.

"Listen, my friend," Quinones said, which was his way of saying we were not friends. "Would I put Ed Bannie above stealing something from an evidence room? Of course not. But there is no reason he'd do it on this case."

"Okay. Maybe I'm mistaken."

He looked like a disappointed father.

"Well, at least I got a free meal and a couple of drinks out of it."

The waiter returned with Quinones' to-go box and the check for me.

"I'm sorry I jumped on you," Quinones said. If you learn something more, call me, and you can take me to lunch again."

This guy was a roller coaster. It made me wonder if his accusations against Bannie weren't taken seriously because of his personality's ups and downs.

"I'll keep in touch," I said.

"Great. See you around," Quinones said.

He left the table and walked out of the restaurant quickly, not even waiting for me to sign the check.

Well, that was fun.

CHAPTER 31

I arrived at my hotel, sat on my bed, and closed my eyes.

I needed a few minutes to absorb everything I'd learned over the last forty-eight hours. If I'd complained that not enough had happened in the first several weeks of my investigation, that certainly wasn't the case anymore.

It started with the call from the modified voice. Undoubtedly, the most important moment of my investigation to that point was surpassed by the information I've ascertained since.

After all, when that call came through, it was just a nameless, faceless, disguised voice. Now, I had an actual suspect.

The turning point was my father telling me about the *Dateline NBC* episode he'd seen and how that had led me to Kira Palova. If I solved this case, my father should be credited with a huge assist.

Knowing what was said in Annie's journal led me to Gina, and then she dropped the nuclear bomb that *'The Other Annie'* was a high-schooler named Wade Bannie, who was two years older than Annie and was either having sex with her or trying to.

That would have been enough, but Gina just kept on giving. She said she'd been afraid to go to the police because Ed Bannie—Wade's father—was a well-known police officer himself.

This led me to research Ed Bannie and eventually to conversations with Cassius Fields and Greg Quinones.

The talks with the reporter and the former cop helped me arrive at my current theory: Wade Bannie killed Annie Ryan and likely had his father help cover it up. The other possibility was that they included Mike Minter in the cover-up, but I wasn't ready to go that far. Why add a third if it wasn't necessary?

If I was able to get the evidence room information back, I could see who went there in the days that followed Annie's murder. If it were Mike Minter and not Ed Bannie, then my opinion would likely change to include him.

If I was playing devil's advocate, here's where I'd poke holes in my theory.

First and foremost, I had no objective evidence that Wade Bannie killed Annie Ryan. I had nothing tying him to the crime scene. All I had was a diary entry from twenty-five years ago that references *'The Other Annie'* and Christmas Eve, but that wouldn't even be close to enough information to get a warrant.

If I went to the police and told them about Kira's work, I'd likely be laughed out of the precinct. Not that I wanted to go to the cops, anyway. First, I needed to determine whether I thought Mike Minter was involved.

So, where did this all leave me?

Ironically, I was a million miles ahead of where I was only three days ago, and yet, I wasn't sure I had the proverbial card to play. I couldn't/wouldn't go to the cops, and I didn't have enough evidence to confront a district attorney.

And possibly the weakest link of all of this. The only woman who knew that Annie Ryan referred to Wade Bannie as *'The Other Annie'* was a nervous wreck named Gina Galasso.

The more I thought about it, the more I wondered if I was jumping to conclusions.

What if Wade Bannie - and, by extension, his father - had nothing to do with this?

∼

I WOKE up the next morning, and the screen name itallstartedwithanAR immediately came to mind.

It all started with.

Did that mean he was saying he'd committed more than one murder?

Was he referring to Kai Butler or other people who had nothing to do with the Annie Ryan case? He also could have just been saying his life had spiraled downhill once he murdered Annie Ryan. But Wade Bannie's life hadn't spiraled downhill, as his Instagram photos showed.

Which is where I went next.

I looked at his photos' time, date, and location and started making a spreadsheet. In the occasional photo, he'd say something like, *'This reminds me of my trip to Puerto Rico in 2002.'*

If that were the case, I'd add Puerto Rico, 2002, to the spreadsheet.

One problem was that Wade started his Instagram page in 2016, and I was in the dark about anything before then—except when he mentioned them like he had with Puerto Rico.

When I finished the spreadsheet, I started Googling about murders in that country during that time.

The Caribbean - especially the very touristy islands - was generally pretty safe, so murders didn't occur all that often. And when they did - like Natalee Holloway - they tended to get much media attention.

My process went something like this:

Wade had a picture of himself in Jamaica in August of 2017, and I found the unsolved murder of a young French girl on August 9th. I added that to my list.

I tried to look for murders that had occurred a few months before or after he posted the picture. One, he might not have been likely to post a photo in the same month he committed a murder. And two, he may have stayed in these countries for months on end.

I only focused on women who had been murdered. Could Wade Bannie have been a serial killer and murdered twenty people, including men? I guess, but I didn't think so. When he said he'd killed between one and how many Conrad Drury had, I tended to believe that it was closer to one and that it was likely attractive women.

Once again, there was a distinct possibility he'd killed Kai Butler and stopped there. Still, I continued on with the spreadsheet.

By the time I finished, it was after one p.m.

∽

Next, I called Cassius Fields.

"You don't give up, do you? Greg Quinones called and told me about your little lunch with him."

"Are you retired or semi-retired?" I asked.

"Why?"

"Would you want to write a tell-all expose if I come to you with enough evidence?"

"I already told you I enjoyed being an old man."

"That's not an answer to my question."

"The evidence would have to be overwhelming," Cassius said.

"Well, I'm not there yet, but that's why I'm calling."

"So, I have to help get the evidence for you and then write the expose? What exactly do you do?"

"I'm your man on the ground, and trust me; I'll be coming to the attention of Ed Bannie a lot sooner than you will."

I still was leaving Wade Bannie out of the conversation.

"What did you need?"

"Okay, here's the thing."

"Stop sugarcoating it, and just give it to me straight."

"I need the name of someone who is still on the police force in the Hollywood division. Someone you trust and can be discreet."

"What do you need him or her for?"

"I need to know who checked things out of the evidence room in the immediate days after Annie Ryan went missing."

"That's it?"

"That's it."

"And what is the end game with this?"

"I'll let you know when I get the results back. Don't take this the wrong way, but it's probably better you don't know too much before I lay it on you all at once."

"You're quite the character, Bobby. Telling a guy who wrote about the LAPD for thirty years what he should and shouldn't know."

He sounded ticked off.

"I understand why you're upset. I promise to tell you all after I get back this information. If I don't get what I'm hoping for, all of my assumptions may have been a house of cards."

"That hardly breeds confidence."

"Then I look forward to changing your mind."

I heard a sigh on the other end.

"I think I can get that for you. It might be a few days. I've been retired for a while now, and I need to find out what active officers I still trust."

"How long should I wait to call you back?"

"You don't call me back. I'll call you when I've heard something."

"Okay, thank you, Cassius."

"And one more thing."

"What?"

"This better be one hell of a story if you're making me come out of retirement."

"It would be massive," I said.

∼

I HAD MORE questions for Greg Quinones, but he was so on edge at the end of our interview that I decided to let him chill out for a day or two.

He had it in for Ed Bannie, and I was afraid he might go shouting his name all around town. He was a wild card—a potential liability. I had to tread lightly with him.

∼

SIMILARLY, I had more questions for Gina Galasso.

Did she know what type of car Wade Bannie drove back then? Maybe someone had seen the make and model driving near William Ryan's house that night. And no, I hadn't forgotten that this was twenty-five years ago.

Did Wade ever brag to her and Kai that Annie had been to his house? If so, Ed Bannie likely knew who she was.

Like Quinones, I let Gina chill out for a few days. My conversation with her had taken a lot out of her, and unless it were a question I needed to have answered immediately, I would give her some space. She deserved it.

CHAPTER 32

By ten a.m. the next morning, I hadn't heard back from Cassius Fields.

The last thing I wanted to do was sit around and wait for people to get back to me.

I knew what I had to do: see Earl Razzle.

The last time I saw him, he made my father a martini. That was a leading contender in a crowded field of 'most surreal moment of the investigation.'

I called ahead just to make sure. His secretary said he was in and would see me in twenty minutes.

Earl Razzle sure was at his office a lot. I wonder if he now delegated more authority than he did as a younger man. He was still a private investigator, or at least, his sign out front of his office said he was.

Then again, he could do most of his work via a laptop these days. I'd certainly spent quite a bit of time investigating online, but I still liked getting out there and meeting with people, as my up-and-down lunch with Greg Quinones proved.

I WALKED OVER, was led in by his secretary, shook Earl's hand, and sat on the couch. This was becoming old hat.

"Don't tell me I'm on martini detail again," he said.

I smiled.

"No, today is business."

"Sounds serious. What do you need?"

"I need a big favor, but I'd prefer if we kept this between us," I said.

"I wouldn't have gotten this far in my business if I didn't know how to keep a secret."

"Okay, good. I want a copy of the evidence room information from the Annie Ryan case. It's not in the summary you gave me."

"You want to know what the police submitted as evidence?"

"If that comes with it, great," I said. "But mostly, I'm trying to get a list of people who went in to look at the evidence in the days that followed Annie's disappearance."

I knew Annie was dead, but sometimes it sounded more appropriate to use disappearance.

"Okay," he said pensively. "That shouldn't be too hard to get my hands on."

"Great, thanks," I said.

"You don't get off that easy, Bobby. It sounds like you might be making some progress. Anything you'd like to share?"

"Can I let you know after seeing the information I requested?"

Earl smiled, but I could tell he was hoping for more.

"Do you think a cop was involved?"

"Why would you think that?"

"One, don't answer a question with a question. And two, police officers are generally who check out things from the evidence room. It's a logical question to ask, so stop being evasive."

His point was spot-on. Why else would I be asking who went into the evidence room? It's not like John Q. Public could just walk in off the street.

"I've narrowed my focus to one critical piece of evidence," I said. "And I want to know who also found it important in the days that followed the Christmas Eve party."

"That's very smart, Bobby. You gave me a little bit of information without giving much away. That's a very private investigator thing to do."

"Maybe your expertise is rubbing off on me."

Earl smiled again, but it wasn't his megawatt version. It was the 'I'm humoring you' version.

"That's all you're going to give me?" he asked. "After all I've done for you."

I trusted Earl Razzle, but I was still trying to limit who knew precisely what I was up to. I was already fearful that the wildcard - Greg Quinones - could be blabbing around town.

Earl was right, however. He had been helpful every step of the way. I decided to give him something.

"What if I told you I was beginning to suspect someone who wasn't even at the party?"

Earl combed his hands through his hair.

"Hmmm," he muttered. "That's interesting. If that is true, it makes me wonder how many months of my life were wasted interviewing people who were actually at the party."

"Hey, me too."

"No offense, junior, but you've been on the case a month. I've been on it for twenty-plus years."

By using the word 'junior,' Earl had lost out on getting more information from me.

"Don't call me junior," I said.

"Calm down, Bobby. I didn't mean it like that. You're doing a hell of a job."

When I didn't respond, he knew he had to apologize.

"I'm sorry, Bobby. That was out of line. Maybe I was just jealous that you were getting somewhere, and I've been stuck in neutral for so long."

"Now, that's an apology," I said, and this time he truly smiled.

"Why don't we meet again this afternoon? Let's say three p.m."

"You think you can get it that quick?"

"I know a great many people in this town," he said.

Yeah, so does Ed Bannie, I thought to myself.

"I'll be here. And one last thing," I asked.

"What is it?"

"Can you try to get it without going through cops who worked the case?"

"I'll try to go through it secretarily. Is that a word?"

"I don't think so," I said.

"Well, you get my point. I'll try to get it through a secretary or someone with a desk job. They might have to get someone higher up, like Mike Minter, to sign off on it."

"See if you can get it without him knowing," I said.

"So, you think Minter could be involved?"

Earl was fishing, but I had a solid response waiting.

"He knows everyone involved," I said. "So, that's my fear with him."

"Good bullshit answer. You really are getting good at this."

I stood up from the couch.

"I'll see you this afternoon."

"See you then, Bobby."

∼

Two minutes later, as I was walking back to the Beverly Hilton, I got a call from William Ryan. I hadn't talked to him in several days. The timing of the call was suspicious. Maybe Earl called him to see if William could get more out of me.

"How are you, William?"

"Bobby, it's been a while."

"It has. I'm sorry, just been busy working the case."

"That's what I'm calling about. Did you realize that tomorrow is one month?"

My heart sank. William wasn't going to kick me off the case right when I was making serious inroads, was he?

"I knew it was coming up," I said. "I didn't know it was tomorrow, though."

"Well, it is. Do you think I should keep you on for another month? Are we making enough progress to make another month worthwhile?"

William didn't know about the garbled phone conversation, my meeting with Kira, talking to Gina, or reaching out to Cassius Fields and Greg Quinones. If he knew any of this, there would be no question. He'd have to keep me on.

"I've been meaning to call you, William. Yeah, I have made some inroads recently."

"Inroads?" he said skeptically.

"Yeah, my puzzle has picked up a few more pieces in the last several days."

"Interesting. Do you have time to come see me?"

I wanted to say no, but William was the guy paying me to do this job. I sometimes forgot that.

"Yeah, I could come up and see you. How about later today? I'm meeting Earl Razzle at three p.m. and could drive to your place afterward."

"That would work. Why are you meeting Earl?"

"There's a file he hadn't included in his summary."

"What file?"

William Ryan didn't beat around the bush. I assumed most people who had made it big in Hollywood didn't pull their punches, and William was no different.

"I'm trying to get a list of things submitted to the evidence room."

That was partly true.

"What evidence specifically?"

He did hire you!

"Annie's diary. There are a couple of passages that interest me. It would probably be easier to show you in person tonight."

There was a pause, and I knew William was exploring his options.

"Okay," he said. "I'll expect a little more candor from you in person."

"Understood," I said. "I just don't want to make it sound like this is groundbreaking if it turns out not to be."

"And I understand that, Bobby. Well, no matter what, you've done enough to warrant another month on the job. How does another ten grand and a free month at the Beverly Hilton sound?"

The first part sounded great. The second part, not so much.

"Thank you. We can discuss the living arrangements when I see you."

"Not a fan of the world-famous Beverly Hilton?"

I laughed.

"We'll talk about it."

"Okay. See you in a few hours, Bobby."

CHAPTER 33

WADE BANNIE

*D*ecember 24th, 1998.
      A day that changed my life forever.
And I know it was my fault, but Annie Ryan deserves a little blame. None of this would have happened if she'd just put out. Dumb bitch.

~

WE MET AT A MOVIE THEATER.

That dork Kai Butler and his ugly girlfriend Gina introduced us. Not that Kai wanted to, but he was scared of me.

When I was a kid, the movie *A Bronx Tale* came out. In it, Chazz Palminteri's character is asked: "Would you rather be feared or loved?"

He answered, "If I had my choice, I'd rather be feared."

And I'd kind of taken that as my motto growing up. I didn't care if people loved me. What the hell did that get me? Nothing. But if they feared me, it got me things.

Plus, it was my father in a nutshell. That man was feared, and I looked up to him. It was only natural I'd grow up to be the way I was.

Anyway, it's what got me my introduction to Annie. Annie was cute.

She was a little more sophisticated than the other high school girls I was having sex with, and she seemed like more of a challenge.

And she proved to be one. I took her out three or four times in October and November of 1998, but she'd never give me more than a kiss. I'd lie to Kai and tell him I was banging his cousin, but I barely got to first base. And I'd become accustomed to getting a lot more than that, so this pissed me off to no end.

We only went out a few times in early December, and once again, it ended with a kiss. Now, part of me could tell she wanted more, but she didn't like the idea of going to my parents' house when they were home. And me going to her parents' house was out of the question. She'd made that abundantly clear.

I was trying to keep Annie a secret from the other girls I was dating, so going to one of my high school parties and finding an unused room wasn't possible.

The clock was ticking. I didn't usually wait around for girls. They waited for me.

But finally, a plan started to emerge.

I knew my parents were flying to Cancun for Christmas Eve and Christmas Day. I was their only child, and obviously, I would be joining them, but about a week out, I told them I needed to stay in Los Angeles.

It's been so long I can't even remember the excuse. Had I said I needed to study for the SAT? No, they wouldn't have believed that crap. Maybe I said it was basketball season, and I needed to practice. Even that sounded like bullshit.

Whatever it was, I got out of going down to Mexico. I was seventeen, and my parents trusted me at home. It's not like I was twelve.

Oh shit, I remember! How could I have forgotten?

I'd told my father in secret that there was this girl I'd been trying to have sex with and hadn't had any luck thus far. I told him if I had the house to myself over Christmas, I could make it happen.

My father loved the idea. It's not exactly father-of-the-year material, but we'll get back to him later.

So, I was able to avoid the family Christmas trip to Mexico, much to my mother's chagrin.

She had tried to be a good mother. I just tended to be more of a bullying asshole like my father. I couldn't tell her my real reason for staying in LA. I told her my girlfriend (I had three, but would never tell her that) wanted me to meet her family for Christmas, and she fell for that. She didn't like that I wasn't going to Mexico, but at least I wouldn't be alone for Christmas. She wouldn't have allowed me to stay home if that were the case.

My father knew what I was up to. My mother didn't. And that was true of just about everything, not only the Christmas of 1998.

I started working on Annie, but she wasn't easy to convince. I knew she still found me attractive. I mean, what girl didn't? I was strong, handsome, charismatic, and all the other things high school girls liked. I think they become choosier as they age, but I was every high school girl's dream.

The thing was, Annie was still a virgin, and she wanted everything to be just right for her first time. She was a brilliant young lady and instinctively knew I was a player. She didn't go to my high school, so she didn't know about the three girlfriends, but she was intuitive enough to know that I was a dog.

But I was a charismatic dog, so I still thought I could pull this off.

I worked very hard on Annie in mid-December. I was on my best behavior and trying to come off as a compassionate guy worried about her feelings. I said I'd make her first time perfect.

That's when she told me she had to be with her parents all day on Christmas Day. They opened presents, had breakfast, and went to a movie together. Blah, blah, blah.

I asked about Christmas Eve, and she told me about the big party at William Ryan's house. I knew who he was—a big Hollywood producer.

Annie said she could invite me to the party. William often allowed people who weren't family to come to these things. I quickly turned down the offer and asked her not to tell Kai and Gina she had invited me.

Looking back, I often wonder why I did that. Did I know that I was going to kill Annie that night? No, it certainly wasn't planned. But something in my subconscious knew it would be better if Kai and Gina didn't know my plans on Christmas Eve.

And it's the only reason I'm still free twenty-five years later. If they'd known Annie was coming over, they'd have told the police, and I'd have been brought in for questioning—either that very night or early the next day.

Those twenty-four hours after Annie died were a terribly stressful time for me, but I'm getting a little ahead of myself.

So, I was still working on Annie, selling her on how perfect I would make her first time. She told me she didn't think she had time to come over with the Christmas Eve party and her plans on Christmas Day.

You see, Annie was only fifteen and didn't have a driver's license yet, so she'd have to leave William's party with her parents.

And that's when I came up with my idea. The conversation went something like this.

Me: "You said there are like sixty people at this party."

Annie: "Yeah, something like that. They are always huge."

Me: "Would anyone notice if you went missing for an hour?"

Annie: "Maybe not. Probably. I don't know."

Me: "My parents live ten minutes from there. I pick you up, we go to my parents, and we have sex. You'll be back at the party less than an hour later. And you'll be a woman at that point."

I REMEMBER SAYING something cheesy like that.

ANNIE: "I DON'T KNOW, WADE."

ON THE NIGHT WE MET, she nicknamed me The Other Annie but called me Wade when we talked amongst ourselves.

ME: "C'mon. No one would have a cooler story about how they lost their virginity. I mean, leaving a Christmas party to go have sex is so cool."

Annie: "Really?"

Me: "Your girlfriends will be so impressed."

ANNIE WAS INTELLIGENT AND INDEPENDENT, but she was still a teenage girl, and shit like this worked.

ANNIE: "ARE YOU SURE?"

Me: "Trust me, you'll never regret this."

Annie: "Okay, let's do it. Just promise you'll be a gentleman."

AND THAT'S when I knew I had her.

. . .

THE OTHER ANNIE

I HAD NEVER ACTED BETTER in my life. And I do mean acted as if I was a Hollywood star in a William Ryan movie. I was playing a role. The nice guy who was going to do everything in his power to make Annie's first time perfect.

It didn't quite go that way.

∼

ANNIE DECIDED that leaving during dinner was the most opportune time.

The dining room was massive, and people constantly got up to get drinks or use the bathroom. Annie said she'd sit with her cousins and not her parents so her parents wouldn't worry when she left the table and didn't return.

Annie said that all the adults would make drinks after dinner before they started doing their Secret Santa tradition. If she weren't back for the game, her parents would start to notice.

I told her that I'd have her back before then.

And I reiterated that she shouldn't tell anyone about what we were doing.

"This will be our little secret," I said.

"I haven't told a soul," Annie said. "The only thing I did was mention it in my diary."

I had laughed at that then, having no idea how important that would become.

∼

ANNIE TOLD me that William always hired valet drivers for his events, and I shouldn't drive to the top of the house.

She would exit one of the rooms that led to the backyard and meet me at the base of the house.

"Don't drive up," she reminded me. "The valet guys will see you. Turn your lights off when you get on William's street. I'll just find you at the end of the street. It's only like fifty feet from his house."

"Okay, " I said.

I was going to agree with anything she said at this point.

∼

When she got in my car that night, she was excited about ditching the party.

"That was so crazy," she said.

About what happened next, she seemed a little more reserved.

"We can just make out if you'd prefer," she said.

I had no plans of only making out. I hadn't missed a trip to Cancun for a make-out session.

We arrived at my parents' house ten minutes later. It was secluded, and no neighbors could see who entered and left the house.

∼

We walked into the house, and I immediately escorted Annie to my room.

At this point, my goal was to have sex with her and then get her back to her party. Nothing more.

I'd put a single rose on the center of the bed.

That's not the person I am, but I wanted to give Annie one last nudge in the right direction.

She smiled at the rose but let out a nervous laugh.

"Like I said, we can just make out," she said.

I figured that's how we'd start, and it would slowly escalate. Shit, it worked that way with all of my other girls.

∼

We lay on the bed, and I leaned in to kiss her.

She playfully kissed me back. It wasn't the kissing that worried her.

We started passionately making out a few minutes later. A minute after that, I grabbed the outside of her breast, which she seemed okay with.

Two minutes later - two minutes too long for me! - I reached for her belt buckle. This was when things started to go wrong.

"Slower," she said. And added, "If it all."

I tried to remain calm, even though I was seething on the inside. There was no way I wasn't having sex tonight. I hadn't gone through all this trouble for nothing.

I continued kissing her and fondling her breasts, even though I was already getting bored with it. I reached for her belt again.

"I'll be very gentle," I whispered. Yeah, right.

She slowly took off her belt, but I could tell it was agonizing for her. I didn't care. I just saw the finish line in sight.

"I don't know if I can go through with this," she said. "Can't we wait till early next year?"

"Every girl thinks what you're thinking right now. Then they go through with it and are happy they did."

"Maybe I'm not like every other girl."

She had removed her belt, but her pants remained on. I grabbed the belt and set it next to me.

"Here, let me help," I said, as if all I cared about was her.

"I don't think I want to do this, Wade."

"C'mon, it's me and you. Annie and the other Annie."

It sounded weird calling myself that name in the moment, but I was trying to do anything to keep this from going off the tracks, which is where it was headed.

"Can I get my belt back?" she asked.

"That's not what we agreed upon."

"This wasn't a signed contract. It's my virginity. I decide."

"When you agreed to come over, it's basically like you signed a contract," I said.

"That's a dumb fucking thing to say, Wade."

My opportunity was slipping away. And underneath my composed exterior, I was starting to lose my cool.

"Let's go, baby. We'll start from the beginning. Here, let's make out."

"I'd like my belt back," she said.

I grabbed it in my right hand.

"You'll get it back after we're done," I said, and that's when things got even worse.

She swore at me and leaned to grab the belt. As I pulled it away from her, it whiplashed back, and the buckle hit her above the eye.

She put her finger up and felt blood.

"What the hell, Wade."

"It was an accident."

"It wouldn't have happened if you gave me my belt back. Now give me my belt back."

"No."

"Now."

"No."

"Give me my belt back and drive me back to the party right now."

"No. We're having sex. I didn't go through all this trouble to feel your fucking tits."

At this point, there was still a chance this didn't have to escalate any further.

"I should have listened to Kai and Gina. You're a scumbag," she said.

Even then, there was still a chance, but not after what she said next.

"I can't wait to return to the party and tell them what you've done."

And that's when I lost it.

I swung the belt at Annie, the buckle connecting with her forehead.

She started screaming.

There was no need to feel for blood. It was streaming down her forehead and into her eyes.

"Please stop, Wade."

"You're going to go tell Kai and Gina what happened, aren't you?"

"No, I promise I won't."

"I don't believe you. You're a lying bitch."

Annie looked into my eyes and assumed I couldn't be reasoned with any longer. She wasn't wrong.

We were both on the bed, but I was between her and my bedroom door. She had no escape. It hit her like a ton of bricks.

"Help," she started screaming. "Help! Help!"

I panicked and straddled her, putting my arms around her neck. She tried to keep yelling, "Help!" and I just wanted that screaming to end.

It did several minutes later.

I NOW HAD a dead body in my bedroom and no idea what to do.

My father would know what my next steps should be, but he was in Mexico with my mother.

I debated calling him and asking what to do.

No one knew Annie was coming to see you!

I reminded myself of that several times.

If you will just be smart, you can get away with this.

I CONSIDERED BURYING her in my parents' backyard but decided against it.

I considered driving out to the desert and dropping her body there but decided against that as well.

I figured the ocean was my best bet.

At two a.m., I put Annie's dead body in my car and drove west toward the Pacific Ocean.

I couldn't just pull up to the beaches of Venice or Santa Monica and drag her body and set it in the water. One, people might see me, and two, the body likely wouldn't float away.

I needed to drop the body where the water was already deep, but I didn't have a boat.

I knew it was usually high tide at night, so I devised a plan. I headed north on the Pacific Coast Highway and passed Malibu. I was looking for an inlet where I could park the car and throw the body off a cliff into the ocean below. Since it was high tide, her body would land in the water, and hopefully, it would be taken out to sea.

About twenty miles up the PCH, I found the type of inlet I was looking for and pulled in. I looked down, and water, not sand, was below us.

It was very late, so there weren't many cars driving back and forth, but I still had to be vigilant.

I took Annie's dead body out of the car and rolled it toward the edge. Even if a car drove by, my car was blocking her body. I looked out on both sides of the PCH, and when I saw no cars coming, I pushed Annie Ryan's body off the cliff.

And then I drove home.

∽

FOR THE NEXT TWENTY-FOUR HOURS, I was a wreck.

I thought it was inevitable the cops would be knocking on my door. I figured Annie's body would wash up on shore.

Neither happened.

And her body didn't wash up on shore the next day. Or the day after that. Or the day after that.

I don't know if the current carried her out to sea or if the sharks arrived at some point, but luck was on my side.

Annie Ryan's body was never found.

∽

I SPENT CHRISTMAS DAY CLEANING.

I started with the outside of my car, which had a small splotch of blood.

I then saw that there was a blood spot on the inside of the car. I spent two hours trying to remove it, but it had soaked into the cloth.

I decided not to get it detailed. If I ever became a suspect, that would be used against me.

Next were my comforter and bed sheets, which I put through the washer and dryer twice.

The sheets were fine, but the comforter still had a small stain. I grabbed an old comforter and replaced it.

~

My parents returned on December 26th.

Annie Ryan's disappearance was front page news in the Los Angeles Times by then.

I got a few phone calls from friends. None of them knew I took Annie out, but a girl from a nearby high school had gone missing. It was news. I pretended I hadn't heard about it.

Kai Butler and Gina Galasso were the only two people who knew I'd taken Annie out a few times. Luckily, they were at the party and knew I hadn't been there.

It was to my advantage they'd been at the party. If not, they might have told the cops to check me out. But knowing I hadn't been there, they had no reason to suspect me.

~

Unlike them, my father was suspicious of me almost immediately.

When they walked in the door, I hugged both parents and asked about their trip. They asked about mine, and for obvious reasons, I was brief and tried to bring it back to theirs.

After we talked for a while, my mother said the fridge was bare and set off for the store.

My father walked outside. I figured he was doing some yard work.

He walked back into the house a few minutes later. I was on the couch watching a football game. Five minutes later, he returned and sat beside me on the couch.

"How was the Christmas party at your girlfriend's?" he asked.

I was nervous. His eyes were piercing.

"It was fine."

"What was her name again?"

"Cindy," I said, making up the first name that came to mind.

"Not many Cindy's your age. A blast from the past, if you will. If I called Cindy's parents, they'd verify you were there?"

"Of course."

"That's odd. You told me that the Christmas party plans were a lie you told your mother. You told me you were trying to get a girl over here."

Oh, shit. In my panic-stricken state, I'd confused my lies.

"What?" I said.

"You heard me," my father yelled.

When I didn't answer, he asked the question he'd been leading up to.

"Did you hear about this missing girl? Annie, something."

"Yeah, I saw it on the news. Horrible."

"You didn't know her, did you?"

"She didn't go to my high school."

"That's not what I asked."

"No, I didn't know her," I said. "You're being weird, Dad."

"Follow me," he said. "I don't want you to talk for a minute. Just listen."

He led me to the laundry room.

"Look over here. There's detergent spilled all over the ground. We both know your mother would never leave a mess like that. Remember, these statements are rhetorical, so don't talk, just listen."

He walked me back to my bedroom.

"You've had the same white comforter for five years. And now, there's this polka-dotted black and white one on your bed? When did you get into polka dots?"

My heart was about to explode.

I'm glad I didn't have to answer because I had no explanation. I'd have probably said I spilled food all over it and ruined it. Maybe he'd buy that.

I had no excuse for what he showed me next, however.

"One more stop," he said and walked me outside.

We approached my car.

Oh, shit.

I saw my father look around to make sure no one was approaching. He whispered, just to be safe.

"After seeing the laundry room and your new sheets, I got suspicious and came out here. The first thing I noticed was how clean the outside of your car was. It certainly didn't look like that when we left."

He leaned in and whispered in my ear.

"And that's when I looked at the backseat."

He grabbed my arm and led me to the seat behind the driver's seat. It's where Annie's head had been resting.

He whispered in my ear again.

"That's fucking blood, Wade. Now, I will give you five minutes to think things over. I'll be in the back of the house. Meet me there. And I want you to remember one thing: If you tell me the truth, I can help you. If you lie, you are at the mercy of the Gods."

CHAPTER 34

<u>WADE</u>

I told my father everything.
 I don't know if it was fear of my father or the fear of getting caught, but I told him every last detail.

His demeanor didn't change much at all. He was very matter-of-fact. When I finished, he looked me straight in the eyes and said, "I can work with this. If you're smart and never say a word to anyone, you won't go to jail and can continue living your life. Let's not have one dead girl ruin your life."

"Thank you," I said.

My father and I had the same mindset.

"One more thing, and I shouldn't even have to tell you this, but don't say a fucking word to your mother."

"I won't."

"Not one fucking word."

"I understand."

"Now, this is your last chance to tell me something you may have missed. Anything that could be crucial to the investigation the cops are making right now."

I thought long and hard.

"Oh, shit. There was one thing I forgot to mention."

"What?"

"Annie said she had mentioned me in her diary."

"Fucking A, Wade. How could you forget that?'"

"A lot is going through my mind right now, Dad."

"Well, whose fault is that?"

I had no good response. I'd killed the darn girl, after all.

"You better hope my fellow detectives haven't combed through that diary yet."

"Would they have?"

"They probably gave it a cursory glance but nothing more. At least, not yet. And that's assuming they already went to this girl's house and picked up her stuff."

"One more thing," I said.

"What?"

"She might have used a nickname for me in the diary."

"What is it?"

"The other Annie."

"What the fuck does that mean?"

I explained it to him.

My father was mulling over his options.

"Are you going to steal the diary?" I asked.

"No. They keep track of who goes into the evidence room. You have to sign in. What I am going to do is get in there and scribble over any mention of you or your stupid nickname. When did you meet so I know where to start reading?"

"In early October."

"Okay. Now, I want you to go lie down, Wade. I want you to sit in that bed and remind yourself - a thousand times if you must - that you will never say a word about her again. Not a single peep. If you see that couple, Tai and Gina or whatever you called them, just say how sorry you are, and then move on. Don't say more than that. There is zero evidence you were at the party, and you won't be a suspect, no matter how much those two don't like you."

"Should we do something about them?" I asked.

"Jesus effing Christ, Wade. You just killed a young girl. Now you want to kill a few more teenagers?"

"No, I just…"

"You need to keep your mouth shut. Let your father clean up this mess."

"What about the car?"

"I'll take care of that, too. You'll be driving something new soon."

"What should I say happened to my old car if people ask?"

"That's the first good question you've asked, son. Just say that your father got a great deal on a newer car and couldn't pass it up."

Even I - a cold-blooded killer - understood the irony that committing a murder had led to me getting a nicer car.

"Okay," I said.

"Last thing," my father said. "This was a one-time thing. Even though she was a tease and leading you on, that girl didn't deserve to die. You will not kill again. I'm putting my life and career on the line for you, and I'm not doing it for some deranged killer. I'm doing it for a teenager who panicked and made a big mistake. Do you understand?"

"Yes, father, I do. I will never do anything like this again," I said.

And I had meant it.

At least, at the time, I had.

∽

THE INVESTIGATION never even got close to me.

How could they? I mean, I wasn't even at the party.

And after my father scribbled out my name in the diary, they had nothing tying me to Annie.

Well, I guess Kai and Gina, but they never said anything. My father would have known. He was like a hawk, circling this investigation from the sky. And he got an even better view when Phillip Chide died and Mike Minter took over.

I was lucky about one thing. This was 1998, and neither Annie nor I had a cell phone. If this happened in 2024, we surely would have texted each other about the Christmas Eve plan, and the cops would have been knocking on my parents' door that next morning.

But it hadn't been 2024. It had been 1998.

And we'd only discussed the plan when hanging out in early and mid-December. Annie had told me never to call her house. Her parents didn't like the idea of guys calling.

If we'd finalized the plan over the phone, the police might have come to my house and asked why I'd called her.

I'd been lucky at every turn of this investigation.

∽

When I graduated high school several months later, I went to live in the US Virgin Islands. My father had arranged all the details, right down to my job as a deckhand on a yacht.

My mother could never understand it. My grades were good, and I could have gone to college.

My father told her it was better to get real-life experience than to sit in a classroom for four or five years. I knew the real reason he was shipping me out of the country.

In private, my father told me the following:

"It's still too fresh in the minds of everyone in Los Angeles. If you leave the country for a few years, people will have forgotten about this Annie girl once you return. Come back as a twenty-one-year-old man and start your life anew. With some real-life experience. You can sleep with some beautiful Caribbean women in the meantime."

And then he added: "Just don't kill them."

It's safe to say we had a majorly fucked up father-son relationship.

∼

I moved to the US Virgin Islands and started working on yachts.

It was fantastic. Beautiful weather. Beautiful women.

I've often heard the phrase, "Karma is a bitch," but I don't buy into that bullshit. If anyone deserved the wrath of karma, it would have been me. But no, I've lived a pretty awesome life in the years since I murdered Annie Ryan.

I've spent my life on boats and in exotic locations, often with beautiful women on my arms. If Karma is a bitch, then it's probably some bitch I fucked. Hahaha.

∼

I killed two more times.

This hadn't been part of some master plan. I wasn't a serial killer in that sense. Both were similar to Annie's death, where the woman turned down my advances, and I couldn't control my anger.

You'd think that someone like me, who had been with ample women, could live with being turned down once in a while. It worked the opposite way. Because women so often threw themselves at me, I couldn't take it when one rejected me.

My second murder happened in the US Virgin Islands in 2001. Her

THE OTHER ANNIE

name was Lola Fletcher. She was a British girl vacationing with her family. She had gotten in a fight with her parents and had ventured out onto the beach around midnight.

I just happened to be there. Talk about bad timing.

We started kissing, and one thing led to another. This was always when I was at my most dangerous. If you turned me on and then soured on me, I was a dangerous animal.

And that's what happened to Lola Fletcher.

She met her demise in the same way as Annie.

Once it was over, I put some big leaves over my hands and repeatedly pushed her body underwater, hoping to wash away any trace of fingerprints.

I must have succeeded because I was never a suspect.

I caught another break as well. In 2000, the internet was not what it is now. Word didn't travel around the world in a matter of seconds.

In 2024, the story of a murdered British girl in the US Virgin Islands probably goes viral. In 2000, it did not. Because if it had, and my father heard about it, I would have had to answer some serious questions.

I started to worry that maybe I was on the path to becoming a serial killer. This was two women in three years.

But I was able to fight off my demon for another ten years before they struck once again.

∽

THE YEAR WAS 2010, and I lived in the Dominican Republic, in a resort city called Punta Cana. Scores of luxury resorts lined the exquisite beaches and ocean, and rich Americans and Europeans flocked to the island.

I was working on a catamaran and would meet gorgeous girls daily. This particular one was a long-legged Tahitian girl with an absurd body and a perfect tan. We only said a few words that day on the catamaran, which was a stroke of luck for me, considering she ended up dead a day later.

I saw her at a club that night. She recognized me immediately.

I didn't go and talk to her.

Instead, I walked toward the beach and made a little follow-me motion with my index finger.

She followed. Girls can be so easy.

We walked along the beach for twenty minutes, getting further and further away from civilization. It was late at night, and no one was around.

We were close to having sex when she got cold feet. Who does that? You can't just wind a guy up like that.

One thing led to another, and by the time the night was over, I'd killed a third woman. I also bobbed her body up and down in the water to remove any potential fingerprints.

The funny part was that Joran van der Sloot was in the Dominican Republic at the same time the woman disappeared, and the authorities questioned him.

What better way to elude suspicion than by having a renowned killer on the island at the same time?

It made me ask myself whether I was all that different from the infamous Dutch national.

I'd decided the answer was no. We were pretty similar.

The difference is that he is rotting away in a prison somewhere while I'm out enjoying my life.

∿

After the murder of the Tahitian girl, I'd been a good boy since.

No murders in fourteen years, and I do hope I'm done. I may be a malignant narcissist with no empathy, but I at least recognize these women didn't deserve to die.

∿

As for the investigations, they have yet to get close to me.

I must have a horseshoe up my ass.

With Annie, my father proved to be a great help.

With Lola Fletcher, there was nothing to connect us. We randomly met on a deserted beach at midnight.

With the Tahitian girl - I don't even remember her name - I did get interviewed, but it was only because they interviewed every member of the staff working on the catamaran.

I had gone to the club alone and never met any of her friends. I just motioned to the beach, and the woman followed me.

Nothing was tying us together.

And you probably won't be surprised to hear that the Dominican Republic was not big on cameras—well, at least not in 2010.

Finally, I'd like to give a tip of my hat to the oceans around the world. The Pacific Ocean took Annie away and never returned her, while the waters of the Caribbean did a great job of wiping off any fingerprints of Lola Fletcher and the nameless Tahitian.

You've provided excellent service to me. Hahaha.

∼

I NEVER RETURNED ONCE I left the US Virgin Islands and the Dominican Republic.

The same can't be said of Los Angeles. I moved back permanently several years ago.

I still constantly travel the world, but LA is my home base.

My father lives in a Hollywood condo, and I see him often.

And it was on one of these visits that I first heard the name of Bobby McGowan.

CHAPTER 35

WADE

"William Ryan hired a new private investigator," my father told me.

It was the second week of June.

I was sitting with my father at his deluxe condo in Hollywood.

My mother was no longer a part of either of our lives. She had soured on my father years ago, and I think she saw me as being too closely aligned with him and cut off ties with me about eight years back. Maybe, in the back recesses of her mind, she suspected me of being precisely what I was, and she just figured a clean break from both of us was the smart move. I can't say I blame her.

My father had sold the house where Annie Ryan had been murdered and was now living at his condo in Hollywood. He had plenty of money to live in a home if he preferred, but he said he enjoyed the simplicity of the condo.

My father had stolen money from drug busts, money laundering, and other crimes, but he'd also been a very savvy investor of that money. He was quite well off in his old age.

The best thing he ever did for me—with the exception of covering up

Annie's murder—was to set money aside for me in stocks and mutual funds. My mother didn't want to take the risk and wanted to let the money earn minimal annual returns. My father said no, let's invest it. Luckily, he won out.

It wasn't until later in life that I discovered my money primarily came from the drug busts I alluded to earlier, but what the hell did I care? I was a killer. Would I now complain that the millions I had been entrusted with came from dirty money? In a word, no.

When I turned twenty-five, I received three million dollars. I gave two million to some stock wizard my father suggested, and he's been a godsend. I never have to worry about money for the rest of my life.

Isn't life grand?

"Did you hear me? William Ryan hired a new private investigator," my father said a second time.

This was after he'd spent ten minutes checking for bugs in his apartment. My father did this religiously every time he knew we were going to discuss the Annie Ryan murder. And from the early days after the murder, he said we should never discuss this over the phone. That included when cell phones became ubiquitous a few years later.

So, if we ever discussed what happened in December 1998, it was in a de-bugged home or condo.

My father knew more about the Annie Ryan case than anyone, including Mike Minter and myself.

What he did not know about was the other two murders I'd committed, and I had no plans on ever telling him.

"How many PIs is that now? 10? 15?" I laughed.

"This is not a laughing matter, Wade."

"It is to me."

I no longer had the fear of my father that I once had. When I had killed Annie, I was almost as scared of him as I was of the LAPD.

Not anymore.

"Shut up and listen," he said.

"Okay, but why is this PI any different?"

"Well, for one, he's not a PI."

"Then, why did you call him one?"

"I don't know what else to call him. He caught his mother's killer after twenty years, though, so he's got some good instincts."

"Yeah, well, so do I. And one of them was having you remove any connection between me and Annie."

"Jesus, Wade. You're becoming even more insufferable."

"Oh, Dad. You're just getting soft in your old age. Remember, you're the guy who stole drugs and money your whole time at the LAPD. Don't tell me I'm insufferable."

"Stop mentioning those things, you idiot."

"Why does it matter? I thought the condo was debugged?"

"Listen to me, Wade. I'm not going to say it twice. Stop talking about my time in the LAPD. Now, back to Annie Ryan."

"Wasn't that during your time in the LAPD?"

My father grabbed the closest pen and threw it at me. It grazed me lightly on the shoulder. I laughed.

"What a sorry-ass throw."

My father looked at me intently. I'd seen that same look from my mother over the years. It was the *'I'm responsible for raising this cretin'* look.

My mother would have a reason for thinking that. She was a good woman who had tried her best. Not my father, though. He was a bullying jerk who lied and stole decade after decade. Just because he was now a washed-up sixty-something doesn't mean he could judge me. He made me. I became who I am because of him.

"Do what you want then," my father said. "I'm just telling you that something feels different about this guy."

"What did you say his name is?"

"Bobby McGowan."

I realized I did recognize the name.

"The guy who caught his mother's killer?"

"Yes, son. I already said that."

I ignored that comment.

"Who has he talked to?" I asked.

"As far as I've been able to gather, William, Earl Razzle, Connor..."

"The usual suspects," I said, interrupting him.

"You didn't let me finish. And I've heard McGowan met up with a blast from your past."

"Who?"

"Gina Galasso."

"That bitch is still alive?"

"Do you have to refer to every girl as a bitch?"

"What happened to you, Dad? I might have to start calling you one."

I got that look again. This time it was more of an *'I raised an asshole'* look.

"To me? Jesus, what happened to you?" he said rhetorically.

"Well, maybe my father was a sexist who always cheated on his wife, and that created my hate for women, and then when I should have gone to jail for what I'd done, you rescued me, and I never learned any life lesson."

He shook his head.

"I don't know what to say."

"Fine, I'll talk," I said. "This Bobby McGowan is just another in a long line of people who will never catch me. Now, is there anything else you want to talk about?"

"No. Goodbye, Wade."

I left without reciprocating.

～

WHEN I GOT HOME to my oceanside Hermosa Beach apartment, I read up on Bobby McGowan.

I'd moved back to California about five years ago, and while I no longer lived in the Caribbean, I needed to live on the beach. So, Hermosa it was.

I hated to admit it, but I was intrigued by Bobby's story. I loved Conrad Drury's interaction with him and wanted to be involved in something like that.

I believed myself to be indestructible. It had been twenty-five years. No pseudo PI was going to catch me.

That was when I decided to send the first postcard.

Which turned into a second.

Which led him to us messaging on my itallstartedwithanAR account.

Which led to me buying a top-of-the-line voice distorter.

Which led to me hiding out at the Beverly Hilton and watching Bobby McGowan from outside as we talked.

Maybe I wasn't indestructible, but I'd sure been acting like I was.

～

ALL OF THIS culminated in another call from my father, several weeks after I first heard Bobby McGowan's name.

"You have to come over right now, Wade."

"What if I'm doing something right now?"

"Yeah, right. Your whole life has been a vacation," he said.

I couldn't help but laugh.

"I'll be there in an hour."

∼

ON THE RIDE OVER, I recreated our last meeting in my mind.

It had been about three weeks since I'd seen him, and I'd been a pretty big jerk. I'd try to be a little nicer today.

As I arrived, he was finishing up checking for bugs.

"No one is bugging your condo, Dad."

"Until they are actually bugging it...and then we'd both be rotting in jail for life. So excuse me if I'm trying to protect both of our asses."

"You done?" I asked.

My attempt at being nicer had gotten off to a rough start.

"I am now."

"Alright, what is it? You invited me over here."

"Things have gotten serious. That guy you wanted to dismiss, Bobby McGowan, has gotten closer than anyone ever has."

Maybe this was more serious than I'd assumed. Sure, he'd lucked into finding me online, but he still had no idea who I was in real life. Did he?

"What does he know?"

"Do you remember an old cop named Greg Quinones?"

"Yeah, you butted heads with him, right?"

"Yes. Same guy."

"What about him?"

"Well, he's always been a bit of a lush, and he went out drinking with some former cops last night. He drank way too much and started talking. He hangs with a group that I wasn't exactly friendly with, but one of them, Gil Castor, always had my back. So he called me this morning. I'm paraphrasing, but this is what Quinones said: 'Some PI calls me and says he wants to take me to lunch. He starts talking about the Annie Ryan case. He asks me like a million questions about it. Then the PI starts asking about that asshole Ed Bannie. The PI even asks a question about who can get into the evidence room. Which got me thinking. Do you think our old friend Ed was up to no good in that Annie Ryan case?'"

"Jesus," I said.

"Yeah, Jesus. Quinones is a bad drunk, and maybe he exaggerated a bit, but it sounds like your guy Bobby McGowan is starting to put a few things together."

"Don't call him my guy. And what could he possibly know? You scribbled over Annie's nickname for me in the diary, and I wasn't at the Christmas Eve party. Those are the only two things that could ever tie me to Annie."

"And Gina Galasso."

That was true.

"How would Robert know to look at the evidence room?"

"Robert?"

"Bobby, whatever," I said,

My father moved on, but I had to watch myself. If he had any idea I'd been conversing with Bobby McGowan, there's no telling what he would do.

"Maybe he got the evidence room signatures," my father said.

"What would that do?"

"It might have him question why I - someone not even officially a detective on the case - needed to see something from the evidence room only a few days after Annie went missing."

"Can't you just say Mike Minter told you to look for something?"

"I could. But I don't want to throw Mike under the bus if it's not necessary. And then he'd start getting suspicious."

My father had always insisted that he never told Mike Minter I had killed Annie Ryan. I'd always been dubious, thinking Minter had to be in on it.

"He never knew?" I asked, for probably the 10th time over the years.

"No. I've told you that a thousand times."

"I know, but I always figured you just didn't want me to know that he knew."

"If it ever got to the point where you were a suspect, I would have told him. But it never got that close. There was no need to let him know. It's better if we are the only two who know. As they say, three's a crowd."

"Did Quinones say if he's meeting Bobby again?"

"No, but it gets worse."

"Damn. What now?"

"There were two requests today for the evidence room. Not one, but two. On a twenty-five-year-old case. That will arouse suspicions, and not just from Mike Minter."

"Who was the second if it wasn't Bobby McGowan?"

"I'm guessing that he's behind both of them. Maybe he tried a few people in case one wasn't successful."

"Do you know who either of the two people are?"

"Not yet, but I will soon."

"So, what do we do now?"

"We wait."

"And if Bobby McGowan continues to creep closer?"

"That's an easy one. We kill him."

CHAPTER 36

BOBBY

*A*fter meeting with Earl Razzle and my phone call with William Ryan, I returned to the hotel and fell asleep within minutes. I hadn't planned it; it was only eleven in the morning.

The last several days had left me exhausted. That had never been more clear.

I woke up at noon, and Earl called me fifteen minutes later.

"This is much earlier than I expected," I said. "Got some good news?"

"Why don't you take a walk from your luxury hotel and find out?"

"You're too much. See you soon."

I ARRIVED at Earl's for the second time in three hours.

He greeted me at the front desk.

"Are we going to your office?"

"Nope," he said. "I've got someone in there. But I've got what you wanted."

He produced a manila envelope from behind his back.

"I hope no one ever says that Earl Razzle doesn't deliver," he said.

"And a lot quicker than expected," I said. "You're like the Domino's of private investigators."

Earl laughed.

"Yeah, I don't think I'll be adding that to my business cards."

"Thanks for this, Earl."

"You got it. Why don't you get back to me tonight."

"I will."

∼

I LEFT his office and called William.

"Hello, Bobby."

"I got the information quicker than I expected. I could look it over and probably head up to see you in a half hour or so."

"Great. I'll be here."

∼

I FIGURED there was no reason to return to the hotel, so I took the manila envelope to my car.

Theoretically, it would only take a few seconds to see if Ed Bannie had been in the evidence room in the days following Christmas Eve of 1998.

I removed the envelope's contents. It was two sheets of paper stapled together. The first entry was from March 2024, and the second was from February 2024. Obviously, these entries were going in reverse order, and I was okay with that. It helped build the tension as I made my way toward December 1998.

By the time I finished scanning the first page, I was already in August 1999. It made sense. The evidence would have been checked out much more in the months following Annie's death than in the years that followed.

I scanned the page, slowly making my way to the first person on the list.

I saw a few names I recognized from the police reports. Mike Minter had been to the evidence room more than everyone else combined. That was no surprise. He had become the lead detective after Phillip Chide passed away.

Speaking of Chide, I arrived at his first entry halfway up the second page. I knew there were less than six months left at that point. I started scanning more slowly.

THE OTHER ANNIE

I wouldn't allow myself to look up at the very top. It's like reading a great book and not letting your eyes glance ahead to see how the chapter ends.

Eventually, I reached the point where there were only about five left. I was covering them with my fingers so I couldn't peek ahead.

Finally, I arrived at the final two.

Phillip Chide was the second person to enter the evidence room on December 28th, 1998.

I removed my fingers from the last entry, and my suspicions were confirmed. Ed Bannie was the first to inhabit the evidence room on December 27th, 1998.

This didn't mean he was the first person in the evidence room. I'm sure they had already submitted a lot of evidence from William's house and Annie's parents' place, but Ed was the first to sign in to look at the evidence.

Why would Ed Bannie, who wasn't even one of the two lead investigators, have to look at evidence a few days after Annie Ryan disappeared? To me, the answer was obvious.

It was the same answer to the question as to why only two of Annie's journal entries were scribbled over in blue.

It's because Ed Bannie had returned home from vacation and discovered that his son had killed Annie Ryan. And I assumed that Wade knew - maybe Annie told him - that he was somewhere in that diary. Even if she hadn't told him, it would be logical that Ed Bannie would look at the diary out of fear that Annie had mentioned his son.

I put the sheets back in the manila envelope. No, it wasn't a smoking gun, but it solidified my opinion of what happened on Christmas Eve and in the days that followed.

I DROVE to William's house, and as I approached, I started to consider where Annie would have met Wade.

I ruled out Wade walking into the house. Whatever his motives were on the night in question, I didn't think he wanted people to know he was there.

Had they met on the lawn outside all of the rooms? Had he met her amongst the trees? Had he parked his car down, away from the top level, and had Annie meet him there? Had he killed her at William's house or waited until later?

While more puzzle pieces kept falling into place, I still had a million questions.

∼

WILLIAM WAS WAITING for me at the top.

I parked my car and went over and shook his hand.

"How do they like this car over at the Beverly Hilton?"

"I always self-park it," I said. "You don't think I'm going to risk the valet handling a car of this magnitude, do you?"

William smiled.

"You're in a chipper mood," he said. "You must have found something."

"Let's talk," I said.

We walked down to the house from the elevated parking area. I had left the manila envelope in the car. I still wasn't sure how much information I wanted to give William Ryan. Did he deserve to hear everything? Yes, but I wasn't sure I was ready. A voice in my head was still somewhat suspicious of William, even though I had zero evidence to back that up.

∼

WE MADE our way to his study, where I'd accepted this job opportunity one month before.

"First things first," William said and handed me a check. "Ten thousand big ones for your second month. I know it's officially a few days away, but since I've agreed to keep you on, I'll pay you now."

And I was withholding information from this guy? It didn't seem right.

"Thank you very much, William."

"You're welcome. Now, since I'm paying you the big bucks, I'd like to hear everything you've learned over the last week or so."

It suddenly hit me just how much I'd kept from him: the distorted phone call, Kira Palova, Gina Galasso, Hearing Wade and Ed Bannie's names for the first time, Cassius Fields, Greg Quinones, and finally, the manila envelope.

"Sorry I haven't updated you as much as I should have," I said.

"That's alright. You're here to do that now."

William Ryan looked stern, almost as if he knew I'd been holding out on him.

"So, it started with a visit from my father," I said.

And then, over the next ten minutes, I told him just about everything that had happened.

I was about to mention what Earl Razzle had just given me when William interrupted.

"Well, you sure have been busy," he said, but it wasn't a compliment. "Maybe I should have clarified this when I hired you, Bobby. When you get important information, you are to relay it to me. Do you understand?"

"Yes, I'm sorry."

"I'm not sure that you are. You had a suspect's name in my niece's death several days ago, and I haven't heard a peep from you. Do you understand why I'm upset?"

We were both still standing, which just added to the uncomfortableness.

William was holding onto a Crystal Rocks glass, and I could tell he was gripping it tight. I thought it might explode in his hands.

"I didn't want to tell you anything unless I was certain," I said.

"Are you certain that Wade Bannie killed Annie?"

"Well, no."

"But you mentioned him, anyway. So there goes that theory."

He was extremely fired up.

In a shock I never expected, he took the Rocks Glass and threw it up against the far wall. I stared in disbelief.

And instead of apologizing, he doubled down.

"What else have you learned?" he yelled.

It was the first time I'd seen William Ryan upset, and boy, was it something to behold. He was furious.

"You better start talking, Bobby."

"I have a working theory," I said, trying to calm my nerves without looking at the shattered glass.

"That's a start. Let's hear it."

"As I told you, the two entries in Annie's diary from December 1998 were crossed out in blue ink. Everything else in the diary had been written in or crossed out with purple ink."

"Keep going."

"And when I learned those entries contained the phrase '*the other Annie*' and who that was referring to, I assumed someone close to Wade Bannie probably scribbled over it. That's the only thing that made sense. Why would anyone else do it? Gina had told me that Wade's father was a big-time police officer, so my thoughts immediately went to him. And today, Earl Razzle got me a list of everyone who checked out things from the evidence room throughout this investigation."

"And let me guess, Ed Bannie's name is on there," William said, his voice returning to normal.

"Yes. He was the first one on December 27th."

"And this does not mean he put evidence in the evidence room."

"No, it means he visited the evidence room."

"So you think Phillip Chide or some other cop went to Annie's parents' house, probably on Christmas Day, and kept the diary as evidence."

"Yes. Ed Bannie was on vacation. If he'd been with the cops at Annie's house, I imagine that journal never would have made it into evidence."

"Why not just steal it from the evidence room?"

"I've pondered that question several times. There are two possibilities. He was worried they'd discover that the diary had gone missing and he'd been in the evidence room. That would certainly arouse suspicion. And two, he probably thought he'd done enough by scribbling over the entries that mentioned *'the other Annie.'*"

"And you believe this Kira woman?"

"She didn't pull the other Annie out of thin air," I said.

"Point taken."

We stood for several seconds in silence.

"I'm sorry about my temper," William finally said. "This is twenty-five years of pent-up pressure. And I felt like you were holding out on me a little bit."

"That's okay. I guess I was." I said.

"Plus, I never did like that rocks glass," he said.

I gave him a courtesy laugh.

"So you really think Ed Bannie's kid might have murdered Annie?" William asked.

"I think it's more likely than not."

"I've known Ed for three decades."

"Do you know him well?"

"No, but we'd see each other at functions around town. Fundraisers and the like."

"What was your personal opinion of him?"

"Nice in person, but I could tell he was tough."

When I didn't answer immediately, William added, "But if he helped his son out, I hope he rots in fucking hell."

"I don't blame you for thinking that," I said.

"The problem I see, Bobby, is that you don't have any hard evidence. Unless I'm missing something."

"Well, there is no body, and it's been twenty-five years, so it was always going to be based on circumstantial evidence. But circumstantially, I think it's pretty strong."

"I'm a little more dubious. I don't think what you have would get him convicted in court."

"You're probably right about that, and that's why I'm going to keep at this and see what I can come up with next."

It sounded like another generic answer, but William didn't jump on me this time. He probably figured I'd seen enough of his temper for one day.

"You've done some great work, Bobby. I look forward to seeing what happens in the coming days. I'd ask for your plan of action, but maybe I should just sit back and let you do your thing. It's working so far."

He was trying to be the nice guy now.

"Thank you, William. Is there anything else?"

"Not for now. Once again, I apologize for my outburst. It was uncalled for."

"No need to apologize," I said.

"Thank you. Now, off you go," William said and smiled.

I walked to the door and remembered something.

"Next time we talk, can we discuss possibly switching hotels? It's a great spot; I just wouldn't mind a change of scenery."

"Let's talk tomorrow," William said.

∼

WHEN I ARRIVED BACK in Beverly Hills, I got a call from Cassius Fields.

"Hello, Cassius."

"I've got some information for you," he said.

"Shoot. I should have called you. I was able to get the list through another avenue."

"So you're telling me I did all this for nothing?"

"I'm sorry. If you want some good news, my suspicions were confirmed, and you're one step closer to writing a groundbreaking article."

"I looked at what I was given."

"And?"

"And you'd mentioned Ed Bannie several times, so I looked for him.

And I saw he was the first to check something out from the evidence room."

"Sort of," I said. "He was the first person to go into the evidence room. We don't know what he quote unquote checked out."

"But you think you do?"

"Yes," I said.

"You know what the thing is about writing a long-form article?"

I could tell where this was headed but decided to play along.

"What is that, Cassius?"

"You need to do your research well before you put pen to paper or fingers to laptop. I need to know the background of the story. To get an overall sense of what I'll be writing about."

"I'd talk to Greg Quinones about Ed Bannie and some of the illegal shit he was up to."

"And what makes you think Quinones will talk to me?"

"He talked to me and didn't know me from Adam. The guy loves to talk, especially if he's had a few drinks. Plus, he told me that you were a good guy."

"Maybe he said that, but he didn't think I went far enough in my articles. He thought my pieces on the LAPD were too saccharine."

"Well, now's your chance to write a more substantial piece," I said.

"How were you so sure I'd want to write this article? Didn't I tell you I wanted to get to this age, and that's why I hadn't written a hit piece on Ed Bannie ?"

"You did tell me that, but now you've already hit that age number. Everything from here on is gravy."

Cassius laughed loudly on the other end.

"Keep in touch."

∽

IT HAD BEEN A FEW DAYS, and I decided to check on Gina Galasso.

"Hello, Bobby. It's nice to hear from you."

That is hardly the reaction I would have gotten earlier in our friendship.

"How are you holding up, Gina?"

"I'm okay, I guess. How's that investigation coming? You looking into Wade Bannie?"

"It's a slow-moving process, but yes, I am," I said, trying to be somewhat vague.

THE OTHER ANNIE

"I'd love to see that guy pay for what he did. He killed Annie, didn't he?"

"I can't be certain," I said.

"But you think there's a good chance?"

"Yes, Gina, I do."

I could hear a quiet sob starting in the background.

"I've started to think how different my life would have been if Annie Ryan had never been killed. Kai would probably still be alive, and maybe we'd still be together. And it's all that jerk Wade's fault."

"Gina, I think it's in your best interest not to get too involved emotionally. I don't know what will happen, and I don't want you getting your hopes up."

"You found his nickname in Annie's journal, and it said he had a bad idea for Christmas Eve. That seems pretty obvious to me."

"It's not exactly evidence of murder," I said.

"Isn't it enough to get a warrant?"

"Probably not. And don't take this the wrong way, but what exactly will a warrant get us? This all happened twenty-five years ago. I doubt Wade has kept any evidence that long."

"Maybe he kept a necklace or a bracelet. I hear of killers doing that all the time."

"That's possible, I guess, but I'm not ready to go to the police or the district attorney yet."

"Okay. Hopefully soon."

"Yes, hopefully soon. Do you need anything?" I asked.

I'd come to care about Gina Galasso. I'd done a 180 on her.

"I'm alright. Trying to cut down on my cigarettes, but it's making me eat more."

"I'll bring a pizza next time, and we'll pig out."

Gina laughed over the phone. It was nice to hear.

"Extra pepperoni and extra cheese," she said.

"Funny, that's what my cardiologist always recommends."

"You're funny. I'm sorry I was such a jerk to you the first few times."

She was apologizing again. I think Gina had been doing a lot of thinking lately.

"Don't be sorry," I said. "You were harboring a terrible secret. And you didn't even know you were harboring it. Wade Bannie wasn't even at the Christmas party. You never could have suspected him."

"Oh, but I did. I should have gone to the police."

It made me quickly ponder what would have happened to Gina if she had. Would they have gotten rid of her? I sensed that Ed Bannie would have done anything to keep his son out of jail. Maybe it was best for Gina that she never said anything.

"You were a scared teenager, and like I said, no one considered him a suspect. You need to stop beating yourself up over it."

"Okay, thanks, Bobby."

She still sounded like a scared teenager.

"Listen, Gina. Why don't we plan on meeting in a day or two? I'll come by your apartment and bring that cardiologist's special with me."

"That sounds great."

"Okay, talk soon."

I heard a few sniffles as she got off the phone.

CHAPTER 37

<u>WADE</u>

*E*verything changed the day my father mentioned Greg Quinones and the evidence room.

I woke up that morning thinking everything was going to boil over soon. After all, it had for twenty-five years. Why would this be any different?

I checked my email, but nothing warranted a reply. I had a few texts from girls in Hermosa Beach, and maybe I'd get back to them later—not at eight in the morning.

I clicked on my Instagram app, not expecting to find anything relevant. I hadn't posted for a few weeks, and the further removed from a post, the less likely people were to comment on it.

I was pleasantly surprised to see that there were two notifications. I clicked on them, and I could tell one was a like, and one was a comment. They both came from the same Instagram handle: GinGal.

Must be a gin-loving gal!

The like was of my latest photo, which I'd taken a month ago while vacationing in Hawaii. I was on a catamaran with a drink in hand and a gorgeous Hawaiian sunset behind me. This was before I knew Bobby McGowan, and I was a bit more carefree.

I scrolled to the bottom to see what GinGal had posted.

I was left stupefied by what I read.

"Wade Bannie, a.k.a. the other Annie, is a killer, and I hope he's brought to justice soon. Annie Ryan deserved better, and so did Kai Butler."

The time stamp read 2:37 a.m.

I immediately deleted the post and then yelled, "FUCK!" at the top of my lungs.

Within seconds, I realized what GinGal stood for: Gina Galasso. She'd taken the first three letters of each name and made it sound like she was a woman who drank gin.

No, this was Gina Galasso, the one fucking woman in this world who knew Annie's nickname for me. She was a more significant threat to me than Bobby McGowan was. She always had been.

But what had changed?

Gina could have gone to the cops any time over the years and had never chosen to. She could have posted on my Instagram at any time.

Why had she chosen now to poke the bear? What evidence had Bobby found to convince Gina that I had killed Annie?

I wracked my brain and couldn't come up with a good answer.

There was no DNA, and the car I used to pick up Annie and eventually dispose of her had been compacted years ago. Could one of the valet drivers have seen my license plate and held on to it all these years? No chance. I was too far down the road. None of them saw me.

What about the news regarding the evidence room?

No, it didn't look good that my father went in there when he wasn't even on the case.

But what did it prove? Nothing.

My father had scribbled over my name in the diary. Maybe they had concluded that my father had somehow tampered with some evidence.

But even that didn't seem like enough for Gina to attack me.

I guess the why didn't really matter.

What did matter was that Gina Galasso had gone on Instagram and accused me of murdering Annie Ryan. This wasn't good.

She even insinuated that I'd murdered Kai Butler, which I hadn't.

If there was any silver lining, the photo was from several weeks ago, and no one likely saw what Gina had posted. If she'd commented immediately after I'd posted a picture, other people would undoubtedly see it. Thank God I didn't post anything yesterday.

I didn't block Gina in case I had to contact her and try to talk her down. Depending on which direction this goes, contacting her could prove useful.

I did turn my notifications on, however, so if she posted something again, I'd see it right away and be able to delete it.

I called my father and told him I was coming to see him.

∼

FOR ONCE, he'd already debugged the place by the time I got there.

And considering the jolt I received that morning, I probably wouldn't have given him shit about it. Something I couldn't quite understand was happening, and being overly vigilant was perhaps a good idea.

"This must be important," my father said.

He was wearing a white t-shirt and army cargo shorts. He looked older than his sixty-five years.

"Yeah, you could say that. Gina Galasso accused me of murder on Instagram."

"What?"

"You heard me."

"When?"

"She posted it at 2:37 this morning. I saw it when I woke at eight and deleted it immediately."

"As you know, I don't understand social media stuff. So talk to me like I'm a third grader."

"Okay."

"Did anyone else see her post?"

"I don't know," I said. "My guess would be no. She commented on a post from several weeks ago, and no one else had commented in at least a week."

"But you can't be sure?"

"No, I can't be sure," I admitted.

"Once you delete it, it's permanently gone, right?"

"Correct. No one can see it."

"Can you ensure that she doesn't have the ability to do that again?"

"I could block her."

"And I'm assuming you did that."

"No."

"Why the hell not?"

"It's the only way I know of getting ahold of Gina. I thought that might prove valuable."

"I get your point, but what if she posts again?"

"I will get an immediate alert, and I'll delete it. And if Gina does it a second time, I'll block her. She posted it at 2:30 in the morning. Last I heard, Gina was kind of a mess these days. There's an outside chance she might not even remember posting it."

"That doesn't make me feel any better. Nor should it put you at ease."

"I'm not at ease. Far from it."

"See, you dismissed this Bobby McGowan guy, and I'm sure Gina's post is somehow related to his investigation."

"So, what do we do?" I asked.

My father thought long and hard.

"If you have any good options other than killing her, I'm all ears," he said.

"I'm trying to figure out how this escalated so quickly," I said. "The only time you went into the evidence room was to scribble out my nickname in Annie's diary. Correct?"

"Yes."

"Is there a chance you didn't scribble hard enough, and they could decipher what was below it?"

"I'd say that's unlikely, but I guess it's not impossible."

"Where is that diary now?" I asked.

"It was returned to Annie's father probably about a year after she died."

"Well, we know that bag of bones didn't have anything to do with this."

"Let's assume it's in Bobby McGowan's possession now."

"I'd say that's a fair guess. Do you remember precisely what Annie said? It's been so long."

"It was something like 'The Other Annie has a scary plan for Christmas Eve.' Something along those lines."

"It wouldn't convict me on its own, but it is pretty damning," I said.

"They'd need a lot more than that. And the car you picked her up in is long gone. The sheets, comforter, and anything else that could have had Annie Ryan's DNA on them are also gone. And maybe most importantly, her body was never discovered. Time is on your side, Wade. They would never try to convict someone based on a diary entry."

"And I'll ask you this one last time: Does Mike Minter know?"

"For the three hundred and fortieth fucking time, he does not."

"I just had to make sure. No one else knows what happened except for me and you. Gina Galasso and Bobby may have their opinions, but they don't have any concrete evidence."

"Correct."

"And there's no secret evidence that could convict me?" I asked.

"No. There's nothing I can think of. Just because you can't be convicted doesn't mean we can continue having Gina Galasso accuse you of this. What if she went to the cops, and Mike Minter was forced to look back over the case with you as a possible suspect? Then, he might start asking our neighbors questions or trying to find out what we did with the car you had in December of 1998. As it stands now, they would never charge you - much less convict you - of the crime. But if Gina Galasso starts yelling all over town, that could change."

I'd committed three murders. I wasn't going to be a shrinking violet now.

"Could you hire someone to do it?"

I didn't have to say what "it" was.

"One man still owes me his life and would do anything for me."

"Archibald?"

"Yes."

We only ever referred to him by his first name. His last name was borderline comical and didn't do justice to how frightening a man Archibald was. Truth be told, neither did his first name.

"Should we call him?" I asked.

"We? If we decide to do this, I will call him."

Archibald was my father's friend - a former cop - and he was laying down the law. If anyone was going to talk to Archibald, it would be him.

"Okay," I said.

"You should consider booking a flight somewhere, Wade. If this goes bad, maybe it's time for you to get out of Dodge. And this time, stop posting on that stupid fucking Instagram. I never understood that."

"I'll take that under advisement."

"Don't be a smart ass. Gina couldn't have posted that if you didn't have Instagram."

His statement hit home.

They might look at her social media if we did away with Gina. I imagine that's pretty standard in murder investigations these days. Since I deleted her comment, I didn't think they could trace it, but I couldn't be sure. Probably better to be safe, I told myself.

"You're getting your wish right now," I said.

"What?"

"I'm deleting my Instagram."

"Do you have any of the other ones?"

"Just Facebook."

"Why don't you delete that also?"

"I will. Give me a minute."

It took me longer than expected, but ten minutes later, I was altogether erased from social media.

"Why don't you take a day trip tomorrow, Wade? Make yourself seen and heard. Get drunk at a bar late at night. Do you get what I'm saying?"

He was referring to what might happen to Gina Galasso.

"Loud and clear."

"Good."

"What are we going to do about Bobby McGowan?" I asked.

"He's nothing without Gina," my father said, echoing my thoughts from earlier.

But now, I wasn't so sure.

It wasn't a singular event that changed my mind. But Bobby had found me on 52solutions. He'd talked to me on the phone. He had spoken to Greg Quinones and Gina Galasso, and who knows who else? I think it's safe to say I'd been underestimating him all this time.

"We couldn't get rid of both at the same time?"

"That would make things even more complicated," my father said. "The guy investigating Annie's murder and a woman he's interviewed both being killed? If it's just Gina, the cops won't draw a connection. It could be anything. If both her and Bobby McGowan end up dead, we're sending them a road map back to us."

It made sense.

"How about scaring Bobby in some way? So when he finds out about Gina, he'll know that if he doesn't stand down, he's next."

"I'll talk to Archibald, but I'm sure that can be arranged."

"Good."

"I shouldn't have to tell you this, Wade, but after you leave my condo today, let's not talk on the phone for a few days. If there is an absolute emergency, come by here, but it would be better if we didn't converse until after this is all over."

"I hear you loud and clear, Pops."

"What a weird thing to say. Do you realize just how serious this is? This is the most crucial juncture since 1998."

I stood up and patted my father on the back.

"It's going to work out. It always does. And we both know that Archibald is the best."

"On that point, I agree."

"I'm going to start looking at flights."

"Make sure you come see your old man before you go."

"I'll come say goodbye. I won't fly out until a few days after Gina Galasso is dead."

"You could leave sooner."

"And miss all the fun?"

We shared a laugh.

CHAPTER 38

BOBBY

For the first time in what must have been a week, Sunday was a somewhat mellow day.

When Monday came around, we officially entered the second month of the investigation and a new month: July.

With the way we were moving, I didn't think there would be a third month.

Now, that might sound like I assumed Wade Bannie would be arrested for the murder of Annie Ryan and my work would be over. That's not exactly what I envisioned. I feared there was an excellent chance that if I laid all my chips on the table, the police or the district attorney might say it's not enough and never arrest Wade Bannie.

I not only thought that was a possibility, I thought it was the likelihood.

~

I WAS TRYING to think outside of the box again.

I'd done this once before, leading me to Adam Toon, a.k.a. Toon the Loon. I hadn't talked to him or Amber Ryan in several days. I'd come to think of them, if not as friends, at least as friendly toward me, but the investigation had gone in a different direction, and I hadn't needed their help as much. I was no longer investigating their family; I was convinced it was an outsider.

But how did I proceed with Wade Bannie?

What to do? What to do? What to do?

Think. Think. Think.

∽

IT WAS ALREADY MID-AFTERNOON, and I had accomplished jack squat, so I decided to head out and grab a late lunch. Maybe that would jar something loose, and I'd formulate a plan.

I took the elevator down to the lobby and passed my favorite employee at the front desk. She always just assumed I was up to no good these days. I reminded myself to call William later and ask about changing hotels.

Over thirty days in the same place is enough for anyone. I don't care if it's at a 5-star hotel in one of the wealthiest zip codes in America.

When I arrived outside, I bypassed the valet stand on my way to the parking garage. I said hi to them, and one of them gave me grief for not using the valet.

"Your car is not so bad," he said. "We see you drive by."

We both laughed.

That's what happens when you are at a hotel for a month. You become friendly with the most random people.

I was almost to the garage when he yelled, "Seriously, park it with us when you get back."

I turned around and yelled, "I just might do that."

As I swiveled around, I noticed an odd-looking guy walking away from the cab stand. He was wearing jeans, a long-sleeve shirt, and a hat.

Someone hadn't told him it was July in Los Angeles, California, and it was supposed to be eighty-seven degrees today.

Why was he walking away from the cab stand without his car? Only weirdos like me had a reason for doing that.

Maybe I was overreacting. I'd been under a lot of stress lately and noticed anything I deemed out of the ordinary.

∽

I ARRIVED at the parking garage and took the elevator up to the fourth floor. I'd tried to keep my car parked in the same section the whole time I'd been there. For the most part, I'd succeeded.

I turned my car on and reversed out of the spot. I headed toward the exit on the first floor. There weren't many cars in the garage. I imagined that would change in the next day or two as we neared the 4th of July on Thursday.

As I rounded the second story, I saw a dark blue van parked in the middle of the parking garage. I slowed down and realized there was no way around it.

I was still a good forty feet from the car's rear bumper and would not be getting any closer. My paranoid mind told me this would be an easy place for an ambush.

It was an odd place for a car to stall. You wouldn't overheat in the thirty seconds it would take to get to the street level. If your car didn't start at all, it would still be in your parking spot, not in the middle of the parking garage. The fact that it was a windowless van only made it more menacing.

I had a bad feeling about this and didn't want to be near the van any longer.

I put my foot on the gas and reversed up the parking garage.

No crazy gunman came running after me, but I wasn't going to take any chances. I continued to reverse until I was somewhere on the third story. Then, I saw two other cars approaching me as they descended the garage. I pulled into a spot and got in line behind them once they passed. I was no longer scared about an ambush with two cars in front of me.

I felt even safer when another car started following behind me. We drove from the third story to the second, and as I looked down, I could see the blue van pulling into a parking spot.

I slowed down and looked in its direction as I passed by it. Just then, the out-of-place man standing by the valet stepped out from behind the van. We made eye contact, and I saw him quickly glance in front and behind me.

I couldn't be sure, but I thought he was eyeing his surroundings. If he had a gun, I would be a sitting duck at the mercy of the cars in front of and behind me.

We continued staring at each other, but he didn't lean to grab anything, which would have made me panic.

A second later, the car in front of me was moving, and I accelerated and got way too close to his back bumper. I looked in my rearview mirror, but the man disappeared behind the van.

I arrived at the first floor and sped away from the Beverly Hilton, only feeling safe once I had made my way out to a crowded Beverly Hills street.

~

I LOOKED at myself in the rear-view mirror.

Beads of sweat were coming down my forehead.

Had I just avoided an ambush?

I couldn't be sure, but it sure felt that way.

The guy hadn't brandished a weapon, so I couldn't exactly go to the cops. What would I tell them? That a van was having car trouble, and two minutes later, several of us drove by the van safely.

They wouldn't exactly put out an APB for that.

Should I call and tell William?

I didn't feel like visiting him after seeing the full extent of his temper a few days previous.

What I was sure of, and no one could change my mind on this, was that I needed to get out of the Beverly Hilton. Wade Bannie had spied on me there, and now there's a chance an ambush had been set up for me.

I needed to find a new hotel, something out of the way, and somewhere they could never find me—whoever they were. I did get a pretty good look at the guy's face and knew I'd recognize him if I saw him again.

That voice in the back of my head made another appearance. He said I needed to drop this case and move back to Santa Barbara today, but I knew I was too stubborn. I was close to solving this case, and there was no turning back now.

That didn't mean I had to be a sitting duck at the Beverly Hilton.

So, as I started taking Wilshire into the heart of Hollywood, I vowed to find a dingy motel to stay at for the rest of my investigation.

Hopefully, one where you didn't have to leave a name or throw down a credit card. I'd often heard about the seedy side of Hollywood. That's where I wanted to be.

~

WHEN I ARRIVED IN HOLLYWOOD, I pulled into a strip mall with a Mexican restaurant, a weed distillery, a donut shop, and a pizza joint.

If the weed did its job, you'd be surrounded by solid culinary options.

I took out my phone and typed cheap Hollywood motels into Google.

As always, there were too many recommendations. I didn't know which one to click on. I wish Google could find a way to streamline it and give us the top five options or something similar. I guess that would lead to too much importance being put into making that top five, but I digress.

By name alone, I knew the motel I wanted to stay at: The Rinky Dink Motel. I'd never heard a better name for a motel. It was perfect.

I called the phone number.

"Rinky Dink Motel."

"Hello, sir. I'm visiting LA, and my wallet was stolen last night. Luckily, I still have cash. Do you guys let people pay with cash and not a credit card?"

"Yes."

"And you have vacancies?"

"Yes."

He was a man of few words.

"Okay, thanks. I'll be there soon."

He got off the phone before risking having to utter a two-word sentence.

∽

THE MOTEL WAS on Hollywood Boulevard, which should be the coolest street in the world on nothing more than name alone.

But it had gone through some tough times over the years and was much more on the seedy Hollywood side. It was the polar opposite of Beverly Hills, and at least for the moment, precisely what I was looking for.

I pulled into the Rinky Dink Motel and intentionally parked my car in the back. Now that the guy in the Beverly Hilton parking garage knew what car I drove, there was no reason to take any chances by leaving my car out front, even in a dilapidated old motel like the Rinky Dink.

I approached the front desk and was greeted by the one-word-sentence guy.

"Hello," he said.

"I called earlier about renting a room."

"Name?"

Without having to put a credit card down, I knew I could make up a name. I wouldn't put it past Wade and Ed Bannie to call every hotel in LA to find out where I was staying once they found out I'd left the Beverly Hilton.

Oh, shit!

I realized Annie's diary was still there. I needed that going forward. It was a massive part of the puzzle. I could also use my clothes and laptop, but they almost seemed secondary. Maybe I'd get an Uber there at about three in the morning and grab everything.

"Name?" he repeated.

"Ernest Hammett," I said, taking my favorite authors' first and last names: Ernest Hemingway and Dashiell Hammett.

It sounded like a fake name from the 1920s, but one-word-sentence guy couldn't be bothered to care.

"It's $100 a night."

Only in Hollywood could you find the nastiest motel on this side of the Mississippi, which still cost you a hundred bucks.

I gave him a hundred.

He didn't mention that I'd taken it out of a wallet that had supposedly been stolen.

"Sign," he said.

Not sign here; just sign.

I signed it, and he gave me an old-school key—that's right, one with a key on the end.

"You're #20," he said.

I left the front office and walked back to Room #20, which I was happy to see was also near the back of the motel, close to my car.

I opened the door, and at the very least, it didn't smell. But the decor was awful, and even Ernest Hammett in 1928 would have thought the same.

The bathroom was tiny as well, but what did I expect?

I was staying at The Rinky Dink Motel.

∽

I SAT BACK on the bed.

Was I being too nonchalant about all of this? Laughing at the motel's name and the one-word guy operating the front desk?

After all, I might have avoided an ambush earlier today. If I had pulled up directly behind the van, he could have shot me and then jumped in his van and driven away.

Was there a license plate on the van? I don't remember seeing one.

What exactly could I do, though? Tell somebody else. Most rational people would tell me I'd overreacted, but they weren't there. I know what I saw, and I know what I felt.

I could no longer sit back and wait to see what happened next. I had to play offense.

I started to formulate a plan.

∼

I FOUND the closest copy shop through Google, and despite it being only a quarter-mile away, I decided to drive.

I'd seen the neighborhood when I pulled into the Rinky Dink Motel. I was going to avoid walking when possible.

∼

"HOW CAN I HELP YOU?"

He was a middle-aged man with a monstrous gut.

"I wanted to type something up and print out a hundred copies. And I wanted it to be the size of a flier, not your standard eight and a half by eleven."

"Okay, that's easy enough."

He led me to one of his computers and told me which printer it would come out of.

I knew my plan, but now that I was at the computer, I didn't know exactly what I wanted to type.

I came up with the following:

"On December 24th, 1998, Wade Bannie killed Annie Ryan. His father, Ed Bannie, helped him cover it up. My name is Bobby McGowan, and I'm looking into Annie's death. If I end up dead, it was Wade and Ed Bannie who had me killed."

When I thought it was sufficient, I specified one hundred copies and the flier size and pressed send. I hadn't noticed the employee walking around the store behind me.

I caught him red-handed, looking at my screen. He looked like a kid caught with his hand in the cookie jar. He quickly looked away, and I wondered how much he'd had the chance to read.

I gathered up my fliers and faced them upside down as I approached to pay. He gave me a look over but didn't say anything besides, "One hundred flyers is seventy-five dollars even."

It sure sounded like a lot for these razor-thin pieces of paper, but I didn't complain. I paid with cash, just like I had with the hotel.

I left the store and was about to drive back to The Rinky Dink when I saw a T-Mobile store across the street.

Having a backup phone that no one knew the number for might be a good idea.

I walked over to the store, and within fifteen minutes, I had my own "burner" phone. It was that simple.

At that point, I returned to The Rinky Dink.

∽

A QUICK THOUGHT came to mind, and it was a menacing one.

If they were trying to kill me, is there anyone else who could have been in the line of fire? My mind immediately went to Gina Galasso. She was the only person - besides myself - who knew who *'The Other Annie'* referred to. And while my testimony would be hearsay, Gina's would not.

If someone had ears to my investigation, it hadn't been a secret I'd met with Gina. Several people knew.

I was on edge as I reached for my phone. Gina probably wouldn't answer a number she didn't recognize, so I used my own phone.

I expected Gina to answer the call, and my nerves would be calmed.

But that didn't happen.

The phone rang and rang and rang to no avail. I left Gina a message asking her to call me immediately. I did the same with a text.

I tried back ten minutes later and then twenty minutes later.

Nothing.

I tried calling an hour later and then two hours later. It was past 8:00 p.m. at this point.

Still nothing.

I was now seriously worried something had happened to Gina Galasso.

CHAPTER 39

BOBBY

I knew what I had to do.

It took me a minute to remember the name of her apartment complex: The Shores. It was ironic, considering the place was a dump, and even though it was in Santa Monica, it was a good half mile from the Pacific Ocean.

"The Shores," a male voice answered.

I had a feeling this guy would be about as talkative as the guy from The Rinky Dink.

"I'm friends with Gina Galasso, a tenant at The Shores, and I haven't been able to reach her for several days."

A little exaggeration was warranted.

"Okay."

"And I was wondering if you could do a welfare check?"

"We ain't supposed to do that ourselves," he said.

"Can you ask the police?"

"I suppose I could."

"Well then, will you? It's been a week since I've gotten ahold of her. I'm worried."

"It hasn't been no week. I saw Gina yesterday morning. Maybe she doesn't want to see you, but she certainly hasn't been missing that long."

He'd caught me in a lie and rubbed it in my nose, but arguing with the guy was unnecessary. He'd probably just take longer if I pressed him.

"Maybe I'm wrong about how long it's been, but I'm very concerned."

"What's your name and number?"

"My name is Bobby McGowan, and my phone number is 805-555-2752."

"Okay, Mr. McGowan, either the Santa Monica police department or I will get back to you. It's already eight p.m., so maybe later tonight, but if not, tomorrow morning."

"Please try your best to make it tonight."

"I'll try," he said, but his voice didn't convince me.

I got off the phone.

I TRIED Gina one more time myself, but she didn't answer.

There was a logical reason why she wouldn't want to talk to me. I'd brought her nothing but grief since coming into her life. It only worsened after I asked her what *'The Other Annie'* meant.

I could hardly blame her if she didn't want to talk to me.

And yet, I felt this was something more ominous. I didn't think it was Gina ignoring my phone calls. Call it a hunch.

If the Bannies were going after me, it would also make sense to go after her.

I had to warn her. I couldn't just sit at my motel, waiting to hear back.

THIRTY-FIVE MINUTES LATER, I was pulling into The Shores.

I walked up to Gina's apartment and knocked on the door. On my way over, I called two more times with no luck.

There was no answer, so I knocked again.

I tried looking in the apartment, but the drapes were mostly closed. I could see through a tiny little section, and I peeked in.

I saw a lamp lying on the ground. It was hardly proof there had been a struggle, but that's still where my thoughts went.

I had to get into her apartment.

I hadn't come all this way not to.

I walked a few feet from the apartment and made a phone call.

"The Shores."

"This is Bobby McGowan. I called earlier about Gina Galasso."

"Listen, I told you this might not happen till tomorrow. I saw Gina yesterday. I'm sure she's fine."

"Do you live on site?"

"Yes. I'm down on the lower level."

"Well, get up to Gina's apartment. I'm up here. And bring your universal key."

"Sir, I can't just let you into Gina's apartment without a good reason."

"Get up here right freaking now and bring the damn key. If not, I'll call the police myself."

I heard him grunt, but I think I'd gotten through to him.

A few minutes later, a man way too old to be looking after an apartment complex approached Gina's place.

"Son, you can't just pop into people's apartments without a good reason."

"Listen to me, old man," I said. "Gina is in danger, and I looked into her apartment. It looks like World War III in there."

A tipped-over lamp was hardly World War III, but exaggeration continued to be warranted.

"Gina's not known for her cleanliness."

"If you don't open the door right now, I will kick the glass window in."

He got the point and fuddled around with his keys.

"If she's in there naked or with some guy, this is on you."

"Fine," I said.

He opened the door and then took a step back.

I took a step into the apartment and called Gina's name.

No answer.

The lamp was on the ground, but besides that, the place looked cleaner than usual. There were no half-filled ashtrays or clothes spread all over the ground. In fact, the lamp had a cord tied around the bottom of it, and it looked like it had been set on its side intentionally.

This should have put my mind at ease, but I still had a sinking feeling. I made my way toward what had to be her bedroom. I shouted her name twice but got no response.

I put my hand on the doorknob. I didn't want to do this, but I knew in my heart that I had to.
Please, please, please don't be dead, Gina!
I slowly turned the doorknob and looked inside.

CHAPTER 40

BOBBY

Gina's body was contorted at a weird angle, and I knew she was dead.

I walked to the bed, and my worst nightmare had come true. Gina was lying on her back, her hands covering her face. One leg was spread out wide, and the other knee was bent upward, partially covering her lower abdomen, almost like she was trying to block something.

She had blood stains all over her chest area. She was wearing a white nightgown, and it was apparent she'd been shot. Because she was wearing nightwear, I figured it happened late last night or early this morning.

More than anything, I wanted to grab Gina's hand and tell her how sorry I was. I'd gotten her into this. Not because of any malicious intent, but I'd still been the one to reel her back into the Annie Ryan case.

But I knew I couldn't touch her hand. I couldn't risk contaminating a crime scene.

So, instead, I just sat on the ground next to her and started crying.

"Oh, Gina, I'm so sorry. You deserved so much better."

I wiped my eyes, knowing this wasn't the right time. Even my tears could contaminate the scene.

A few seconds later, I heard the old man.

"Is everything alright in there?" he yelled.
"No, it's not. Call the Santa Monica Police right now."
"Are you sure?"
"Do you want to come back here yourself?"
My point got through.
"I'll call them right now. Should I say there's a dead body?"
"Yes."
I turned my attention back to Gina.
"I'm going to find whoever did this to you, and they will suffer. I can promise you that, Gina. I'm so sorry."
I couldn't help myself and continued to weep for a few more seconds. I snapped out of it when I heard the old man talking on the phone outside.
"Yeah, I think there's a dead body. The guy won't let me go look myself."
I had to make a quick decision.
Did I want to hang around and be grilled by the Santa Monica police all night? Would my name get out to other branches of the LAPD? Could Mike Minter notify Ed Bannie that I was being interviewed? Could they detain me overnight? Could they have me killed in jail?
So many questions popped into my mind. Some were probably a little outrageous, but I was a nervous wreck. And who could blame me? I was kneeling next to a dead body.
I stood up.
"I'm sorry, Gina, but I have to go. I'm going to find the people responsible and make them pay."
I quickly walked out of her bedroom and then out of the apartment. The old man was still there.
"Is Gina dead?"
"Yes."
I started heading toward the stairs.
"Where are you going? You have to wait for the police."
"Tell them I'll call them."
"You can't just leave."
"Watch me," I said and leaped down the stairs two at a time.

∽

I ARRIVED AT MY CAR, took a side street to Wilshire Boulevard, and then headed east on Wilshire back toward Hollywood.

Had I made a mistake?

While the Hollywood precinct of the LAPD had jurisdiction over the Hollywood Hills - where Annie was killed, and Beverly Hills - where I was potentially targeted - they did not have jurisdiction over Santa Monica.

I wouldn't have had to deal with Mike Minter.

Maybe if I told the SMPD my theory of who killed Gina, they would listen.

And yet, I knew I wasn't going to turn around.

I would contact the SMPD and talk to them by phone. Something told me that I should avoid going to a police station, even if it was just to answer questions.

Two police cars with their lights on flew by me.

When Santa Monica turned into Brentwood, I grabbed my phone.

"Hello?"

"William, this is Bobby. I'm coming up to your house."

"You realize it's past nine p.m. I'm an old man and getting ready for bed."

"It's important."

"Alright, I'll meet you outside of my study."

I made my way to the Hollywood Hills and parked in my usual spot.

I walked down the steps, and William waited outside.

"Come in," he said.

We walked into his study. William sat down at his desk. I remained standing. I had too much nervous energy to sit.

"They killed Gina Galasso," I said.

I held back tears. By saying it out loud, it made it all the more real.

"What? Gina Galasso is dead?"

"Yes. She was shot in the chest. She had her arms and one of her legs up, trying to protect herself, but that didn't do any good."

Maybe I was giving William too much of the gory details, but the visual wouldn't leave my mind.

"Who did this?"

"I think you know."

"Wade or Ed Bannie?"

"It has to be," I said. "Maybe they hired that goon I saw, but they are behind it."

"Goon?"

I realized I hadn't told him.

"What happened?" he asked.

I told him about seeing the guy outside of the valet and then his van blocking the parking garage five minutes later.

"That could just be a coincidence," William said.

"Tell that to Gina Galasso."

William just shrugged.

"I don't think any of this is a coincidence," I continued. "They were trying to ambush me. I'm sure of it."

"By ambush, do you mean kill you?"

"What do you think?"

I felt defeated. Gina hadn't been my responsibility, but I still felt massive guilt over her death.

I continued to be a nervous ball of energy, walking the room's perimeter. I started looking at some of William's framed photos on the wall—anything to prevent Gina's body from popping into my head.

"Did you find Gina's body?" William asked.

"Yes. She didn't answer my phone call, and I got suspicious. Especially after what happened to me today."

I looked at another of William's photos, trying to distract myself. It wasn't working. The visual of Gina's arms crossing her face kept coming back to me.

"If you found the body, why aren't the police talking to you?"

"Because I left the crime scene."

"Bobby, Bobby, Bobby. You can't just leave a crime scene."

"Well, I just did."

"They will find out who you are."

"I'm sure they will. I just couldn't do it tonight. I'll call them in the morning."

"How long ago did this happen?"

"I came straight here."

"Then it's not too late."

My anger got the best of me.

"Listen, William. I'm not freaking going back to that crime scene. Not tonight. Seeing Gina's body like that was too much for me."

I looked up at another photo on the wall. This one was of William and the Mayor of Los Angeles.

"Alright, calm down, Bobby. This is hitting you hard. That's easy to see."

"Gina opened up to me about who *'The Other Annie'* really was, and it cost her her life."

"You don't know that for sure."

"You got another explanation?" I asked.

"Didn't Gina have a bit of a drug problem?" he asked.

"She may have. Why?"

"Maybe it was a drug deal gone bad."

It wasn't impossible.

"All I'm saying, Bobby, is you don't know for certain that her death is related to your investigation. That's why you should return to the crime scene and talk to the police."

"Stop bringing that up. It's not going to happen."

William was still sitting at his desk. I continued to walk around the other side of his expansive study like a chicken with my head cut off.

I looked up at another framed photograph. There were seven men, and in front of them was a shovel in the ground. They were breaking ground on something.

William was on the far left. The guy on his immediate left looked familiar.

Who was he? I wracked my brain.

And then, my whole body froze.

It was the guy from earlier today. The guy at the valet. The guy who stepped out from the van.

How the fuck did he know William Ryan? Or, more importantly, how did William know him?

I started to tense up. I felt a sudden urge to get out of there. People had alluded to William's temper - which I had seen firsthand - and others had suggested I was just a pawn in his scheme.

Had William been involved this whole time? I had to get the hell out of this study.

I looked over, but William wasn't looking in my direction. I quickly grabbed my phone and took a picture of the photo, putting the phone back in my pocket before William looked over.

"Would you like a drink, Bobby? You've had a tough day."

"Listen, I have to go," I said.

William rose from his chair.

"But you just got here."

"It's been a long day. I should sleep."

It certainly had, but that's not why I needed to leave.

I beat William to the door of his study and opened it.

"I really have to go," I said.

"You look like you've seen a ghost, Bobby. Are you sure you don't want to stay a while longer? Come have a drink."

GET OUT OF THERE, my mind yelled.

"I can't. I have to go."

I sprinted up the stairs toward my car.

William walked outside of his study but remained on the lower level. He was seventy years old and couldn't keep up with me.

"Are you still at the Beverly Hilton?" he asked.

After what I'd just seen, there was no way in hell I was telling William about the Rinky Dink Motel.

"Yeah, why wouldn't I be?"

"Well, because of this guy you saw. Maybe it scared you."

"I'm still at the Beverly Hilton," I said.

And with that, I opened my car door, got in, and sped off like a driver in the Indianapolis 500.

WHEN I ARRIVED BACK at the Rinky Dink, I reversed my car into a spot so no one could see my license plate. I went into my room, turned off all the lights, and snuck into bed.

With the exception of the day my mother died, this had been the longest day of my life.

I turned my phone off. I'm sure the SMPD was asking the old man who I was, and if they got a name, maybe they would track my phone.

I could deal with all of that tomorrow.

For now, I was a man in need of some sleep.

As I lay down, my immediate thoughts went to Gina. I couldn't believe she was gone. She'd opened up to me on our last two visits, and I was starting to see the sweet young girl she'd been once upon a time.

I hope you didn't suffer for long, Gina.

And even while thinking about Gina, another thought was never far from my mind: Was William Ryan somehow part of all this? Had he been pulling the strings all along?

CHAPTER 41

BOBBY

I awoke at five am. Maybe my internal body clock was warning me that I had another long day ahead. Shouldn't it have let me sleep in if that were the case?

I said a quick prayer for Gina, knowing it was time to get to work.

I turned my phone on and was expecting a barrage of messages. I don't know if I'd call it a barrage, but they were important.

I'd received two messages from the Santa Monica Police Department. The first one said, "This message is for Bobby McGowan. We know it was you at Gina Galasso's apartment. Please call us back as soon as you get this."

The second one is: "If we don't get a call from you by nine a.m. tomorrow morning, we will issue a warrant for your arrest."

Finally, William Ryan had left a message: "You didn't seem like yourself tonight, Bobby. You left in a rush. Is everything OK? Was it something I said?"

I WENT to my photos and pulled up the last picture I took with William Ryan and the man I'd seen at the Beverly Hilton.

THE OTHER ANNIE

I had no doubt. The man on William's left was the man I saw at the Beverly Hilton.

I scrolled to the bottom of the photo. There was some writing I couldn't quite make out, and I was hoping it was the name of everyone in the photo. I moved my fingers on the iPhone to focus on that part of the photo.

It read: *"From left to right: William Ryan, producer. Archibald Dickey, LAPD. Ed Bannie, LAPD."*

I looked back at the photo and into the eyes of Ed Bannie. They were intense; there was no doubt about that. Not to be outdone, Archibald Dickey held a gaze that I could only characterize as unrelenting. You weren't winning a staring contest against him.

I scrolled the phone back to the bottom of the photo.

"2004. Breaking ground on the new Little League field in Hollywood. Thanks to William Ryan for his generous contribution and the LAPD for getting this off the ground."

I started to backtrack a little.

This could just be an innocent photograph of William and the LAPD. Maybe it was a photo-op, and William had no idea who this Archibald Dickey was.

Maybe what I should be taking from this was that Ed Bannie and Archibald Dickey were standing next to each other. Maybe it was the those two who were thick as thieves.

Maybe I'd jumped the gun in trying to connect William with Archibald Dickey.

∼

I HAD no choice but to call the Santa Monica Police Department.

If I didn't, they'd put out a warrant for me.

I decided to show up unannounced at the Santa Monica Police Department rather than schedule a time and risk that word would spread.

∼

I ARRIVED at the Santa Monica Police Department on Olympic Avenue at 7:30 a.m. on July 2nd.

The upcoming 4th of July holiday was the last thing on my mind.

I walked into the precinct and told the woman at the desk who I was.

"Hawthorne," she yelled.

A police officer on the younger side approached me. He wore glasses, his hair was gelled, and he had that no-nonsense look that so many cops had. He reminded me of Guy Pearce's character in LA Confidential.

"You're Bobby McGowan?"

"Yes."

"I'm Detective Hawthorne. You're a hard guy to get ahold of. Theoretically, I could place you under arrest right now, but I won't."

"Thank you," I said.

I was going to try my best not to be combative this morning. I'd do anything to remain a free man.

"Follow me," he said.

I was led to an interrogation room and asked to sit.

Detective Hawthorne - he'd only given me his last name - left for a few minutes and returned with a much older cop.

I know they did good cop, bad cop. Maybe they had a new version: young cop, old cop.

Hawthorne spoke first.

"This is my partner, Detective Childs."

"Nice to meet you," I said.

He nodded in my direction.

"Why did you flee Gina Galasso's crime scene last night?"

It was time to decide. Did I let it all hang out and tell them everything? I still wasn't sure exactly how much I was ready to divulge.

"Because I was scared," I said. "I'd been interviewing Gina for an investigation I'm conducting, and I worried if they got to her, they could get to me."

"Wouldn't you rather be in police custody than roaming the streets where they could get you?"

"Sorry, but no."

"Why is that?"

Here we go.

Fuck it, I told myself. Let's let it all hang out.

"Because I fear that some police officers are involved in the case I'm working on."

They shared a quick glance.

"Which case is that?"

"Have you heard of Annie Ryan?"

They both nodded.

"I've heard someone was investigating that case again," Childs said. "I didn't know it was you."

"In the flesh," I said.

"And who do you think killed Gina Galasso?"

There was no backing down now.

"I think Archibald Dickey killed her at the behest of either Wade Bannie, Ed Bannie, or both."

"Who are these people?" Hawthorne asked.

The elder Childs tapped him on the shoulder as if to say, "I've got this."

"Archibald Dickey and Ed Bannie, the former cops?"

"Yes. Do you know them well?"

I sure hoped not.

"No, by reputation only."

And I knew what he meant by that. It wasn't a compliment.

"Is Wade Bannie Ed's son?" Hawthorne asked.

"Yes."

"And why do you suspect them?"

I spent the next ten minutes reviewing my entire investigation. I only left out a few things, including seeing William in the same picture with Archibald Dickey.

I didn't want to make it sound like I suspected William. Plus, I was starting to believe that I might have overreacted.

"That's quite a theory, Mr. McGowan," Childs said. "Why haven't you laid this out at the Hollywood precinct?"

"Because Ed Bannie still casts a big shadow over that department, and I couldn't risk it getting back to him."

I was more forthcoming than I'd anticipated. Something told me to trust the two guys in front of me.

"Do you have any actual evidence that Archibald Dickey killed Gina Galasso?"

"Nothing direct, no. Unless you count him trying to ambush me at the Beverly Hilton."

"That's hardly evidence he killed Gina Galasso," Childs said.

"I understand that. Did you know Dickey?"

"Like I said, only by reputation. The Santa Monica and Hollywood divisions of the LAPD don't always see eye to eye."

That was good news.

"Too bad you guys can't just take over the Annie Ryan murder case," I said.

"That's not how it works, Mr. McGowan," Hawthorne said. He'd been mostly quiet to this point; a big part of that was just age itself. Detective Childs knew more of the names I was dropping.

"And you said William Ryan, the producer, is the one who hired you?"

"Yes."

"What does he think about all this?"

"He just wants to find out who murdered his niece."

"Let's go back over what you saw when you entered Gina's apartment," Hawthorne said.

I spent the next ten minutes rehashing things I'd already said.

When I concluded, they looked at each other.

"Listen, Mr. McGowan. We don't think you had anything to do with Ms. Galasso's murder. You contacted the super and brought it to our attention, after all. But you can't just leave the scene of a crime. That's a chargeable offense."

"I understand, and I'm sorry."

"We are not going to charge you, but I suggest picking up our phone calls on the first ring."

"I will," I said.

"And we will be calling you in the coming days."

"I'll answer," I said.

"Okay, we're going to let you go."

"Thank you," I said.

"Be careful. I don't know if everything you've told us is true, but look both ways when you cross the street."

It was the same warning that Adam Toon had given me. That seemed like a year ago, but it had barely been a month. This case was aging me in dog years.

"I will. Thank you, detectives."

I was escorted to the front of the SMPD and released as a free man.

CHAPTER 42

WADE

My father requested that I not see him for several days.

I didn't listen. Too much was going on, and I needed to be in the loop. I didn't like the idea of my father talking to Archibald Dickey without my input.

It was midday on Tuesday, July 2nd when I knocked on my father's condo door.

The Fourth of July was a monster event in Hermosa Beach. Thousands of beautiful girls descended on the beach and The Strand, a local stretch of watering holes.

Usually, I'd be right there amongst the masses, eyeing the beauties walking by, but something told me this 4th of July would be different. I might even be catching a flight out of the United States.

My father was pissed when he saw me approach the door. You could always tell by his expression.

"What the fuck are you doing here?" he asked. "Didn't I tell you to steer clear from seeing me?"

I pushed by him and walked into his condo.

"This is my life, too," I said. "If you're planning something new with Archibald, I want to know about it."

When he didn't answer, I said, "Aren't you going to debug?"

"I already did this morning."

We both sat down.

"When was the last time you left the house? Days? Weeks? I'm sure your condo is safe from bugs."

"Why are you here, Wade?"

"I told you. Gina Galasso is dead, correct? I saw something on the news about a woman murdered in Santa Monica."

"Yes, she's dead."

"And did we scare Bobby McGowan?"

"Yes, Archibald did, although I'm not sure that was such a good idea. He's now on McGowan's radar. Hmm, whose idea was it to scare McGowan? Oh, yeah, yours."

"Shut the fuck up, Dad. You've never made a mistake?"

"None as grave as the ones you've made."

We were more combative than usual.

"It was one mistake twenty-five years ago."

"It's the mistake that never quite goes away."

I was tempted to finally tell him about the other two girls I'd murdered. Just to stick the knife in a little bit.

Your son is way worse than you think.

It wouldn't affect me. I already knew I was evil, but he thought I'd only made one big mistake decades ago. Seeing his face drop when I told him about the other girls would be fun.

"Can we call Archibald?" I asked.

My father dialed his number, put the phone on speaker, and set it on the table between us.

"Hey, Ed."

"Wade is here, too."

"Hello, Wade."

"Hi, Archibald."

"Alright, that's fucking enough," my father said. "This isn't a freaking meet-and-greet. So, what's the latest?"

"I tried calling you this morning, Ed, but you didn't answer. We've had an interesting day."

I gave my father a look, and he glared back.

"I was busy. Let's hear it now."

"Well, I've been tracking McGowan's phone since our run-in at the Beverly Hilton. I have to say, it's nice to still have the amenities of being a cop without still being one. It looks like I put quite the scare in him because he checked into some shithole in Hollywood: The Rinky Dink Motel. I find it amusing that you think this guy is some Grade-A PI. He's an idiot if you ask me. He checks into a sleazy motel to get off the grid but then keeps his phone on?"

"He probably doesn't know he's being tracked," I said.

"No shit, Wade," Archibald said.

I was getting it from him and my father.

"He was the one who found Gina's body," Archibald said. "He must have become suspicious when she didn't answer. He didn't hang around until the police got there, though. He got the hell out of there. So, anyway, fast forward to today. He went to the Santa Monica police station this morning. He must have felt guilty after fleeing the crime scene last night. That, or the SMPD found out who he was, and he had to turn himself in."

"That's not good if he's talking to the Santa Monica PD," my father said. "I've got no pull with them."

"Nor do I," Archibald said.

"What do we do next?" I asked. "Is it time to put Bobby McGowan out of his misery?"

"It's certainly an option."

"It might be getting to that point," my father added.

"Ed, if I do this for you," Archibald said. "I will be taking a vacation in the next few days. That will be two murders in three days, and these are two people whose connection will be easily established. They will bring the heat down like you wouldn't believe."

"I think that's a good idea, Arch. Get out of the city for a while. Shit, get out of the country. I'm going to have my son do the same."

"Is that a confirmation to get Mr. McGowan out of the picture?"

I thought my father would look at me, and we'd decide together.

"Yes. It is," my father said.

He'd said it without even a glance in my direction. My father was getting on my last nerves.

"Just a heads up, "Archibald said. "I'm going to wait until very late tonight. It's a seedy motel in a bad part of town. People don't go to sleep until three a.m. This will be an early morning job."

"No problem. You know what's best. Call me when it's completed."

And with that, my father ended the phone call.

"Why didn't you confer with me about killing Bobby McGowan?" I asked.

"The adults were talking, Wade."

I stood up and kicked over the table in front of us.

"Fuck you," I said.

Just a few days back, I remember thinking that my father was old and I was now the family's alpha male. Not the way that phone call had gone. I felt emasculated.

"Simmer down, Wade. We're doing what's best for all of us."

"I can't wait to get the fuck out of this country. And away from you."

"I'd book that flight soon," he said. "Shit is going to hit the fan tomorrow morning when they find Bobby McGowan dead."

"You know I've talked to him?"

I'd like to claim I didn't know why I brought it up, but I knew. I was tired of being treated like a red-headed stepchild by my father. I hated how he looked down on me. How he always made decisions without conferring with me.

"To whom? To McGowan?"

"That's right."

"Why the fuck would you talk to him?"

"Don't worry, I had one of those voice distorters."

My father just shook his head.

"Why? Give me one good reason."

"That guy who killed his mother, Conrad Drury, well, he used to poke Bobby's buttons, and I thought I'd do the same."

"Bobby? You're on a first-name basis now?"

"Technically, it's Robert."

"You're such a buffoon, Wade. Shockingly, you haven't been nailed for the Annie Ryan murder. You commit one murder, and everything has to fall in place for you to avoid getting caught."

I was bubbling with rage.

My father continued.

"Honestly, you belong on America's dumbest criminals or whatever that show is called. You use a voice distorter to talk to the guy investigating your murder? What the fuck is wrong with you?"

"You're wrong," I said.

"About what?"

"About me getting away with one murder."

I looked over and saw my father's face sink, just as I'd hoped.

"What are you talking about, Wade?"

"You just think I'm some dummy who got away with one murder. But you're wrong."

"What are you saying, Wade?"

"Do I have to spell it out for you, Ed?"

I was tired of him calling me Wade every two seconds. He didn't deserve to be called Dad, so I used his first name.

"What did you do?" he asked.

"Maybe you're the dummy. You didn't notice that women were going missing in the Caribbean countries I stayed in? Some cop you are."

My father put his hands over his face.

"Please tell me you're kidding."

"Nope. I'm dead serious."

"How many?" he asked.

"I don't know. Eight or nine."

That was a giant lie, but I wanted to make him feel even worse.

"Jesus, Wade."

My father's head remained in his hands.

"I should have never protected you," he said. "You were seventeen. You would have gone to Juvie and maybe to some county jail. You could have made something of yourself when you got out."

"Oh, I made something of myself. I traveled the world and always had pretty girls with me."

"That's not making something of yourself, Wade. And by the way, you traveled the world because of the money I gave you and had you invest. Do you know why I stole drug money from horrible people? To give you a better future. Instead, you murdered young women."

I remained furious.

"Oh, you're some great father because you took money from drug dealers? Oh look, it's fucking Robin Hood."

"Get the hell out of my house," he said. "And I want you to listen to me, Wade. If you are not out of the country by the end of the day tomorrow, I'm going to the police myself."

"You wouldn't do that."

"Why not?"

"Because then you'll spend the rest of your life in jail for covering up Annie Ryan's murder."

"To get you off the streets, it might be worth it."

"Fuck you," I said.

"Get out of my house," he said. "And then get out of the country."

"If you want to know the truth, it was only two other women."

"And that's supposed to make me feel better?"

My father raised his eyes toward me, and they were moist and on the verge of tears. I'd never seen my father cry. Not once.

"Please leave, Wade. I don't ever want to see you again."

I grabbed his cell phone and threw it as hard as possible toward one of the sliding glass doors. The door shattered, and the glass came tumbling down.

My father looked at me and was speechless.

"You should have gotten thicker glass, Ed. This place fucking sucks."

And with that, I stormed out of his condo.

CHAPTER 43

BOBBY

As I left the Santa Monica Police Department, I took out my phone and called William Ryan. It was still only 8:15 a.m.

"Hello?"

"How do you know Archibald Dickey?" I asked, getting right down to it.

"Who?"

"Don't play dumb," I said.

"I have no idea who you are talking about."

"You have a picture of you, him, and Ed Bannie in your study."

"I have thirty framed photos in my study. Which one is it?"

"It was for breaking ground on a new little league field."

"Oh, that. That was fifteen years ago. Maybe longer. I don't know every person in all of my photos. Come on, Bobby."

He sounded convincing. People had alluded to William's temper and said he might be a bit power-hungry, but no one had ever suspected him of being involved in Annie's murder. I should probably be giving him more of the benefit of the doubt.

"Who is he, anyway?" William asked.

"He's a former cop, but more importantly, he's the one I saw at the

Beverly Hilton, and if I had to guess, he's the one who killed Gina Galasso."

"Oh, wow. That's him? Well, I don't know the man. I swear to you. I'll take a polygraph if you want. I'll swear on the souls of my kids. Whatever. I have no idea who he is."

"Okay, okay. I believe you."

"And you said Ed Bannie is in that same picture?"

"Yes. How do you not remember?"

"Do you know how many photo-ops I've done over the years? Hundreds. Maybe thousands."

As a Hollywood producer, that was believable.

"Plus, it was my wife who put all those pictures up. Check next time you're here. There won't be a photograph from the last ten or twelve years."

He continued to sound believable.

"I'm leaving the Santa Monica police department right now," I said.

"You wisened up and went in?"

"Yes."

"How did they treat you?"

"They were more accommodating than they had any reason to be."

"Did you tell them everything?" William asked.

"Pretty much."

"Then they aren't done with you yet."

"I know."

"If you accused a former cop of being involved in a murder, it will surely get back to Mike Minter and those guys in Hollywood."

"Good. It's time we put all our cards on the table."

I was getting tired of using that phrase.

"You said you pretty much told them everything. What did you leave out?"

"I didn't mention you and the photo of Archibald Dickey. I didn't want you to come under suspicion."

"Thank you. Once again, I don't know the guy."

"I said I believe you. Now, let's hope Archibald Dickey left a fingerprint at Gina Galasso's. And then the cops can build a connection between Dickey and Ed Bannie."

"Ed Bannie would still have to turn on his son. Remember, I hired you to find Annie's killer. Not the father of Annie's killer."

"You don't have to tell me, William."

"Alright, keep me posted from here on in. You kept too many things from me early on. And I'll tell you what, I'll give you a $10,000 bonus if they arrest Wade Bannie."

"With all due respect, I'm no longer doing this for the money."

"Okay, then I rescind my offer."

I laughed. I was pretty sure it was the first time I'd done so since finding Gina's body.

"I'll be in touch," I said.

Maybe I'd made too quick a reversal on William, but my gut told me he had nothing to do with hiring Archibald Dickey.

And I had to go with my gut.

I DROVE BACK to the Rinky Dink motel, sat down on the bed, and just started thinking.

I thought about Gina and how, if this had turned out differently, she might have been able to turn her life around. The burden of getting Wade Bannie off her chest would probably have been good for her in the long run. Sadly, we'd never know.

I thought about my options. One was to go to the DA's office in Hollywood and drop off the fliers I'd made. Several DAs would see them, and maybe one or two would take it seriously.

I hated being in this position, but I knew I needed the help of the DA's office or the police going forward.

There was not going to be a smoking gun in this investigation. If it ever went to trial, this case would be based on circumstantial evidence. Decades-old murders are solved all the time these days, but the difference is that they have a body to test for DNA.

Annie's body was never found, and I didn't think it ever would be, which meant no DNA.

Now, maybe I was wrong, and it was buried in the Bannies' backyard, but I doubted it. Ed Bannie had been a cop and a renowned one at that. He would know better than to bury a body in his backyard. He would have found somewhere to dispose of it forever, assuming Wade hadn't done that by the time Ed returned from his vacation.

I HADN'T GIVEN much thought to Ed Bannie's wife, but maybe I could contact her. I didn't know if she was still alive or if they were still together, but perhaps she would be willing to talk. Doubtful, but worth a shot.

And I needed to find out just how close Ed Bannie and Archibald Dickey were.

I thought Greg Quinones just might be the guy.

Let's hope he was in the talking mood.

∼

"Quinones here," the familiar voice said.

"Hello, Mr. Quinones. This is Bobby McGowan again."

"You ready to buy me another lunch?"

I wasn't sure if going out on the town with Greg Quinones was advisable at the moment, but I knew how important he might end up being. I decided to see what the phone call produced first.

"We could do that," I said. "Let me ask you a few questions over the phone first."

"Alright, what do you want to know?"

"First off, is Ed Bannie still married?"

"No, his wife left him years ago."

"But she's still alive?"

"Yes, I think so."

"Any idea where she lives or how I could get ahold of her?"

"Sorry, but I don't. As you know, me and Ed ain't exactly on speaking terms."

"Do you have any idea if she'd talk to me?"

"Like I said, I don't know anything about her. And don't go after a man by going behind his back to his ex-wife. Come on, man."

I wasn't sure I agreed with Quinones on this, but I knew it wasn't going over well, so I changed the subject.

"Did you tell anyone about our conversation? Specifically regarding Ed."

He laughed, which I didn't take as a good sign.

"Well, I might have told a few former cops that night. We'd had too many drinks, and they managed to get it out of me. You're kind of to blame. Making me have all that Scotch at lunch."

Shit.

"Please tell me none of them are still friendly with Ed Bannie."

"No, none of them. Well, maybe this one guy, Gil Castor, but he probably didn't say anything."

"Probably? I asked you to keep this conversation between us."

"Whoops."

"What kind of cop are you? I thought you'd know how to keep a secret."

"Tread lightly, Mr. McGowan. I'm getting close to hanging up on you."

What else could I get from Mr. Quinones? Think. I wanted to broach Archibald Dickey, but I didn't want to get hung up on.

"You've always wanted to take down Ed Bannie. Correct?"

"Yes, you know that."

"You said everyone knew he was dirty."

"They did."

"Then why wasn't he ever held accountable?"

"Because he was smart about it. He'd only take his guys with him if he knew they were looking at a big drug bust. He had his own little circle. It was small, but they were super tight. So he'd give them a taste of the drug money, knowing they'd never rat on him. On the outside of the circle, we had suspicions, but we couldn't prove them."

He'd set me up. Now was the perfect time to ask.

"What were the names of the guys in Bannie's inner circle?"

"There were three others. Brad Neely. Matthew Chance. And Archibald Dickey."

Bingo.

"Quite the last name."

"Sure is."

"I'll bet you guys gave him a lot of shit."

"Not exactly."

"I'm shocked," I said.

"Archibald wasn't a guy you wanted to needle. He's one of the toughest SOBs I've ever known. Maybe he got teased as a kid, I don't know, but he developed leather-like skin at some point. That guy is bad news and always has been."

"Do you know if Dickey and Ed Bannie remained friends?"

"As far as I know, they are still best friends. They are probably having a drink together right now."

"Mike Minter wasn't part of the inner circle?" I asked.

"No. Mike was younger, and although he looked up to Ed and they were quite friendly, I'm not sure Ed ever trusted Mike with his life as he did with the others."

Maybe Mike Minter wasn't involved at all. I'd been on the fence about him for a while now.

"Do you know if the other three are still alive?"

"Archibald and Brad are. Matthew died a few years back."

"Could you get Archibald or Brad's number for me?"

"Did you not listen to a word I said? These guys were thick as thieves. There is zero chance they would help you get to Ed Bannie. Less than zero, actually. And Archibald would probably break your neck just for asking."

"Sounds like a pleasant guy."

"Count your blessings you haven't crossed paths with him yet."

Oh, but I have.

"I have a few things to do, Mr. Quinones, but I might be calling you back."

"Your next talk will cost you a free lunch," he said.

"It's a deal."

~

I GOT off the phone and looked down at the fliers on the side of the bed.

It was time.

I'd told the Santa Monica Police Department basically everything I knew. Why was I keeping it from the Hollywood precinct and the DA's office? It was time to go full-on scorched earth and see what happened next.

No, this flier wasn't a smoking gun, but maybe continuing to put pressure on Wade and Ed would create a powder keg, and they'd make a crucial mistake.

I called for an old-school yellow cab, and they said they'd be there in twenty minutes. I didn't want anyone tracking me through my credit card, and that's what my UBER was connected to.

I then looked down at my iPhone and realized my mistake. They could be tracking me through that.

You idiot!

I wrote down several numbers, including William, Quinones, Cassius, and others, and then turned my phone off. From now on, I'd use the burner phone whenever possible.

~

THE YELLOW CAB arrived fifteen minutes later.

I'd kept my phone off but was looking at the front entrance of The Rinky Dink. When the cab arrived, I walked over.

"Are you Bobby?" he asked.

The driver was a Hispanic guy in his fifties.

"Yes. Listen, I've got four stops I have to make. I'll tip you generously. Is that okay?"

"That sounds great, my man. Where are we going first?"

"There's a copy shop up the street on the right-hand side. Let's go there first."

"A coffee shop?"

I shook my head.

"No, a copy shop. Like FedEx/Kinko's. I'll show you when we get there."

∼

At the copy shop, I made a second set of fliers, this time adding that Gina Galasso had been killed and that Archibald Dickey was likely the man responsible.

As I said, I was going full-on scorched earth.

∼

The next stop was the Hollywood division of the LAPD.

I went into the precinct with about forty of the fliers. I approached the front desk.

"Please give each and every one of your cops one of these fliers," I said.

"What? What are these?"

"Give one to everyone," I said and walked out.

For good measure, I dropped several by the front door.

I got into the yellow cab.

"I think you dropped a few of those."

"It's okay. Just drive."

∼

Our next stop was the DA's office in Hollywood.

The head District Attorney for all of Los Angeles had his office downtown. However, he had no affiliation with the Annie Ryan case. Hollywood DA's would.

This building also housed a courthouse; the DA's office was on the third floor. I took the elevator up and found the entrance to the office.

"How can I help you?" the receptionist asked.

"I have information on the most important cold case in Hollywood history," I said.

"Wow, that's great. What is it?"

"I need you to give one of these flyers to every Assistant District Attorney who works here."

"Wouldn't you rather drop these off individually?"

"No, I'll trust you to do that. Thanks so much."

And I turned to go, dropping a few more leaflets on the ground as I walked out.

∼

I ARRIVED BACK at the cab.

The driver seemed to be having a good time

"This is like some great adventure," he said. "Where are we going next?"

"To the Beverly Hilton."

∼

I HAD him park in the front, right next to the valet. I didn't want him sitting in the garage if I had to make a quick getaway.

I told him to stay where he was and that I'd be down in a few minutes.

I made my way up to my room on the sixth floor. I filled my duffle bag with as many clothes as possible.

I also grabbed my laptop and Annie's diary and set them on my clothes. I didn't want to make two or three trips, so I decided the rest of my clothes and Annie's childhood toys could wait until a later visit.

I returned to the lobby, my head still on a swivel.

The front desk woman who didn't trust me looked up as I passed.

"Hello, Mr. McGowan. Are you checking out?"

"Nope, just grabbing a few things," I said.

∼

"THIS IS FUN. What's the next stop?"

"This adventure is over, my friend. Back to The Rinky Dink Motel."

"You got it."

～

I had him drive me to my room at the back of the motel so fewer people would see me exit the yellow cab.

I tipped him very generously, and he thanked me profusely.

I think I'd made his day.

～

It was now 2 p.m., and it was time to sit back and wait for the shit to hit the fan.

CHAPTER 44

BOBBY

The rest of the day was a slow-moving one.

For that, I was grateful. I needed a few stress-free hours to recharge my battery.

I spent most of it online, looking for breaking news. I saw nothing. I watched the local news on the off chance they mentioned something—also, nothing. Even Gina's death was no longer in their news cycle.

It's sad how quickly a murder in Los Angeles moves aside and makes room for whatever's next.

∽

I GOT into bed at about nine p.m.

Well, I'd spent most of the late afternoon and early evening in bed, but this time, I was ready to go to sleep. Whether I'd achieve sleep, considering all that was going on, was a different subject altogether.

Finally, at around eleven, after a few hours of tossing and turning, I fell asleep.

∽

THE OTHER ANNIE

At 2 a.m., I woke back up.

There was just too much on my mind. It's almost a shock that I managed to sleep for three consecutive hours.

I turned on my laptop to see if I'd missed anything. There was nothing about some random guy dropping off fliers to the LAPD and the DA's office.

I wondered what was going on behind the scenes. I had to assume that several police officers and DAs had seen them. They couldn't just ignore what they saw. Maybe they were saying I was just a crackpot and ignored the fliers, but even if that were the case, at least they were talking about Wade Bannie, Ed Bannie, and Archibald Dickey.

That was a good thing.

~

At 2:45, I tried to fall back asleep, but it wasn't happening. I switched my pillows around, and I even tried to count sheep. Nothing worked.

~

A little after 3:00, I heard a slight rustling outside my door.

It wasn't loud, but it was unmistakable.

I ever so quietly got out of bed and stood up.

Less than five seconds later, I heard a key - or something similar - going into my door lock.

As silently as I could, I tiptoed toward the door. If someone were about to enter, I'd rush and slam them up against the wall.

I thought about screaming, but if they had a gun, they'd just shoot into the room. I thought the element of surprise was more valuable.

I heard the lock opening up. I quickly lamented choosing a motel without an electronic key. It's incredible where the human mind will go under duress.

The door started to open ever so slowly.

I had to wait until he'd fully stepped into the room. One advantage I had was that my eyes had adapted to the darkness. His would take several seconds.

I told myself to look for a gun and focus on that arm.

Half of his body slowly entered the room, and then, as he slid his other half past the door, I attacked him.

With as much force as I could muster from five feet away, I tackled him into the door he'd just opened. The door hit the side wall with great force, and the man hit the door and fell to the ground.

He had a gun in his right hand, a long silencer attached to it.

With my left hand, I grabbed his wrist so he couldn't fire the gun. With my right hand, I started pummeling his face. I don't know if I'd knocked the air out of him, but he didn't put up much of a defense.

I punched his face five consecutive times, and his grip started to loosen on the gun.

"What's going on?!" a neighbor yelled.

"Call the police," I screamed.

I was able to remove the gun from his hand, but I continued to punch him with my right hand. I didn't care that I had the gun. I didn't know what other weapon the guy might have hidden. I had to hammer him until he was incapable of doing anything.

I heard some grunts from adjoining rooms.

"Call the police," I screamed for a second time.

Enough light was coming in from the motel's lights that I could make out the face of the man on the ground in front of me. Sure enough, it was Archibald Dickey. I punched his face two more times for good measure.

He slumped over, and I knew he was no longer a threat.

Someone approached the door and saw me holding a gun.

"He attacked me," I said. "This is his gun."

"I believe you," he said. "I called the cops."

"Good."

It all happened so fast that I was barely able to contemplate that I'd nearly been killed. I could be an overthinker at times, but when I heard the key, saw the man, and then the gun, my primal instincts took over.

I looked down, and Archibald Dickey was still on the ground. It didn't look like he'd be getting up any time soon.

But I still had the gun pointed at him, just in case.

The LAPD arrived a few minutes later.

I asked the guy still standing outside my room to tell them I'd set the gun down on the bed right now. I wasn't taking any chances.

Three officers approached the room. They escorted me out and started to put handcuffs on me. They then laid me on the ground.

"He's not the bad guy," my new friend said.

"This will only be for a few minutes."

They asked me my name and wanted a quick explanation of what had happened. I gave it to them.

They stood Archibald Dickey up. He was wobbly, and his face was a bloody mess.

"His gun is on the bed," I said.

"We were told, sir. Please be quiet and let us do our job."

They handcuffed Dickey and put him in the back of one of the cop cars. I looked out, and there were probably three or four cop cars sitting in The Rinky Dink's parking lot.

One of the officers turned to me.

"We're going to take you back to the station for some questions, okay?"

Without much choice, I just said, "Alright."

"And we'll get these handcuffs removed soon."

"Thanks," I said.

One-word front-desk guy had meandered over to the crime scene. He had a name tag on, signifying he worked for the motel. He looked down at me, handcuffed on the ground, with an expression that said, "*I knew you were trouble.*"

The cops pulled me to my feet and had me look in the direction of one-word guy.

"He says his name is Bobby McGowan, and he's staying here. Is that correct?"

"I don't remember his name, but he's staying here," he said.

He didn't recognize my name because I'd given him a fake one.

"And this man, in the backseat. He's not staying here, is he?"

"No. I've never seen him before."

"You can return to your desk now. We'll be out of here soon."

"Thanks."

They removed my handcuffs and put me in the back seat of one of the police cars.

It looked like I was headed to another police station.

Much better than the morgue, I told myself.

I'd been very fortunate.

If I'd still been asleep, I'd have met the same fate as Gina Galasso.

CHAPTER 45

WADE

My father called me at 5:30 a.m.

I knew something was up. He'd never called me this early. Not once in his whole life. Plus, when we did argue, and the previous day was an all-timer, he'd usually let things simmer for a few days. Not this time.

"What is it?" I asked.

"The shit has hit the fan."

"How bad is it?"

"Have you booked that flight yet?"

"No."

"I'd do it right after you get off the phone. Depart today. If you wait any longer, you might be on the no-fly list."

"Are you sure we should be talking on the phone?" I asked.

"There's no other choice; now shut up and listen."

"Okay."

"Yesterday, Bobby McGowan went to the LAPD and the DA's office and dropped off fliers saying you were responsible for Annie Ryan's death and that I helped cover it up. He also said Archibald was likely responsible for killing Gina Galasso."

"How could he know all this?"

"Shut up and listen, Wade. It gets worse. As you know, Archibald planned on killing Bobby last night. Well, it didn't work out that way. McGowan overpowered him, and the LAPD was called. As far as I know, they are both in police custody right now."

"Fuck. Archibald won't talk, will he?"

"No, he won't. But he was accused in those fliers of killing Gina and then is caught with a gun, breaking into McGowan's motel room. It doesn't look good."

"No, it doesn't."

"And it gets worse again," my father said.

"Stop saying that. What this time?"

"I've been talking to Archibald over the phone in recent days. Shit, you were with me when we called him yesterday. That's going to be a tough one to explain away."

"We're fucked, aren't we?" I asked.

"That's why you need to book that flight. I know we had a horrible fight yesterday, but you're still my son. Get out of the United States and enjoy the rest of your life. I'd suggest flying to somewhere you can go unnoticed for a while. Your name will be coming up in connection with Annie Ryan. Soon."

"They still have no real evidence."

"Wade, they now have circumstantial evidence coming out of their ass. And now, they have Archibald."

"You said he won't talk."

"I don't think he will, but you never know. And it almost doesn't matter. They will realize that everything Bobby McGowan has told them is true. So, they'll start to think that maybe he's also right about who killed Annie Ryan."

"God dammit. What about you? Are you going to get out of the country?"

He didn't answer for a few seconds.

"Dad?"

"I'm too old to go on the lam."

"So, what, you're going to go to jail?"

"No, I don't think I'll be doing that, either."

"Then, what?"

"Figure it out, Wade."

I then realized what he was trying to tell me, but I didn't want to believe it.

"No, you don't have to do this."

"Yes, I do. I'm not rotting away in some jail. And you know why? Because cops don't last long in jail. Especially dirty cops, and once they go digging on me, I'm royally screwed. All the former cops who hated me will come out of the woodwork."

"Maybe they won't have enough to convict you. Or maybe they'll give you a break because you're a former cop."

"I'm not going to hang long enough to find out."

"Don't you believe in the rule of law?"

It sounded dumb, but I was just trying to throw things out there.

"Yeah, and we broke the law. Over and over. You may not see it yet, Wade, but this is all over. The avalanche has started. Bobby McGowan won. The LAPD is coming for us. Sooner rather than later."

"No. I don't believe it."

"Open your eyes, Wade. It's over."

"Let's talk this out," I suggested.

"You take care of yourself now, Francis Wade."

I was getting desperate. This was his goodbye to me.

"There's got to be another way," I said.

"There's not. I'm going to hang up now."

"Dad, please don't."

"Goodbye, Wade. And good luck."

With that, my father hung up the phone.

We'd spoken for the last time.

CHAPTER 46

BOBBY

I was released from the police station at 5:45 a.m.
It was now July 3rd.
They said they'd be in touch. When I left, my two cell phones, laptop, and duffle bag awaited me.

"Your motel room is still considered a crime scene, so I'd find somewhere else to stay," the officer said.

"Gladly," I replied.

~

I TURNED on my regular phone.

I was no longer worried about being tracked with Archibald Dickey in jail, and Wade and Ed Bannie would probably get a visit from the cops soon. Maybe I was being naive, but I wasn't worried about them.

I ordered a UBER back to the Beverly Hilton.

~

I ARRIVED BACK in my hotel room and laid down on the bed.

My body probably wanted to sleep for twenty hours, but I wasn't sure my busy mind would allow it.

I was able to fall asleep, however, as my body won out.

When I woke at 12:30, I called William Ryan and told him everything that happened, including the fliers and, more importantly, Archibald Dickey coming to kill me.

He was mesmerized.

"Hopefully, Mr. Dickey had been talking to Ed or Wade Bannie recently. I'm sure the police are going through his phone." I said.

"Everything is coming together, Bobby. All because of you."

"And they aren't going to see your name on Dickey's call log, are they?"

"This again? No, they will not see me on there."

"I believe you," I said. "I wouldn't have called you if I didn't."

"So what's next on the docket?" William asked.

"I don't know if there's much I can do now. The cops know pretty much everything."

"You could do one thing for me."

"What is it?"

"I know the head DA up here. Could I have him give you a call? You can explain everything you've learned and why you think Wade Bannie killed Annie. It might help to expedite what we're looking for."

"Wade Bannie being arrested?"

"Exactly."

"Sure, have him call me," I said.

"Thanks, Bobby. I'll have him call you soon. Report back to me after you hear from him."

∼

Ten minutes later, the Hollywood district attorney called.

His name was Max Collier.

I spent twenty minutes telling him everything I had learned since taking the Annie Ryan case.

"So, what do you think?" I asked.

"If this were thirty-six hours ago, I would have said this case was too circumstantial, and being that it was twenty-five years ago, we'd be unlikely to get a conviction."

"And now?"

"Well, if the cops can connect Archibald Dickey to Wade or Ed Bannie, that changes everything."

"Thank you. You have no idea how good that feels to hear."

"Why don't we talk again tomorrow, Bobby? I have a feeling momentum is on your side."

I was getting a call from an unlisted call.

"Sounds good. Talk then," I said and clicked over to the other call.

∽

"Hello?"

"You've proved a formidable opponent, Robert," a voice said.

It was not being disguised.

"Is this Wade?"

"Not many people can outduel Archibald Dickey."

He'd ignored my question.

"Who am I talking to?" I asked.

"Aren't we past that? You've put my name on flyers and accused me of murder. Do you have to hear me say it? And does it matter anyway? I'm not going to admit to anything."

"I guess you're afraid to admit your first name is Francis."

He laughed.

"You'll have to do better than that, Robert."

"Oh, I think I've done quite well. You'll be hearing from the police quite soon," I said.

He laughed again; I hated his smugness.

"Doubtful," he said.

"You keep laughing, but you're now the one on the defensive."

"I just wanted to say goodbye and congrats."

"Congrats on what?"

"On being better at this than I initially assumed. You still didn't catch your man, but you deserve some credit for how you played the game."

It's like he was holding a trump card. How could he be so confident with all that was going on?

"Why don't we meet up in person?" I asked.

"At one point, I would have liked that."

"Not anymore?"

"Sorry, Robert, but no. And I really was just calling to say goodbye. You take care now, you hear?"

"Hold on, I have a few more quick questions."

"Nice try. Goodbye."

And he hung up.

I THOUGHT back on our conversation.
   I didn't like when he said, "Doubtful," when I mentioned the police.
   This was a guy who'd gotten away with everything in his life.
   And he thought he was going to do so again.
   I thought I had an idea why.

"DETECTIVE PATCHETT SPEAKING."
   "I need the biggest favor you've ever given me. And please don't give me grief about it. Time is of the absolute essence."
   "Hey, Bobby. What is it?"
   "Can you find out if someone named Francis Wade Bannie has a scheduled flight out of LAX today or tomorrow? If you can't get this information yourself, I know you know someone who can. It's crucial."
   "You're taking advantage of our friendship, Bobby."
   "This is the last time, I promise, but I need this."
   "Spell out his name for me."
   I did.
   "Keep your phone close," Patchett said. "I'll see what I can do."
   "One more thing."
   "You're killing me, Bobby. What?"
   "Get me his address too."

TO MY AMAZEMENT, Detective Patchett called me back in less than fifteen minutes with the information.
   My suspicions were proven correct.
   Wade Bannie was booked on a flight from LAX to Mexico City at 6:00 p.m., four and a half hours away.
   He was trying to flee the country, and if he did, I feared he would never be brought to justice.

For a guy I was suspicious of only a day before, I sure was getting chummy with William Ryan. It felt right. He'd hired me, after all, and had been there since the beginning.

I told him about my discussion with the DA, the call with Wade Bannie, and the information Detective Patchett had just relayed.

"What are you going to do now, Bobby?"

"I fear he'll vanish if he leaves the country."

"And the DA won't put a hold on his passport?"

"I highly doubt it. Not this quickly. They are probably still trying to tie Archibald Dickey to Wade and his father. And his flight is in less than five hours. Hermosa Beach is less than ten miles from LAX, so it's not like he has far to go. But Mexico City is an international flight, so he might try to get there in the next two or three hours."

"You're talking in circles. What's your plan?"

"Wade has lived all over the Caribbean but also spent a lot of time in Mexico. He probably knows how to go underground and hide in plain sight. I fear we may never see him again if he gets down there."

"Stop saying that. Come up with a plan."

"I was thinking about breaking into his house and stealing his passport. If we can just give the DA another two or three days, I do think they may red flag him from flying."

"You're never one to run out of ideas. Passport stealing is a new one."

"Listen, William, I should go. If I'm going to do this, I need to head down to Hermosa Beach soon."

"Maybe you should just let the authorities handle this."

"By the time they handle it, he'll be in Mexico with dreads and new tattoos and looking nothing like he does now."

Another long silence followed. It felt like William was weighing his options.

"Can you wait a few minutes before you go? I have something I want to check up on."

"The clock is ticking. I'll answer from my car."

CHAPTER 47

WADE

I'd booked my flight after getting off the phone with my father.

He was gone, and I knew it. I had to save my own ass.

I chose Mexico City. I'd spent a lot of time in Mexico and always found it easiest to make myself invisible in Mexico City. Sure, it still had American tourists, but nothing like Cabo, Cancun, Acapulco, Playa Del Carmen, or a handful of other more touristy cities.

I could pay for an apartment in Mexico City with cash upfront and become a hermit for a few months until the temperature died down.

And that was all assuming I became an international fugitive.

I wasn't ready to concede that yet.

But I wasn't dismissing it, either. My father had been calling Archibald, so I knew it was now a distinct possibility they'd tie us to the Gina Galasso murder.

I wasn't taking any chances. I had to get out of the United States.

I looked down at my watch.

2:30.

My flight was in three and a half hours. I was going to pack and then leave the house around 3:00. I'd get to LAX around 3:30, giving me two and a half hours before the flight. That was plenty of time. I'd move some money around with my phone, and then right before I boarded the plane, I'd drop it in the garbage.

I knew better than to let them track me through my phone.

I did have one regret. It was a shame I couldn't have had one last 4th of July in the United States.

Then again, maybe July 3rd had become my personal Independence Day.

It was time to be free again.

I started to pack.

CHAPTER 48

BOBBY

For about a minute after my conversation with William, I debated whether to go to Hermosa Beach.

William had been trying to talk me out of it. There were some good reasons why I shouldn't go. A desperate criminal, one who had killed at least one person and maybe several more, was about to flee from justice. He would do anything to avoid capture. That could include killing me if I got in his way.

On the other hand, I couldn't just let him catch a plane and potentially disappear forever. Are these international fugitives usually caught? Yes, but sometimes it's ten or fifteen years down the line. I couldn't take that risk. Wade Bannie deserved to be locked up for the rest of his life.

I came to my decision.

I couldn't just sit idly by.

∼

TEN MINUTES LATER, I was heading toward Hermosa Beach. It was 1:45, and the traffic in Los Angeles was brutal. It didn't help that the 4th of July was the following day. Tens of thousands of people were on the road, arriving a day early to their destination.

I feared that maybe I'd taken too long, and by the time I got to Hermosa, Wade Bannie would already be gone. Would I then go to LAX? And if so, what exactly could I do there? Walk up to him and steal his luggage? I wouldn't get far without being arrested.

Hopefully, it wouldn't come to that.

I looked at the clock on my cell phone every few minutes as if that would suddenly make the LA traffic disappear.

My plan wasn't complicated.

I would wait for him outside his place and attack him when he walked out. I'd punch him into submission, just like I'd done to Archibald Dickey if need be. I'd then grab his wallet from his pocket and take his luggage, which likely had his passport.

I'd then run to my car and drive away, knowing Wade would never call the cops.

My only goal was to prevent Wade Bannie from getting on his flight.

∽

Traffic continued to be a slog.

At 2:30, I passed LAX. I knew Hermosa was about seven to ten miles from there. Traffic eased up a bit.

At 2:44, I took the exit that led me into Hermosa, but there was still a wall of cars in front of me. I had Wade Bannie's address programmed into my GPS.

Was I even sure he lived at this residence? It was what Detective Patchett had given me, but no, I couldn't be sure.

Maybe I'd arrive at the house, and some random couple would be living there, and I'd have lost my chance at catching Wade Bannie.

Stop it, Bobby!

My GPS said I was a mile away, but I still had seven minutes.

I did something I should have done earlier. I typed in his address and brought it up on Zillow.

It was a two-story house with amazing views. The wraparound deck overlooked the Pacific Ocean.

There were neighbors, but they weren't cramped together like an apartment complex. If I was lucky, I might be able to commit my crime and get the hell out of there without being seen.

When my GPS said I was two-tenths a mile away, I started looking for parking. I couldn't just pull my car into his driveway.

There was very little parking, so I said screw it and double-parked. I gave the guy enough room to exit, but if I got a ticket, could the cops use that to confirm I was in the area where Wade Bannie had been assaulted? Sure, but that was about tenth on the list of things I was worried about.

I walked towards Wade Bannie's place. The house was now directly in front of me. Maybe it was just the sun's reflection, but the house's paint was the whitest white I'd ever seen.

There was a fancy lime-green sports car parked in the driveway. Wade may have had five sports cars for all I knew, but I found it encouraging that one was sitting directly in the front of the house. Maybe he hadn't left yet.

On the right of the house was a big fence, and from looking at Zillow, you could follow that down to the wraparound deck in the back of the house. The front of the house was wide open, and there was no place to hide.

So, I hid behind a few trees and headed down the right side.

Thirty seconds later, I'd passed the front of the house and was now walking along its perimeter. Wade hadn't stormed out with a gun, so I was off to a good start.

The fence was only about six feet tall, so I tried to slump down as I walked along it. I didn't need any neighbors IDing me after the fact.

After another minute, I'd reached the end of the side of the house. The Pacific Ocean was now below me. It had been partially blocked from the house and the trees, but now I could see it in all its beauty.

I was only a few feet from his back patio.

The problem was that when I stepped onto that patio, I would be in plain view of anyone watching from inside the house. I had to move very slowly. If Wade heard a noise coming from the patio, he might grab a gun or head for his car and drive off. I didn't like either possibility.

I got to the right angle where the edge of the house ended and the patio began. I peeked around the edge and saw two huge sliding glass doors. Maybe one of them would be open.

I methodically climbed a few steps onto the deck, shielded by a white brick wall. I took a few more steps until I was mere inches from the sliding glass door.

I thought I heard someone crying.

I tilted my neck so my eyes could get the slightest look inside the sliding glass door. I didn't see anything.

I thought I heard another whimper, but I couldn't be sure. The Pacific Ocean was loud below me.

This time, I went for a better look and leaned my eyes about six inches past the door. I still didn't see anything.

The first sliding glass door was about fifteen feet long, and then there was a break before the second.

The entire patio was probably sixty feet long and twenty feet wide, and several lounge chairs were scattered about.

I didn't plan on going out to that part of the deck. You'd be seen too easily.

I peeked inside one last time and, once again, saw nothing.

I decided to risk quickly walking across that first door and getting to the white brick wall. As I did it, I heard a scream. There was no mistaking what I heard.

Was Wade Bannie killing another woman before he fled to Mexico City? I'd thought it sounded more like a male screaming, but I couldn't be sure. I had no idea what was happening, but somebody was suffering in that house. I couldn't just sit out here on the deck.

I leaned my eyes over the second sliding glass door and quickly glanced inside.

I couldn't believe what I saw. There were two masked men wearing balaclavas standing over another man. The man on the ground was hog-tied, his mouth duct taped, and his face looked to be a bloody mess.

I should have called the police, but curiosity got the best of me. I leaned past the door a second time and peered in.

Instantaneously, I knew I'd made a mistake. This time, one of the guys wearing the balaclavas saw me looking in.

"Get him," was all I heard.

I started running but didn't get far. One of the men had arrived at the first sliding glass door and side-swiped me as I ran by it. I had no chance. The second man was out there a split second later.

I was a pretty tough guy, but not when I was on the ground and someone pointed their gun at me, which is what the second man did.

"What should I do?" the first guy asked.

"Duct tape his mouth," the other man said. It was apparent he was in charge.

I thought they were both white, but I couldn't be sure. They'd be impossible to pick out of a lineup, that's for sure.

The guy in charge was about a foot taller than his partner.

The shorter man duct-taped me and guided me inside.

Once there, they told me to sit on the ground. That's when I looked at the guy across from me, and there was no mistaking who it was: Wade Bannie.

He looked nothing like the guy in his Instagram photos. He'd been worked over, and his face was a bruised and bloody mess. He was hogtied, lying on the ground, and had a look of outright terror.

Was I going to be next?

I looked up at my captors.

"Check his wallet," the tall guy said.

The shorter man reached into my pocket and grabbed my wallet.

"It's him," he said.

It's him?

How the hell did they know who I was?

He returned the wallet to my pants, which I thought was odd.

"Tie his hands behind his back."

With a small piece of rope, the shorter man did so.

The taller man spoke again.

"Go get the van and reverse it down the driveway. Try to get it as close as possible to the front door, and then open the van's back door. Got it?"

"Got it."

"I'll have these two up there, ready to load into the van."

The shorter man walked out of the first sliding glass door, pulling his balaclava down as he exited.

Wade Bannie looked over at me. I caught his eyes for one second and then looked away.

He was in pretty bad shape, but if he was looking for sympathy, he was looking at the wrong guy.

"Don't even think about moving," the taller guy told me.

He grabbed the hog-tied Bannie and slid him along the tile floor toward the front of the house.

I knew I wouldn't get far with my hands tied behind my back. I couldn't even open a door. The taller man was back in under five seconds, so the point was moot.

He leaned toward me, the gun flailing in his hand. Was I going to be shot right then and there?

Instead, he grabbed me by my tied wrists and slid me along the ground for about fifteen seconds until I'd almost reached the front door, and then he dropped me there.

Wade Bannie continued to glance in my direction, but I didn't give him the satisfaction of looking back.

A minute later, I heard a truck reversing down the driveway.

The taller guy opened the house's front door and lifted Wade Bannie by his wrists. He walked him outside, and I heard him shove Wade into the van.

He came back for me a few seconds later and threw me in the back of the van as well. There were no seats—just the bottom of the van and Wade Bannie.

∼

ABOUT FIVE MINUTES into the ride, Wade thrashed about, trying to free his arms or legs from the rope. He was hogtied, and it was a lost cause.

A voice came from the front.

"If I hear you moving around again, I'm going to come back there and cut one of your eyes out."

The thrashing ceased after that.

∼

THE VAN WAS WINDOWLESS, so I had no idea where we were going.

Were they going to kill us both? Just Bannie? Just me? Neither?

I had no idea what was going on or what to expect.

I tried to start loosening my wrists from the rope. If I was successful, maybe when we slowed down, I could open the back of the van and jump out—if the van could even be opened from inside.

It didn't end up mattering. My wrists were tied so tight behind my back that I didn't have a chance.

At some points, the van was driving quite fast; at others, it slowed to a crawl. I could hear other cars on the sides of us.

If I had to guess, we were headed north on Interstate 405. Traffic wasn't as bad going that direction, and we never would have reached the higher speeds if we had been going south on 405.

One thought kept springing to mind: I didn't want to die in the back of a van.

Let me get out. Give me a fighting chance.

∼

ABOUT THIRTY-FIVE MINUTES into the drive, a voice came from the front. I recognized it as the taller man.

"Mr. McGowan, I want you to crawl into the next row. Put your body weight on the divider and roll over it. You shouldn't need your hands."

I was able to get on my knees. The divider wasn't much taller than that. I leaned my body weight into it and rolled over. I landed on the top of the divider, and then gravity took over, sending me into the next row. I hit the seats and tumbled down on the ground in front of me, but I was quickly able to get back up on one of the seats.

It probably would have been comical if I wasn't fighting for my life.

I could now see the front windshield, and to my shock, we were on Wilshire Boulevard approaching the Beverly Hilton.

The shorter man was driving. They were still both wearing their balaclavas. I'm assuming the van had tinted windows because if a cop saw two guys wearing balaclavas, they'd inevitably be pulled over.

"When we get there, drive into the parking garage," the taller man said.

A few minutes later, we did just that. They drove up to the third floor and pulled into a parking spot.

"I want you to listen, Mr. McGowan. If you do just as I say, you will remain alive. I'm going to come back there and remove the duct tape from your mouth and cut the rope holding your hands together. You are then to walk into the Beverly Hilton and not leave your room for the rest of the day. If that is understood, you may nod."

I nodded.

"I am going to take your wallet, cell phone, and anything else from your pocket as safekeeping. Now, I know you could call the police from the hotel's phone, but if you do that, we will find out and come back and kill you. We will then go to Santa Barbara and kill your father. If that is understood, you may nod again."

I nodded again.

As the taller man opened the front door, I took one last look back at Wade Bannie. He stared at me but didn't try to say anything through his duct tape. He knew I was being released. Maybe he was registering defeat for the first time in his adult life. I didn't know, and frankly, I didn't care. I had a feeling Wade Bannie's remaining hours on earth were going to be some rough ones.

The tall man came back and, using a knife, cut through the rope that tied my hands together.

"I'm going to remove the duct tape now. Don't say a word, not even to Mr. Bannie. Just go. If you understand, nod."

I nodded.

He took the duct tape and ripped it from my mouth.

It was painful, but I remained stoic.

He stepped back out of the van, and I scooted to the edge and hopped out. I said nothing and started walking toward the exit of the parking garage.

I heard the tall man shut the door behind me, get back in the front, and then the van sped off a few seconds later.

I didn't even turn around to look.

CHAPTER 49

WADE

I was five minutes from heading to the airport when my two eventual killers broke into my house.

I tried to run, but they tackled me immediately. My gun was mere feet from me, but I never had a chance to get to it.

They duct-taped my mouth and hogtied my arms and legs behind my back.

They started asking me yes and no questions; I could only nod or shake my head.

They'd alternate between that and punching me in the face.

I figured I was going to be beaten to death in my own house.

IRONICALLY, my one moment of hope was when I saw Bobby McGowan looking through the sliding glass door. The guy whose investigation had led to me fleeing the country and my father deciding to take his own life.

Maybe he'd call the cops, and I'd live to fight another day.

Unfortunately, my two captors caught him as well.

Maybe they'd kill Bobby, also.

I could have lived with that.

~

But, no, that wouldn't prove to be the case.

They let Bobby McGowan out of the van, and I knew I was a dead man.

At that moment, I'd prayed for a quick end.

It would not come.

~

They drove me to some secluded house and started asking me more questions. If they thought I was lying, I was beaten unmercifully. Even when I told the truth, I was beaten. It felt less like a fact-finding mission and more like revenge. I guess I couldn't blame them, whoever the hell they were.

~

This went on for two ruthless hours, and just when I thought my body was going to give out, the taller man approached me with a gun by his side, and a few seconds later, everything went black.

CHAPTER 50

BOBBY

*A*t 7:18 a.m., there was a knock at my door.

With everything that had gone on, I had no idea who to expect. The hotel staff? The cops? The guys who let me go?

It was none of the above.

A guy in his mid-fifties wearing a black suit and black top hat was at the door. He looked like a chauffeur.

"I've been paid to drive you to William Ryan's estate."

I had no phone, keys, or wallet, and my car was still in Hermosa Beach.

"Sure. Why not?"

HE WAS DRIVING a black Lincoln Town Car, and we headed toward the Hollywood Hills.

He had me sit in the back and told me I had one of those dividing windows if I wanted to roll it up. I kept it down.

That was likely a subconscious decision after being forced into the back of the van yesterday.

The driver dropped me off at the top of William's driveway, and once I got out, he parked in the far corner of the lot. I guess his job wasn't done.

As was now customary, William was waiting for me at the bottom of the stairs. We shook hands, and he led me to his study.

"There's something I want to show you," he said. "Sit down."

I took the seat he offered. William sat behind his desk, and a TV lowered from the wall.

I hadn't seen that feature before.

He pressed the button on his remote, and the frozen screen came to life.

It was the local news channel KTLA, and the time stamp was from 5:01 that morning.

The reporter—an Asian woman in her thirties—was outside a condominium. Several police cars were on each side of her.

"I'm standing outside the condo of Ed Bannie, the well-known former LAPD detective. Mr. Bannie called the LAPD this morning and said that he was about to commit suicide and they should come and retrieve his body. The LAPD arrived at his house less than an hour ago and found Mr. Bannie dead inside, reportedly from a gunshot to the head. And just a few minutes ago, the LAPD released a statement saying they now consider Ed Bannie's son, Wade Bannie, a suspect in the infamous Annie Ryan disappearance. There are reports that the LAPD is looking to locate the younger Bannie. This is a developing story; I'm sure we'll have more as the day goes on."

I was dumbfounded.

Ed Bannie had killed himself, and the LAPD had admitted that Wade was a suspect in Annie Ryan's murder.

William Ryan walked toward me and handed me a check.

"What's this for? I said I didn't need a bonus."

"It's yours. You earned it."

"I thought I'd only get this if they arrested Wade Bannie."

William Ryan raised his eyes to mine.

"I've got this gut feeling they aren't going to find Mr. Bannie."

And then, ever so slightly, William Ryan smiled. It was something I easily could have missed, but now that I'd seen it, there was no denying what it meant.

William Ryan knew about the fate of Wade Bannie.

Maybe he'd orchestrated it, or perhaps he'd just heard about it, but he knew.

"What makes you say that?" I asked.

"Intuition. Let's call it that."

"You sure it's just intuition and not inside information?"

The slight smirk appeared again.

"You've done your job, Bobby. Magnificently. You've earned every penny of that. Now, take that check."

I slid it into my pocket since I had no wallet.

"Would you like to play a game?" William asked.

"What type of game?"

"It's called the Game of Hypotheticals. None of it means anything. It's all make-believe. But it's fun to hypothesize about how something might have happened."

"Sure, let's play."

"Great. And remember, these are all hypotheticals and not meant to be the truth. So, obviously, these statements could never be used in a court of law. Do you understand?"

"Yes," I said.

"Why don't I start by asking you a hypothetical?" William asked.

"Alright. Go ahead."

"When you found out where Wade Bannie was, why did you go to his place? What had you planned on doing once you got there?"

"This is all hypothetical, right," I said.

William smiled.

"Yes, that's the name of the game."

"Well, in that case, hypothetically, I was going down to Hermosa Beach to prevent him from getting on a flight out of the country. I feared we might never see him again if he caught his flight to Mexico City."

"But what did you plan on doing when you got there? Confront him?"

"If need be. I feared what I'd probably have to do was confront Wade when he left his house. I'd knock him on his ass if need be. I'd then leave with his luggage and passport, knowing he wouldn't call the cops because he wouldn't want to draw any attention to himself."

"Thank you. Now you can ask me a question."

"Hypothetically, when did you decide to send people to abduct Wade Bannie?"

"Well, that is just a wild theory, Bobby."

William smiled again. He'd probably smiled more in the last three minutes than over the five weeks I'd known him.

"Placate me," I said. "Remember, this is all hypothetical."

"Yesterday, when I got off the phone with you. Like you, I couldn't fathom Wade fleeing, especially when his arrest felt imminent. As Annie's uncle, I just couldn't let that happen. So, I would have called a few friends to ensure Wade never reached the airport."

"And hypothetically, what friends would you call?"

"Nice try, Bobby. You'd been playing the game so well, but that question is off-limits. Try another one."

Before I could ask another question, he continued.

"In totally unrelated news, you should check out this documentary I produced. It's called *Convicts to Citizens*. It's all about hardened criminals who get paroled from jail early. Sadly, some of them return to crime. Good friends to have, though, you know."

Another smile from William. He was enjoying this.

"Hypothetically, what did these two guys learn from Wade Bannie?"

"You'd be surprised just how much. Wade described in detail how he killed Annie on Christmas Eve after picking her up from my house. He'd started kissing her when they arrived at his parents' house, and when she turned him down, he strangled her. That's all I will say about that. It boiled my blood when I heard it. Wade Bannie is lucky I wasn't there. Hypothetically, of course. Wade claims that he did not kill Kai Butler, and considering the duress Wade was under, I'm going to assume he was telling the truth. He did own up to killing two young women in the Caribbean. In a similar fashion to Annie."

I bowed my head.

"Damn. He killed two other women?"

"Yes. I will send an anonymous letter to the police in those countries," William said.

"So, Annie was never killed at your house?"

"In this hypothetical game, no."

"We can stop with the charade now, William. And don't worry, your secrets are safe with me. I'm not going to tell anyone."

He extended his hand, and I grabbed it. We shook. That was enough.

"Whatever you did, I know it's because you've had this bottled-up anger and sadness for twenty-five years. I'm not here to judge you," I said.

"Thank you, Bobby. And it's good for you that those two guys were there."

"Why is that?"

"Wade Bannie had a gun on the counter. And despite your cute little plan, you wouldn't punch him a few times and escape with his luggage and passport. It wasn't going to be that easy. It may well have ended with one of you dead. And either you're dead or being investigated for murder. Neither option sounds appealing."

I nodded.

"Did Wade's father help cover up Annie's murder?" I asked.

"Yes."

"Was Mike Minter part of it?"

"No."

"Where did they dispose of Annie's body?"

"The Pacific Ocean and that was all Wade. Ed wasn't back from his vacation yet."

"Did they hire Archibald Dickey to kill Gina Galasso?"

"Yes."

"And to kill me?"

"The first time at the Beverly Hilton was just to scare you. The second time, he intended to kill you."

"Wow, they asked all the pertinent questions, didn't they?"

"Yes, they did."

I tried to think of some other unanswered questions I'd had throughout the investigation. I couldn't come up with any on the spot.

"Did Wade suffer?" I asked.

"Why don't we end this little game now," William said. "There are some things that you shouldn't know about."

I nodded.

"So, what now?" I asked. "You can't exactly have a big party since Wade will never be found."

"When the LAPD confirms that Wade likely killed Annie, that will be enough for most people in the family. It will be a relief that no family member was involved in her death."

"You know, it's too bad."

"What is?"

"When I played out the end of this in my head, I imagined you hosting a big party and everybody being able to put Annie's death behind them."

"That will still happen. Just not tonight. We'll have to disguise tonight's festivities as a 4th of July party."

"You're having a party tonight?"

"After yesterday's events, yes, I am. You're free to join if you'd like."

I understood all the reasons William had to celebrate, but the fact that Wade was tortured took a little bit of the shine away for me.

"With the information I'm now armed with, I think it's better I get back up to Santa Barbara," I said.

William smiled.

"You're not armed with anything. You can't gain any information from the Game of Hypotheticals. It's all make-believe."

"I still think I'll pass on the party. If you have one when the LAPD confirms that Wade Bannie killed Annie, I'll come down. But please, give Amber, Adam Toon, and Earl Razzle my best."

"I will."

"And anybody else I forgot."

"You got it."

"No regrets on what went down yesterday?" I asked.

My question came out of left field. I hadn't been planning on asking it.

"Listen, Bobby. I've had regrets for twenty-five years over Annie's death. Was it a member of our family? Was it related to my money? Why did it happen at my house? These all bothered me greatly, but one thing I will never have regrets over is how Wade Bannie died."

"I understand," I said.

He looked at me with a curious expression.

"You know I did a lot of studying up on your mother's case before I hired you."

"I assumed so."

"And there was one part that particularly fascinated me."

I had no idea where he was going with this.

"What was that?"

"Near the end, when you found out where Conrad Drury was, you didn't call the cops and wait for them to arrive. No, you went after Drury yourself. I admired that, and it showed that you had some dog in you, that you were tougher than your exterior. And maybe a little meaner. And I didn't blame you for one second. This guy murdered your mother, and you wanted him dead. Nor should you blame me. Wade Bannie killed my niece, and I had to hear in detail how he strangled her. He also effectively killed my brother, Connor, as well. He'd even killed a part of this family forever. And I wanted answers to all those questions you asked earlier. So, if Wade Bannie had to go through a few things for me to get the answers to those questions, I'm okay with that. In fact, I'm just fine with that. I'm glad the bastard suffered."

I nodded at him, letting him know I understood. Nothing more needed to be said.

William picked up the phone on his desk and made a call.

"Mr. McGowan will need a ride back to the Beverly Hilton. He'll be up in a few minutes."

He then walked back toward me.

"Is this it?" I asked.

"Yes, Bobby, this is it. This is where we part ways. You've done a spectacular job. Thank you for everything."

He extended his hand, and we shook again.

"Oh, shit, I almost forgot," he said. He went back to his desk and grabbed something.

A large Ziplock bag held my wallet, iPhone, and keys.

"Thank you, William."

"No, thank you, Bobby."

I opened the door.

"If you'd prefer, he can drive you to Hermosa Beach to pick up your car," William said.

"You know everything, don't you?"

"Let's just say I like to keep my eyes on how things are going."

"Was that why I was hired? I was easy to keep track of?" I asked.

"You're reading too much into it. I hired you because I felt you had the goods, and I was proven right. You should be very proud of yourself. A vicious murderer will never have the chance to kill again."

"When you put it that way…"

He smiled.

"Take care now, Bobby. Don't be a stranger."

"Goodbye, William."

CHAPTER 51

BOBBY

William's chauffeur drove me to Hermosa Beach, where I picked up my car.

There was a ticket on it.

Would the Hermosa Beach cops look at who received parking tickets on the day Wade Bannie went missing? It was unlikely but certainly not impossible. Maybe I wasn't 100% done with this case.

Jeez.

I DROVE BACK to the Beverly Hilton and decided to valet my car for the first time.

The guy gave me a big smile.

"About time!" he said.

I grabbed my bags and checked out of the hotel. My favorite woman was at the front desk, and I think she was happier than me when I was finally leaving.

I WENT BACK OUTSIDE to retrieve my car.

He gave me a funny look.

"Back already?"

"I was afraid you might scratch up my car."

"Would probably be an improvement on that hunk of junk."

I laughed pretty loudly.

"You're funny. Maybe I should have valeted it this whole time."

"Next time you're back."

"It's a deal," I said.

My car arrived a minute later, and I left the Beverly Hilton for the final time.

As I headed toward the freeway, my thoughts raced.

I realized I owed Cassius Fields a call. I'd give him what I could, but that last day would obviously be off-limits.

I would also eventually say goodbye to Adam, Amber, and Earl, but for the moment, there were too many questions I didn't want to answer.

They could all wait a few days.

I'd decided to leave the party without anyone knowing, a.k.a. an Irish Goodbye.

It seemed apropos for a McGowan surrounded by a bunch of Ryans.

I ENTERED Interstate 405 heading north, and then fifteen minutes later, merged onto Highway 101.

I was an hour from home.

I looked down at my phone.

It was 12:53 on the 4th of July.

I could go home and just chill out; after the last several days, no one would blame me. I could lament the losses of Annie Ryan and Gina Galasso, and curse myself for ever having taken the case.

But, no, that's not what I wanted.

I was tired of focusing on the sadder aspects of this case. I'd achieved my goal and identified Annie's killer, something numerous people told me would never happen.

I'd met quite the cast of characters, and been paid handsomely.

I'd accomplished the impossible, and had every reason to celebrate.

So, I came up with a different plan.

I wasn't going to go home and sulk.

Screw that!

I would drop my car off and then UBER to downtown Santa Barbara.

I'd find a bar near the ocean and order their signature drink.
I wouldn't care if it was the most outlandish drink you've ever seen.
It could be a blended Pina Colada with multiple umbrellas in it.
I didn't care.
I was going to drink one or two of them - maybe three! - and then sit in awe of the fireworks.
Maybe I'd even get a little drunk.
I had a big check burning a hole in my wallet; maybe I'd buy a drink or two for neighboring tables. I'd talk to the people around me and focus on all that's good in life.
It was the 4th of July and I was going to enjoy myself!
After all I'd been through over the last month, I think I'd earned that.

THE END

PLEASE CLICK THROUGH TO THE NEXT PAGE TO LEARN ABOUT MY OTHER BOOKS. THANKS!

ALSO BY BRIAN O'SULLIVAN

Thank you so much for reading THE OTHER ANNIE!

I'd be honored if you left a review :)

My next novel will be the 8th - and final! - book in the QUINT series. I hope you'll pre-order by clicking her: **THE FINAL CHAPTER.**

If you are not caught up on the QUINT series, now is the time. Here's a link to all 7 novels: **QUINT SERIES.**

And here's a few of my favorite standalone novels: **THE MASTERMIND** and **THE BARTENDER.**

Finally, from the bottom of my heart, I just wanted to say thanks to each and every one of you. You make this all possible - and worthwhile!

And I hope you'll keep telling your friends about my books, posting about them on Facebook groups, nominating them for book clubs, or anything else to keep this momentum going.

Thank you, everyone!

You're the best.

Sincerely,

Brian O'Sullivan